AN ACT OF PATRIOTISM OR AN ACT OF TERROR . . .

Corman's hand tightened on the trigger. "You're not going to launch this missile, General," he said, his words sounding hollow in the vault.

"Maybe not," the general said, "but sooner or later it'll have to be done. The Reds must be stopped. I was in Germany at the time of Munich, and there were a lot of sound, bright men who said Hitler should have been stopped when we had the power to do it easily. But there were too many idealists—and their way seemed easier. So we paid a hell of a price . . ."

"I'm not going to discuss politics with you. Your boys have worn me down, General. I'm too tired to listen."

"We're all tired," the general said. "It's been a long, hard, dirty grind."

"And now it's over," Corman said. "I've stopped you, General."

"That remains to be seen," the general said . . .

THE
February Plan

Robert L. Duncan

Writing as

James Hall Roberts

BALLANTINE BOOKS • NEW YORK

Copyright © 1967 by William Morrow and Company, Inc.

All rights reserved. No part of this book may be reproduced or utilized in any form or by any means, electronic or mechanical, including photocopying, recording or by any information storage and retrieval system, without permission in writing from William Morrow and Company. Published in the United States by Ballantine Books, a division of Random House, Inc., New York, and simultaneously in Canada by Ballantine Books of Canada, Ltd., Toronto, Canada.

Library of Congress Catalog Card Number: 67-11634

ISBN 0-345-27170-X

This edition published by arrangement with William Morrow and Company, Inc.

Manufactured in the United States of America

First Ballantine Books Edition: September 1978

Part One

1

CORMAN came awake slowly and it took him a moment to remember where he was and why he was here. He rolled out of bed, his feet probing for the slippers the maid had left beside his bed the night before. He walked over to the window and looked out at the steel-gray rain slanting down over the leafless trees of Hibiya Park, driven by a cold wind off Tokyo Bay. Foolish, he thought, that he should be here at all. Paul was dead, beyond his help. There was nothing he could do to change that.

He heard the clatter of a typewriter in the sitting room and he checked his watch. Eight o'clock. He had overslept, and his secretary was already hard at work. He took a shower and shaved and dressed, and as he went into the sitting room and saw Finley on the telephone, his depression began to lift. She was not a beautiful woman, but only, he thought, because she did not allow herself to be. It was as if she had decided quite early in life how a secretary should look and conformed herself to that mental pattern, drawing her ash-blond hair back in a chignon, dressing in tailored suits, as if her primary concern was to look efficient. She smiled at Corman and then spoke quite firmly into the telephone. "No, Mr. Corman is not available for interviews. He's here gathering material for a new book.

No, I'm not at liberty to say what the subject matter is going to be." She put down the telephone and stood up with a sigh, smoothing the wrinkles out of her skirt. "I don't know how in the hell it happened," she said, "but they know you're here."

"The Japanese reporters go over the passenger lists on all incoming flights," he said, sorting through the stack of mail on the desk. "I'm surprised it took them this long to find me." He paused to read a cable from New York, a blistering denunciation from his lecture agent: YOUR WHIM WILL COST YOU FIFTY THOUSAND DOLLARS. YOUR FAILURE TO NOTIFY UNFORGIVABLE. It was signed "Max."

There was a polite tapping at the door and Finley opened it, admitting a Japanese waiter with breakfast. She had him put the tray on the desk, dismissed him, and then gently removed the stack of letters from Corman's hands. "You can take care of those after you've had your breakfast," she said.

"Then they must be pretty bad," He sat down at the desk and took the silver cover off the plate of scrambled eggs.

"Terrible," she said. "Your publisher's angry because he doesn't know what to do with the galleys. Max is giving you hell because he's had to cancel a dozen lectures on the spur of the moment. There's a letter from him, by the way, that's even hotter than the cable. And your literary agent is fretting in a gentlemanly way because he thinks you should have gone to Hollywood yourself."

"Have you heard from Mitsu this morning?"

"Not yet," she said, sitting down across the desk from him. "But it's a little soon. There must be a million girls in Tokyo named Suzuki."

"Have some coffee," he said, filling a cup from the silver pot, sliding it across the desk to her. "Have you eaten?"

"At the crack of dawn." She sipped at the coffee thoughtfully. "You mind if I meddle?"

"That's what I pay you for," he said, smiling. "Go ahead."

"This is a different kind of meddling. There's a letter from Phoebe in the pile."

"I see," he said, his smile fading. "And what does she have to say?"

"She wants you to give up this probing. She doesn't think anything can be gained by it."

He nodded silently, finishing the eggs. Phoebe's reaction surprised him, but he knew objectively that he should have expected it. The Phoebe he had been married to would have demanded answers, seizing the problem like a terrier and shaking it until the answers were torn loose. But she was married to a banker now—what was his name? Corman had met him once, a dignified, conservative man with graying temples. Mason, yes, that was his name, and Phoebe was in her forties now instead of her early twenties, and somewhere along the line she had taken on a desire to protect the respectable illusions of life, and Paul was one of those.

Corman filled his cup and tasted the coffee. It was scalding, bitter. "And what's your opinion?" he said. "Do you think I should give up?"

"Paul's dead," she said simply.

"Yes," he said. "Paul's dead."

"I know that's hard for you to accept."

"I don't have any choice about it," he said. "It's a fact. Paul is dead and I saw him buried. But you still haven't answered my question. Do you think we should go home?"

"It's going to cost you a lot of money if you don't."

"That's still no answer."

She shifted slightly in her chair, a little uncomfortable now, as if she suddenly regretted being on this subject at all. She had been with Corman ten years, and from the very beginning she had drawn definite lines in ther relationship beyond which she would not go. Now one of those lines had been crossed and it made her uneasy.

"All right," she said finally. "For what it's worth, I think you should give up and go home. Whatever you find isn't going to be very pleasant, and it could be quite unsavory. It can't possibly do Paul any good, so it just doesn't make any sense." Her polished fingernail tapped the handle of the cup slightly, repeatedly, and the cup turned almost imperceptibly in the saucer. "I don't have to tell you how it's affected you. You haven't worked an hour since this whole thing started, not good, productive work. I can understand how upset you've been, but you don't have anything to gain by whipping yourself with it. Something terrible happened. You say you accept it. Well, I don't think you really do or you wouldn't be here." She stood up now as if to signal that the conversation was finished and she was withdrawing behind the security of the line again. "There, now, I've had my say. And now that I'm through meddling for the day, would you like to get started on the correspondence?"

Before he could answer, the telephone rang. She picked it up, listened a moment, and then turned to him. "It's a Major Henshaw from the American Embassy. Do you want to talk to him?"

He nodded, taking the telephone from her. "This is Phillip Corman," he said.

The voice on the line was smooth, practiced. The major was obviously a government trouble shooter whose job it was to soothe storms and calm the irate. "Good morning, Mr. Corman. I hope I'm not calling you too early?"

"What can I do for you, Major?"

"I'm a military attaché with the embassy here and I had word from the States you were coming. I think it might be a good idea if we get together."

"Why?" Corman said flatly.

The major was unperturbed. "I thought we might talk about your son, Mr. Corman."

"I see."

"I'd consider it a personal favor if you could come out here sometime this morning."

"All right," Corman said. "Where are you?"

The major gave him the address of a building in Minatoku, near the American Embassy, and Corman agreed to meet him in half an hour. When he put the telephone down, he was a little surprised to find that his hands were sweating. "I'm about to get another government run-around," he said to Finley. "They're about to try a new fiction on me, forgetting that I'm an expert at it."

"Keep an open mind," Finley said. "You can't be sure."

"No, I can't be sure of anything it seems." He took his overcoat out of the closet and slipped it on. "You'd better send some cables this morning. Tell Jones to hang loose and take the best price he can get. Apologize to Henderson and have him send the galleys here."

"Then we'll be staying here for a while?"

"Yes. I owe Paul at least that much."

Her voice stopped him at the door. "What shall we do about Max?"

"Send him a cable," he said, with a half-smile. "Tell the old bandit, in a polite way, to go to hell."

2

He caught a taxi in front of the hotel, handing the driver the address which the doorman had written out in Japanese characters, and then he sank back in the seat, intending to have a look at the city on the way to the major's office. But the rain was too heavy, smearing the windows of the taxi and allowing him only a fleeting glimpse of the traffic and a diversity of people scurrying along the sidewalks, women in kimonos and men in Western business suits. Finally he gave it up.

He had been here before, in the first year of the Occupation, and he had been curious to see how Tōkyō had changed, but most of the old familiar reference points had either been altered or obliterated; the wrecked city had been rebuilt, and the miles of gutted buildings and wooden shacks had disappeared. The people had changed as well. There seemed to be a commercial arrogance in the Japanese he had met during the past three days here, a reflection perhaps of the aura of unsteady affluence which seemed to hang over the city.

In less than a half hour the taxi reached Minatoku and the driver pulled up the curb, turning around to tap the paper with the address on it to show that they had arrived. Corman fumbled with the wad of oversized bills in his pocket, peeling off five one-hundred-yen notes and stuffing them into the outstretched hand before he climbed out into the drizzling rain.

The Temporary Annex was a small, gray stone building surrounded by a low wrought-iron fence. He made a run for the awning and the glass doors, pushing them open to enter the foyer, a drab waiting room decorated by a limp American flag on a standard against the wall. The no-nonsense woman behind the desk recorded his name in a book and then led him down an antiseptic hallway to a door marked with Major Henshaw's name.

The major was not what Corman had expected. He was a tall, lean man with a gray cast to his face, as if he were convalescing from an illness, and his glib cordiality was an effort for him. He took Corman's coat, hanging it from the horns of an iron coat rack which already held a dripping umbrella, then he turned to an automatic coffeepot which sat on a table near the single small window. There was a stock portrait of the President on the wall behind the desk. It was unsigned.

The major poured out two cups of coffee. "I apologize for asking you to come all the way out here on a day like this," he said. "But I've been too swamped to get away from my desk for weeks now. Do you take sugar, cream?"

"Black," Corman said, accepting the cup, watching the major as he sat down on the edge of his gray metal desk, opening a humidor, offering Corman a cigar before he lighted one himself.

"While I'm thinking about it," the major said, rolling the end of the cigar in the flame of the match to establish an even coal, "I happened to mention your being here to the ambassador. He's a great fan of yours. He'd like to meet you while you're in Japan."

"Thank him for me," Corman said, "but I'm not here for social events."

"No, of course you're not," the major said. "Needless to say, you have our deepest sympathy."

"I don't mean to be rude, Major, but I've had just about all the official condolences I can stomach,"

The February Plan

Corman said. "You said on the telephone you have some information concerning my son. Now, if you're going to give me the straight government line again, you can save us both a lot of time by telling me so."

"I understand how you feel," the major said, going around the desk to open a drawer and remove a folder. "There's always a good bit of confusion surrounding something like this. I get fed up with it myself at times. But I hope you'll bear with me." He sat down on the desk again, his face screwed up against the smoke, thumbing through the papers offhandedly as if to acquaint himself with the contents. "The report from the States is pretty sketchy," he said, "but then, Air Force Intelligence didn't have much time to put it together."

"You have an Intelligence report on this?" Corman said, startled.

"That's a typical reaction," the major said with a smile. "But Intelligence covers a lot of routine matters. When they found out you were coming to Japan, they made a report to fill me in, hoping I might be able save you some time and trouble." His eyes dropped to the paper in his hands. "According to the information I have, your son was fatally injured in a helicopter accident at Vandenburg Air Force Base on the second of January. That's correct, isn't it?"

"I can hardly question that," Corman said.

"Then perhaps you will tell me what you are questioning, Mr. Corman."

"That's in your report, isn't it?" Corman said. "I made the same charges in the States. The Air Force lied to the boy's mother about the whole matter."

"In what way?"

"My son was a launch-control officer at Vandenburg," Corman said, trying to control his irritation. "On December first he wrote to his mother, telling her he planned to spend the Christmas holidays with her. A week later he wrote a letter asking her to set up a party for some of his old school friends who were planning to get together in Connecticut over the holidays. But he never showed up. And then, on the third of January, both she and I got telegrams from the government saying he had been killed in an accident."

"Regrettable."

"I'm not through. During the holidays his mother was frantic because he didn't show up and she hadn't heard from him. She sent telegrams, she called his commanding officer, and she got no answers at all except that his unit had been alerted for some military exercise or other and that he would be inaccessible for a while."

"Things happen," Major Henshaw said, flicking the cigar ash into a bronze fish on his desk. "You were in the army. You know that."

"During the time when the Air Force said he was at Vandenburg," Corman said, "he wasn't in the States at all. He was here, in Tokyo."

"And what makes you think that?" the major said reflectively.

Corman took the folded paper out of his wallet, opening it and reading it again, feeling an old, familiar pain at the sight of the penciled scrawl. "December 23," it read, and then, without a greeting (how should a son address a father who has not acted like a father?), "Goddamnit, you have to do something, you have to. They are going to kill us all. February 5. The Blue Ants. You can't sit on your ass any longer. They're . . ."

The major read it twice and then turned the paper over in his hands as if to see if anything was written on the back. He thought about it a moment, his lips pursed speculatively, and it seemed that he was more on guard now, although Corman could not be sure. "What are the Blue Ants?" the major said.

"I don't know."

"What's supposed to happen on February fifth?"

"I don't know that either."

The major shrugged. "I don't see that it has any significance."

"It was written by my son. It's his handwriting."

"But you don't know what it means."

"I received it on the fifth of January, three days after his death. It was sent from Tokyo."

"Via the APO?"

"Through the Japanese mails. There's a woman's

The February Plan

handwriting on the front of the envelope. And she's obviously written her name and return address on the back flap, but the envelope got wet in transit and everything except her last name was smudged out."

"So you have no idea who she is?"

"No."

"Why should you be disturbed by a note like this? Why should it upset you?"

"Why in the hell wouldn't it upset me? Obviously he was in some sort of trouble and he was appealing to me for help."

"If it was intended for you at all," the major said calmly. "It's possible it was, of course, I can't deny that, but at the same time it could have been meant for somebody else, since there's no salutation on it and he didn't send it to you himself. Or perhaps it was meant for nobody at all. He could have been drunk when he wrote it. It might have been a practical joke. Who knows?"

"It was no practical joke. Paul didn't have much of a sense of humor."

"Didn't he?" the major suggested. "Can you be sure of that? How many times have you seen him in the past few years?"

"That has nothing to do with it."

The major put down his cigar and sipped at the coffee. "When it comes right down to it, Mr. Corman, and I don't say this to be argumentative—I'm only interested in getting at the truth—you can't have any way of knowing what his intentions were when he wrote this note, if indeed he did write it at all. I don't mean to be offensive, but if my information is correct, you scarcely knew the boy at all."

"Did Air Force Intelligence tell you that?"

"You're a public figure, Mr. Corman," the major said. "There were a number of stories in the papers after your son died. They went to great lengths to spell out the trouble between you and your wife, the divorce, your alienation from your son."

"I didn't come here to argue with you, Major." Corman said, suddenly tired. "And I don't intend to defend myself."

"You're not being attacked," the major said. "We're not the ogres you seem to think we are, Mr. Corman. It was my duty to see if you would accept the status quo. Since you're obviously not going to, then I can say you haven't been told the full truth, not because there was anything mysterious about it, but simply because it was to everybody's advantage to keep it quiet. Too, there was no point in subjecting you and your former wife to a lot of unnecessary grief."

"I'm grateful there was so much government concern about my feelings," Corman said with irony. "But I'm a mature man and I don't like being lied to, not for any reason."

The major shrugged. "Lies are sometimes necessary," he said. "I've been authorized to give you all the details, Mr. Corman, but there are some parts of the story which could prove embarrassing to the United States. I have to ask you to keep those confidential."

"I'm not out to embarrass anybody. I just want the truth."

"All right," the major said. He finished the coffee in his cup and went over to the pot to refill it. "It's true. Your son was here in Japan during the last two weeks in December. We couldn't admit that, we couldn't let you know, because there's a delicate negotiation taking place between our Defense Department and the Japanese government and we don't want it made public yet. And to have released the full story would certainly jeopardize that negotiation."

"My son was a first lieutenant," Corman said testily. "Are you trying to tell me he was involved in a high-level diplomatic incident?"

"Yes," the major said, "not as a military officer, but as a man." His cigar had gone out. He took the time to relight it. "Last October the Pentagon asked a Japanese diplomat over to Vandenburg to witness a missile launch and tour the facilities. I won't mention his name for obvious reasons, but he's a member of the Diet, high-ranking. The diplomat brought his wife along and since she was thirty years younger than he and not particularly interested in missiles, the Air

Force assigned an officer to show her around the base."

"My son?"

The major nodded. "He showed her the sights and took her to lunch and afterward they had a few drinks at the officers' club. Well, to make a long story short, they ended up at a motel near the base. I don't have to explain these things to you—it was one of these East-meets-West things—but it caused a hell of a row at Vandenburg. The wife wanted to leave her husband for the lieutenant and the lieutenant was all for that. But the Pentagon apologized profusely to the dignitary, the dignitary took his wife back to Japan, the Air Force put the fear of God into your son, and everybody thought the matter was settled."

"But it wasn't."

"No, unfortunately not." The major pulled at the cigar thoughtfully. "Your son continued to write to the woman and she answered him. We found the letters after the accident, when we went through his things. They made plans to meet in Japan during the Christmas holidays. He applied for leave to go back to Connecticut and even wrote to his mother concerning his plans just on the off-chance that somebody might check up on him. He lined up a ride on a military plane to Japan. Military flights often carry service hitchhikers, and since the lieutenant's affair with the Japanese woman had been carefully hushed up, the captain who agreed to take him along had no reason not to."

"That doesn't sound like Paul," Corman said. "He must have known his mother would raise the roof when he didn't show up."

"He had covered that possibility too," the major said. "He drafted out another letter to his mother and a wire. One of his friends on the base was supposed to send that wire on December twenty-second, telling Paul's mother that his leave was canceled and that a letter would follow. The letter explained that he had been put on special duty and wouldn't be home until sometime in the spring. It was a very convincing letter, full of regrets."

"She never got it."

"It was never sent. The friend's wife was involved in a car accident and he went on emergency leave. By the time she was out of the woods, it was already after Christmas and too late to send either the letter or the telegram. Paul's mother was already raising hell at the base, and Air Force Intelligence was on it immediately. It didn't take them very long to find out what happened."

Corman felt a sourness in his stomach now. "Where did they find him?"

"He turned himself in. The wife spent a week with him at an inn near Izu and then decided to go back to her husband. Your son was quite bitter about the whole thing. It completely unhinged him. One minute he turned himself in and the next he changed his mind and almost killed a sergeant in his desire to get out and see the woman again. Anyway, he was subdued. On the first of January he was flown back to the United States." The major fell silent now, a commiserating sadness in his eyes. "I know how you must be feeling, Mr. Corman, I'm sorry the whole thing happened, needless to say."

"I don't want your sympathy," Corman said, "and I still don't see why it was necessary to withhold the truth."

"I think they could have handled it better, but that's only my personal opinion, Mr. Corman. I don't make policy." His eyes were gauging now, as if he was trying to decide whether to go farther than he already had. "I think I can rely on your discretion, Mr. Corman," he said. "The reason for all this covering up is that the American government is negotiating with the Japanese to establish missile bases here. Nothing nuclear, of course, only defensive missiles, but you know how sensitive the Japanese are to such things. At the moment it's all top secret. If anything leaked out concerning the connection between your son and this woman, a good newspaperman could unravel the whole thing. So it was necessary to make it seem that your son had been at Vandenburg all last month, that he had not gone to Japan."

"That sounds very conclusive," Corman said. He

picked up the scrawled note. "But how do you explain this? Why did the woman send it to me?"

"I can't explain it," the major said painfully. "Your son was a very unstable boy, Mr. Corman. In his last days he was raging, incoherent much of the time. I think that's a pretty good description of the note you have. Raging, incoherent. I haven't the slightest inkling what it means. It probably didn't make sense to anybody except himself."

Corman's anger was gone now. It had drained out of him, leaving him with a numbness that approached despair. "I'd like to see the letters he exchanged with the Japanese woman," he said. "I also want to see the letter he wrote to his mother."

"I'm sorry. All that material was sent to Washington. I imagine it's been destroyed by now. There was no point in retaining it."

"Then you can't prove a word of what you've told me."

"No," the major said. "But considering the circumstances, I don't think anything needs proving. You can always press the matter, but I don't think you really want to make an issue out of something which will be harmful to everybody concerned, just because I can't document what I say."

"So I'm to accept on faith."

"It's to your advantage," the major said reluctantly. "There's one thing more. I hesitate to mention it because it might seem that I'm trying to pressure you. In a way I suppose I am. But your son's death was no accident, Mr. Corman. On the second of January he was taken out of the guardhouse and put in a helicopter to be transported to a psychiatric examination. Midway in the flight he attacked the pilot, trying to get control of the helicopter, and when he failed, he opened the door and jumped."

Corman shook his head, stunned. "Suicide?"

"I have children myself," the major said. "I could no more believe that one of my children would be capable of something like that than you can believe it of yours. But things like this happen all the time. And if you insist on pushing this, Mr. Corman, we will have to release all the facts."

Corman stood up. "You've made your point," Corman said.

"It had to be done," the major said. "Now, when are you going back to the States, Mr. Corman?"

Corman retrieved his overcoat from the rack. "I don't know."

"If there's anything we can do to make your stay here more pleasant, give me a ring." He picked up the telephone. "I'll have a car drive you back to the hotel."

"I'd rather walk."

The major glanced at the rain drumming against the window. "It's really coming down."

"I intend to walk."

The major shrugged, returning the telephone to the cradle. "Again, Mr. Corman, I'm sorry about all this. But both of us have to be realistic."

Corman said nothing. He looked toward the major, fixing in his memory the positioning of the spare man behind the desk, the glow of the fluorescent ceiling lights on the thinning scalp, the bushy eyebrows slightly raised. Despite his protestations of sympathy, there was no give to the man, Corman decided, no resiliency at all. Corman knew he was not to blame for any of this; he was an instrument of communication like a telephone or a telegraph key, but Corman could not bring himself to separate the man from his function.

"I'll let you know what I decide," Corman said, "but I think you had better get one thing straight, Major. Until I am sure in my mind what happened, until I'm absolutely convinced, I intend to keep asking questions."

The major said nothing. Corman turned and went through the door.

3

Standing on the sidewalk, he turned up his collar against the rain and momentarily regretted refusing the offer of a car. There were no taxis in sight, and he had no desire to take the subway. It was an aimless time; he did not know what he wanted to do. The confusion within him had almost reached the point of physical pain. Paul was not only dead, but he had killed himself as well, and Corman could not keep from blaming himself for what had happened, at least partially. There was no way to fix the total responsibility for something like this; there were too many vagaries involved, too many twists to the road, but Corman knew beyond doubt that if he had acted differently, kept open the lines of communication, the end result would not have been the same.

He had never really known Paul, that was the trouble; he had never taken the time to find out what made him tick. He had seen the boy last on his eighteenth birthday when Paul and one of his friends from Princeton had come to New York for the day and stopped by Corman's apartment. They came late in the afternoon, and Corman was close enough to finishing his dictation that he felt free to put off the rest of it, and all in all, it had the makings of a pleasant evening. Finley was warm to the boys and mixed drinks all around and then retired to the study to type up her notes. Paul's friend looked after her, a quizzical look on his face, while Paul stared straight ahead, obviously embarrassed, and Corman realized it was not going to be such a pleasant evening after all.

He suddenly felt ill at ease in the presence of his son, and his subsequent attempt to compensate was a poor one. He had not seen the boy in three years and Paul was more like a stranger than his own flesh and blood, a brooding adolescent with a confusing mixture of traits and physical characteristics. He had Corman's slightly Roman nose and Phoebe's wide eyes and a way of pursing his lips thoughtfully at times, before he answered a question, a mannerism Corman supposed that he had picked up from his stepfather. Paul maintained an air of wary disapproval, never looking at his father directly, and Corman had to work to keep his irritation in check.

Paul was wearing a letter jacket. The conversation, for the most part, centered on the rowing team and its chances that year. There was also a divergent discussion about what Paul and his friend had or had not seen in New York, and a few inquiries from the friend (who fancied himself a writer) about Corman's techniques. But Paul was clearly as uncomfortable as Corman was, and after an hour of small talk he stood up abruptly and said they had to be going. Corman caught the surprise in the friend's eyes; quite obviously they had planned to spend the evening. Corman ushered them to the door. The friend left first and Corman could see him through the leaded pane of the door, standing on the sidewalk, swinging a key chain in a glittering golden arc.

Corman took a fifty-dollar bill out of his pocket, putting his hand on Paul's arm and trying to press the money into his hand. "I want you to have a night on the town," he said, smiling.

"No," Paul said, not looking at him, anxious to be gone. "No, thanks."

"Come on, don't drag your feet," Corman urged. "Take it. You can always use fifty dollars."

Abruptly Paul jerked away and Corman heard him say something like "You can't buy it," but he could not be sure of the actual words because he was so startled. The boy's eyes were full of a sudden, shining hostility, an open hatred, and for a moment Corman thought the boy was going to take a swing at him. But he did not. He turned and went down the steps without a backward glance. Stupefied, Corman stood by the door until the fragmented images of the boys had disappeared from the beveled glass, then he went back into the living room and poured himself a double shot of scotch, waiting until the whiskey had eased him before he called Finley from the study and went back to work.

He had handled the whole thing badly, he knew that now. He should have gone after the boy, pressed the issue, ripped open the lines of communication, aired their mutual grievances. But he had not done it, of course, and nothing would be gained by stewing about it. He would put it out of his mind. He walked for fifteen minutes, skirting the edge of a deserted park, and the tension began to drain out of him. He was soaked through now; the overcoat was a soggy mass against his shoulders, and his shoes were full of water.

He walked a few more blocks, hoping to spot a taxi, but there was none. Finally, finding himself in front of a small Japanese bar, he went in out of the rain, taking off his overcoat and hanging it on a rack near a booth where he sat down. He summoned a waitress and remembered enough of his long unused Japanese to order a bottle of Suntori. All of the people in the bar were Japanese, middle-aged men in business suits for the most part, and the hostesses were pretty girls in flowered kimonos. One of them drifted up to his table, a bright, expectant smile on her face, and he murmured his apologies to her. Her smile did not diminish; she bowed and moved away, apparently understanding enough English to know he wanted to be left alone.

When the Suntori came, he poured himself a drink, trying to purge his mind of the persistent image, that final moment when Paul's hand had fumbled with the latch on the helicopter door and he had pitched himself out into the empty sky. After the first drink Corman felt better. He poured himself another and picked up a copy of the English edition of *Asahi* which someone had left behind in the booth, scanning the lead stories in an attempt to divert his thoughts, reading accounts of border skirmishes and minor conflicts, debates in the U.N., the progress of the trouble in Southeast Asia, the endless cycles of international adjustment. There was an item about a Japanese fishing boat that had been rammed by an Australian freighter, killing twelve men. He passed it over quickly; he had already had too much of death today.

And then his eyes fell on the photograph of a man who looked vaguely familiar, an American general with graying hair and a stern face caught by the camera in a moment of anger as he stood addressing a dinner meeting. His mouth was half open; one of his fists was upraised. The lead caption read: GENERAL GIBSON DENOUNCES CHINESE REDS. Corman read on, intrigued, the memories flooding back into his mind now, the photograph yielding to the image of the man as

Corman remembered him, the major who had occupied the office next to his at SCAP, "Old Grumbling Gibson," as the rest of the officers used to call him.

Gibson must have been close to forty then. That would make him somewhere in his sixties now and account for that iron-gray hair. God, how the years went by. Corman had come to know Gibson quite well in those days of occupation, not because he was particularly drawn to this dour-faced man who groused at everything. But Corman had been working on his first book at the time and was patterning a character after Gibson and therefore needed to know more about him. Eventually he had come to appreciate Gibson's virtues, although he couldn't say he had ever enjoyed him as a person. There was not an ounce of humor in Gibson's personality; life was a grim business which absorbed all of his energies. He had no time to spare for frivolous pursuits.

He was a large, bearlike man who, despite great outbursts of profanity, was a true Victorian in the best sense of the word. He refused to tolerate the evils he saw about him, the conditions which most of his fellow officers accepted as inevitable, and he was always fighting something, storming into the offices of his superiors at least once a day to demand action against one social injustice or another.

The biggest battle in his life when Corman knew him was over the disposal of the garbage from the Eighth Army mess halls. As he said to Corman one day, stopping by his office to let off steam, "Goddamnit, Corman, they're selling that garbage to hog contractors when there are a million kids going hungry in his country."

As far as Corman knew, Gibson had never made any headway with the military establishment in this particular battle despite the hundreds of vitriolic memorandums which he poured out. The army structure was too vast, the practical rules too rigidly set, and his protests were vague cries in a bureaucratic wilderness. In their time together they had become friends. When Corman's first book was finally published, Gibson sent him a telegram of congratulations, and

Corman had always meant to write back to him, to keep in touch, but somehow, in the hectic confusion of those days, he had not.

Now he had run across Gibson again, still protesting, still fighting, the issues larger now, befitting his rank as a brigadier general in the Air Force. Corman filled his glass again and drank it halfway down, concentrating on the article. Gibson was commanding officer at Wheeler Air Base now, and the account was of a speech he had made to the Press Club in Tokyo. Always controversial, he was attacking Japanese trade with Red China, calling it unethical and immoral, putting himself out on a limb by questioning the official policy of a friendly nation. However, he did not limit himself to the subject of trade. Fired up by the warm reception his remarks received and the strength of his convictions, he had plunged on into more dangerous areas, heaping invective on Red China and any nation that aligned itself with the Red Chinese position on anything. Red China was a "communist cesspool," a "cancer to civilization," a grave threat to the security of the world. The Red Chinese were close to the point of demonstrating a new missile capable of delivering nuclear weapons anyplace on earth, and their intent was clear. Had not the Chinese Defense Minister, Lin Piao, called for the destruction of "U.S. imperialism, piece by piece"? Had not Mao Tse-Tung said, "We are not afraid of atomic bombs. What if they killed three hundred million Chinese? We would still have plenty more." The handwriting was on the wall; the eventual holocaust would stagger even the most pessimistic imagination unless steps were taken to prevent it.

The questions that followed the speech were inevitable, Corman realized, because Gibson had stopped just short of an aggressive commitment and the reporters could not let it rest there. *Asahi* reported the post-speech questions and answers:

Q: Are we to assume, General, that you advocate some sort of military action against Red China?

A: I'll answer that this way. If somebody's sworn he's going to kill you and you believe he means to try, then you hear he's gone out and bought a high-powered rifle, hell, you're not going to sit still and wait for him to come after you, are you?

Q: Do you advocate a preventative military action, General?

A: I'm saying that Red China has to be disarmed.

Q: By force, if necessary?

A: It's obvious they're not going to enter into any disarmament negotiations, and the stupidity of their public pronouncements is appalling. They don't understand the ramifications of nuclear warfare. In their twisted way of thinking, they're perfectly willing to start a holocaust because they think they'll survive and we won't. They're not afraid, so deterrents are useless.

Q: That leaves only military action, doesn't it, General?

A: I won't quibble with you. Yes, the only thing that will stop them, remove the threat, is military action.

Q: On the part of the United Nations?

A: On the part of anybody big enough and strong enough to get the job done.

Involvement, Corman thought; Gibson had always been involved, trying to change things, to alter, to rectify, vitally concerned about what was happening in the world. Corman envied his vitality, his willingness to commit himself because this was something he himself had never been able to do. He lived, he experienced, but there was no real commitment involved to anything except his work and all else was subordinate to that, grist for his literary mill. Even during those most intimate times, when he was making love to one of the innumerable women who had drifted in and out of his life in the past ten years, he had never been carried away by the heat of passion. There was always one detached, alert corner of his mind which was busy observing, recording, noting the details, the postures, artifices, the texture of flesh, the words, sighs, exclamations, and his own sensate reactions, all of it translated into words and stored away against the time when he would need it.

If he had been able to commit himself all the way, Phoebe would not have divorced him and he would not

The February Plan

have lost his son. He found himself analyzing his own self-pity, putting it into words. This disgusted him. He finished the glass and poured himself another.

At three o'clock he decided he had had enough and he tried to stand up, only to realize that he was not going to be able to make it. He raised a hand and summoned one of the hostesses off her stool at the bar. She came over to his booth, her moon-shaped face slightly expectant, her tiny mouth puckered up in a piquant smile. *"Nani?"* she said. Her voice was musical. It had a bell-like ring to it.

"Do you speak English?" he said.

"Yes," she said, starting to sit down.

"No, I don't want company," he said hurriedly. "You would probably be very good company, but that's not what I want. No, I want you to make a telephone call for me. Call the Imperial Hotel, Miss Finley. Tell her where I am and to come and get me." He paused, waiting for the girl to move, groaning inwardly at the puzzled expression on her face. "You don't speak any English at all, do you?"

"Yis, I speak," she said. "I speak."

"I won't argue with you. If you say you speak, you speak." He fumbled for the small notebook he carried in his pocket, hauling it out to the table with numb fingers, taking out his pen and printing in large letters: IMPERIAL HOTEL, MISS FINLEY. *"Denwa,"* he said, going through the motion of picking up a telephone. "You call for me, all right? *Denwa.*"

"Hai," the hostess said, nodding, her face lighting up. She picked up the piece of paper and retreated toward the back of the bar. He followed her with his eyes, watching her as she summoned the bartender for a hasty conference. Then she disappeared into a back room.

In twenty minutes Finley arrived at the bar. He spotted her the moment she came through the door, her face screwed up as her eyes adjusted to the light, water dripping from her translucent raincoat. Then she located him and came across the bar to his booth, eying first the bottle and then him, without comment.

"Would you like a drink, Finley?" he said.

"No," she said. "How drunk are you?"

"I'm feeling pretty good."

"Can you walk?"

He stood up. His knees threatened to give way but did not. "I think so."

"I have a taxi outside."

He nodded, taking the wad of bills out of his pocket and putting them all on the table. "I want to leave something for the girl who made the call."

"That's too much," she said. She left two of the hundred-yen notes and stuffed the rest of the money in his pocket. "Is that your coat on the hook?"

"Yes."

Once they were outside, the sting of the rain against his face brought him alert. He held the taxi door open for Finley, and then ducked inside, almost falling across the seat before he caught himself.

"You want to talk about it?" Finley said, once she had instructed the driver and the cab was underway.

Corman shrugged. "What's there to say? He killed himself," he said in a monotone.

"Paul?"

"Yes. He was mixed up with a woman and he killed himself."

"Are they sure?"

His face was very tight now. He felt that it was about to break, to shatter into a million pieces. "They're sure."

"Then I can see how you'd want to tie one on," she said sympathetically. "How did it happen?"

He told her, reciting the facts, compressing them, editing them to leave out everything extraneous, feeling numb inside, as if he were outlining a book he intended to write, blocking in the main flow of action and leaving the embellishment for later.

"It's a terrible thing," she said, when he was finished, "but you can't blame yourself for it. There was nothing you could have done about it."

The taxi pulled under the Imperial Hotel's porte-cochere and she signaled the doorman who hurried toward the car. Then she turned her attention to Corman, straightening his tie and smoothing down the collar of his overcoat. "I don't think we should go through the lobby," she said. "I spotted a couple of Japanese reporters on my way out, and you're in no shape for interviews. We'll go downstairs through the arcade and take the elevator from there."

She led the way into the arcade, the rows of subterranean shops, and he held onto her arm as she pushed through the congested crowds, guiding him into the elevator. Once they reached the fourth floor, she left him standing in the hallway while she surveyed the corridor outside his suite. Only when she was sure it was clear did she come back for him, taking him to his room, unlocking the door, depositing him in a chair while she turned down his bed.

"There's no point in sobering you up," she said. "You can use some extra sleep. Take off your clothes. Do you want a hot bath?"

"No bath," he said, watching her as she rummaged through a bureau drawer for his pajamas. She put them on the foot of the bed and then knelt down to take off his shoes. He put his hand on her shoulder. "I want to make love to you," he said.

"Sure you do," she said matter-of-factly, grimacing at the wet socks. "It wouldn't do any good, you know that. You might get rid of your troubles for a few minutes, but they'd come right back. Now, stand up." He stood up and she took off his overcoat and his suit jacket, hanging them on the door to the sitting room. "Just leave your clothes on the floor. I have to send your suit out to have it cleaned and pressed."

"Don't be in such a hurry," he said as she headed for the sitting room. "Stay awhile. Talk to me."

"You'll be better off if you can sleep."

"I'm not going to be able to manage that."

She nodded. "All right. Put on your pajamas. I'll get some coffee."

The coffee was hot and bitter. As he drank it, he could feel his mind clearing. A matter of chemistry, he thought, alcohol and antidote, toxin and antitoxin, and how much of moods and stresses and attitudes would one day be reduced to chemical formulas. He put the cup down and leaned back against the low headboard of the bed, looking toward Finley who sat in an overstuffed chair near the window, facing him, wearing a speculative frown.

"I'm sorry about today," he said.

"You don't have to apologize to me," she said.

"You're the only person I care enough about to apologize to," he said. "But to be frank, I don't know what in the hell you're doing here with me. You should be married."

She smiled slightly. "Now you're sounding like my mother. But I've had enough of marriage. I tried it once, when I was twenty. It didn't work."

"And you let that sour you?"

"I'm not bitter, if that's what you mean. I enjoy my work and that's half the battle."

"You shouldn't be willing to settle for that."

"You keep me pretty busy," she said, "and I enjoy it. The money's good, I like the travel, and I get a certain satisfaction out of your being successful." She was retreating now; he could see it in the way she held herself against the chair. She had not become defensive. No, she was simply pulling back behind one of her damned restrictive lines again. "And speaking of work," she said, "do you want me to make the plane reservations for tomorrow? If you want them, I'll have to call this evening."

"You don't like talking about yourself, do you?"

"There's really nothing to say," she said pleasantly, standing up now, smoothing out the wrinkles in her skirt. "I'm thirty-six, doing a job I enjoy. I take life one day at a time. And that's all there is to it."

He nodded, swallowing another mouthful of coffee. He would accept her limits; he would not push it farther. "I don't want the reservations," he said. "We'll be staying here awhile."

"Are you going to work here?"

"No."

"Then you're still not satisfied about Paul."

He shook his head. "I think the major told me the truth. But I want to know what Paul went through, what he was thinking."

"Then I suppose I should tell you," she said. "Mr.

Mitsu called this afternoon, about an hour before I got the summons from the bar."

"Did he find the woman?"

"Yes," she said quietly. "He's located her."

"Call him back," Corman said. "I want to see him first thing in the morning."

"All right."

"Tell me something," he said, curious now. "If I had decided to go back to the States tomorrow, would you have told me about the call?"

"I don't know. Frankly, I don't think that seeing this woman is going to do you any good. But that's your decision to make, after all." She clicked on the lamp by his bed and turned off the overhead light. "If you're not going to need me any more this evening, I think I'll go down to my room."

"I won't need you," he said. "I have to write to Phoebe and then I'm going to follow your advice and get some sleep."

She paused at the door, stopped by an afterthought. "Oh yes," she said. "The representative of some Japanese literary society called this morning. They want you to give a lecture while you're here. I told him I didn't think you were interested, but I promised to relay the request."

"You're right. I'm not interested."

"I'll let him know. If you need anything, just whistle."

Once she was gone, he started to get out of bed, but he still felt unsteady and a little nauseous and there was really no point in making the effort now. He would write to Phoebe after he had talked with the woman and had more to report. He turned off the light and lay back on the bed, waiting for sleep.

2

MITSU called promptly at eight o'clock the next morning, and Corman arranged to meet him around the corner at the *Naka-Saiwai-mon* entrance to Hibiya Park, between the library and the sprawling public hall. Leaving Finley behind to catch up on the correspondence, he took the elevator down to the arcade and went out a side door to find himself in a different city. Sometime during the night the rain had turned to snow, and the heavy flakes continued to drift down, slowing traffic to a standstill and blanketing the streets.

With the wind at his back he crossed the avenue and walked down the sidewalk flanking the park, passing the great white expanse of the deserted baseball field. Once he had rounded the corner, he saw the black Datsun, and as he approached it, the door swung open to receive him. He slid into the seat. Without a word Mitsu shifted into gear and the car moved away from the curb.

Mitsu was close to fifty, a physically small man with a hairline mustache, In his black overcoat and homburg hat he looked more like a diplomat than a private investigator. "If you don't mind, Mr. Corman," he said in impeccable English with a trace of a British accent, "there is a teahouse in the park where we can talk in more comfort and complete privacy."

"That's fine with me."

Mitsu nodded, turning the car into the park at the next intersection, almost running down a shaggy-headed student who was negotiating the treacherous street on a bicycle, his cape billowing out behind him. Apparently Mitsu was known at the teahouse. A diminutive woman in a kimono led them past the public room to a smaller private room which was furnished Western style, serving them tea and then leaving them alone.

Mitsu sat down at a table, opening his attaché case and removing a folder of papers. "We had very good luck," he said. "Ordinarily something like this could have taken a few weeks."

"I want to see the woman," Corman said. "That's going to be possible, isn't it?"

"No problem there," Mitsu said. He handed the folder of papers to Corman with a slight bow.

Corman rubbed his hands together against the chill in the room. "We might save time if you just tell me about her."

"If you prefer," Mitsu said. "Her name is Akiko Suzuki. By the Japanese standard she is twenty-two years old. By Western chronology she is twenty-one. She works in the documents section of the Meiji Memorial Gallery. Some of the old Imperial Household documents are going to be published in English, and she is one of the translators on the project. She lives in an apartment in Shinnanomachi."

"Her husband," Corman said, interrupting. "What's his official position?"

"Husband?" Mitsu said. "She's not married."

"Then you must have the wrong woman," Corman said flatly. "The woman my son was with had a husband who was a high-ranking official in the Japanese government. They visited California last fall."

Mitsu's fingers laced around the fragile teacup as if to draw warmth from it. "She's not married," he said again, "and she never has been. And she hasn't been out of Japan. I'm positive of that. But she's the woman who addressed the envelope to you."

"Did she tell you that?"

"We have had no direct contact with her."

"Then how can you be so sure she's the right one?"

"My staff is quite thorough," Mitsu said, unperturbed, "and this was a relatively simple matter. From the woman's handwriting it was apparent she had been well trained in writing Western script. Too, she signed her name in the English fashion on the flap of the envelope. Since the letter was postmarked from the Shinjuku post office substation, we concentrated our efforts in that area. It was possible, of course, that she had mailed the letter when she was passing through Shinjuku. If that had been the case, our task would have been more complicated. But the simple explanation is usually the right one, or so has been our experience. And she was making no effort to hide herself; her address had been erased by accident." He paused, lifting the cup as if to study its delicate markings. "I won't bore you with the methods we use to cover an area, but in our business persistence is a greater virtue than cleverness. Once we had located the woman, we compared her handwriting with that on the envelope, and there was no doubt about it. She is the right person."

Corman opened the folder. The report was concise, apparently complete, typed single spaced on three sheets of paper. He read the first page and then looked up at Mitsu. "It says here that her father is with Tokyo University. What does he do?"

"He's a physicist," Mitsu said. "and he is connected with the Institute of Space and Aeronautical Research. As far as we know, he is working at the Japanese Space Center in Satsuma, on a project which is guided by Tokyo University."

"I don't doubt your efficiency," Corman said, "but none of this makes any sense." He went on to tell Mitsu of his conversation with Major Henshaw, not identifying him by name, including only those parts of the story which concerned Paul and the woman, leaving out any mention of the American-Japanese negotiations. "So if my information is correct, this can't be the right woman."

Mitsu permitted himself a smile. "Isn't it possible there were two different women connected with your son? Or perhaps the Suzuki woman simply mailed the letter for him as an act of accommodation."

"It's possible," Corman said. "How long have you been in this business?"

"Twenty years," Mitsu said. "I went to the States intending to become a lawyer, but I didn't like it there. So I went to Great Britain and I studied criminology and came back intending to work for the Tokyo Metropolitan Police. But the pay scale was very low at the time and there was a long list of applicants. I was married and I needed money, so my brother and I went into business for ourselves."

"Apparently you've done well at it."

"Yes," Mitsu said, with some reluctance. "I'm pleased we are successful and I enjoy having many comforts for my family, but when investigators do well, it is a bad time for society in general. There isn't much trust left in Japan. A man applies for a position with a bank and I am hired to investigate him, to see if he is a good risk. Or a man doesn't trust his wife and I'm employed to see what she's doing. Or business partners don't trust each other. And all of industry is full of spies. I don't think there is a single man left any more who is not investigated at least once in his life without his knowledge or approval. Personally I don't like that, but our firm does very well because of it." He looked at his watch. "If you would like to meet this woman now, I will drive you out there."

The trip took the better part of an hour. Mitsu drove cautiously, threading his way through the snarls of traffic at the intersections, the chains on his rear tires rattling against the ice-covered pavement. Finally he turned off a wide avenue into the deserted drive of the Outer Garden of the Meiji Shrine.

Corman remembered the Outer Garden well. He had been here once before with Major Gibson, investigating a report that an unknown GI had broken into the gallery and slashed the face of the Emperor Meiji in a number of paintings. From the adamant tone of the complaint to GHQ, they had expected to be confronted by a very angry curator, but they had not reckoned with the reverse temperament of the Japanese. The curator was undoubtedly incensed, but he never showed it for a moment, leading them through the halls and pointing out the damage with a broad smile, at times breaking into a nervous giggle as he showed them how this painting had been slashed and that one gouged. It had been a curious afternoon, ending with the three of them getting drunk on sake in the curator's office and Gibson staggering back to GHQ to write a report recommending an official apology and the repair of the canvases from the reparations fund.

As Mitsu drove into the long oval in front of the gallery, Corman felt momentarily displaced. The gallery was larger than he remembered it, whiter, with two wings extending from the massive central dome. Mitsu parked the car near the reflection pool, now frozen solid. Three Japanese boys stopped sliding on the ice, staring after them as they climbed the stairs to the arched entranceway.

"I'll find out where she is," Mitsu said. He bought the tickets and then stopped to talk to the guard for a few moments before he turned back to Corman. "Her office is the third one down the east wing. She's there now. Do you want me to come with you?"

"No, thanks."

"Take your time. I'll have a look at the pictures."

The paintings were as bad as Corman had remembered them, heroic and massive canvases in the European style, complete with resplendent uniforms and prancing horses and long descriptive titles such as "Return to the Throne of the Administrative Authority by the Tokugawa Shogunate." There were few people in the gallery, a uniformed student or two and a herd of very small children in quilted robes shepherded by a pair of governesses.

The legend on the third door was written in Japanese, and he rapped on it lightly. The chatter of voices inside quieted immediately and then the door opened to him. There were two women in the room, working at a long table heaped with partially unrolled scrolls and old papers. The older of the two, a woman in her fifties, wearing a gray kimono, bowed slightly in his direction.

"I'm looking for a Miss Suzuki," he said. "Akiko Suzuki."

The older woman nodded, bowing again as she left the room, leaving him alone with the younger woman who regarded him with slightly apprehensive eyes, brushing the long black hair away from her face with the back of a thin hand. "I am Miss Suzuki," she said.

"I'm sorry to disturb you like this," he said, "especially since I'm not sure you're the person I'm looking for." He took the scribbled note out of his wallet and held it out to her. "Does this mean anything to you?"

She took it, adjusting the heavy-rimmed glasses on her nose, a hesitant glint in her eyes. She read the note and then handed it back to him, her face composed. "Where did you get this?" she said.

"I think you sent it to me," he said quietly. "I'm Paul's father."

"I see," she said. She picked up one of the scrolls and began to reroll it, compressing it in her thin fingers. She was a delicately boned girl, dressed in a baggy black wool dress which did not become her. She was not a pretty woman, Corman decided, much too frail, her features too angular, her hair drab, not at all the kind of girl he had thought would appeal to Paul. "What do you want of me?" she said at last.

"I want to know a lot of things. But first you can tell me what this note means."

"I don't know."

"But you sent it to me. You must have some idea."

"I knew he meant it for you," she said. "So I looked up your address in *Who's Who* and I sent it to you."

"Did he ask you to send it to me?"

"No. He didn't ask."

"I'm sorry," he said, "but I'm confused by all this. Did you know Paul very well?"

"Quite well," she said. "Do you have a cigarette?"

He handed her a pack and she took one out, moving away from the table to light it. "We're not supposed to smoke in here," she said, "but sometimes I do it anyway. I stay away from the worktable so there's no danger to the manuscripts." She exhaled the smoke. "I don't think I want to talk about Paul," she said. "He's in enough trouble as it is."

"Trouble?" Corman said, startled by her use of the present tense.

"He must be or you wouldn't have come to see me,"

she said. "He doesn't like you very much, do you know that? He is very bitter toward you."

"You don't really know about it, do you?" he said, almost to himself. "Paul's dead, Miss Suzuki."

She looked at him sharply, the cigarette freezing in her hand. He had never seen such a look of pain as he saw now in her eyes, in the reflexive grimace of her mouth, and he thought she was going to cry out. But she made no sound. She just stood there, looking at him.

"I didn't mean to shock you," he said. "Paul was killed in a helicopter accident in California early this month. I came to Japan to find out why he was here in December, to talk with anybody who knew him."

She looked away, smoking the cigarette again, trying to conceal the tremor in her hands. "I was afraid he was dead," she said. "I had a dream one night and I saw him dead."

"You say you knew my son very well. Can you tell me who the other woman is?"

"Other woman?"

"My son was having an affair with a married woman," Corman said quietly. "Maybe you didn't know it, but that's why he came to Japan."

She turned to Corman now, snuffing out the cigarette in an ash tray which she took from a drawer, replacing it the moment she was through with it. "There was no other woman, Mr. Corman," she said.

"Maybe you don't understand what I'm trying to say."

"I understand," she said, "but there was no other woman, believe me. I was in love with Paul and he was in love with me."

"Where did you meet him?"

"Here, in Tokyo. There was a scientific meeting of some sort and a reception afterward. My father took me. Most of the professors took their wives, but my mother is dead. During the evening I became ill, a very bad headache, so an American officer offered to drive me home. It was Paul. After that we met very often. And we fell in love."

"When was this?"

The February Plan

"I met him in November, the last of November."

He shook his head, incredulous. "That's hardly possible," he said stubbornly. "He didn't get to Japan until late in December. He was following a woman he met in the States."

"I'm sorry," she said, "but it did not happen that way."

He had difficulty thinking now. The room was unbearably close and the smell of the old papers was overpowering. He sat down on a chair against the wall, occupying his hands with the lighting of a cigarette. "You said Paul was in trouble."

"The trouble was not until later," she said, "and I never knew exactly what it was. When we met, no, not then, but when we fell in love, he was very happy." Paul had not wanted to fall in love, she went on, and neither had she, especially with an American, but both of them were lonely and ready for it and so it happened. When they were together they talked incessantly and they found that they had a great deal in common. She was not close to her father. He worked at Satsuma, and in his infrequent visits to Tokyo he was absorbed in his studies and conferences so that there was no real communication between them. Paul was equally withdrawn from his parents. He was bitter toward Corman, never really close to his stepfather, and his mother never really understood him. Paul had showed Akiko one of her letters once in which his mother was advising him to go down to the Los Angeles County Museum to see a certain exhibition, not because she thought he would enjoy it, but because it would fill a gap in his education.

"And when was this," Corman interrupted, "the letter about the art exhibit?"

"About the first week in December, I think."

"So she thought he was in the States."

"Yes," she said. "He wrote letters telling her he was in California and those letters were sent back to be mailed from there."

"Where was he stationed here?"

"Somewhere in Tokyo. I never knew exactly where."

"The reception where you met him—where was it held?"

"In Shimbashi, at a new American company called American Electronics. They had just gone into business. My father said the scientific meetings they held and the reception were just publicity, because they hoped to sell electronic items to the Japanese space program."

He took out his notebook and recorded the name of the company. "Now," he said, "about this trouble Paul was in. I want to know everything you can remember."

"It began about the middle of December," she said. "Paul wanted to go back to the States to tell his mother about us and to take care of some personal business." He thought the Air Force would let him go, she continued, because there was a delay in the project he was working on and consequently he was just killing time anyway. He was so certain he could go that he wrote his mother, asking her to arrange a party for some of his old school friends. Akiko was upset about his plans, but he promised her he would be back in Japan shortly after New Year's.

Then, on December nineteenth—she remembered the exact date because she had the afternoon off—he came to see her at her apartment. He was upset, angry because the project schedule had been accelerated and his leave had been canceled. Too, there was trouble in his outfit. Some of his fellow officers had been arrested, for no reason that he could see, and rumor had it that they had been sent to a special detention camp in northern Japan. He had made it his business to find out what had happened to them, the charges against them, but all of his inquiries were rebuffed. She calmed him down. He spent the evening and then went back to his base.

They had not planned to see each other for a week, but on the afternoon of December 23 he showed up at the gallery, in a foul mood. He had been drinking. He came in the back way, swearing very loudly, and she was afraid the guards would hear the noise and call the military police. She took him into her workroom and made him promise to stay there while she went to the

The February Plan

gallery director and asked for the afternoon off, pleading a sick headache. She managed to get Paul out of the gallery without incident, hoping the fresh air would sober him up.

It didn't work. He had the bottle with him, and when they reached her apartment, he finished it off, sitting in the middle of the floor, wearing his overcoat. He asked for a sheet of paper and a pencil, saying he was going to write to his father, but he scribbled no more than a few lines and said to hell with it. His father wasn't going to do anything about this. He was going to have to take care of things himself.

She talked him out of his overcoat, and while she was hanging it in the closet, she felt something heavy and cold through the material. There was an army pistol in the pocket. Frightened, she hid the pistol in a small writing desk and then sat down beside him on the floor, trying to get him to talk. She knew he was in trouble and wanted to help, but there was nothing she could do unless he told her the truth. Finally he took a paper out of his pocket and handed it to her, asking her if she recognized any of the names written there. She looked at them, a list of names numbered one through eight, but they meant nothing to her.

When she asked him to explain, he changed his mind and took the paper back, telling her she would be safer if she didn't know what was going on. She talked him into lying down awhile and made him a pot of black coffee, but the first cup made him violently sick to his stomach. Afterward he lay down on the floor again and went to sleep.

At seven o'clock he got up and retrieved his coat from the closet, moaning in despair when he found the pistol missing, knowing instantly that she had hidden it. He was not abusive, but he was insistent. He had to have that pistol; if she didn't give it to him, a lot of people were going to get hurt.

At this point she was trembling with fear and indecision. She knew that something terrible would happen if she gave him the pistol. He argued that he was already in serious trouble. He had found out something about the project and refused to go along with it.

Consequently they had tried to arrest him, and even now the military police were looking for him. It had been a mistake coming to her place because they would track him here and he didn't want to get her into trouble. He had to leave immediately, but he couldn't go without the pistol. When he had done what he had to do, he would surrender himself to the authorities.

She broke down and wept, determined not to lose him, finally proposing a bargain. He could have the pistol back if he agreed to take her with him. She knew where she could borrow a car—from one of her co-workers who lived in the next block—and she would drive him wherever he wanted to go. It made sense. He couldn't afford to expose himself by taking the train or subway. And he couldn't speak enough Japanese to take a taxi.

After some argument he gave in, but she refused to give him the pistol until she came back with the car. It took her fifteen minutes to get it and drive back to the apartment. She prayed all the way that he would not be gone and breathed a sigh of relief when she saw him sitting in the low entryway, putting on his shoes. She got the pistol from the writing desk for him. Without a word he put the pistol in his overcoat pocket and climbed into the car.

He told her to drive to the American Electronics Company in Shimbashi, and she made the trip in terror, torn between wanting to have an accident to keep him from using the pistol and the certain knowledge that he would be taken into custody if she did. She avoided the Ginza, taking a purposely long route, killing time while she talked to him. She loved him, she said, she wanted to marry him. If he loved her, he would balance what he was about to do against their future together. He said little. He loved her, but this was something he had to do. He had no choice.

American Electronics was housed in a long, concrete, modernistic structure in the warehouse district not far from Shimbashi Station. She drove down the narrow street which fronted it, then Paul directed her to turn into an alley just beyond the building and stop the car. He got out and studied the fence that protected the side and the rear of the building. He just stood there with his hands in his pockets, his back to the wind, his shoulders hunched up against the cold. The exterior of the building was floodlighted, and the fence bore a large red warning sign in Japanese and English.

Muttering to himself, he climbed back into the car and told her to follow the alley as it curved to the left. In a few minutes they were back on the street in front of the building, and he had her park in the shadows just beyond it. He sat in the car a long time, smoking a cigarette in silence. Despite the lateness of the hour, the company was still open, and through the large plate-glass windows which framed the foyer he could see the pretty American receptionist at her desk. She was wearing headphones, working at a typewriter, transcribing something from a dictating machine.

Paul watched for perhaps fifteen minutes, then he kissed Akiko and told her to take the car and go home. He would get in touch with her as soon as he could. Once again she begged him not to go, but he paid no attention to her, getting out of the car and going into the building. The receptionist took off her earphones and Akiko could see that they were talking together. Then the receptionist got up and led him through a door into a corridor.

Akiko could not leave without knowing what was happening and she stayed where she was, watching the building. The receptionist did not come back into the foyer. The building seemed deserted; no one went in or out of the large glass door. Finally Akiko could stand it no longer. She got out of the car and was just going into the building when she heard the shots, four of them, from somewhere deep in the building, muffled, like the sounds of firecrackers. In that second she panicked. She ran across the foyer to the door Paul had gone through. It was locked. She pounded on it with her fists and then, suddenly afraid for herself, she ran out of the building and into the street just as four men came running around the side of the building. She ran for the car, but she stumbled and fell on the sidewalk. The four men caught her.

"Were they American?" Corman said.

Her face was very pale now. "Three were American. One was Japanese."

He stood up, holding the cigarette over his open palm so the ashes would not fall on the floor, opening the drawer to get the ash tray. "What did they do to you?" he said.

"Nothing," she said. "They frightened me, but that's all." One of the men had held her arm, she went on, not roughly, but enough to restrain her while the other three men split up, two going down the street one way and the third in the other direction. There was no traffic at all; the street was too narrow for the large trucks which serviced the furniture warehouses, and they were all closed at this hour anyway. In a few minutes the men were back. The Japanese began to question her in Japanese, but she answered in English and one of the Americans took over, asking her where she had parked the car. When she pointed it out, two of the Americans walked with her to the car and climbed in, one in the front seat with her and the other in the rear. The other two men went back into the building.

She was almost hysterical by now. The Americans were very calm, very polite. They examined her identification papers and seemed impressed by the fact that she was Professor Suzuki's daughter. They would not tell her what had happened in the building. They deluged her with questions. They wanted to know her connection with Paul, assuming she knew what he was doing and had come here to help him. She denied it. In her desperation she grabbed a lie and held to it. She scarcely knew Paul at all. He had stopped by the apartment looking for her father and then had forced her to go with him. She knew nothing.

They talked to her for about an hour and then drove her back to her apartment, going in with her, one of the men searching the two rooms while the other continued to question her. He wanted to know everything about her, where she worked, where she had gone to school, the names of her friends, her political and religious affiliations, how long she had known Paul, how many times she had seen him, everything.

The February Plan

But she stuck to her story. She had seen Paul only once before tonight, the time when he drove her home from the reception. She might have caught a glimpse of him from time to time when he came around looking for her father, but she had not spoken to him. After a while the man finished searching the apartment. They warned her to mention what had happened to no one and then they left.

"So they believed you," Corman said.

"No," she said with a trace of irony in her voice. "They knew Paul and I were in love. They knew we had been having an affair. But they were satisfied I didn't know what he was doing at the electronics company. And that's all they were interested in."

"How do you know that?"

"My father told me. He came back the next day, very upset. I think the Americans told him about what had happened. He questioned me and became very angry, and then he cried and told me to forget everything that had happened. He said that if I ever mentioned it to anybody, Paul would be killed."

"Killed?"

"That was the word he used."

"So you never found out what Paul was doing there."

"No," she said. "For a week I was too ashamed to do anything, not because of my father, but because I had betrayed Paul. Maybe there was nothing I could have done for him that night, but I should have tried."

"Yes," he said. "You should have tried."

"And then later, when I didn't hear from him, I took the note he had written for you and I found your address and I sent it to you." She was too restless now to sit still any longer. She went back to the worktable, beginning to rearrange the scrolls. "But one thing still troubles me. Did I send the note to you because I really wanted to help Paul? Or did I send it to you because I wanted to relieve my conscience, so I could say to myself, 'There, I did something, it's not my responsibility any more'?"

"Nothing's ever clear-cut," Corman said. "But I can

tell you this, I don't think there was anything you could have done to help him."

"But why do we have to protect ourselves, to be so selfish? Or maybe it's just me, I don't know. I loved him, but he didn't come first."

The universal problem, Corman thought, the universal disease. "It's not just you," he said gently. "Everybody suffers from it. You're just more honest with yourself than most." He ground out the cigarette in the ash tray. His mouth tasted stale, dry. "Those men who picked you up that night, were they in uniform?"

"Only the Japanese."

"Was he a policeman?"

"No, I think he was a plant guard."

"And the Americans—they didn't identify themselves?"

"No. I thought perhaps they worked at the company."

"Were they armed?"

"I don't know. I thought they were, but I didn't see any guns."

"And they never contacted you again?"

"No."

"One more thing. The list that Paul showed you—what kind of names were on it?"

"They were Chinese, I think."

"But written in English, a romanized script?"

"Yes."

"Do you remember any of them?"

"No, I . . ." she began, and then she caught herself. "Yes, there was one," she said. "I remembered it because it was the French word for 'dog.' I don't know why I should have remembered it, but it didn't seem to belong in the list."

"Chien," he said.

She nodded. "Chien," she repeated. "Chien San-Chiang. Yes, that was it."

He wrote it down. "But it doesn't mean anything to you."

"No." The telephone rang. She gave it a reluctant glance, then composed herself and picked it up. She said a few words in Japanese and then put it back on the cradle. "I'm sorry," she said, "but I have a staff meeting. I have to go."

"Can I talk with you again later?"

She did not answer immediately. She opened the windows a crack to clear out the smoke and then took the ash tray from him, emptying it into a wastebasket before she cleaned it with a cloth and replaced it in the drawer. "I've told you all I know," she said.

"I may have some more questions when I've had time to think."

"Tomorrow, then, you can call me here." She wrote a telephone number on a slip of paper and handed it to him. "This is my number here, my extension." She followed him out of the room, closing the door behind her. "Paul was really a very nice person," she said. "It makes no difference what you find out about him. You should remember that." She looked at him a moment longer and then turned away, walking across the exhibition hall toward the director's office, her low heels clacking against the polished floor.

2

"What kind of licensing system does Japan have for private investigators?" Corman asked Mitsu on the way back to the Central District.

"Very strict," Mitsu said, keeping his eyes on the road. The snowfall had thickened and he kept the car at a crawl. "We register with the government and then their investigators investigate us. We have to post a bond, a very large one, and then we have to pay a licensing fee."

"Are you required to file reports with the government about the cases you're working on?"

Mitsu shook his head. "On our tax reports we are required to list our sources of income, but since we are in a highly circumspect profession, we are allowed considerable latitude. In some cases I have listed income under miscellaneous to satisfy a client who did not want his name connected with my firm in any public record. The government tax auditors have never questioned this."

"Suppose you run across evidence of an unprosecuted crime in the course of one of your investigations. Are you required to report it to the authorities?"

Mitsu brought the car to a halt at an intersection, waiting until a streetcar passed before he urged the car forward again. "What you are asking me, in essence, is how confidential the law allows me to be."

"Yes."

Mitsu smiled tolerantly. "My conscience is a stricter governor than the law. I deal only with information. Mr. Corman. One party desires facts about another, and I supply it. What is done with that information is none of my affair. If I ever broke a confidence, I would be finished in this business. I would also be subject to prosecution." He frowned at the road now. They were on the gentle downgrade of the street flanking the Diet Building and the traffic had increased quite suddenly, the cars jammed together, one behind the other, horns blaring as they were slowed to a complete stop. "I'm afraid we've hit a traffic jam," Mitsu said. "It may take us some time to get back to your hotel."

"I'm in no great hurry," Corman said thoughtfully. He did not really understand Mitsu and he was not sure that he could trust him. But when it came right down to it, he had no choice. He would have to take the chance. "I have something I would like you to do for me." Corman said, as the cars began to move again. "But I think you should have the opportunity to turn it down. In any event, whether you do it or not, I have to ask you to keep what I have to say in the strictest confidence."

"That's fair enough," Mitsu said.

Corman told him the whole thing, everything the major had told him and a full account of his conversation with the girl. "I don't know why the American government has chosen to lie about this," he said, "and I don't know what they're trying to hide."

"Governments lie for the same reasons that individuals do," Mitsu said. "Sometimes they really have something to hide, sometimes they simply make a mistake and don't want to admit it, and sometimes a lie gets

The February Plan

started by accident and grows out of proportion before anybody can stop it. What do you want me to do?"

"I want to know what happened to my son," Corman said flatly. "I want to know what he did at the electronics company that night, just for my own information, without stirring up anything that could reach the papers. I have the feeling you may run head on into government resistance and you may be risking your license by getting involved."

"That's true," Mitsu admitted. "And because of that risk my fee would have to be proportionately higher. There's a Japanese tradition against the open discussion of money matters, and many people consider it to be bad taste, but I've found that I have much less difficulty when there is a clear-cut understanding."

"I appreciate that. How much do you want?"

"I can't say, at the moment. First, I have to make a few preliminary inquiries to see whether I will be able to help you. Then I must talk to my brother and my accountant and draw up a cost estimate. When I have that, I can quote you a price." They had reached the hotel now and Mitsu stopped the car, asking a few questions about Paul, a general physical description, his full name, rank, and serial number, writing down the answers.

"When can I expect to hear from you?" Corman said.

"Tomorrow morning."

"Fine."

He went up to his suite to find the galleys for his new book awaiting him on the desk, the long printed sheets neatly aligned along one side of the blotter and his notes for some contemplated changes in a balancing stack on the opposite side, with a sheaf of blank paper and some newly sharpened pencils in the middle. It was Finley's delicate way of prodding him, but she was nowhere around. He ignored the work in front of him. Taking off his overcoat, he rubbed his hands together to restore the circulation in his cold fingers, then he picked up the telephone and asked the operator to get him Major Henshaw at the American Embassy. It took a full minute for the call to go through, and then there was no answer from the major's office. He left his name and hung up, just as Finley walked in, her arms full of packages.

He helped her deposit them on the divan. "It looks like you bought up the town," he said.

She smiled, taking off her coat and putting it in the closet, shaking her hair loose after its confinement in the hood. "I just went for a walk," she said. "I hadn't intended to buy a thing, but I saw some silk in a shopwindow and I was hooked. Have you been back long?"

"Not long," he said. "I see that the galleys are here. How in the hell did Henderson get them here so fast?"

"Special messengers and a direct flight," she said. "There is also another cable from him. He wants them 'soonest.'"

"He'll have to wait. Do you feel like taking some dictation?"

"Sure." She got her pad from the desk and sat down, crossing her long legs.

"There's no heading on this. I just want to put down everything before I forget it." He began to dictate and the pencil whispered against the paper. He recorded the conversation with the major and the girl, his memory emptying itself automatically, and with a start he realized quite suddenly how cut off from any meaningful human relationships he really was. The thought distressed him. This woman who sat taking his dictation was the only person in the world he was really close to, but even that relationship was insubstantial, dependent on money.

He finished the dictation and then stood looking at the street and the park beyond and the Tokyo Tower in the distance, its lights winking through the gloom of snow.

"Do you think the girl is telling the truth?" Finley said.

"I think so. She has no reason to lie to me."

"What are you going to do about it?"

He shook his head. "I don't know yet," Suddenly, on impulse, he turned to her. "What are you doing tonight, Finley?"

She laughed, startled. "What I do every night, I suppose. I'll do my nails and read."

"Let's change the routine," he said enthusiastically. "I think we should see Tokyo. Hell, I don't know, maybe we can have dinner someplace and go to a night club. How about it?"

"All right," she said. "But I didn't come equipped for anything too dressy."

"You look fine," he said. "Eight o'clock."

"Eight o'clock." She smiled. She looked at her watch meaningfully. "That should give you about five hours to work on the galleys. I'll take the portable down to my room and type up the dictation."

When she was gone, he sat down at the desk, intending to work on the galleys, but he found that he could not get interested in them. He had worked two years on this book, off and on, with varying degrees of excitement, and he had looked forward to making some final changes in the galleys, the last chance he would have to touch the book before it was published. There was one scene in the book that still bothered him, and in the week before the news had come about Paul he had blocked out the new direction he wanted to pursue. But now the notes were stale and his enthusiasm had fled. He made a half-dozen efforts to get started, pacing the room, sitting down to write a single line, and then pacing again. At four o'clock he gave up. He put on his coat and went out, stopping by the Japan Travel Office in the arcade to get directions to the American Electronics Company.

A girl in a kimono gave him a map of the Central District and wrote out the address in Japanese characters for him to hand to a taxi driver, but once he was on the street he realized he was not going to be able to get a taxi. The rush hour had begun; the street was clogged with vehicles. He decided to walk. Consulting the map, he set out. It was only four-thirty, but the heavy snow deepened the twilight and the street lights had already come on. According to the map, Shimbashi Station was only a short distance to the south and the electronics company was near the station, but he chose to follow the Ginza instead.

He barely recognized the street. The flashy neon signs burst against the overcast in great whorls and loops of colors. Nothing was familiar to him except the trees which still sat in their square boxed holes along the sidewalk. As he walked along the street, pushing through the crowds of people, he began to have second thoughts about the wisdom of taking off on his own. It was unlikely he would learn anything at the company, and his premature questions might complicate Mitsu's investigation. Corman was reasonably sure Mitsu would take the case; Corman was a firm believer in the power of money to overcome obstacles.

Shimbashi Station had not changed much. It was still crowded with throngs of commuters battling to get up the steps to the train platforms; the same façade of dirty stone and concrete still remained, the same deep rumble of the trains on the overhead tracks. Across the street from the station, there had once been a night club known as the "A-1." The building was still there, but according to the sign, it was now occupied by a Japanese printing company.

He turned off into one of the narrower side streets, moving more briskly now as darkness fell and the air grew bitterly cold. The electronics company was just as Akiko had described it, a low, modern building which looked out of place in the setting of decrepit stone buildings which surrounded it. He pushed through the large glass door and went into the foyer, cleaning the snow off his feet on the mat before he approached the desk and the pretty young American receptionist who smiled up at him. "Good weather for penguins, isn't it?" she said.

"Yes," he said, returning her smile.

"May I help you?"

"I'd like to see one of the officers of your company," Corman said, temporarily disconcerted, not knowing how to phrase his business. *My son stormed in here with a pistol one night last month and now he's dead and I want to know what happened.*

"Yes, sir. Are you interested in some of our electronic equipment?"

The February Plan

"No, it's a personal matter," Corman said. "Do you have a public relations man?"

"Our Mr. Wilkinson handles that. May I have your name, sir?"

"Corman," he said. "Phillip Corman."

"Thank you." She turned and pressed a button on the telephone and then picked it up and spoke into it, nodding before she turned back to Corman. "Would you go right in, sir?" she said, indicating a door to her left. "Mr. Wilkinson's office is the first one to the right after you enter the corridor."

He turned toward the door which she indicated, noticing that there was a second door leading off the foyer, this one marked "No Admittance." with a string of Japanese characters beneath it. He wondered which of these doors Paul had gone through that night.

Corman had seen Wilkinson's type before, in publishers' offices, along Madison Avenue, young, vigorous, good-looking men with crew-cut hair and tanned faces (an implication of involvement with the great outdoors), and as Corman entered his office, Wilkinson stood up to meet him, shaking his hand, asking him to have a seat.

Corman looked at the illustrations on the wall, large framed pictures of rockets blasting off and multi-horned satellites drifting around in space. "Coals to Newcastle," Corman said.

"Beg pardon?"

"I thought the Japanese were masters in the electronics field. What's an American company doing over here?"

"The Japanese are pretty good," Wilkinson confessed. "But some of the components we make are unique and we're really not in direct competition with any of the Japanese firms. They wouldn't have let us operate in Japan if we were. But we use exclusive American designs and Japanese labor, so you might say we have the best of both. Now, what can we do for you, Mr. Corman?"

The right tone had now been set, an atmosphere of easy cordiality between Americans in a foreign country.

"Well, I'm a writer," Corman said. "And I'm doing some research over here."

"Not *the* Phillip Corman?" Wilkinson said, his eyes suddenly interested. "I've read most of your books. They're really first-rate."

"Thank you," Corman said.

"We'll be glad to help you in any way we can. Are you researching another book?"

Corman shook his head. There was nothing to be gained by pretense, in beating around the bush. "I'll be frank with you, Mr. Wilkinson," he said. "I'm looking for information about my son."

"Your son?"

"The Air Force lieutenant who one night last month forced his way in here with a gun."

"The what?" Wilkinson said, a baffled smile on his face, as if he had not heard Corman correctly.

"My son came in here with a gun," Corman said grimly. "Now, that's a fact, Mr. Wilkinson, and I can prove it, so we can drop the pretenses. He came in here; there was trouble of some sort. I want to know what happened to him."

"You're really serious, aren't you?" Wilkinson said, his smile fading.

"Yes."

"And when did you say this happened?"

"The night of December twenty-third."

Wilkinson shook his head, perplexed, flipping back through an appointment book, checking an entry. "I thought so, but I wanted to be sure. I was here on the night of the twenty-third—a couple of appointments—and believe me, nothing like that happened. This is a small company. If anybody had stormed in here with a pistol, I'd know about it."

"I'm not here to make trouble for you," Corman said. "I just want the truth."

"The truth," Wilkinson said with a mystified shrug. "In the first place, Mr. Corman, why would anybody try to hold us up? We don't deal with cash here. Oh, there's some in petty cash, I suppose, but not enough to justify a robbery. He couldn't have hoped to steal

The February Plan 51

any of our electronic components. They wouldn't have been of any earthly use to him."

"Then you deny the whole thing."

"I'm not denying anything," Wilkinson said patiently. "I'm just saying it didn't happen. What led you to believe your son was here?"

"I won't go into that."

"Perhaps it was some other electronics company. If I were you, I'd go to the Japanese police. Any happening of that sort would certainly have been reported."

Corman shook his head. He was wasting his time here, but there was one more question he had to ask. "You held a reception last November, a scientific meeting, an open house. That's true, isn't it?"

"Yes."

"My son was invited to it. That means you must have a record of his address in your files."

"I'm sorry," Wilkinson said regretfully. "We didn't issue individual invitations except in a few special cases, and all of those went to Japanese scientists who wouldn't have come unless they were singled out. We sent a notice to the University of Tokyo and there were a couple of items in the paper. If your son came, he must have seen one of those."

"And I suppose you didn't keep a guest list?" Corman said sourly.

Wilkinson shook his head. "No, sir."

Corman stood up. "I'm wasting your time and mine," he said.

"Not at all," Wilkinson said, rising at the same time. "I wish I could help you, Mr. Corman, believe me. If I were you, I'd go to the police. The Japanese police are very efficient." He walked down the hall with Corman, chatting all the way, promising to check with some of the other electronics companies and report back if he could find out anything more tangible, inviting him to come back and have a drink any time.

And then, just as they reached the foyer, Corman saw a man going out the door and he stopped short, craning his head to one side to minimize the reflection of the foyer lights in the glass door. The man was of medium height, stocky, and there was something about the way he walked that struck Corman as familiar. A kind of bustling swagger. The man went to the curb and turned slightly for a moment, looking down the street toward an approaching car, and Corman caught a glimpse of his face in profile. With a start of recognition Corman pushed open the door and went out into the street. But he was too late. The man had already climbed into the car and it had pulled away into the falling snow. Corman stood looking after it, very curious now. The man had been dressed in civilian clothes; he had gained considerable weight since Corman had seen him last, but there was not the slightest shred of doubt in Corman's mind as to who he was. The man in the car was his old friend, General Gibson.

3

"I'm sure it was old grumbling Gibson," he said, having to raise his voice against the blare of the orchestra. "I couldn't have made a mistake about that."

"There's nothing so strange about that, is there?" Finley said, finishing her drink. "After all, an American company is bound to do business with the American military."

"But why should they lie about Paul's being there that night?"

"Can you be sure the Japanese girl told you the truth?"

"I believe her," he said, his voice drowned out by the passage of a miniature train. It was filled with bare-breasted chorus girls and it ran on a platform track around the walls of the night club. That was the trouble with the modern Japanese, he thought; they never knew when to quit. If one of anything was adequate, then a hundred would not be too much. The night club itself was a case in point, vastly overdone, with a myriad of stars projected on a black ceiling and hundreds of spinning satellites hanging from invisible wires against a background of mirrored walls. The orchestra was too big and too loud, the girls too flamboyant, the drinks too large, the tariff too high.

The February Plan   53

He was not distracted, but Finley seemed to be enjoying herself, and perhaps the dissatisfaction he felt was not with the city at all but with the riddle that continued to nag at his mind, making a lighthearted evening impossible. They had gone to a geisha house for dinner, but it was not the kind of place he remembered from the old days, and he found himself bored. After dinner he had taken her to a club where a dozen "go-go" girls gyrated on a stage high against one wall, each girl framed in a three-way mirror. It was much too frantic for his tastes, and after a couple of drinks they had come to this place.

"Would you like to dance?" he asked, standing up, pushing his chair back.

"Yes, I think I would," she said.

There was too much of a mob on the dance floor and they could do little more than stand close together, eddying around in the tides of dancers, most of them Japanese and most of them drunk. He was surprised to find how relaxed she was against him. They stayed on the dance floor until the next show started and then they went back to the table and had another drink. The floor show was terrible, again too much. "Are you ready to leave?" he said to her.

"Any time."

In the taxi on the way back to the hotel he sat with his arm around her and her head on his shoulder. She smiled at him happily. "Doesn't it strike you as being pretty darned strange?" she said.

"What?"

"All this," she said. "I mean, less than three weeks ago you were getting ready to go on a lecture tour and I was all set to hole up for a couple of months and transcribe dictation, and then, well, here we are. You just never can tell what direction life is going to take, can you?"

"No," he said. She was extremely vulnerable tonight; the tone of her voice told him that. For the moment her defenses were gone and she was no longer a protective secretary operating according to the strict rules she had set for herself. "Do you mind being here?" he said. "Do you mind having your well-ordered life interrupted?"

"My well-ordered life." She laughed slightly. "Do you know what I do with myself in New York when we're not working?"

"No. I've wondered."

"It's a regular dog path," she said. "On Monday nights I take adult education classes. The subject doesn't really matter; I've been through everything from sewing to modern art. On Tuesday night I answer letters. Wednesday night I do my hair. On Thursday night my sister Ethel—she lives in Manhattan—drops by the apartment to complain about her husband and kids. On Friday night I go out, usually to a movie or a concert, sometimes on a date, sometimes alone. On Saturday morning I clean my apartment and then I go to Brooklyn to spend the weekend with my mother. She's widowed and she cries a lot, and when she's not crying she's lecturing me on finding a husband and becoming respectable. On Sunday morning we go to Mass, and in the afternoon my brother Howard drops over with his wife and stays just long enough to satisfy his conscience. Sunday night I go back to my apartment and work to make myself look presentable on Monday, and then I start the dog path all over again."

"It never varies?"

"A little sometimes, but not much." She laughed again. "Do you know what a fuss my mother made when she found out I was going to Japan with you? She called Howard—he's a lawyer—and tried to talk him into telling me about the Mann Act and white slavers. When he wouldn't do it, she called a priest. And when she couldn't interest any of the men of the cloth in the pit her daughter was about to fall into, she came all the way to Manhattan to tell me about men."

"And what did you say to her?"

"That she was just about twenty years late with her advice. She never recognized my marriage. It wasn't in the church, so it didn't count. She still sees me as a virginal girl of fourteen. She still has my confirmation dress tucked away somewhere." She raised up slightly,

The February Plan

looking out the window at the lights haloed by the swirling snow. "That's really Japan out there, isn't it?"

"Yes."

She sank back against his shoulder. "I should never drink anything," she said. "I do all right when I don't have anything to drink."

"I think you're doing all right now," he said.

"No, not at all. You're my employer, my boss." She giggled slightly, remembering something. "Once in a while I have lunch with a group of secretaries and we all sit around talking about our 'bosses' as if we were serfs or something. It's positively feudal." Her smile faded.

They had reached the hotel now, and the doorman scurried to the taxi to open the door. Corman paid the fare and then looked around to see Finley standing at the entrance, watching him, and he felt a quick, sharp pang of physical desire at the sight of her, the mink stole around her shoulders, the long slim legs set off by the black lace of her cocktail dress. He tipped the driver and then took her elbow and ushered her across the lobby to the elevators, knowing that the decision was imminent. He would have to commit himself in the number of the floor he gave the operator, three if he intended to see her to her room, four if he intended to take her to his. They entered the elevator. The uniformed Japanese boy looked up at him, waiting. "Three, please," he said evenly, looking to Finley. There was relief in her eyes, and just a trace of disappointment.

4

At three o'clock in the morning he came suddenly awake, completely disoriented, the dream still clinging to his mind. He had been dreaming about Paul, and his present concern had distorted the past into something terrifying.

Even after Phoebe had married again and Corman did not see Paul very often, he always remembered his birthday. He did not pick out the presents personally; he had left a standing order with Macy's to have their personal shopper pick out something suitable each year and have it sent to him on June ninth. One year, however, on Paul's thirteenth birthday, Phoebe had called Corman to give him her own subdued brand of hell. The present had not arrived and Paul was heartbroken because his father had forgotten him. She suggested that Corman make amends by taking Paul out to dinner for an impromptu celebration. Corman turned her down.

He was extremely busy; he had an appointment with a photographer and a publicity man which he could not break. He called the department store and jumped all over them, and they apologized for the oversight and promised to send out something by special messenger. His conscience appeased, Corman had gone on to his meeting.

In the dream, however, he had not. He had picked up Paul and they had gone to dinner and had a marvelous time together. The boy was bright, alert, good company, full of a prideful love for his father, and Corman was touched by it, full of wonderment that after all these years he could feel such a glow of parental affection. In the dream he had rented a hansom cab for the ride back to Phoebe's apartment house, and he and the boy had agreed to do this every week. And then, as he reached out to embrace his son, quite suddenly Paul was no longer there. Full of a baffled rage, Corman grabbed for the driver, intending to pull him off his high seat and force the truth out of him, but his hands closed on empty air and he came awake, a sour taste in his mouth, the frustration stirring within him.

He could not go back to sleep. He went into the sitting room and he turned on the lights. The galleys were still on the desk, and he approached them with a feeling of relief. Sitting down at his desk, he picked up his notes, diverting his mind into the familiar, comfortable channel of his work. He began to write in longhand, the pencil covering one sheet after another, and by the time he had finished the scene he was startled to find that the night had gone and the sunlight was streaming through the windows. The door opened

The February Plan

and Finley came in, ready to begin the day, a little surprised to see him sitting at the desk in his pajamas.

"Have you been up all nght?" she said.

"Most of it," he said. "I couldn't sleep so I rewrote the scene. Have you had breakfast?"

"Bright and early," she said, picking up his penciled pages. "I'd better get on the typing right away. The galleys need to go back."

"I enjoyed last night," he said. "More than anything I've done in years."

"Except for a slight hangover, I can say the same," she said. "I'll go down and get the mail and give you time to get squared away. Will an hour give you enough time?"

"Plenty."

"Shall I have breakfast sent up?"

"I'll eat later."

She smiled, and left, and he was aware that there had been a change in her, a softening of her defenses, and this disturbed him. His feeling of last night had been correct; she was an especially vulnerable woman, and the balance of their relationship, established over the years, was changing, as much on his part as hers. He had been very close to taking her to his room last night, and he knew that she would have gone with him and he did not really want that. Sex would only complicate things. She was the one emotional constant he could depend on, and he did not want to see that jeopardized.

He put it out of his mind, turning to his work again, but he had not gone through half a chapter when the telephone rang. He picked it up to find Mitsu on the line.

"I'm sorry to disturb you so early, Mr. Corman," Mitsu said, "but I have just heard from a friend of mine who works for the American government." This friend, he went on, was a Japanese who translated offical documents passing between the American and Japanese governments. He was an extremely responsible man who would never divulge secret information, but occasionally his opinions served Mitsu as a kind of weather vane, letting him know which way the political wind was blowing. Mitsu had asked him what difficulty might be expected if Mitsu undertook the task of finding out why the United States Air Force had gone to such lengths to conceal the presence of one of their lieutenants in Japan for the month of December. Mitsu gave his friend Paul's name. Within an hour the friend had called him back. Mitsu was going to run into a great deal of difficulty, the friend said. The area of inquiry was a highly sensitive one.

"I see," Corman said thoughtfully. "Then you've decided not to take the case."

"I didn't say that," Mitsu said. "After so many years of routine industrial and divorce cases this offers a very pleasant challenge. But the cost will be high."

"How high?"

"I will need a retainer of ten thousand American dollars," Mitsu said.

"A retainer?" Corman said. "Do you think it will cost more than that?"

"It shouldn't cost that much," Mitsu said. "My fee will come to about fifteen hundred dollars. Another two thousand will go to my operatives, and the rest will be a reserve against expenses. We will have to pay for some of the information we get. Whatever is left will be returned to you."

"All right," Corman said. "You have the case. But there may be difficulty in getting American currency into Japan. I understand the Japanese government is pretty strict about that sort of thing."

"There won't be any problem," Mitsu said. "You can have the money deposited to my account in the Bank of Tokyo in Los Angeles."

"All right. I'll cable my agent today."

"Then I will go ahead immediately," Mitsu said.

"Without waiting for confirmation?"

"I trust you, Mr. Corman."

"When can I expect to hear from you?"

"As soon as I have anything to report," Mitsu said. "And I hope that will be soon."

Once Corman had replaced the telephone on the cradle, it rang again. This time it was Major Henshaw.

His voice was positively cheerful. "Good morning, Mr. Corman," he said. "Have you had breakfast?"

"No," Corman said. "I want to see you, Major."

"I was sure you would," the major said, "and I thought I'd save you some trouble. I had some business in the Central District and I thought I'd stop by on the off-chance I could buy you some breakfast."

"Where are you?"

"In the lobby."

"I'll meet you in the coffee shop in thirty minutes," Corman said. He shaved and dressed, but the delay did nothing to diminish his irritation, and by the time he reached the coffee shop, he was openly angry.

Major Henshaw stood up as Corman approached. "Well, it's nice to see you again, Mr. Corman," he said, smiling.

Corman sat down. "I wish I could say the same for you," he said. "I've met a great many liars in my time, Major, but I think, just offhand, that you outshine them all."

"I'm sorry you feel that way," the major said, unoffended. "I took the liberty of ordering for you. Ham and eggs. The eggs here are particularly good. Most of the eggs in Japan have an off-taste because the poultry growers keep the chickens on a diet of dried fish. But these eggs are not like that."

"I didn't come down here to discuss Japanese poultry," Corman said, easier now, realizing that his anger put him at a disadvantage against the major's unemotional attitude. "Let's get right to it. You know my son came to Japan in November, don't you?"

"December," the major said evenly, correcting.

"That won't work any more," Corman said. "I found the girl, Major. I know there wasn't any wife of a Japanese dignitary. So let's drop all the nonsense."

"What girl is that?"

"Her name is Suzuki. You know that as well as I do."

"I don't know what you're talking about," the major said quietly, his fingers unfolding the napkin, smoothing it out on his lap.

"How in the hell do you manage it?" Corman said.

"How can you be caught in an obvious lie and continue to stick to it? I suppose you don't know anything about American Electronics either."

"No," the major said.

The breakfast was served now by a phalanx of uniformed waiters, and the major waited until they were gone before he began to eat. He ate as if he did not taste the food at all, as if the whole process was a matter of refueling himself. "Do you consider yourself a patriotic man, Mr. Corman?"

"If you're getting ready to wave the flag, you can forget it."

"No flag waving," the major said. "I'm simply asking you, in the name of your government, to go home."

"I see. In the name of the government." Picking up his fork, Corman began to eat, startled to find that he was ravenously hungry.

"You can have it straight from the ambassador or the State Department if you want it that way. But it's vital that you go back to the States."

"And I'm to accept the importance of this matter on faith."

"Yes. Something very critical has developed here, Mr. Corman, something so critical that the future of the United States could depend on it. Your presence in Japan just now is very unsettling."

"My presence," Corman said, turning his attention to the iced fruit in the compote. "That's supposed to make me feel very important, isn't it?"

"You are important in this affair."

"Just my being here."

"No, Mr. Corman, it's your prying that we don't like," the major said.

"Then it's my prying that bothers the government, not my presence. What if I agreed to give it up, would the government still want me out of Japan?"

"I think that's a rhetorical question. Even if you made such an agreement, we couldn't afford to take the chance." The major wiped his mouth with his napkin and began to fold it, first in half, then in quadrants. "Perhaps I'm dense, Mr. Corman, perhaps it should be

The February Plan

obvious to me, but I still don't understand exactly what you're after over here."

"It's quite simple," Corman said. "I gave up my son when he was a small child, Major. Now, I'm realistic enough to know he was better off with his mother than he would have been with me. But I was his father, after all, and he expected something out of me. I never gave it because I didn't even know what it was. Love, support, maybe guidance, I don't know. And he never demanded anything out of me, not once, not until he wrote that note."

"Which meant nothing."

"No, he was asking me to do something. God knows what he wanted me to do, but he was asking. By the time I knew anything about it, he was dead and it was too late to save him. I'll give it to you straight, Major. I intend to find out why he wrote me that note. And I'm stubborn enough that I won't be dissuaded."

"I can't blame you for that," the major said, his face hard-set, intrenchant. "And there's nothing wrong with stubbornness, not if it's applied at the right time. But this isn't the right time, Mr. Corman. It seems to me that you take your country for granted."

"There's no reason why I shouldn't."

"But there is. Nobody can afford to take their country for granted, not in times like these. The country comes first. Whether your curiosity gets satisfied or not is completely unimportant."

"Your generalities don't move me," Corman said, finishing his coffee. "And your patriotic pleas don't sell me, not one bit. Now, I don't know whether you're speaking for the United States or not, but I'll give you a piece of advice. If you want my cooperation, you treat me like an intelligent man. You tell me why and how my finding out about my son will complicate things. No lies, no fictions, just the truth. Then I'll decide what I'm going to do."

The major thought for a moment. He held one hand over the steam rising from his coffee cup as if to warm his fingers. "We're both in awkward positions," he said at last. "I understand your point of view, but I can't tell you a thing. And to be completely realistic, you don't have any decision to make. You will be going back to the States within the next week."

"You think you can force me to leave Japan?"

"Yes."

"I don't see how," Corman said firmly. "My visa is in order. I have a valid passport. I haven't broken any laws."

"For all your accomplishments, you're a very naïve man," the major said. "With the stakes as high as they are, it's not the least bit important to the government how you are removed. But you will be."

"Am I to consider that a threat?"

"If you like. There are times, Mr. Corman, when the individual doesn't count. This is one of them."

"I don't believe that," Corman said. "And I'll tell you something else, Major. I'm not your average man. I've worked hard and I've made something of a reputation, and you can't take me out without making waves." He stood up. "I'm going to stay here until I find out why my son wrote that letter. When I'm satisfied that I have the real reason, I'll go home. Not before."

The major's eyes were passive, emotionless. "You think about this for a day or so. Just give it some thought. And if you change your mind, call me."

"I won't change my mind," Corman said. "Thanks for the breakfast, Major."

5

By the time he reached his room, there was a hard knot of apprehension in his stomach, and the fact that he was frightened made him angry. Finley glanced up from the typewriter when he came in and then went back to the transcription of his longhand changes in the chapter while he prowled the room, restless, thinking. He had put up a bold front with the major, refusing to accept the major's appraisal of the situation, but now that he had time to think it through, he knew the major was not bluffing. If the American government wanted him out of Japan, they would get him out, by

The February Plan

whatever means happened to be expedient. He knew it, but he refused to accept it.

"Finley," he said. The typewriter stopped, and she looked up at him. "Do you have the name of the literary society that wanted me to speak?"

"It's sponsored by the *Chuo Koron,*" she said. "I think that means the *Central Review.*"

"Did they suggest any specific date?"

"Any time that's convenient with you."

"Then set up an interview right away and a lecture date for later, say the middle of February."

"Why did you change your mind?"

He told her about his breakfast conversation with the major. "I don't know how he means to go about it," he added. "But I don't intend to make it easy for him. I want you to set up interviews with the Japanese press this afternoon. I want it well known that I'm in Japan, that I came over to research a new book, and that I intend to stay for a while."

She shook her head in disbelief. "He actually threatened you with violence?"

"He was extremely careful in his choice of words. He just said I was going to be removed from Japan, one way or another."

"You don't have to take that from a military attaché," she said. "I think you should call the ambassador."

"If the major's telling the truth," he said, "then talking to the ambassador wouldn't do any good. And if he's just bluffing, then it's not necessary."

"Do you think he's bluffing?"

"I don't know whether he is or not. I'll take a few precautions and let it go at that. I don't think it's anything to worry about." Now that he was beginning to formulate a definite plan of action, the knot began to dissolve in his stomach. Foolishness, he thought. There was no real reason to be afraid. The major was most certainly exceeding his authority. Corman had met many men exactly like him in Washington, petty officials who overdramatized their projects to exaggerate their self-importance. If Corman had indeed represented any threat to American security, it would not have been left to a man like Henshaw to handle it. It was reasonable to assume, therefore, that the major was bluffing, protecting himself. Perhaps he had loused up an assignment, and maybe his career was threatened by what Corman might uncover. And he had amplified this into a matter of international politics, hoping he could intimidate Corman into dropping the matter.

"On second thought," Corman said, "I don't think I'll meet with the Japanese press. But go ahead and set up the literary society."

"Which means you're not sure whether to believe him or not," Finley said, reading his mind.

"I'm too suggestible," he said with a smile. "It's an occupational hazard."

"I don't think you should take any chances."

"There's not going to be any trouble," he said, and then he changed the subject. "I'm going to need some funds transferred in the States," He told her about Mitsu and the Bank of Tokyo. "Send Jones a cable and have him handle it."

"All right," she said. "Where will you be?"

"I'm going to find a library somewhere and do a little research," he said, "and then I'm going back out to the Meiji Gallery."

"Do you want company?"

"No," he said. "I'd like to have the chapter ready to go over again by tonight. And if you feel like it, maybe we can have dinner together."

Her eyes turned to him briefly. "All right," she said.

6

Once he left the hotel, he had a feeling of extreme well-being. The storm had stopped sometime during the night and the normally dirty city was covered with a mantle of dazzling white. The sky was cloudless, the sunlight so brilliant that his eyes ached with the intensity of it. The day was considerably warmer, almost springlike, and in the streets the torrents ran along the curbs from the rapidly melting snow.

He walked to Shimbashi Station and took the electric train to Yotsuya, knowing that if there was any-

The February Plan

where in Japan he could find out who Chien San-Chiang was, it would be at the National Diet Library. The train was packed with Japanese and the air was foul. He felt vaguely uncomfortable, his head towering above the crowd of students around him, boys in blue uniforms with their billed caps pulled down over shaggy hair and gauze masks tied around their faces to protect themselves from contaminating germs.

He left the train at Yotsuya with a feeling of relief, enjoying the short walk to the library. The building itself had been erected as a palace for the Crown Prince in 1909 and used as a provisional Imperial Chamber. It was deserted after the war, and he and Gibson had inspected it for possible use as an officers' billet, but it was a national historic site, a marvelous building in the French style, with ornate ceilings and glittering floors, and both of them knew what would happen to it if it was converted to quarters. They had turned in a negative report and the matter was dropped.

The great Hall of Flowers had been modified into a reading room now, and Corman was relieved to see that the famed rococo ceiling was still intact. He approached the desk and was greeted by a middle-aged man who directed him into one of the small rooms off the main hall. Within a few minutes a bright-eyed young man came up to the table where Corman was sitting and asked if there was any way he could help him.

"I'm not sure," Corman said. "I'm looking for two specific pieces of information, and frankly, I don't know where to begin. The first is the meaning of the phrase, 'blue ants.'"

"Blue ants?" the young man said quizzically. "You are speaking of Formicoidea, the insects?"

"I don't know," Corman said. "I ran across the phrase and I'm trying to find out what it means."

"In what context was it used?"

"It wasn't in any context," Corman said.

"Ah." The young man scribbled something on a note pad. "I will be glad to check that for you."

"The second item is what I suppose to be a Chinese name. Chien San-Chiang."

The young man wrote that down, too, before he left. He was back within five minutes, his arms full of books. He put them on the table, very carefully, and then he opened the first one and spread it in front of Corman. The color plate showed what seemed to be millions of ants in every conceivable size and color. "As you can see," the young man said, "there are no species of Formicoidea which are blue in color. There is one Tasmanian species which often takes on a purplish hue, and that is the closest approximation I could find. But, if the name is taken in context with the name which you gave me, we have a totally different meaning. 'The blue ants,' is a euphemism for people who live in the People's Republic of China."

"The Red Chinese?"

"Yes. The uniform of that republic is blue. According to my information, the phrase originated when a journalist, an Englishman, observed thousands of people building a dam, all of them dressed in blue coats, all of them industrious as ants."

"I see," Corman said. "Then the name is Chinese?"

"Yes, sir. Chien San-Chiang is one of the most renowned of the Chinese scientists. There are references to him in all these books, but one is more complete than the rest in terms of biography." He opened a thick volume to a place he had marked. "This is a recent volume pertaining to science which the Chinese government published last year. The binding on their books is most elaborate, don't you think? Their government must subsidize printed works as their volumes are most inexpensive." He spoke precisely, each word separate and distinct, like beads on a verbal chain, and Corman realized he was using the occasion to practice his English.

"Thank you very much," Corman said. "You've been most helpful."

"You are welcome. If you wish more assistance, please call upon me."

Once the young man had left the room, Corman pulled the heavy volume to a position in front of him. The librarian was right—the book was a fine job of production with heavy, glossy paper and a leather binding, but once he began to read he found that the writer's use of English left a great deal to be desired. There was a repetitive use of the adjective "glorious," and it was used to modify both the People's Republic and the scientist himself.

Chien was a man of fifty-two who had taken a Ph.D. in physics from Cal Tech in 1950. From 1951–55 he had been employed by the American government at Los Alamos. In 1955 he had left the United States for Russia where he worked four years. The book went into no detail about this emigration, but Corman had a vague recollection of the circumstances which had prompted it. In the mid-fifties a Chinese scientist had been expelled from the United States for security reasons, either because he had tried to steal classified documents or because of his communist affiliations, Corman could not remember which. He had no doubt this was the same man.

He read on, mentally deleting all the descriptive adjectives. In 1959 Chien had returned to his homeland. During the early 1960's, with the help of Russian scientists, he had been instrumental in planning the gaseous diffusion plant at Lanchow. He had headed the nuclear tests at Lop Nor. At the moment he was Director of the People's Institute for Nuclear Research, in Lanchow.

Corman closed the book, taking out Paul's note to read again, hoping it would somehow make sense in the light of this new information.

"December 23, Goddamnit, you have to do something, you have to. They are going to kill us all. February 5. The Blue Ants. You can't sit on your ass any longer. They're . . ."

Was Paul trying to warn him of a possible act of aggression by the Red Chinese? That was not likely. After all, Paul had only been a first lieutenant and not in any position to pick up exclusive military intelligence. And even if by some freak of chance he had stumbled onto something that important, he would have reported it to his superiors immediately. He would not have entrusted it to a cryptic note. That made no sense at all.

He took the train to Shinnanomachi Station and

walked to the gallery, going directly to Miss Suzuki's workroom, but she was not there. In her place he found the woman in the gray kimono who had been here before. She turned from the manuscripts she was cataloguing, giving him a brief and respectful bow. When he asked for Miss Suzuki, the woman gave him a blank smile, shaking her head as if to signify her inability to speak English.

"Suzuki-san," he said, frowning, trying desperately to remember enough of his Japanese to ask where she was. *"Suzuki-san, doko desu-ka?"*

"Ah," the woman said with obvious relief, beginning to chatter in Japanese, and Corman thought how ridiculous this must seem to her, that he could ask the question in Japanese without knowing enough to understand the answer. Finally, with a shrug of his shoulders, he gave it up. Apologizing, he backed out of the workroom and went down the gallery looking for the director's office.

He ran into the same trouble with the director's secretary, a pretty girl with incredibly large and stricken eyes, and he was trying to explain to her what he wanted when the director himself came out of the inner office, a slight, spare man with sallow skin and streaks of gray in his hair. He grinned nervously at Corman, hunching his shoulders beneath an ill-fitting gray suit. "I am the director here," he said. "Are you having difficulty?"

"A little," Corman said gratefully. "I seem to be having a communications problem."

"Maybe I can help you," the director said. "Will you step into my office, please?"

Corman followed him into a cubicle with narrow slot windows overlooking the snow-covered grounds. The director apologized for his secretary. Japan was in the throes of a boom, he said, and skilled personnel were hard to come by, especially those who were proficient in English. The private industries hired these people immediately and the government wage scale was not high enough to offer any competition. So the gallery had to take what it could get. All of these statements were delivered with the same nervous smile he had displayed in the outer office, a mannerism which struck Corman as oddly familiar.

"I'm looking for Miss Suzuki," Corman said.

"Ah, Miss Suzuki, yes," the director said. "Unfortunately she is not here today."

"Can you give me her home address? I was supposed to get in touch with her."

"No," the director said, continuing to smile. "It is contrary to government policy to release the addresses of employees."

"I was afraid of that," Corman said. "But maybe you can make an exception this time. It's vitally important that I see her today."

"That would be difficult in any event," the director said. "She is no longer employed here."

"She isn't?" Corman said, startled.

"No, sir. This was a family matter with her, I believe. It was necessary for her to terminate very quickly to see to her father. I did not like to have her go. Such workers are difficult to obtain. But in Japan the sense of family is very strong."

"Where did she go?"

"To the south of Japan, I think," the director said, his smile not wavering for a moment. "Her father is working there."

"And she left no forwarding address?"

The director nodded. "Yes, she left no forwarding address."

"Is there anybody around who might be able to tell me where she went?"

"I think not."

"Perhaps her landlord?"

"No, sir."

"But you can't be sure."

"Yes, sir. I have the fortune to own the building where she resides." Her decision to go had been quite sudden, he went on, in the middle of the night. Perhaps she had received a telegram from her father, a telephone call—the director didn't know. By morning she had packed all her belongings and was ready to go, notifying him of her decision, expressing her regrets that her departure had to be such a hasty one, implying that her father was ill and needed her.

"I see," Corman said, his hopes evaporating. "If you hear from her, I'd appreciate it if you'd give me a ring."

"Certainly."

Corman wrote his name and the number of his room at the Imperial on a piece of paper. The director continued to grin as he accepted it and walked Corman to the door. It was only when Corman was halfway to the railway station that he remembered where he had seen that grin before—on the face of the Japanese curator who had led him and Major Gibson through the gallery twenty years ago, giggling over the damaged canvases. Twenty years and a different set of circumstances, it was no wonder he had not recognized the man. Everything changes, he thought to himself; he has changed and I have changed and time passes. God, how it passes.

7

It was dark by the time he reached the hotel. He went up to his rooms to find the neatly typed pages of the revised chapter on his desk and a note from Finley saying that she was tired and had a headache and wanted to beg off from dinner. She would see him in the morning. He was relieved to have the evening to himself. The day had left him tired and depressed, no closer to an answer than he had been before. But that was only part of it.

He had always pictured himself as being immensely adaptable and he often cursed the self-imposed discipline that kept him tied to the typewriter and prohibited any real involvement with the world. He could see now that he had been deceiving himself. There was a security in the familiar, a protection in routine, and he did not like being in Tokyo, caught up in a network of lies and frustrations, in a country that aroused long dormant emotions and made him dissatisfied with himself. He was beginning to feel the itch to go back to work again, to lose himself in a project, the

The February Plan

next book. He had already made the notes for it and the characters were coming alive in his mind. He had a nagging suspicion that if he waited too long to begin it, it would go sour and he might not be able to write it at all.

He took off his clothes and had a hot bath, still chilled from the afternoon, then he put on his robe and ordered a bottle of bourbon and a steak sent to his room. He ate slowly—the food here was excellent—then he poured some bourbon in a glass and settled down to read the typed draft of what he had written that morning. But no sooner had he picked up the manuscript than there was an interrupting knock on the door. He answered it to find a Japanese bellboy with an envelope for him.

At first he was tempted not to open the envelope at all; he had the feeling it was from Henshaw and he was in no mood for one of the major's pressuring afterthoughts. He put the envelope on the table and settled down to work again, but the force of his curiosity was too strong and he picked it up again, running his thumb beneath the flap, removing the single sheet of paper. It was from Mitsu.

> I need to talk to you. When you receive this, come out of the hotel through the arcade and cross the street into the park. Come in through the Hibiya entrance and follow the road to your right. My car will be parked in front of the bandstand. Make sure you are not followed.

He groaned inwardly, having no desire to get dressed and go out again, but he really had no choice. Mitsu was the kind of man who would sit in his car for hours, waiting, and Corman couldn't very well send a bellhop to tell him it wasn't convenient. He dressed again, putting on his overcoat, making sure the hallway was deserted before he approached the elevator.

Once he reached the street he stopped, stepping back into the shadows, shivering in the cold night air, until he was absolutely sure no one was paying the slightest attention to him. He hurried across the pavement, almost tripping on the streetcar rails. Once he had reached the shelter of the park entrance, he lighted a cigarette, watching the traffic around the hotel, feeling rather foolish.

He stayed there for five minutes and then he followed the road around to the right and found Mitsu's car. The moment he climbed in, Mitsu shifted into gear and the car crawled forward.

"What's the urgency?" Corman said, warming his hands in the blast of hot air from the heater. "And why all the secrecy?"

"One of my operatives was picked up this afternoon," Mitsu said.

"Picked up? By whom?"

"American Intelligence."

"What was he doing?"

"He had arranged to buy information from one of the Japanese technicians at American Electronics," Mitsu said. "They met in Yurakucho this afternoon and that was where they were arrested. My man would admit nothing, of course—he has been well trained—but they already knew he was working for me. They told him to inform me that my agency would be in serious trouble if I continued this investigation. They threatened to take steps with the Japanese government to have my license revoked."

"Then they know I hired you," Corman said.

Mitsu nodded in the darkness. "I think there is a listening device on your telephone. Or it could be something as simple as replacing one of the operators on the hotel switchboard with one of their people to monitor all your calls."

"Your man is sure he was picked up by Intelligence men?"

"Yes."

"Did they identify themselves?"

"They didn't need to. He's been in this business long enough to recognize them."

"But what stake could American Intelligence have in all this?" Corman said. "And why in the hell would they go to all this trouble?"

"Do you know what 'cover' is?"

The February Plan

"Vaguely."

"It's really quite simple," Mitsu explained. "If something happens and you want to keep it quiet, you take the known facts and interpret them in a different way, create another story around them, one you hope people will accept. In this case your son was involved in something they don't want known. Perhaps he stumbled into it by accident. Perhaps he was a part of it and defected, I don't know. But they don't intend for you to find out anything about it."

Corman was quiet a long moment. "If you continue this investigation, do they have enough influence with the Japanese government to put you out of business?"

"It's possible," Mitsu said. "But you're paying me to take risks. And if we aren't seen together, if you do nothing to arouse their suspicions, then I don't think there will be any official action against me. Now that I know what we're up against, I can be more circumspect with my agents."

"Do you know what we're up against?"

Mitsu nodded. "An operation of the Central Intelligence Agency." He paused now, his face illumined briefly by the flare of a match as he lighted a cigarette. They were in the northeast part of the city now, somewhere in the maze of back streets along the canals that fed into the Sumida River. Corman could see a barge in the distance, a light glinting through the window on a scum of dirty ice that was beginning to cover the canal.

"You're sure about that?"

Mitsu smiled slightly. "I'm never sure of anything, Mr. Corman. To be sure is to take unnecessary chances. But my men have watched American Electronics very closely. They've checked the trucks that go in and out of the company. The trucks that go in are driven by Americans and they carry electronic equipment into the plant. But the trucks that leave carry empty boxes. But even more conclusive has been the action of the Japan Electronic Machinery Industry Association. This is a very zealous and powerful group, Mr. Corman. They have refused to allow any American electronic company to gain a foothold in Japan.

They went to the government, asking that American Electronics be denied a license. They were told, very discreetly, of course, that American Electronics would not be in competition with them. They were asked, in the interests of their country, to drop the matter, and they did. As far as I can find out, American Electronics has made no contracts with the Japanese space program or anybody else. And finally, the establishment of the company was an overnight operation. It went into business in a great hurry."

"So it's a front for the CIA."

"Probably," Mitsu said. "The CIA likes to operate behind bogus companies. It gives them an excellent reason to assemble many men in one place. It makes a good communications center and a place to store and distribute equipment." It was a familiar pattern, Mitsu went on, and the CIA had used it quite often. The famous Gibraltar Steamship Corporation and the Double Check Corporation during the abortive Bay of Pigs affair were two cases in point, though neither of these companies had the elaborate refinements which had been built into American Electronics.

"I have enough information to conclude that American Electronics is a dummy company," Mitsu said. "And there is something else. Before my man was picked up, he learned a number of things from the technician, including some information about the night your son was there."

"Then he really was there," Corman said reflectively.

"Yes," Mitsu said. "The technician didn't see everything that happened, but he did see enough to let us know you have not been told the truth." As a matter of fact, Mitsu went on, it was only by chance that the technician saw anything at all. He was one of the twenty men who worked in the large assembly room at the back of the building, and all of them were kept completely in the dark about the company. None of them had the slightest idea what they were working on. They were given specifications for small electronic components which they were to wire by hand, very intricate pieces of equipment which took a long time to

The February Plan

finish, and there was much speculation among them as to how these finished components were to be used. The technicians were told the components would be used in the Japanese space program, but most of them did not really believe it. As far as they could see, these finished components were never shipped out, only stored away in cartons. Mitsu was convinced these components had no practical value at all; they were simply busy work, something to keep enough men busy to create the image of a legitimate business.

The workers were well paid and had enough company loyalty not to ask too many questions. But to this particular technician, any pay scale was too small because he had a large number of debts and was supporting a mistress from one of the Ginza clubs. He needed more money, and since Christmas seemed to put the Americans in a good mood, he decided to stay behind one evening and try to get a loan, an advance against his wages. This was on December 23.

His shift was over at six-thirty and he left the building and went down the street to a bar to have a drink. It made him feel confident and he went back to the building, but by the time he reached the alley, doubt had begun to set in again and he couldn't make up his mind whether to ask or not. While he was standing there in the shadows, a car drove up in the alley and stopped at the rear entrance. An American general got out with a couple of other officers and went in. A few minutes later a second car arrived, disgorging a load of Japanese and Americans dressed in business suits. The technican interpreted this to mean that there was going to be a party in the building and he decided to wait awhile. His boss would be in a better frame of mind if he gave him time to have a few drinks.

The technician went back to the bar and returned to the company at eight o'clock, just in time to see an American lieutenant going into the foyer. The technician went around to the rear of the building and was just about to ring the night bell when he heard four shots from inside. Frightened, he ran down the alley and ducked into a walled trash enclosure. In a few moments the security men from the company ran down the alley. The technician was scared to death, certain they would search the alley inch by inch and find him and blame him for whatever had happened inside the building.

He climbed up on an overturned box which allowed him to see over the wall. As he was trying to fix the location of the guards in the darkness, the rear door of the company building opened, spilling a wash of light into the alley. A car drove up just as three men came out of the building, one to either side of the general, holding him up. The general had been wounded. There was blood all over the left side of the general's uniform. The men hustled the general into the back seat of the car, the general almost falling as he stooped over to get in, and then the car sped away. Within a few minutes a second car arrived and four more men came out of the building, half dragging the same American lieutenant the technician had seen going in the front door. The lieutenant's hands were tied behind him and he was almost out on his feet, stumbling along, making no show of resistance. They threw him into the back seat of the car and drove off.

The technician was not very bright. Something terrible had happened in the building and he was sure they would try to implicate him in it. He sank down in the refuse, hearing the footsteps of the security men as they came back down the alley. They stopped right outside the trash bin, so close to him he could hear their breathing. He closed his eyes and held his breath. But they did not look into the enclosure. Soon afterward the door closed and the alley was enveloped in darkness again. He did not move for a long time, afraid they had left someone behind to watch, trying to trick him into revealing himself. He did not feel safe enough to leave the alley until shortly before dawn.

"Then Paul shot somebody," Corman said, his voice flat.

"I think so," Mitsu said. "And I presume that was the reason he took a gun there, either to kill somebody or to threaten them. Considering everything, I think we can rule out theft. From the physical description of the wounded general and other information we have been

The February Plan

able to identify the general. His name is Gibson and he is the commanding officer at Wheeler."

"Gibson?" Corman said with a start.

"Do you know him?"

"Quite well. I worked with him over here during the Occupation. But I think you must be mistaken. He's been quite active the past few weeks."

"It was a minor wound in the shoulder," Mitsu said. "He received emergency treatment at St. Luke's Hospital for what was listed as an 'accidental gunshot wound.' There was no publicity about it, and he was sufficiently recovered from it to go back to work the day after Christmas." Mitsu paused slightly. "Were you and the general good friends?"

"I don't think he had any real friends."

"But he would remember you, wouldn't he?"

"Are you suggesting I go see him? He's not going to tell me anything," Corman said, "not if the whole damn government is trying to keep it secret."

"Perhaps you could go to see him as an old friend," Mitsu said. "It's a short cut, of course, but perhaps he might agree to help you. You never can tell about these things. And it never hurts to try."

3

FOR over an hour now Corman had been enduring the questions of the young man from the *Chuo Koron* who sat in judgment on the edge of a straight chair in the sitting room, smoking a cigarette in an ivory holder, a petulant smile on his face. Corman wondered how many hours he had had to spend in front of a mirror to achieve that look of disdain. His name was Hosoi and he was incredibly naïve, Corman thought, to think he could outparry an old hand at the buisness, provoke him into a foolishness of some sort which would be duly reported in the pages of the literary magazine.

"Then you disagree with the critics who say that your *Wind in the Evening* should not have been published?" Hosoi said with a practiced disinterest.

"I didn't say that," Corman said. "And I don't recall any critics who said that it shouldn't have been published."

"Not in those words, perhaps. But they accuse you of cashing in on the success of *The Conquerors,* prostituting your reputation. The implication is that they think it should not have been published. But it did sell seventy thousand copies in the original edition, didn't it?"

"I've never felt the need to be vindicated by anything or anybody," Corman said, restraining his irritation. "The critics had their judgment and the public had theirs. I was displeased by the former and pleased by the latter, but neither judgment had anything to do with the success or failure of the book as far as I'm concerned. I set up my own standards for what I do. And no critic has ever been as hard on me as I am on myself."

As if by signal, Finley came into the room from the hall, interrupting the interview, carrying a handful of papers as a tactful indication that Corman was a very busy man. Corman could tell that the young man resented her presence. He regarded her with subdued hostility, but he did not show it directly. He thanked Corman for agreeing to speak at the literary society. It was the custom, he said, for the speaker to set his own topic and then answer questions from the floor after the lecture. "We are delighted to have you," he said finally, taking one last look at Finley as if to gauge her permanence in the room. Apparently she was here to stay. The interview was over. He stood up, shaking hands with Corman, and then he left.

"Thank God," Corman breathed, looking after him. "How did you know things were getting sticky?"

"From the look of him," Finley said. "I thought his good manners would last about an hour before the venom took over."

"He's venomous all right," Corman said. "I can just imagine getting up in front of three or four hundred young dilettantes like him and trying to defend the fact that my books make money."

"Then you've changed your mind about staying?"

"I think so," he said, lying back on the couch, closing his eyes.

"Any particular reason?"

How could he explain to her how he felt, the strong desire to be back within the protective shelter of a familiar routine? He decided not to try. "I don't think I'm going to be able to do any good here," he said. "There's no way I can help Mitsu, and I might get in his way if I stay around."

"Have you talked to General Gibson?"

"I called Wheeler," he said. "They said he wasn't available. It didn't surprise me." He raised himself up, taking the newspaper off the desk and handing it to her. "Gibson's going to have his hands full."

She sat down beside him with the paper and he read the lead story again, an article concerning a discovery made by a Japanese reporter which had already set off demonstrations in front of the American Embassy and the Japanese Diet. The United States, with the full consent of the Japanese government, was establishing a missile base in the Japanese Alps, in Fukushima Province, northwest of Nikko. The base had been under construction for six months and was near completion. At first the Japanese government had insisted this facility was nothing more than a static-test site for the boosters to be used in the Japanese space program, but the reporter had uncovered enough evidence to make his charges stick and the government had been forced to change its story, admit the truth.

An agreement had been signed with the United States to bolster Japan's self-defense forces against the increasing threat of Red China's nuclear capability. The construction of the missile base was under the supervision of General G. V. Gibson, but once it was completed, it would be manned by Japanese personnel under the complete control of the Japanese government. The article contained quotes from a number of high-ranking officials in both governments, assuring the Japanese people that there was no possible danger to the people of Fukushima Province. The story did not say what kind of missiles would be installed at the base or whether they would be armed with nuclear warheads.

She read the story and then put the paper down. "I can see why he doesn't have time to talk to you," she said. She gave him an appraising frown. "You didn't get much sleep last night, did you?"

"No," he said. "I spent four hours going over the suite looking for electronic devices."

"This place is bugged?"

"I don't think so. I couldn't find anything. But I couldn't sleep and I needed something to keep me occupied."

"The trip here has been a wild-goose chase for you, hasn't it?"

"Grist for the old mill," he said sourly. "Maybe when I get back to the States, I'll go to work for the CIA. Their fiction writers have one hell of an advantage. If nobody believes the stories they put out, they can change them in midstream."

"You mind if I ask you a question?"

"No, go ahead."

"Are you really giving up or is this just one of your moods?"

He smiled thinly. "You were against this whole thing in the first place, remember?"

"I didn't think it could change anything. After all, Paul's dead, and I thought you'd just be stirring up frustrations after the fact. I don't believe in starting anything painful unless something good can come out of it."

"That says it pretty well," Corman said, standing up, restless, having no desire to sit and analyze. "Nothing good can come out of this poking around, and I want to get back to work. When we get back to the States, I'll see if Max can't set up another tour for a while, and I want to get to work on the new book." Even as he said it, he knew that was not quite true, that somewhere in the dark complex of his rationalizations there

The February Plan

was a spark of apprehension that warned him to back off. As long as he had thought he was jousting with the windmills of bureaucracy, he had felt competent to handle it, but the CIA was a different matter. He was coming dangerously close to getting involved in something larger and he wanted none of it. That was what it amounted to. Whatever the CIA was doing, he would not interfere. He would go home. Sooner or later Mitsu would let him know what had happened to Paul, and that would be that. "Let's take the day off and go down to Kamakura," he said impulsively. "You can't leave Japan without seeing the big fat Buddha, old Daibutsu."

The thoughtful expression had not left her face. Her finger tips were touched together under her chin. "You're a funny man," she said. "Sometimes I think I know you pretty well, and then a time comes when I know I don't really understand you at all."

"Writers are peculiar," he said. "They often do irrational things. You know that. How about it? You want to go to Kamakura?"

"I'm game," she said. "I'll have to stop by my room and get my coat."

"Fine. I'll pick you up in ten minutes."

Once she was gone, he picked up the telephone and called the desk, arranging for a car and driver to meet them in front of the hotel, then he went to the bedroom to change into a heavier suit. He was feeling considerably better now that he had made the decision to go home. The telephone rang and he finished knotting his tie before he went into the sitting room to answer it. It was the overseas operator asking him to hold on a minute for a call from New York, and then Jones's voice came on the wire, sounding tinny and faraway. Corman was delighted to hear from him. John Paul Jones was the best literary agent in the business, a gentleman with an illustrious past, a shrewd mind, and an illogical paternal feeling toward all the writers he handled.

"Hello, John," Corman said cheerfully. "How are you?"

"A little sleepy," Jones said, and from the reluctance

in his voice Corman could tell that the news was not going to be good. "It's the middle of the night here. How are you feeling?"

"Curious," Corman said. "What kind of trouble am I in now? If it's the galleys, they're finished."

"No, it's not the galleys, but we have run into a little trouble here. I'd better let Roy Blakely explain the first part of it. We're on a conference line."

Blakely? Corman thought. Why would Jones have lined up a lawyer? He had met Blakely only once at Jones's house and he remembered him as a beefy man with a broad Midwestern accent and a disarming manner that covered one of the shrewdest legal minds in New York. Blakely wasted no time in greetings.

"We have a problem here, Mr. Corman," he said. "This morning Max Adams filed suit against you in superior court for a hundred thousand dollars."

"What in the hell for?" Corman said incredulously.

"It's a standard breach of contract suit," Blakely said, unruffled, as if he were discussing a herd of cows that had broken down a fence. "He's after thirty thousand actual damages, seventy thousand punitive. I won't go into the legalese, Mr. Corman, but he claims he had a contract with you that called for you to give thirty-one lectures in the next three months. He claims you willfully walked out on that contract."

"I can't think Max is really serious about this," Corman said. "Hell, he may have filed a suit out of pique, but I don't really think he means to go through with it. We've been friends a long time."

"We can't count on friendship," Blakely said. "And I don't see how any of the standard protective clauses are going to do us any good. By protective clauses I mean those parts of the contract that say you don't have to meet the terms of the contract if prevented by acts of God, illness, accident, and so forth."

"I don't need any of those things," Corman said. "I'll call Max right away and straighten this whole business out."

"It won't work," Jones said, interrupting. "I spent all afternoon with him, and he's solid as a rock on this. It's not just the money involved, although he's a sharp man with a dollar, but he feels his reputation has been injured. He promised you to a large number of organizations and he's hell-bent to deliver."

"People have canceled out on him before," Corman said. "As far as I know, he's never sued any of them."

"Be that as it may," Blakely said, "he's sure suing you. He claims he's out for damages, but I don't think he really wants that. According to the schedule I have, you've only missed five of the dates so far. Now the next date is in Billings, Montana, on February seventh, and he hasn't approached them with a substitute yet. To my way of thinking, he's trying to force you to keep the rest of the engagements."

"Then if I keep the rest of the dates, there's no suit, is that it?"

"That would cut the ground right out from under him," Blakely said. "Now, he could always go after you for a smaller amount on the basis of your non-performance on the dates you've missed, but I don't think that's very likely."

"So all I have to do is come back to the States," Corman said.

"I know that what you're doing over there is very important to you," Jones said. "But a couple of other things have come up and I think you should know about them. First, I had a call from the Bureau of Internal Revenue this morning. They want to get in touch with you."

"Why?" Corman said. "Is something wrong?"

"I'm sure it's just routine. Manny's the best accountant in the business, and I'm sure all your records are in order. I told them you were out of the country and they've agreed to wait. But the worst bit of news—I don't even know how to soften it—is that we lost our deal on *The Breakers*."

"Lost it?" Corman said. "I thought it was all set, just a matter of some final details."

"I thought so too," Jones said ruefully. "But something happened to jinx it, and they didn't even bother to explain. Their attorneys just called and said they were no longer interested. I've been trying to get through to the head of the studio, but his secretary says he's in Europe and won't be back for six weeks."

"They must have given you some hint," Corman said.

"None, but you know how these film people are. They like something and then they just go cold, just like that. Maybe somebody's wife didn't like it, maybe the bankers wanted to cut back on production—who can explain these people? But we're trying to stir up some interest elsewhere."

"What do you want me to do about this other matter?" Blakely said, breaking in. "If you're coming back to the States right away and can keep the rest of those dates, I'll talk to Max about it. But we don't have much time to spare. He already has your letter saying that you're canceling, and that's really all he needs to press the suit. And if he fills those dates with other speakers, then you're up a creek."

All I have to do is go home, Corman thought. He had already made the decision to return to the States, but now a cloud of suspicion had begun to form in his mind and he felt outraged, They were doing this to him, they were manipulating him.

"Are you still there?" Jones said, after Corman had been silent for a long moment.

"I'm still here," Corman said. "Look, give the tax people authorization to begin whatever kind of audit they want to make. And I'll call you tomorrow about my plans."

"Just don't let it ride too long," Blakely advised.

"I appreciate your interest, Mr. Blakely."

"I'm sorry all of these things hit at the same time," Jones said, "but I'm sure everything will work out. Have you found out anything about Paul?"

"I'm beginning to," Corman said. "Thanks for calling me, John."

The palms of his hands were cold and wet as he put down the telephone, and he felt a deep and visceral anger. He picked up the telephone and called Finley, telling her they would not be going to Kamakura, then he had the operator connect him with the Embassy Annex. "Major," he said, once Henshaw was on the line, "I want to see you."

"I'll be here all day," the major said pleasantly. "Come at your convenience."

2

A block from the Temporary Annex the taxi ran into a police barrier. Corman paid the driver and went the rest of the way on foot, pushing his way through the crowds of people on the street, most of them carrying signs protesting the missile base. He had seen demonstrations in Japan before, but none as noisy as this one. Most of the demonstrators were from the universities, uniformed students and girls with stringy hair, the new radicals, thousands of them, filling the street with a snake dance, shuffling in a writhing line, three and four abreast, pressed close together, their feet shuffling against the pavement with a hissing sound like the pistons of a locomotive. They were chanting and their voices matched the rhythm of their shuffling feet and their breath condensed and steamed in the cold air until it seemed that they were all part of some monstrous machine. He pushed his way into the building, past a row of helmeted Japanese policemen who stood watching the demonstration with impassive faces.

Inside the annex business was being carried on as usual. The receptionist informed him that he was expected. He found the major standing at the window, looking out into the street, a curious, rather detached expression on his face, as if he were watching a movie. "The poor, frustrated bastards," he said to Corman. "They're all steamed up and they don't know where to put their anger. They would feel much better if this was a unilateral action; they could throw a few rocks at the Americans and go home. But their government's involved in it, and that splits up the target."

"I know how they feel," Corman said. "But I have a target."

"Do you?" the major said evenly.

"No pretenses this time," Corman said indignantly.

"You weren't bluffing when you said you'd get me out of Japan, were you?"

"I don't understand," the major said. "Maybe you'd better fill me in."

"I got a call this morning from New York," Corman said angrily. "I am being sued by an old friend who never would have sued me unless pressure was put on him. I have just lost a hundred and fifty thousand dollars in a movie sale that suddenly went sour, for no reason at all, no explanation. And after years of quiet coexistence the Internal Revenue has decided to start needling."

"That's quite a lot for one morning."

"Too much to be coincidence, and all of it designed to bring me running back to the States to keep myself from going bankrupt."

The major sat down behind his desk, taking a cigar from the humidor, biting off the end of it. "And you think I had a hand in this?"

"I know damn well you did."

"Aren't you overestimating my capabilities?" the major said, lighting the cigar.

"No, I'm not, Major," Corman said, walking to the window, turning his back to the crowds. "It was a clever move, I have to admit that, but your timing was just a little off." His anger had become diffused now. "And you went just a little too far. Because I was all set to go back to the States this morning, partly because I was beginning to get a vague picture of what was going on, of what this is all about. And I have to admit, it scared me. But this pressure of yours didn't have the right effect, Major. It made me realize a number of things about myself. They may not be of the slightest importance to you, but they mean a hell of a lot to me. I've always run when the going got tough, when there was really anything to be faced, and it's been convenient for me because I happen to have a talent, a knack for words, and I learned a long time ago that people can forgive anything of an artist as long as he's producing and as long as he's successful."

The major eyed him speculatively. "This really isn't

necessary," he said. "You don't have to explain yourself to me."

"Oh, but I do," Corman said vehemently. "Because you'd better understand me completely. You have to know that I mean what I say."

"And just what is it that you're saying, Mr. Corman?"

"I'm a citizen of the United States," Corman said, his voice hard now. "I happen to know what my rights are. Theoretically I am one of the people who run the government. It does not run me. It does not tell me where to go or what to do or how to go about doing it, not as long as I obey the law. And I have obeyed the law."

"I have no reason to doubt that."

"And if you think you can force me out of Japan, you're dead wrong."

"Oh?"

"If you don't stop this financial harassment back in the States, I'll go straight to the Japanese papers."

"And tell them what?"

"That American Electronics is really a front for the CIA, that they don't manufacture one damn thing, that the whole thing is a sham engineered by the American government. There's no way you can cover that any more."

"There's really no need to," the major said, unperturbed, a slight reproof in his eyes. "In the first place, Mr. Corman, a good many things have happened since we talked the last time. The situation has changed. And you're underestimating the Japanese government. They know that American Electronics is a cover."

"Then you admit it."

"Of course I do. It would be foolish not to. It was set up to cover the transportation of technicians into Japan for work on the missile base up in the mountains. That took a considerable number of men, and we would have had a hard time getting them into the country without the Japanese press getting wind of it. The Japanese reporters are uncanny at sniffing out a story. So we brought the men in for American Electronics, and it worked rather well. They stayed in Tokyo awhile, and then we shuttled them off to the mountains. Now, I'll admit that the newspapers still don't know the company was a dummy, and they will undoubtedly print your story. It might cause a little embarrassment to our government, otherwise it really doesn't make any difference. We only needed the company while the missile base was being built. And now the cat's out of the bag anyway."

"I think you're bluffing again," Corman said.

"Am I?" the major asked with a smile.

"I know my son went to the electronics company, Major. He shot General Gibson and then he was arrested."

"That's true," the major admitted. "I can tell you that. Your son was brought over to work on the missile base, Mr. Corman. We try to screen our personnel very carefully, but sometimes we can't catch everything. Your son, I'm sorry to say, was mentally unbalanced. He developed a rabid feeling against the establishment of a missile base here and decided to try to force the general to call it off. I don't know whether he really meant to shoot the general, but the fact is that he did. He was overpowered by the security guards and we sent him back to the States under heavy guard because he might have talked inadvertently and exposed the real purpose of the company. He was about to undergo psychiatric treatment when he killed himself."

"I don't believe you," Corman said, but the doubt was beginning to creep into his mind now, that damned persuasive hint of doubt. "You're too facile at these shifting stories."

The major leaned back in his chair, the springs creaking with the shift of his weight, the cigar smoke curling about his head. "It happens to be true, Mr. Corman. We've only been interested in maintaining security about the missile base. But now it's wide open and we don't care what you do. As far as we're concerned, you're perfectly welcome to stay in Japan as long as you like, do as much digging as you wish."

"But you say this only after you've created enough financial pressure to get me out of here."

The February Plan

"The auditing of tax records is a fairly routine thing," the major said. "Millions of people go through it every year. And movie studios back out on deals without any government pressure. And how could we arrange to have you sued? You're a fair man, Mr. Corman. I sympathize with what's happening to you, but I know you can't hold us accountable."

"We'll let that pass for the moment," Corman said abruptly. "Let me get one thing straight. If I decide to stay here, I will get no more interference from you?"

"None." The major stood up, smiling blandly. "As a matter of fact, the ambassador's having a reception in the middle of February for some visiting congressmen. If you're still around by then, I know he'll be delighted to have you and your secretary for dinner."

So this is it, Corman thought, and as far as the major was concerned the whole affair was settled and the final explanation had been made. Corman had the feeling he was being manipulated again, subtly, skillfully, but he did not know how. "I have no desire to have dinner with the ambassador," he said. "And I don't know what my plans are yet."

"I can understand that," the major said. "I'm sorry I couldn't tell you the full truth in the beginning."

Corman approached the door. "I'll be in touch with you, Major."

"You do that. And if you can possibly stay for the reception, be sure and let me know."

Once Corman was outside, he found the sharp air bracing and the confusion in his mind began to clear. He did not believe the major for an instant. The major possessed that unordinary instinct of the born storyteller, the ability to pick up little threads of fact and weave them into a convincing tale, so adroitly, so expertly that it was difficult to unravel them. And now the major would feel certain of success, accomplishing his objective through a reverse psychology, to send Corman home with all his suspicions quieted.

Corman pushed through the crowd of Japanese. It would be best to let the major think he had been successful, for the moment anyway. He went back to the hotel. Finley was in the sitting room, proofing the galleys. He shrugged off her questions and then retired to his bedroom with a scratch-pad and pencil, sitting down on the edge of the bed to examine his current financial position.

For years now he had left his financial affairs in the hands of his agent and an accountant who also served as his business manager. Jones deposited his royalties in a special account from which Manny paid the bills and sent Corman a monthly check for his expenses. He was not sure exactly how much money there was in any of the accounts, but he had no doubt that the lawsuit was going to be expensive. His reason told him that a claim of a hundred thousand was much too high, but he had a hunch that Max could get fifty thousand out of a jury. This being the case, he probably wouldn't settle for much less than that figure.

Then there was the matter of Blakely's fee. He would not come cheap. He would undoubtedly earn his money, but Corman could expect to pay him five thousand dollars at the least. Well, there was nothing to be done about that. He would advise Blakely to settle out of court as quickly as possible, paying the settlement and the costs out of available funds, making up the difference with an advance from his publishers. In order to assure his liquidity, he decided to cable Manny immediately and arrange a mortgage on the Connecticut place.

He drafted out a cable on the notepad and then went into the sitting room to call it in, but he stopped short at the last moment. If his telephone was monitored, the major would know he had decided to stay, and Corman did not want that to happen. He jammed the cable in his pocket. He would find an Overseas Telephone Office and make a direct call to Manny.

"I want you to book us a couple of seats back to New York for the end of the week," he said to Finley. "Make it Saturday. That should give us time for a little sight-seeing."

"Then we're definitely going home?"

"Yes."

She did not question him further. She nodded and

The February Plan

picked up the telephone and called the travel service. Then she turned to him. "The Saturday flights are filled up. But they can give us two seats on Sunday morning, ten o' clock."

"That's fine," he said. "Are the galleys ready to mail?"

"I'm just finishing them. I'll get them off tonight."

"Then there's nothing more for us to do here," he said. "What would you like to do for the rest of the day?"

"How about the Kabuki Theater?" she suggested.

"That's fine with me," he said. "See if you can get us some tickets, and I'll meet you in the lobby. Ten minutes."

Once she had gone, he picked up the telephone and asked the operator to try General Gibson at Wheeler for him again. In a few minutes the general's adjutant was on the line, a Major Allenton. "I'm sorry, Mr. Corman," the major said, "but the general's out of town. Is there anything I can do to help you?"

"Is General Gibson up at the missile base?" Corman asked flatly.

"I'm afraid I can't answer that," the major said after a moment's hesitation, caught off guard by the bluntness of the question.

"You don't have to tell me," Corman said. "I just want you to pass along a message for me. I'm an old friend of the general's from Occupation days and I want to see him before I leave Japan. I'm going up to Nikko tomorrow and I'll call the missile base from there. Just make sure he understands that I intend to see him before I leave Japan."

"I'll pass the message along," Major Allenton said.

Corman put on his coat and went downstairs to meet Finley, deciding not to discuss his plans with her. "There are a couple of things I have to do before we go to the theater," he said when they were outside the building.

"The afternoon performance starts in an hour," she said.

"That's plenty of time. Let's walk awhile and pick up a cab farther in."

They walked past the park in the cold afternoon sunshine, stopping at the corner while Corman checked the street behind him. The traffic was heavy and the sidewalks were crowded. There was really no point to evasive tactics, he decided. The major was convinced he was going to return to the States. Corman spotted a taxi in the swarm of cars, and hailed it, helping Finley in, noting with relief the small sign tacked to the back of the front seat: I SPEAK ENGLISH.

"I want to go to the nearest Overseas Telephone Office," he told the driver.

"Why didn't you make the call from the hotel?" Finley said.

"I don't want to share it with Major Henshaw," he said, smiling. "It'll only take a minute."

Once they reached the Overseas Telephone Office in Yurakucho, he left Finley in the cab and went in alone, stopping at the counter to give Manny's home number to the Japanese clerk. "This call is a 'Want Now,'" Corman said. The woman nodded and directed him to one of the oversized telephone booths along the side of the room. He closed the door behind him.

It was ten minutes before he had Manny on the line. His voice was lethargic, sleepy.

"Did I get you up?" Corman said.

"You got me up," Manny said without rancor. "What can I do for you?"

Corman told him what he had in mind. "If you can get more than twenty-five thousand on a first mortgage, take it. And then get in touch with Jones and ask him to get as much of an advance as he can from Underhill."

"You're not playing the Japanese stock market, are you?" Manny said reprovingly. "You can lose your shirt at that sort of thing."

"I'm not playing the stock market," Corman said. "Did Jones tell you about the suit?"

"He told me." Manny's voice was fully alert now; it always took him a little while to get awake. "Look, you really don't want me to get you a mortgage. You're going to have to pay points, and the rates are too high.

And what the hell do you want a loan for anyway? You're coming home right away, aren't you?"

"Not right away, no. And I'm going to need more money over here. But I don't want it sent until the first of the week." He paused, thinking. "All right, hold off on the mortgage until you hear from me. But I want a financial statement, a listing of everything I've got and what we can get out of it. You might check the cash value of my life insurance policies."

Manny's mental groan was almost audible. He specialized in artists and performers and he had often described his role as that of a shepherd leading a flock of woolly, irresponsible sheep through a world that was out to fleece them. Obviously he felt that way now. "Just remember," he reminded Corman, "we have an agreement. Any time you get ready to take a flyer, you consult me first."

"This is no flyer," Corman said. "I'm about to go through a hurricane and I want to know how stout my sea wall is."

"You and your lousy damn metaphors," Manny said. "Now, this statement of your financial position, it's for your information only, right?"

"Right."

"I'll get it to you at the Imperial. And how's a thousand?"

"Make it two."

"Fifteen hundred? You're cutting it pretty thin as it is."

"All right. Fifteen hundred."

"You'll have it by next Tuesday."

"Fine. What kind of trouble are we in with the tax people?"

"No trouble. They've just got the eye on your entertainment and travel deductions for last year. One of their men'll come in and we'll have lunch together and do a lot of arguing and a little adjusting. That's all there is to it. Don't worry about it."

"If you say not to worry, I won't."

"Then I said the wrong thing," Manny said with a chuckle. "A heavy spender like you, maybe you should worry just a little. Keep in touch."

By the time Corman reached the counter, his bill was ready for him. "Six minutes," the Japanese woman said. "Eight thousand, six hundred and forty yen."

Corman counted it out in thousands, aware that his resources had just gone down by some twenty-four dollars. Once he had a receipt, he asked the receptionist if she would place a local call for him. He gave her the number at Mitsu's office, going back into the booth to pick up the telephone. Mitsu was not there, but Corman talked to his brother and left word that he would be at the Kabuki-za.

When Corman and Finley reached the theater, the performance was already in progress. An usher led them to their seats near the runway. Corman had never cared much for Kabuki; the music of the whanging samisens and wooden flutes was much too strident for his taste, the choruses always chanted in a high, nasal whine, and he was not much impressed with the spectacle of flamboyantly costumed actors in grotesque make-up who did more posing than acting. The play today was a *shosagoto,* a Kabuki drama adapted from a Noh play, which meant that there was even less physical movement than usual. Corman watched for a while and then allowed his mind to drift, wondering what had happened to bring Max to the point of a lawsuit.

There had always been an easy feeling between him and Max since the evening they had dinner together to discuss the possibility of Corman's filling in some lecture dates left vacant when a senator came down with the flu. Max was a middle-aged, portly man who had wanted to be an impresario and had ended up as a lecture agent and a good one, living in a midtown apartment crammed with mementos his clients had sent him, wood carvings for the most part, a veritable menagerie of exotic animals from all over the world.

Max had been especially fond of Phoebe, charmed by her Southern accent and her beauty (she brought out a mellow, courtly quality in him; perhaps that was the reason he had been so fond of her), and when Corman and Phoebe came to their amicable separation and eventual divorce, Max had been quite upset about it, scurrying back and forth between them, trying to effect a reconciliation. That had been years ago, and as Corman thought about it, he could see that there had been a subtle change in the relationship after that. The phone conversations were pleasant enough, their meetings were without strain, but somehow the personal concern had been drained off and there was no longer anything except business between them.

He was still not convinced that Max had instigated this lawsuit on his own, and it wounded him somewhat to think that Max held him in such low regard that he would be susceptible to a government plot against him. But then Corman had handled the whole thing badly and he knew it.

Corman stirred slightly, looking around to see Mitsu in the aisle. "I'll be back in a few minutes," Corman whispered to Finley, standing up, following Mitsu into the lobby. He filled Mitsu in on his conversation with the major. "I'm going up to Nikko tomorrow," he said finally. "I've made it clear that I don't intend to leave Japan until they let me see the general, and they're not going to arouse my suspicions by letting me think he's avoiding me. But I need directions to the missile base."

Mitsu nodded. "I'm expecting one of my men back from Nikko this afternoon," he said. "Perhaps you and your secretary can come to my house this evening for dinner. We can talk there without being interrupted."

"What time?"

"Is seven-thirty all right with you?"

"Fine."

Mitsu wrote out the address on a slip of paper. "Just hand this to any taxi driver. He'll bring you there."

3

When they left the Kabuki Theater at five o'clock, Corman remembered a small bar near the Dai-Ichi building and decided to have a drink there if it was still in business. It had been something of a marvel in occupied Japan, an exact replica of an old bar in some hotel in St. Louis, complete down to the smoky wood paneling and old tables off a Mississippi steamboat. He was disappointed to find that the Steamboat Bar was no longer in business, but there was another cocktail lounge occupying the space and it was relatively uncrowded, so he decided to have a drink anyway.

They sat in a booth as far from the piano as they could get, and Corman ordered martinis. There was a kind of special glow about Finley this evening, Corman decided, a flush to her cheeks, an excitement in her eyes. She was enjoying herself, perhaps because she thought they were going home and she could afford to relax a little.

It was only after they had finished the first round of drinks that Corman decided to tell her the truth. "I think I'd better level with you, Finley," he said. "The reservations I had you make were just window dressing. I want the major to think I'm going home."

"I see," she said.

"And that's all you're going to say?"

"It's your decision to make."

"Are you disappointed?"

"A little. I'm not particularly anxious to go back to the old grind, but maybe I'm a little disappointed that you're stalling."

"Stalling what?"

"Getting back to work," she said, sipping at the martini the waitress had just put in front of her.

"I'm not stalling," he said. "I don't have any reason to stall."

"Starting a new book is always hard for you."

"It's not the new book."

"Then what is it?"

"Stubbornness," he said flatly. "Stubbornness, pure and simple. They're determined to run me out; I'm determined to stay."

She nodded, accepting it. "It's hard on you, being back here, isn't it? I don't mean the business about your son, I mean just being in Japan."

"I feel disoriented much of the time. It's not like I remembered it. How could you tell?"

"I know you pretty well. You keep looking at things with a funny little twist to your face as if they don't belong here. You had the expression when you came into this bar. You weren't actively unhappy about it, but it just wasn't right somehow. You used to come here—not to this bar, but the one that was here before—with Phoebe, didn't you?"

"Once in a while, yes. But it really doesn't have anything to do with Phoebe."

She finished her drink and ordered another, more relaxed now, her mind more reflective as the drinks began to take effect. "I know the feeling," she said. "There was a church up in Yonkers where I used to go as a little girl. They tore it down one summer when I was away and put a supermarket in its place. I knew they had done it so there wasn't any surprise, but I felt uncomfortable when I went up there again. Every time I go past that neighborhood I feel uncomfortable, as if there's something that's just not quite right about it." She looked up now, her fingers keeping time to the piano across the bar. "I wonder if, for tonight anyway, you'd mind calling me Elaine?"

"That goes against a habit of long standing," he said, "but I'll try. How did people start calling you Finley?"

"Protective coloration," she said, smiling. "It's harder for men to make passes at somebody they call Finley. The first boss I had started calling me that and I encouraged it. So finally it stuck."

She glanced at him and then looked away, finishing her drink, watching the Japanese piano player and the people sitting at the bar, most of them Japanese men in the company of long-gowned hostesses. "Don't they ever bring their wives to a place like this?"

"Who?"

"The men."

"It's a long-standing Japanese tradition," he said. "A man never tells his troubles to his wife. She probably wouldn't know what to do if he did, but these babies, they're trained in gin and sympathy. I remember in the old days there was a hostess in the Steamboat Bar named Rosie. She wasn't good-looking and she didn't speak a word of English, but hell, she had a regular line-up of GHQ officers who used to stop by here and tell her their troubles. She'd get the damnedest look on her face, like she was the one person in the whole world who could really understand their problems, even if she couldn't understand their language."

"Did they sleep with her?"

"Some of them, I guess. But the smart ones didn't. They knew that the kind of magic she had wouldn't work if they got too involved with her." He snapped his fingers at the waitress, a young Japanese girl in tight black slacks. "You want another one?" he said to Finley.

"One more and I'd never make it out of here," she said.

He ordered another martini for himself, feeling a slight strain settle between them as if she had something she wanted to say and could not quite bring herself to do it. "I've changed my mind," she said. "I think I will have one more, if it's all right with you."

"Certainly." He called the waitress back and amended his order. "Why the change of heart? You feel the need to tie one on?"

"I'm not the type," she said, a little too brightly now. "I'm all business, you know, a real efficiency machine. If I have a problem, then I think it through, just feed it into the old mental computer and see what comes out. But every once in a while something comes along that the machine can't handle. So a few drinks help me see things in a new perspective."

"What's the problem your machine can't handle now?"

"Let's put it in fictional terms. Now, let's say we have a heroine who gets hurt in a bad marriage, deeply hurt, and afterward she flounders around for a while, looking for a man who's going to soothe the wounds and prove to her that life doesn't have to be all bumps and bruises. But she doesn't find him, of course, because her standards are too high, and she begins to believe he doesn't exist at all. She doesn't like that because she's a romanticist at heart. So in order to avoid the total proof of this black fact, she sets up a system."

"A system?"

Her mind groped for the right word. "A routine, yes,

that's better. Everything in it's proper place, a life with no surprises. And that works pretty well. But we have to complicate the story. Occasionally our heroine meets another man she thinks might be a possible faith healer and she sees him just long enough to have a good look at him and she shies off, just short of disillusionment. And then she goes to work for a man she admires very much; and he seems to respect her system, her attitude toward life, let's call it. She enjoys her work and they get along swimmingly over a period of years." She fell silent now as the waitress brought the drinks to the table. Her eyes followed the Japanese waitress as she left.

"What kind of life do you suppose she has?" she said.

"I have no idea. I've never been an expert on Japanese women."

"But you're an expert on a great many other kinds."

"No," he said. "And let's get back to your heroine."

She nodded, removing the plastic toothpick from the glass, examining the olive pinioned on the end. "All right, our heroine has fallen in love with her boss. Now, that's no big deal. The world doesn't stop spinning; people still go on with their daily lives, and it's just not very important, not to anybody except our heroine. But it's very important to her. Because she had a nice professional relationship established."

"Strictly professional?"

"Not strictly. My heroine and her boss get along very well. He tolerates her occasional interference and accepts her advice once in a while, and she feels needed, and in a way it's a professional friendship, if you know what I mean."

"And this is a pretty terrible predicament, is it?" Corman said.

Her fingers closed around the martini glass, carrying it up to her lips. "She understands this man," she said. "She knows all of his weaknesses and some of his strengths, and she knows that she loves him and nothing can ever come of it. Because he's pretty well tied to his work, and even if he wasn't, he'd make a lousy husband. So she can't expect anything in that direction. Still, she has to do something and do it fast."

"I don't know," Corman said tentatively. "Situations like that have a way of taking care of themselves."

"That's what she's afraid of," she said. Her shoulders shrugged. She grimaced and tasted her drink. "There's no point to this. When I get back to the States, I'll find you another girl and I'll take another job. It's as simple as that."

"It's not that easy and you know it."

She finished the third martini with a toss of her head. He knew her very well. She was close to a final decision now, and once she had made it, she would stick to it, come what may. He could not allow that to happen. He had come to depend upon her; she was extremely important to him, and the thought of her leaving was an impossible one.

She saw his confusion. "I don't mean to upset you," she said, "but you're the literary expert. You've handled situations far more desperate than this for your heroines. All right, give me an ending."

"I don't want you to leave me," he said flatly.

"I can get you an excellent replacement, any one of a dozen girls who can take hold and master your blue funks and your wild enthusiasms within thirty days."

"It wouldn't be the same."

"Wouldn't it? All that's required of me is to do the job of an efficient secretary and to prod you a little from time to time to keep you producing. I may be a habit, but little more than that. That's all you need, isn't it, a glorified girl Friday?"

"Hell, you know how I feel about you," he said uncertainly. "You're a fine secretary, probably the best in the business. You're also a damned attractive woman . . ."

"And after the bulging catalogue of assets comes the stinger," she said, interrupting.

"The time's not right for this. I don't know how I feel about anything right now, but I want to be honest with you. I don't think I have any great capacity for personal relationships."

She shook her head slowly. "Please, don't explain."

The February Plan

"To love somebody takes selflessness," he said insistently. "I've never had it and I wish I did. I get lonely as hell. I want to keep you around, but I suppose that's not fair. You'd probably never get what you wanted out of me, and if you stay with me, you may miss your chance to have it altogether."

"That spells it out," she said, self-contained, withdrawing now. "I wanted things clear-cut, and now they are. I thank you for that." She pushed back from the table and stood up, picking up her purse. "I'm sure Mr. Mitsu won't mind if I beg off this evening. I'd like to go back to the hotel and put the galleys in the mail."

"I'll drop you off. I have to take a cab anyway."

"It's only a few blocks, isn't it? I think I'll walk."

"I'm sorry about this, Elaine."

"So am I," she said.

He watched her as she disappeared through the crowded bar, then checked his watch. It was ten minutes after six, and it would take at least an hour to get out to Chiba and Mitsu's house. Leaving enough yen on the table to cover the bill, he went to find a taxi.

4

The drive to Chiba was not a pleasant one. Corman's last trip to the district had been on a hot summer day when he was to meet a visiting colonel at one of the beaches on the eastern side of Tokyo Bay, and he remembered a delightful journey through the countryside with the neatly terraced farms to the east, rising step on step to the crest of the timbered ridges. And on the west, hugging the coves and inlets along the bay, were the fishing villages with their nets strung out on racks to catch the sun, and the vast brown shallows planted with seaweed awaiting harvest, and beyond them the boats at anchor, so many of them that their masts formed a leafless forest on the water. But what he remembered most vividly about that day was the smell in the air, the earthy, richly decadent smell of the steamy land and a hint of salt blowing in from the bay on a west wind.

On this trip he saw nothing of the Chiba he remembered. By the time the taxi had crossed the river, the early twilight had deepened into night, blotting out everything except the lights of the boats reflecting on the black waters. Once they passed the village of Chiba, the driver got lost, driving all the faster because of his uncertainty, blasting his horn to scatter a covey of bicycle riders who happened to get in his way. Finally, his patience exhausted, Corman grabbed the driver by the shoulder and ordered him to stop. The driver pulled off to the side of the road.

"*Koko wa nan to iu tokoro desu-ka?* Corman said sharply, trying to find out if the man had any idea where he was.

"*Shiranai*," the driver said abjectly, shaking his head.

"Then ask somebody, damn it. *Hanasu* somebody."

The driver shifted into gear and drove on, pulling into the next narrow side road he came to, stopping near a farmhouse with a thatched roof. Flicking on a flashlight, he walked up to the door and knocked. The door opened and an old man in a heavily quilted robe peered querulously into the darkness, bowing formally when the driver came close enough for the old man to see him. Through the open door Corman saw a bare room with a firepit in the center of it and an old woman sitting with her feet down in the square, a blanket about her to trap the heat from the charcoal burner at her feet. Beyond her was a television set, and Corman recognized the flickering familiarity of an American Western.

In a few minutes the driver came back to the taxi, nodding happily, chattering in Japanese as if to assure Corman that he now knew the way. Within a half hour they had reached another village, and the cab edged its way down a narrow lane flanked by high wooded walls on either side, stopping finally in front of a gate. The driver turned to Corman with a pleased expression on his face, tapping the note of directions to indicate they had arrived.

"You wait," Corman said, climbing out of the car, but the man did not understand at all, and as Corman walked toward the gate, he clutched at Corman's

The February Plan

sleeve, pouring out an obsequious tirade. Corman shrugged him off. "Damn it, I'm going to pay you," he said, pulling the bell wire and hearing the distant tinkle. "But you're not going off and leave me stranded until I'm sure this is the right place."

He heard the crunch of footsteps in the snow beyond the gate, and in a moment the gate creaked open and a man appeared, his hand held up to shield his eyes from the glare of the headlights, his long kimono flapping about his legs. It took Corman a moment to realize that the man was Mitsu. Mitsu spoke a few words in Japanese and the driver began to calm down. They talked briefly, then Mitsu turned to Corman. "You owe him seventeen hundred yen," he said. "For an additional twenty-five hundred he will wait in the village and drive you back when you're ready to go."

"All right," Corman said, counting out the money from his wallet. "I'm giving him twenty-five hundred now, and tell him I'll give him another three thousand if he's back here at ten o'clock sharp."

Mitsu nodded, relaying the instructions to the driver, who bowed and went back to his taxi. Mitsu led the way through the gate, closing it behind Corman, locking it before he followed the garden path toward the house. The stone lanterns were dead black against the snow. A pond in a miniature landscape glinted with ice. "I should not have been so thoughtless as to have you come all the way out here," Mitsu said as they reached the entryway and Corman removed his shoes. "I have an apartment in Tokyo that I use sometimes when I'm working late. We could have talked there."

"I don't mind," Corman said, following him down a hallway, pausing while Mitsu slid back a shoji which screened the living room. "I've always liked Chiba. I was just sorry I had to get out here after dark."

"Chiba has changed," Mitsu commented. "We still have our fishing villages, of course, and they are still pretty, but we have industry also, canneries, food-processing plants, and the smell is terrible sometimes, especially in the summer." He took Corman's coat while Corman looked around the room. It was traditional Japanese, with the reed mats soft and springy beneath his feet. In the far corner was a low writing desk and a lamp, and near it was the traditional alcove with a hanging scroll of delicate birds on a leafless bough.

"I keep forgetting how beautiful Japanese architecture is," Corman said. "When I was over here before, I had an ambition to live in a house like this."

"This is really a compromise," Mitsu said, putting Corman's coat in a closet. "My wife is the traditionalist in the family and she would have been out of place in a strictly Western house. But these houses are very cold, and I refused to suffer through the winters any longer. So I had a central heating plant installed. The water for our bath comes from an electric water heater and it no longer takes a day to get it hot with charcoal. As for the clothes"—he indicated his gray kimono—"I'm not trying to preserve any special tradition, but I've never been comfortable in Western business suits." Mitsu paused. "It just occurred to me that you were going to bring your secretary."

"She told me to give you her regrets."

Mitsu nodded. "I'm sorry she couldn't come. Would you like a drink before dinner?"

"No, thank you," Corman said.

Mitsu led the way into the next room, sliding back the shoji and leaving it open. His wife was a lovely woman in a black and white kimono, and she bowed formally from her position next to a *hibachi* where she was beginning to cook sukiyaki, smiling up at Corman and murmuring a greeting in a soft voice. Mitsu indicated where Corman should sit at the low table and then sat down himself, adjusting the pillow beneath him. "I wanted to buy a Western kitchen for my wife," he said. "We went into Tokyo to the department stores, but all the appliances only scared her. She said she had spent forty years learning to cook Japanese style and it was foolish to begin again at her age."

The wife said little during the meal, preserving the delicate smile on her face, seeing to Corman's needs. He ate hungrily, enjoying the conversation with Mitsu, the anecdotes Mitsu had to tell about his life as a private investigator and the decisions he had to make concerning his daughter. She was now twenty-two (he showed Corman her picture, a striking girl with a wistful expression on her face) and she was currently studying in Paris, enrolled in the Institute of International Relations.

Ironically Mitsu had worried about her education from the time she was twelve, trying to decide whether to have her educated in Japan in one of the strict private schools or whether to send her to the United States for a more liberal, Western education. In the end, of course, he had no choice at all; he had overlooked the determination of the new generation to make their own decisions. When she was old enough, she rejected both of the alternatives he offered her and went off to Paris on a scholarship. Mitsu did not really mind. He was obviously proud of her independent spirit.

Once dinner was over, Mitsu's wife cleared the table and retired from the room. Mitsu poured two shallow cups of sake. "Times change," he said, "and a wise man changes with them." He lifted his cup. "*Kampai*, Mr. Corman."

"*Kampai*." The sake was hot and sweet and Corman had another, waiting for Mitsu to broach the subject which had prompted the invitation here tonight, but Mitsu seemed hesitant, reluctant to get down to business. Finally Corman had to do it himself. "Did your man get back from Nikko this afternoon?" Corman said.

"Yes." Mitsu nodded. "I would advise you against going directly to the missile base itself as it is under heavy security, but it might be wise for you to acquaint yourself with the way it is laid out." He stood up, went into the other room, and came back with a map which he unfolded on the table. "You have been to Nikko?"

"Yes."

"Lake Chuzenji?"

"No."

"Very well, then. There is a toll road here that goes west from Nikko to Lake Chuzenji," he said, following the line on the yellow tourist map with his index finger. "It joins with another road which goes along the upper side of the lake and then goes north toward Lake Yunoko. About halfway—here, at this point—there is another road that turns off to the west. It is a new road, so it is not on the map." He sketched it in with a pen. "The road is open across the river and a bridge has been constructed. It is very popular with fishermen. The road crosses a plain for a few miles and then it enters the rough, mountainous country near Mount O-take. As the road enters the mountains, there is a gate. This is guarded at all times by the American military. The base itself is beyond that."

"And that's the only access road?"

"Yes," Mitsu said. "But as I say, it would be foolish to go all the way out there on your own. I think you should take a room at one of the hotels on Lake Chuzenji—some of them stay open during the winter—and then call General Gibson at the base. If he agrees to see you at all, he will probably come to your hotel. No extraneous personnel are allowed onto the base, absolutely none. Now, the base telephone number is Lake Chuzenji seven-five. It is not listed on the Chuzenji telephone exchange, so I suggest you remember it. It's a foolish policy, but even though there is all this publicity about the base in Tokyo, the officials there still deny its existence."

Corman smiled admiringly. "If the number's secret, how did you get it?"

"There are no real secrets in the world, Mr. Corman," Mitsu said. "No impenetrable ones. There are only things that some people know that other people don't know, and there are always methods of finding out." He was thoughtful a moment. "One other thing which you should know. About a mile past the gate there is a cutoff to the right and some quonset huts in the center of a compound surrounded by a barbed-wire fence. My agent talked to some of the local Japanese workmen who were hired to build this place, and they say it was designed for use as a detention center, or, to be more precise, a concentration camp."

"For whom?"

"That's not quite certain. Some of the residents of

Chuzenji have seen trucks filled with American soldiers under guard going up the base road. We can only presume they were being taken to that compound."

"But you're sure they were prisoners?"

Mitsu nodded. "There are trucks built especially for the transportation of prisoners. These were that kind. I have reports of at least six trucks on that road since the first of January. That, by the way, is where I have reason to believe your son was taken."

"They took Paul there?" Corman said, startled.

"I can't be sure," Mitsu said. "Life is full of coincidences, and many times I have been certain of something only to find out that it only had the appearance of truth. So I never say I know anything absolutely, finally."

The reason he believed Paul had been taken there, he went on, stemmed from something that had happened near Lake Chuzenji in the predawn hours of December 24. An innkeeper on the Lake Yunoko road had been awakened by a pounding on the door about four o'clock that morning and had stumbled to answer it, only to find himself confronted by two American civilians who wanted to use his telephone. He invited them in and showed them to the telephone, and one of the men called someplace local—the innkeeper was sure it was local because he did not have time to get long distance—and he seemed quite agitated and upset in his conversation. When the American was through with the call, he explained to the innkeeper that his car had broken down and that he had called for another one which would be there within the next half hour.

Being a courteous man, the innkeeper offered the hospitality of the inn to the Americans until their help arrived. It was a bitterly cold night, and without the engine running in the car they would have no way to keep warm. The Americans thanked him and declined, telling him to go back to bed. There was nothing more he could do. By now, however, the innkeeper was wide-awake, so he put a kettle of water on the stove to boil for tea. A half hour later he saw the lights of another car coming down the road, and because he had nothing else to do, he sat down at the window to watch.

The car approached and stopped, its headlights burning, and three Americans got out of the disabled car, half dragging an American officer who appeared to be sick since he had to be supported on either side. When the lieutenant had been taken about halfway to the other car, he suddenly broke away from the men supporting him and tried to run toward the inn, but his legs would not support him and he fell sprawling to the ground. The other Americans were after him in a second, picking him up and carrying him to the car which drove off to the north. Within a half hour a military tow truck arrived to remove the disabled car.

"Considering the weather, the time element would be just about right," Mitsu said. "If they had left American Electronics at, say, ten o'clock, they would have reached Lake Chuzenji shortly before dawn. Again, it is only presumption, but I think the lieutenant was your son and that they were taking him to the detention camp."

"But why did they take him all the way up there?" Corman said. "And why a detention camp? Why not one of the more convenient guardhouses?"

"Are you familiar with detention camps, Mr. Corman?"

"I inspected one once," he said. "The Eighth Army set up one near Yokohama as a deterrent to fornication. If a man caught VD, he was sent to that hellhole and the word was passed around what could happen to a man if he fooled around with the pompom girls. It didn't do any good in the end. Sex is sex, and a man wasn't going to pass up a lay just because that camp was there."

"Were there ever any political detention camps?" Mitsu said thoughtfully. "Camps for dissenters from official policy?"

"Not military ones," Corman said. "Hell, there was always too much pressure from the mothers of America and the militant congressmen for the army to get away with anything like that. But intelligence could have maintained camps like that. There's supposed to

The February Plan

be one operating in Texas even now, but I don't know that the existence of such a camp there has been proven. I do know there was a detention camp set up by the CIA in Guatemala for dissenters against the Bay of Pigs operation."

"The camp in the mountains may serve a similar function," Mitsu said.

"Why would they need it," Corman said, "to keep the word from getting out that a missile base was being established on Japanese soil?"

"It's possible," Mitsu said, "especially if the missiles on that base are to be armed with nuclear weapons."

"Neither government has admitted that."

"It is not necessary for them to admit it. There would not have been all this need for secrecy if they had intended to use it as a base for conventional weapons. And I share the same fears as my countrymen in this regard. We had Hiroshima and Nagasaki. We are the only nation that has had direct and horrible experience with atomic power. As for myself, I had two uncles who lived in Hiroshima, and after the bomb was dropped there was nothing left of them or their wives or their children or their houses. Nothing. Everything had been completely vaporized, Mr. Corman. They didn't come out with scars or fears of radiation sickness or shattered homes that had to be rebuilt. The bomb dropped and they didn't exist any more, not a scrap of them, nothing. The ground was completely bare where their houses had been, not a trace of anything except pieces of earth that had been so heated it bubbled and congealed and turned into glass which was dug up as souvenirs by foreign visitors. . . ." His hand was trembling now; his face was flushed, and he was having difficulty controlling himself. He stopped abruptly, draining his sake cup, pouring himself another one. "I apologize, Mr. Corman," he said, quieter now, "but I was very fond of my uncles and I am very much afraid of the bomb, not in an abstract, general way, but personally." He refilled Corman's cup. "And this fact leads us to another point, Mr. Corman, a clarification of our business dealings."

"If you need more money, I'll see that you get it."

"Not money, no." Mitsu's hands fluttered in a vague protest. "The money you have already paid will be more than enough. This is something else. We made an agreement that whatever your son did, whatever crime he committed or attempted to commit, would be treated confidentially."

"Yes."

"I may not be able to guarantee that," Mitsu said.

"Why not? He's dead, Mr. Mitsu, and no official charges have been filed against him that have to be cleared. What difference could it make to the world what he did?"

"That's true," Mitsu admitted. "But my concern is a larger one now. I intend to find out what kind of missiles are concealed on that base. I intend to prove that they are armed with nuclear warheads."

"And if they are?"

"Then I will do everything I can to see that they are removed from Japan."

"You won't get anywhere," Corman said. "Even if you confirm your suspicions, what can you do about it? You'll be up against two governments."

"I have given that a lot of thought. I'm just one man and I have little influence in government circles. But I have a reputation for honesty, and if I release the information to the newspapers—the proof—it will be published. And you must not mistake the depth of the feeling my country has against nuclear weapons, Mr. Corman. The students are rioting now because a treaty has been made behind their backs, and it's more or less an intellectual demonstration. But let the people know that this is nuclear, the same power that demolished Hiroshima and Nagasaki, and there will be riots in Japan as no one has ever seen before. Everybody will take to the streets. All work will stop. That missile base will be besieged by public opinion and swept away."

"I don't see how my son is involved in your campaign."

"What happened to him is incidental. But I would have to explain how I became involved in this, what things led me to the suspicion and the discovery, and

The February Plan

everything I've done will have to be revealed. If I conceal anything, it will be used as a weapon against my integrity. So when the time comes, I must be completely frank and open. Now, that leaves you with a choice, Mr. Corman."

"What choice?"

"Right now I know very little about your son. It has been said that he went to American Electronics, that he shot a man. We think your son was picked up by your Intelligence and taken perhaps to the detention camp. But this is presumption, hearsay. Everything is inferential, there are no hard facts, and even a Japanese court would throw out any indictment against your son on the basis of insufficient evidence. So nothing I currently know could hurt the memory of your son. But suppose I find proof that your son was a traitor who sold military secrets to his country's enemies? If you wish me to drop my investigation of your son's case, then the truth will remain hidden and I will use a different approach to the larger problem. What your son did or did not do will no longer be an issue."

"Suppose you drop the case," Corman said after a pause. "What happens to the ten thousand dollars I put in your account?"

"What has not been spent will be returned to you. I would accept no compensation at all for my services."

Corman finished his sake, thinking it over. "I want to know what happened to my son," he said. "And I really don't have much chance of finding out by myself. I want you to go ahead. If it turns out that you have to make public what you find, then I'll take my chances."

Mitsu nodded, obviously relieved. "I'm glad we understand each other," he said. "This is the first time I have been faced with such a conflict of interests. I am pleased to have it resolved."

Corman studied him curiously. "Tell me something, Mr. Mitsu," he said. "When I first met you, I sized you up as a polite but very hardheaded businessman. But I never would have taken you as a patriot."

"I don't pretend to be a patriot," Mitsu said solemnly. "I just happen to find myself in a position where I can do something for a cause I believe in. And my sense of honor compels me to do it." He looked up as he heard the bleat of the car's horn outside, then checked his watch. "Ten o'clock," he said. "Your taxi is very punctual. I wrote down the train schedules out of Tokyo for Nikko and I have listed two or three hotels where you might be comfortable." He handed the list to Corman. "I would appreciate your letting me know where you are staying. When you call my office, use a public phone booth. Fortunately, I have enough influence so that my lines have not yet been tapped."

Corman put the paper in his pocket, slipping on the overcoat which Mitsu brought him from the closet. Mitsu followed him out into the cold entryway and waited while Corman put on his shoes.

"I hope you'll thank your wife for me," Corman said, extending his hand. "The dinner was delightful."

"She will be most pleased that you enjoyed it," Mitsu said. "I will be waiting to hear from you."

When Corman reached the hotel, he thought about stopping by Finley's room for a moment, but it was almost midnight and there was no sense stirring up a matter which had already been resolved. When he reached his room, he poured himself a drink and then sat down to write out a list of the things he wanted her to do in his absence. Midway through the list he changed his mind. He wadded up the paper, dropped it in the wastebasket, and reached for a fresh sheet.

"Dear Elaine," he wrote. "There's really nothing more for you to do here, since I'm leaving for Nikko in the morning. I'll be staying at the"—he consulted the list Mitsu had given him and picked out the first hotel— "Chuzenji-Kanko until I can persuade the general to see me. Now, I want you to use one of the reservations you made for Sunday and go back to New York. Just leave the other ticket at the hotel desk and I'll pick it up when I get back. I'm sorry things had to work out this way, but I'll call you when I get back to New York. Maybe we can see things in a different light then."

He left the note propped up on the desk where she could see it and then he checked the train schedule.

The February Plan

There was a semi-express leaving for Nikko at seven in the morning out of Tokyo Station, arriving in Nikko at eight fifty-eight. He lifted the telephone and asked for the desk. "I'm going to Nikko in the morning," he told the clerk. "Is it necessary to get a train reservation in advance?"

"No, sir," the clerk said. "The trains to Nikko are not crowded this time of year."

"Fine," Corman said. "Then I want to leave a morning call. I want a pot of coffee served in my room promptly at five o'clock. Tell the waiter to knock until he wakes me up."

"Yes, sir," the clerk said. "It shall be done."

4

BY the time the train reached Nikko, the sky was overcast and it was raining again, dampening the spirits of the crowd of skiers who had come north for a holiday. Pulling his collar up around his neck, Corman threaded his way through the people on the platform, stopping in the station to check the return schedules, and by the time he reached the street, the Lake Chuzenji motorbus was already pulling away.

There was only one taxi at the stand and it had been cornered by an American sailor who was getting soaked as he stood in the rain, arguing with the driver. As much as Corman disliked getting involved, the lone taxi appeared to be his last chance of getting to Chuzenji for some time, so he walked over to the sailor and asked if he could help.

"Hell, this goddamned gook is trying to rob me," the sailor said angrily. "He wants two thousand yen to take me over to Lake Chuzenji."

"He may be a thief," Corman said, "but he's also

the last cab. Look, I'll pay the fare if you'll let me share it with you. I have to get over there this morning."

The sailor considered this a minute, then nodded. "Okay," he said. "You got yourself a deal."

Once the taxi had pulled away from the station, the sailor began to talk, overjoyed to run into a fellow American, assuming instantly that Corman would share his prejudices and be interested in the plans for seduction which had brought him up here. It was ironic, Corman thought, looking out the window, that in this perfectly incredible place with its profligacy of temples and pagodas, in the center of the greatest treasures in all Japan, both cultural and scenic, this sailor should be prattling on about the girl he was planning to bed down with at Lake Chuzenji.

The taxi groaned up the steep switchbacks, through heavy stands of cedar and fir trees with the ethereal beauty of a Hiroshige print, but the sailor did not notice, caught up as he was in his sexual monologue, his tale of classic frustration. His name was Herbert Fields, and he had met a girl in Tokyo who was really stacked and she had been leading him on and putting him off when it came to making out (how many evasive phrases were there for the act of sexual intercourse? Corman wondered, and each generation had its own), but finally Herbert told her it was either now or never, because he wasn't going to go on being frustrated by her, and she said her parents were taking her up to their country house at Lake Chuzenji for a week and that if he found a hotel room nearby, she would come to him. Well, Herbert had located a hotel room all right and paid a week's rent in advance, and he had a bottle of Suntori in his ditty bag and he was all set.

When he found that Corman was staying at the same hotel, he insisted they would have to have a drink sometime. Corman was grateful when the cab finally reached Chuzenji and Herbert Fields departed, leaving Corman behind to settle the bill.

The hotel was about what Corman had expected it to be, a Western-style structure with fifty-three American-style rooms. He had no trouble registering. Most of

The February Plan

the sports addicts had gone on to Lake Yunoko for ice skating and skiing. He was able to get a room with a telephone and a connecting bath. He followed the bellboy up the stairs. The room was small but comfortable, with a beamed ceiling and a large window overlooking a hill of pine trees near the lake. He unpacked and ordered breakfast sent to his room. Then he picked up the telephone and asked the operator to get him Lake Chuzenji 75. The call was answered immediately.

"Chuzenji seven-five," a male voice said.

"This is Phillip Corman. I want to speak to General Gibson. He's expecting my call."

The line went dead a moment, then the voice returned. "I'm sorry, sir, but you have the wrong number. This is the Seven seventy-fourth Weather Detachment."

"Weather station or not, just give him a message for me. Tell him I know what happened at American Electronics and the CIA operation there. Now, I don't want to cause trouble for anybody. I simply want to talk to the general as an old friend about an urgent personal matter. I'm at the Chuzenji-Kanko Hotel."

The connection was severed from the other end. Corman settled back on the bed to wait. Within ten minutes the telephone rang. He picked it up to find Major Allenton on the line.

"You were very foolish to come all the way up here, Mr. Corman," Major Allenton said. "In the first place, the general isn't here. And even if he were, he wouldn't have time to see you. You're wasting your time."

"I don't think so," Corman said. "I hate to interfere with his plans and I know how busy he is, but I'm going to see him. You tell him the lieutenant who shot him was my son. I'm scheduled to go back to the States the first of the week, but I'll stay here all winter if I have to. I'm a very stubborn man."

"It may be a very long wait."

"No," Corman said. "I think it's going to be a very short one. You let him know my plans."

Corman put the telephone down and fought the temptation to lie down for a while. The night had been a long one and he had slept little; the dash to Tokyo

Central and the subsequent train ride had tired him. He decided against it. He was too restless to sleep. He left word with the operator that he was expecting a call and wanted to be paged when it came through, and then he went downstairs, picking up a newspaper from the desk, wandering out into a glass-enclosed porch. The rain was beginning to slacken now, but the light on the porch was gray and gloomy, and he went back to the lobby, settling down in an overstuffed chair near the fireplace.

He was just opening the paper when he spotted the sailor coming across the lobby and he pulled the paper up in front of his face, hoping that Fields had not seen him. He was not in luck. The sailor came over and sat down in the chair next to his, rubbing his hands together, lowering his voice, his expression gleefully salacious.

"God, have I got all the luck," he said to Corman. "Her folks have gone back to Tokyo on business for a couple of days and they're going to let her stay up here and go skiing. So we're going to have that whole house to ourselves, just her and me, baby, just her and me."

"I hope it works out for you," Corman said.

"I got it made either way. Her folks come back, we switch over here. I'm all set for a week, man, seven beautiful days and nights. You want a drink? Hell, there's no use my hoarding it. She's got a bar there, a whole damn bar."

"It's a little early in the day for me."

"Then later maybe. I'm in room three-twelve. I won't be going over to her place until afternoon. So any time before then."

"Thank you."

The sailor grinned, self-contained, a little smug, as if nothing on earth was quite as important as his impending success with this girl. Corman watched him as he disappeared up the stairs, and it occurred to him that the sailor was just about Paul's age, early twenties, and he wondered what Paul had been like, whether he had ever felt the same surge of high animal spirits which moved the sailor.

The thought depressed him. He picked up his newspaper again and was glancing at the front page when he felt a presence at his shoulder. He looked around to see a Japanese bellboy bowing with extreme politeness. "Telephone, please," he said.

Corman thanked him and took the call in the telephone room off the lobby. Major Allenton's voice was both crisp and a little angry. "General Gibson will see you tomorrow morning," he said.

"Fine," Corman said. "How do I get there?"

"A car will pick you up at your hotel at nine-thirty."

"Tell the general I'm looking forward to it," Corman said.

Once he had finished the call, Corman did not know what to do with the long hours of the day and evening that yawned in front of him. Ordinarily he enjoyed walking, but the day was wet and cold, and through the window he could see a fog creeping in as the rain slackened. He could always go into Nikko and tramp around the temples and the shops, but that did not interest him greatly. Finally he went up to his room and lay down, intending to sleep, taking two aspirins in the hope they would relax him.

He lay on the bed and his thoughts turned to Mitsu and the situation which confronted them both. There was a parallel in the actions; both were pitting themselves against the sluggish behemoths of bureaucratic officialdom, and neither really had a chance of winning. Their motives were different perhaps, with Corman operating out of anger and stubbornness and Mitsu out of personal duty and persuasive fear, but there was little hope that either of them would be successful. Mitsu's cause was the more hopeless of the two. If the American government had decided to arm Japan with nuclear weapons, there was nothing Mitsu could do about it. None of the demonstrations, the strikes and the riots, would prevail against that decision. The sense of public outrage would be vented and lose force. Eventually the people would get used to the idea and in the end they would accept it.

Corman would fare no better. He would meet the general and receive another version of Paul's adventures, and perhaps it would be the truth, more likely not, and having used up his last tangible resource, Corman would go home. He was amazed that they had gone to so much trouble to cover a comparatively simple matter. It was doubtful that he could learn anything which would endanger the security of the United States. He was no threat to anybody. Why couldn't they tell him the truth and let him go on his way?

He found his mind drifting now as the aspirins began to take effect. Soothed by the hissing of the steam radiators along the wall, he fell asleep.

He was awakened by the jangle of the telephone and for a moment he was disoriented by the twilight in the room, until he checked his watch and realized he had slept through the day. It was now five o'clock. His mind was still furry when he picked up the telephone. It was Finley and she was extremely upset.

"Phil," she said, "I have to see you. Something's happened. It's terrible. I don't know what to do."

"What's the matter?" he said, his mind clearing. "Where are you?"

"Downstairs, in the lobby."

"Come on up." He hung up the phone and dressed hurriedly. He was buttoning his shirt by the time the rap came on the door. He opened it, and she all but fell into his arms, out of breath, her face pale. He led her to the bed and she sat down while he brought her a glass of water from the bathroom. She drank it slowly, calming by degrees. Some of the color came back to her face. "We have to get out of here," she said. "Right away. Tonight."

"What's going on?" he said. "What are you doing up here anyway?"

Her right hand was shaking as she handed him the water glass. She put her hands in her lap, bringing them under control. He had never seen her so badly shaken. "Mitsu's dead," she said quietly.

"Dead?" he said, stunned, incredulous. "Are you sure?"

"I was there," she said. "God, I was right there when it happened." She was on the edge of tears, but they did not come. Her panic was beginning to yield to her discipline; her hands were clutched so tightly together in her lap that the knuckles were white. It had happened that morning, she went on. She had gone up to Corman's room about half-past eight and found the note waiting for her. It did not surprise her too much because she had been thinking along those lines herself. If she was to take the Sunday plane, there were a few loose ends to tidy up, enough work to keep her busy for the morning.

She went down to the desk to pick up the morning mail, sorting out the important messages in case there was anything she might need to call Corman about. There was a letter from Jones—bad news; Henderson had not seen fit to give Corman any sizable advance at this time. While she was sorting the mail, a cable arrived from Manny, a long, no-nonsense message advising Corman to come back to the States immediately. The Internal Revenue boys were taking Corman apart, piece by piece, insisting on the verification of every penny, in no mood either to conciliate or overlook. They were concentrating on the two costly research trips Corman had taken to Europe last year.

She had just decided to call Corman about this when the telephone rang. It was Mitsu, wanting Corman's address at Lake Chuzenji. He was very upset. She gave him the name of the hotel and then volunteered the guess that Corman would still be somewhere en route. Corman was not habitually an early riser; he had probably caught a train sometime between eight and nine.

Mitsu was extremely alarmed at this. Time was running out and Corman was in grave danger. Mitsu had discovered the answer to the riddle; it was all there, in the morning's English edition of *Asahi*. He knew it with complete certainty, but there was nothing he could do about it, not without Corman's help. He could not even call the papers; the whole thing was too staggering to be credible. Corman would have to help him get the proof.

"He was almost incoherent," Finley said, catching her breath. "He was so upset he was rambling, and I couldn't make much sense out of it. But I'm trying to remember exactly what he said, everything he touched on, because some of it might be important to you."

"You're doing very well," Corman said. "Go on."

"He was more than upset," she said. "He was scared, frightened. I asked him to give me the details and I told him I'd take them down in shorthand and get them to you. But he said he couldn't talk on the telephone because our wire might be tapped and he was taking a terrible chance by just calling. He told me to go out the Hibiya entrance to the hotel and turn left and keep walking and he would pick me up. He wouldn't say when or where, just that he would pick me up."

She had done as he requested. She followed his instructions, leaving the hotel, walking down the street, more curious than concerned at this point. She walked for perhaps half an hour, expecting to be picked up at any minute, but there was no sign of Mitsu. She reached Shiba Park, waited around for a while, and then decided to catch a cab back to the Imperial. As she was crossing the street, she heard someone call her name and she looked back to see Mitsu standing on the side of the street she had just left, about a hundred yards farther down. Apparently he had just come out of an alleyway where he had been waiting for her.

The traffic was heavy and she was isolated on an island in the middle of it, waiting for the light to change. And as she stood there, she heard the blaring of a horn and the screech of brakes. A woman screamed, and Finley's heart caught in her throat. A crowd was gathering near the place where she had seen Mitsu. Without thinking, she dashed across the street, almost getting hit by two cars, pushing her way through the crowd until she saw Mitsu. He was lying in the alleyway, crushed out of shape, covered with blood, obviously dead.

Sick to her stomach, she backed away, leaning against a lamppost, listening to an American soldier describing the accident to a buddy. A heavy truck had swerved into the alley off the street, crushing the man before he could move, roaring on up the alley without slowing down for an instant. At this point she remem-

The February Plan

bered what Mitsu had told her over the telephone, and the fear struck her with full force. She was certain this was no hit-and-run accident. Mitsu had been murdered.

Two cars pulled up, the first a Japanese police car and the second full of Americans in business suits who dispersed immediately, moving into the crowd. She panicked. If her line had been tapped, if they knew where to find Mitsu, they would also be looking for her.

She moved away from the accident immediately, trying to be casual and unhurried about it, losing herself in the crowd of people on the sidewalk. A block away she darted into a curio shop and pretended to examine a row of brass Buddhas, but all the while she was fighting the panic within her, trying to get organized, to figure out what she was going to do. She could not go back to the hotel; that was the first place they would look for her. She thought about calling Corman, but that was risky. If the line had been tapped at the Imperial Hotel, they knew where Corman was and all the calls going into the Chuzenji-Kanko would be monitored. But she had to get in touch with him, to tell him what Mitsu had said, to let him know he was in danger.

From her vantage point in the store she saw two of the Americans coming down the street, so she went out the back door of the shop into a narrow lane, following it until she found herself on a canal full of filthy gray water and a barge or two. She rested by a stone wall a moment and then crossed a footbridge and kept walking until she came to a boulevard.

She managed to catch a taxi, telling the driver to take her to Tokyo Central. On the way she went through her purse and found that she still had a considerable amount of yen left over from her shopping expedition. When she reached the station, she bought a ticket for Nikko and, having a few minutes to wait, used the time to call the airline, hoping there had been a cancellation on an earlier flight. She was in luck. There were two seats available for Friday night. She had the reservations switched.

"Then I came up here," she said. "We have to get out of here, Phil. I've had time to think it through. If we can get back to Tokyo and catch that plane, if we show them we're going home, there's no reason for them to interfere. That makes sense, doesn't it?"

"They can't touch us in any case," Corman said grimly. "We haven't broken any laws, done anything illegal."

"You don't understand," she said urgently. "As far as I know, Mitsu didn't do anything illegal either, but they killed him just the same."

"We can't be certain of that," Corman said. "It could have been a hit-and-run, a simple accident."

"And the Americans?" she said. "All those men? Can you explain that away too?"

"I'm sure they had Mitsu under surveillance," Corman said, "and it might have taken them a few minutes to reach the scene of the accident." He put his arms around her now, but he could feel the stiff rebellion in her and he released her. "All right," he said. "I'll admit that you may be right. I don't believe it, but as long as there's any chance at all that they had Mitsu killed, I want you out of here."

"No, I . . ."

"I'm not giving you any choice. In a way you'll be my insurance. You take the plane back to New York. If there's not a call from me within three days, go to Jones and Blakely and let them know what happened. They'll find a way to trace me."

She shook her head adamantly. "I don't want you killed."

"Nothing's going to happen to me. And we can make doubly sure of that if you'll do as I say." She was beginning to weaken now; he could see the doubt in her face. "You go back to Tokyo on the next train. Get a room near the airport and stay in it. Tomorrow night, just before your flight time, I want you to call me here and let me know that you're all right. Then you get on that plane and go home."

"If that's what you think we should do . . ."

"It's what we're going to do," he said. "I don't think all these precautions are necessary, but we won't take any chances." He picked up the telephone. "Give me the desk, please." And then, when the desk clerk answered: "This is Corman in two-fourteen. I want to hire a car to drive to Nikko. No, change that. I want to arrange for a car all the way to Tokyo."

"Yes, sir," the clerk said, a little hesitantly. "But it may take a little time."

"How long?"

"An hour perhaps. It is necessary to rearrange the drivers who work for the hotel."

"Fine. Go ahead and arrange it." He put down the telephone. "We'll have a car for you in an hour. And right now I want to go down and see if I can locate a copy of today's *Asahi*, and then we'll get something to eat."

"I can't eat anything," she said. She took off her coat, then she opened her purse, rummaged around in it, and handed him a folded newspaper. "And I picked up a copy of the paper at Tokyo Central while I was waiting for my train. I went through it, but I couldn't find anything significant."

"I'll take a look at it after a while," he said, minimizing it, folding the newspaper and putting it in his pocket. "But right now I think you'd better eat something. You have a long night ahead of you." He called room service and ordered two steaks and a small pitcher of martinis.

In a few minutes the Japanese waiter knocked discreetly at the door and brought in the pitcher and two glasses on a small lacquered tray. Corman poured one for Finley and handed it to her. "Go ahead, drink it," he insisted. "It'll do you good."

She drank it dutifully. "I've never seen a man killed before," she said, grimacing. "One minute he was standing there, waving at me, and the next minute he was dead, just like that." She looked at him directly now. "I'll go back to Tokyo. I'll do as you say, but I want you to tell me the truth, what you really think. Am I letting my imagination run away with me?"

"I don't know," he said. "If the CIA wanted him out of the way, I think they would have picked him up, questioned him, even jailed him for a while, but I don't think they would have run him down with a truck. But I can't be positive. Sometimes I think the world's gone crazy."

"Maybe I'm just being foolish," she said, sighing. "God, enough's happened lately to keep me on edge for the rest of my life." She finished her drink. "I'll tell you the truth. I don't like it over here. I like to think I'm cosmopolitan, and when I get home I'll lie my head off to make the other girls envious, but I don't like Japan one bit."

There was another knock on the door. "You'll feel better when you've had something to eat," Corman said to her, crossing to the door and opening it. A young man in a camel's-hair coat stood in the corridor, a pleasant smile on his face. "Good evening, Mr. Corman," he said. "Do you remember me? We met down at the electronics company."

"Yes, I remember," Corman said warily. "Wilkinson, isn't it? What are you doing here?"

"I'd like to talk to you," Wilkinson said, but he was not asking for permission. He came into the room and closed the door behind him, taking advantage of Corman's startled inaction, nodding respectfully to Finley who stared at him apprehensively. "Miss Finley, isn't it?" he said quietly. His eyes flicked around the room. He stood with his back against the closed door.

"What in the hell do you think you're doing?" Corman said, irritated.

"I'm with the Central Intelligence Agency, Mr. Corman," Wilkinson said patiently. "I'm sorry I can't offer you any credentials to back that up, but I don't think you really need them, considering everything. I hate to take you out in weather like this, but I'm going to have to ask you to get your coats."

"We're not going anywhere with you," Corman said. "And you're going to have a hell of a time trying to force us."

"You're a reasonable man," Wilkinson said, unperturbed. "I'm armed and I'm not alone, Mr. Corman. And there's no need for you to fight us. We're all Americans, all on the same side, after all. It's a routine matter, no cause for alarm." He smiled now, taking

Corman's acquiescence for granted. "Now, if you'll get your coats, I have a car waiting."

2

By the time the car left the lake, moving north on the road to Yunoko, the last vestiges of daylight were fading, and Corman had no more than a glimpse of icy plain and snow-covered trees before darkness set in and he could see nothing.

Wilkinson sat next to the driver, turned sideways in the seat so that his peripheral vision included the back seat. He was perfectly relaxed. The car moved slowly, its chained wheels rattling over the ice-covered road.

"Where are you taking us?" Corman said.

"Up to the base," Wilkinson said. He smiled. "Actually it's not very far, but it takes a hell of a long time to get there. While it was raining down here, it was snowing up there, and the roads aren't in very good shape. I hope you're not too uncomfortable, Miss Finley?"

She said nothing.

"I want to know by what authority you're arresting us," Corman demanded. "I want to know the charge against us."

"This isn't an arrest," Wilkinson said. "It's protective custody, as much for your benefit as ours. But we'll go into that later." He said no more, taking out a pack of cigarettes, offering them to Corman and Finley before he lighted one for himself. "It's inconvenient all the way around, but it happens to be necessary."

He was just finishing his third cigarette when the car slowed and turned off on a side road to the west, creeping across the river bridge and the frozen marshland. Wilkinson filled in the silence, chatting about nothing in particular, as if to reassure them that there was no reason for apprehension and that within an hour, two at the most, they would be heading back for the hotel, with no harm done. In another fifteen minutes the car slowed again as the searchlight caught it, glowing against the ice on the side windows. Grimacing, as if he resented having to leave the warm car, Wilkinson opened his door and climbed out. Corman heard the murmur of voices, and in a moment a guard opened the front door and flashed a light into the back seat.

Apparently the guard was satisfied. He withdrew, and Corman could see him in the headlights as he raised the heavy wooden arm of the barrier, a stocky man in an Air Force uniform, his breath pluming in the cold air. He waved the car through. On the other side of the barrier the car stopped and Wilkinson climbed in again, shivering against the cold, motioning the driver to move on. The darkness closed in again. The road steepened perceptibly, the engine laboring to make the grade. "All of this must be a damned nuisance for you, having to come all the way out here," Wilkinson was saying, "but it's a technicality of the law and we have to observe it. Under Special Directive Number Seven of the National Security Council we are only allowed to question American civilians on American soil, and that's been enlarged to cover military bases abroad. I think we can make you comfortable while you're here."

"I doubt that," Corman said flatly. "You're taking us to your detention camp, aren't you?"

Wilkinson smiled. "That just goes to show you how much real security there is any more. The existence of the camp was supposed to be completely 'black,' as we say in the trade."

"I assume that's a roundabout way of saying yes," Corman said.

"It's not like you think it is," Wilkinson said, lighting another cigarette. "A detention camp isn't a prison. It wasn't set up to punish anyone or to rehabilitate them. It's exactly what the name implies, a temporary center where people can be detained for security reasons."

"And you think we're security risks?" Finley said.

"Let's say we have to make sure that you're not," Wilkinson said. He terminated the conversation then, peering through the windshield as the driver turned off on a road to the right. In a few minutes they were

The February Plan

halted at another checkpoint, but this time Wilkinson did not bother to get out of the car. He rolled down the window, exhibiting his identification badge. Corman saw the glint of the lights on barbed-wire fences. The car passed through the gate, and Wilkinson turned to Corman again.

"You might be interested to know, Mr. Corman, that in this age of electronics we still rely on some of the old-fashioned protective techniques," Wilkinson said, matter-of-factly, as if he had been asked to explain a working mechanism to a new recruit. "I laid it out myself. The camp sits down in a hollow and it's thoroughly fenced and cross-fenced. Around the camp itself we cleared all the underbrush in an area a hundred yards wide, and we patrol that strip with dogs. Personally I think all these precautions are unnecessary, considering the roughness of the country around here. Even the most experienced mountain climber would be foolish to try the slopes. Have you ever done any mountain climbing, Mr. Corman?"

"No," Corman said. "And you've made your point."

Wilkinson ignored his comment, smoking in silence a moment, his face washed with the red glow from the coal of his cigarette. "Some of the boys in the outfit were really tickled to get sent up here. They like to ski. But they were pretty sore when they got the word. We've had heavy snows all winter and the ridges are dangerous, just ready to bust loose. We've had two or three avalanches since I've been here."

He was interrupted again by another checkpoint, and five minutes later the car rolled into the camp itself, pulling to a stop next to a brightly lighted quonset hut. As Corman helped Finley out of the car, he tried to get his bearings, but he caught no more than a glimpse of other quonset huts scattered about an open clearing, and then Wilkinson was at his side, ushering him past the guards into the building.

The room was small, containing a desk and chairs, dominated by an old-fashioned oil-burning stove that flooded the room with an overpowering heat. Wilkinson grimaced at the man who stood up behind the desk as they came in, a big, lumbering officer with a red face. "What are you trying to do, roast yourself alive?" Wilkinson said with a pained smile. "Miss Finley, this is Lieutenant Maynard. And this is Mr. Corman."

Maynard nodded and said nothing. Wilkinson took off his overcoat and helped Finley with hers, placing both coats on the rack against the wall. "Lieutenant Maynard here is from Houston, Texas," Wilkinson said, "and he operates under the belief that the whole world's going to freeze unless the temperature is kept at a constant hundred degrees." He smiled at his own humor. "If you don't mind, Miss Finley, I'd like you to wait here. See if you can't scrape up some fresh coffee for the lady, Maynard."

"None for me, thanks," Finley said, looking to Corman, more bewildered than frightened now. Wilkinson had opened a door leading into a central corridor and was waiting for Corman to follow.

"It's going to be all right," Corman said. "I'll be back in a few minutes."

Wilkinson led the way down the corridor to the first door, opening it for Corman, permitting him to enter first, then closing the door behind them. The room was cluttered with a pair of overstuffed chairs and a small plain wooden table. There was a worn flowered rug on the floor and a single framed print of a desert landscape on the wall. "Have a seat, Mr. Corman," Wilkinson said. "This is the dayroom for our staff here. We had to do considerable scrounging to get the furniture. There's a winter lodge on the base that was used during World War II by Japanese officials who wanted to get away from it all, and it happened to still be furnished when we took it over, but most of the pieces were in pretty bad shape."

Corman sat down, accepting a cigarette from the pack Wilkinson offered him. Wilkinson did not sit. He stood near the small window which was shuttered from the outside. "It was stupid of me," he said suddenly, "not to offer you coffee too. If you like, I'll have the lieutenant bring you some."

"No," Corman said. "Let's get on with the interrogation."

The February Plan

Wilkinson smiled pleasantly. "No interrogation," he said. "Just a few questions."

"Which I won't answer," Corman said. "Despite your special directive, whatever the number is, you don't have the right to ask me anything."

"In a strictly legal sense we do," Wilkinson said. "I can get you the directive and let you read it, if it would make any difference, but there's no point to that. We don't use coercion. Whether you answer the questions or not is strictly up to you. You should understand, Mr. Corman, that neither you nor your secretary is in any jeopardy. We're not threatening you with anything. Quite honestly, we need your help."

"We?"

"Your country."

Corman grimaced slightly, showering ashes onto the floor. "I've heard quite enough of that phrase from Major Henshaw. You know him, don't you?"

"Yes."

"Then you can understand how I feel. For the moment let's leave patriotism out of it, Wilkinson. You represent the CIA, not the whole government, so when you say my country needs my help, what you really mean is that the CIA wants my co-operation."

"I won't argue semantics with you, Mr. Corman."

"Because all you're interested in is results." He studied Wilkinson for a moment. "You're Ivy League, aren't you?"

"That's right."

"Princeton?"

"I can't say."

"And Wilkinson probably isn't your real name, is it?"

"No."

"My son went to Princeton," Corman said. "He went into the service before he graduated. I don't think you could have known him there. I'd say, just offhand, that you've been out of school for seven or eight years."

"That's not important one way or the other," Wilkinson said.

"I think it is," Corman said. "You know all about

me. If we're going to do some verbal sparring, I ought to know something about you as well. If you're a product of the Ivy League, I can guess you're reasonably bright and perceptive. I can assume you know damn well you're not going to get anything out of me I don't care to give."

"Very good," Wilkinson said, sitting down now, his politeness evaporating. "Then we won't waste any time. You're important to us only because you've stumbled into a top-secret project and we have to know the extent of your knowledge. We also have to know how much Mitsu knew about it and whether it's possible he could have passed the word along. If there's any knowledge outside our organization, we have to contain it and keep it from spreading. Now, if you co-operate with us, if we're absolutely certain we can trust you, we can release you."

"You're straying," Corman said. "You're wandering away from the truth. You can't con me; you'd better get that straight now." He crushed out the cigarette. "You know damn well you can't release me now, and what I know or don't know won't influence that in the least. The mere fact that there's a top-secret project here is enough to insure that."

Wilkinson smiled. "Touché," he said. "All right, then, we'll drop that pretense. You're right, we're going to have to keep you and Miss Finley here for a while."

"How long?"

"I can't tell you that. But no more than a few days, let's put it that way."

"One more thing," Corman said. "If you expect me to be frank with you, then you're going to have to be frank with me. Was your agency responsible for all my trouble back in the States?"

Wilkinson thought the question over a moment. "Yes," he said.

Corman blinked slightly. "How did you accomplish it?"

"It wasn't very difficult. The word got out in New York that the government looked with displeasure on your book, *The Barriers*. It was pretty doubtful that any movie based on it would get an export license, on the grounds that your book represented an image of the United States that was damaging to our national prestige."

"That's all it took?" Corman said, startled.

"Most large corporations have a secret fear of the government, Mr. Corman, you know that. The government has the power to control business, and business knows it. Hollywood is bankrolled in New York, and the money men there aren't about to do anything to antagonize the government, not unless they think it can be turned to a large enough profit. In this case they apparently didn't think it was worth the risk."

"And the suit over my lecture contracts—that was the handiwork of your agency, too, was it?"

"Yes. We worked through a senator who knows your lecture agent. But we didn't have to use any pressure. We just suggested to your agent that the government favored any legal action that would force you to come back to the States. He took it from there."

"That bastard," Corman said. "I suppose I don't even need to ask you about Internal Revenue, do I?"

"They received a tip that there were irregularities in your returns. They're required to check these things out."

"That makes me very angry," Corman said calmly. "I knew it couldn't be coincidence, but I rather hoped it was. And that changes things. I think I'm going to put a few conditions on my co-operation, Mr. Wilkinson. I want some guarantee that all these financial pressures are going to be relieved."

Now it was Wilkinson's turn to be taken aback; Corman could almost see the machinations of his mind as he thought it through. "I'll be frank with you, Mr. Corman. First, I don't have the authority to make any deals, and secondly, I'm not so sure what anybody can do at this point. If there are no irregularities on your returns, the tax situation will take care of itself. We might be able to have the suit called off, a settlement of some sort, perhaps—he has a lot of clients in the government. As far as your movie deal is concerned, the best we could do there is to let the right people know that the government no longer has any objections. Whether or not they decide to carry through with your contract, or however they handle things like that, well, that's going to have to be up to them. I can't guarantee anything, understand. The best I can do is pass the suggestion along."

"And I'm left with the short end of the stick."

"That's possible," Wilkinson said. "Now, will you answer some questions?"

"That depends on what you ask."

Wilkinson had begun to relax now. He lighted a cigarette and crossed his knees, leaning back in his chair, assuming a conversational attitude as if all strain had disappeared and he could afford to be at his ease. "First, I'd like to know what you and Mitsu discussed last night."

"Another point of clarification first," Corman said. "Did you have him killed?"

Wilkinson shook his head, exhaling the smoke. "No, that was an accident."

Corman shrugged. It was a foolish question and he could not expect a straight answer. "All right," he said. "We talked about a great many things. He suspected that you have nuclear weapons here. If he could verify that suspicion, he was going to make a public issue out of it. He offered me a chance to get out of our deal, because if what he suspected was true, he couldn't keep my son's name from being mixed up in it."

"And what had he found out about your son?"

"He suspected that you boys brought Paul up here, to the detention camp. He couldn't prove it."

"Nothing more than that?"

"Nothing more."

"Did you accept the chance to disassociate yourself?"

"No."

Wilkinson nodded, apparently satisfied. "Why did he call your secretary?"

"You monitored the call. You know as much as I do."

"Unfortunately not," Wilkinson said. "After you left for Nikko, we closed down the tap on your phone at the hotel. We jumped the gun a little, I think, but it

The February Plan

didn't seem necessary to maintain it. We had a man covering Mitsu's office, and we didn't think Mitsu could get past him. But Mitsu was a clever man. Evidently he knew he was being watched and went to some trouble to get out of his office unobserved. By the time we tracked him down, he was already dead. Our men saw your secretary on the street, and so we just put two and two together."

"Mitsu didn't tell her anything," Corman said. "He was afraid the telephone was tapped. He wanted to get in touch with me, and when he couldn't, he made arrangements to meet her and give her the information to pass on to me. But he was killed before they could get together. That's all there was to that."

Wilkinson scratched his chin thoughtfully. "It must have been pretty urgent or he wouldn't have gone to all that trouble," he said, almost to himself. "Well, whatever he knew, it apparently died with him. There would have been some reaction by now if he had passed the word along." He looked up now, encouraged, Corman supposed, because all the facts seemed to be falling neatly into place. "If you don't mind, Mr. Corman, I'd like to know everything you did today, step by step."

"That's very simple. I got up at five this morning. I had coffee served in my room. At six-thirty I took a cab to Tokyo Central where I caught the seven-o'clock train for Nikko. I came to Nikko by car and stayed in the hotel until you showed up this evening."

"And who did you talk to, Mr. Corman?"

"You mean conversations, telephone calls?"

"Anybody you even spoke to."

"Hell, I don't know," Corman said. "I imagine I said something to the waiter, the bellboy who carried my bags to the lobby, the doorman, the cabdriver who took me to Tokyo Central. I didn't talk to anyone on the train. I may have said something to some of the hotel employees at Chuzenji, I don't know. I made one telephone call to your so-called weather station and talked to the operator. And then later Major Allenton called me back."

"That's all?"

"Yes, I think so."

"How about the sailor?"

"The sailor? How'd you know about him?"

"We had a man on the train with you as far as Nikko. But unfortunately you and the sailor took the last cab. It took our man a little while to catch up with you."

"He should have introduced himself," Corman said dryly. "He could have shared the car with us."

Wilkinson smiled slightly. "What did you and the sailor talk about?"

"Sex. Only it was a monologue on his part."

"What's his name?"

"Fields, I think. Herbert Fields."

"His rank?"

"Beats me. I know he wasn't an officer."

"What was the girl's name?"

"How in the hell would I know her name?"

"All right," Wilkinson said, taking a new tack now. "You made reservations for Sunday morning to fly back to New York. JAL, Flight two twenty-seven. Did you really intend to use those reservations?"

"If I was successful, if I found out what I wanted to know."

"About your son?"

"Yes."

"And that was the reason you wanted to see General Gibson?"

"I still want to see him. I have an idea I can persuade him to tell me the truth about what happened to Paul."

"What makes you think he knows the truth?"

"A general usually knows what's going on. And he's got a personal reason for having kept up with Paul."

Wilkinson stood up now, crushing out his cigarette. "I guess that takes care of everything for now."

"For you, maybe, but not for me. I'd like to talk to the general."

"I'll be glad to relay the request, but again I can't promise anything." He looked around at the room rather apologetically. "I'm sorry we can't offer you any better quarters than these," he said. "I'll have a bed brought in for you. There's a toilet down the hall that you'll be allowed to use whenever we can spare a guard to go with you."

"What about Miss Finley?" Corman said. "What are you going to do with her?"

"I really don't know," Wilkinson said. "We hadn't made provisions for any women on the base. But I'm sure we can convert something. We'll make her comfortable."

"Can I see her?"

"I doubt it," Wilkinson said. "Not that I have anything against it, but we're pretty shorthanded here. We'll see."

Corman stood up, restless now. "All right, Wilkinson. I've leveled with you," he said. "Now suppose you do the same with me. What's this all about? What's the government doing here?"

"I wish I could tell you," Wilkinson said. "But I can't, of course. And anyway, you'll know the details soon enough."

"One more question then. How long am I going to be held here? There's no reason not to tell me that."

"A week," Wilkinson said. "No more."

"Thank you."

"If you need anything, just let the guard know," Wilkinson said, as if he were the host here, anxious that his guest should be comfortable. "I'll have dinner brought to you after a while, and some magazines if you'd like to read. Nothing current, I'm afraid, but they may help to pass the time."

"All right," Corman said.

Wilkinson nodded. All of the arrangements had been made, everything taken care of, and he was free to leave. The door closed behind him as he went out. Corman heard the rasp of a key as the door was locked from the outside. He suddenly felt desperately fatigued, despite the fact that he had slept most of the day. It was logical, he thought; anxiety and defensiveness emptied a man far more quickly than physical effort.

He sat down again, feeling the pressure of time. He was absolutely sure Wilkinson would be questioning Finley now, and he was reasonably sure she would have enough presence of mind not to mention the newspaper, but he could not be positive. He took the paper out of his pocket and unfolded it on his knees, beginning to scan the tightly packed columns, looking for whatever it was that Mitsu had seen here, the words that had frightened him enough to send him looking for help, the words that had inadvertently caused his death.

Part Two

1

IT was midnight before Wilkinson left the detention camp, driving the jeep up the frozen slope to the main road, following it for three miles to the cutoff which led to the lodge. He was tired and half frozen and he wanted nothing more than to have a drink and to sack in for the night, but he knew he was still hours away from that luxury. The major was a stickler for paper work and he would insist on a full written report on Wilkinson's interrogation of Corman and Miss Finley. It was quite unnecessary, of course. When it came right down to it, Wilkinson could only report that two uninvolved people had stumbled into the project by accident and knew nothing about it. Well, there was always the chance that the major would accept an oral report on this one. It was a very small chance, perhaps, but nothing would be lost by trying, and it was possible the effort might save him three hours of work.

He drove down the winding road between the tall stands of fir trees and finally rounded a sharp curve to be confronted by the lodge, standing on a slope, the lights shining out of its arched windows and giving the building form against the dark forested hill behind it. The lodge was huge, an example of Gothic Swiss architecture with a multiplicity of needle-pointed gables and carved exterior beams, now peaked with snow.

When Wilkinson had first seen it, it had reminded him of a ski lodge in the White Mountains where he had vacationed many times, a place with small, snug rooms and a spacious lobby with a roaring wood fire and community sings. There had been a protective atmosphere about that place, an elemental comfort which was entirely lacking here.

This lodge was a conglomeration of a few large and drafty rooms, heated only by wood-burning fireplaces, some of which did not draw well. The best of the rooms had been taken by communications and as quarters for the general and the major, and the larger rooms on the second floor had been converted into dormitories for the temporary use of the project technicians until the Hole was completed. Wilkinson had been assigned one of the smaller and less desirable rooms on the third floor. When the technicians moved to the Hole, Wilkinson had considered taking one of the larger rooms, but he had decided it was not worth the trouble. He spent little time in his quarters anyway, and his room was relatively warm and there was no point in trading comfort for convenience.

Parking the jeep in the circular driveway, he pulled a tarp over it against the forecast of heavy snow, and then he went into the reception hall, showing his identification badge to the uniformed guard at the entrance to the beamed living room. There was a fire crackling in the massive hearth, and General Gibson and the major were listening to a lean man named Beardon who stood by the fireplace talking. As Wilkinson came in, Major Henshaw glanced up at him briefly and then returned his attention to Beardon, who paused in his report long enough to allow for the interruption and then swept on, picking up where he had left off.

Wilkinson had met Beardon only once before, a number of years back, when Beardon had been called into Washington for a special debriefing and Wilkinson had been on the evaluation team. At the time he had felt an antipathy toward the man, and he could not say that time had changed his first impression. Beardon was much too arch in his manner, almost supercilious. He was a man of mincing affectations with a perpetual and

The February Plan

effete curl to his lip, but he was an expert on the Red Chinese, operating inside Red China as a British journalist, and Wilkinson respected his efficiency. Wilkinson had long since learned to work with men he did not like, and sometimes there were positive advantages. There could be no feeling of personal involvement here to complicate the mission.

Beardon stood lounging against the carved rock facing of the fireplace, one long arm draped along the high mantel. He was wearing a heavy tweed jacket which fell away to reveal a black turtle-necked sweater, and he spoke in a tailored journalese, each word clipped and precise. "And that's all there is to it, really," he was saying. "It's all open and aboveboard, exactly what they've announced it to be. They're very literal-minded people. That's revealed by their poetry; it's not nearly as mystically abstract as most Westerners suppose. Mentally they follow a straight line. They like things one, two, three."

"And this surprise they've announced," Major Henshaw said, bringing him back to the point. "You haven't been able to find out what it is?"

"I have a great many ideas, formulations really, but absolutely no hard facts, not one. I was at the Peking Institute last week, and they trust me there—as much as they trust any foreigner, I should say—but I couldn't get a rotten peep out of anybody. Maybe some of them knew what was going on, or maybe they were as much in the dark as I was, but the end result was the same. I couldn't dredge up anything except a few bloody rumors, and most of them were stirred up by the official announcements."

"Then give us your educated hunch," the general said.

"That's easy, really," Beardon said with a smile. "They've gone to great trouble to let the foreign press know that they've made a break-through and that they plan to unveil it. That was the word they used, 'break-through,' and they usually describe anything even remotely newsworthy as an 'achievement.' It's my guess that they have come up with a delivery system beyond the old Soviet planes we know they have, a missile probably. I suspect it's in the medium range, but I know they've been working on something more ambitious, and we mustn't be surprised if it's larger."

The major frowned, and Wilkinson had the feeling this was not so much intended for Beardon as it was for the general, who sat in an overstuffed armchair, his hand toying with a cigarette lighter. He turned it over and over in his fingers like a talisman. The major looked to Beardon again. "But they will all be there, you're absolutely sure of that?"

"All of the arrangements call for it. Twenty-three hundred and sixty-four of them, to be exact. That's somewhat higher than we estimated, I think. Barring the possibility of illness, which could reduce that figure by six per cent, I think they'll all be there, every precious one of them. The Republic has elevated them to a kind of religious pantheon; actually there's a whole mystique centered around them, a new image, created, I suppose, to give the younger generation a new set of heroes. They've put up special barracks to house them near the Glorious Science Hall. Really beastly facilities. But they make a flaming miracle out of running water and electric lights, and if you have hot water, it's a positive smash. And these facilities have hot water. They're really escalating this thing. If the weather permits, they'll have to move it outside, into the Workers' Gymnastic Stadium."

The general stirred now, shifting his weight in the chair, pocketing the lighter. "Who have you got set up over there to handle things on that end?"

Beardon looked startled for a moment, as if he had not really expected to be questioned by the general and did not much want to answer. The old rivalry, Wilkinson thought, the agency versus the military. "His name is Chao," he said. "I trained him myself, General. He's a good man."

"I'm just asking who he is," the general said. "Where does he fit into things from their point of view? What does he do for a living?"

"He's a student," Beardon said. "He studies physics at the Peking Institute. He's twenty-five years old."

"How well do you know him?"

The February Plan

"Quite well. I met him last year when I was there. I've seen him a number of times since, very circumspectly, of course, and I know he's sympathetic toward our point of view, not only sympathetic toward us, but avidly against communism."

"Do you have a dossier on him?" the general said.

Beardon sputtered slightly, looking at the major, a quizzical smile on his face as if to ask if he was required to take this seriously. The major made no move to get him off the hook. Beardon shrugged. "Certainly there's no dossier as such, General, because there are no real provisions for making an investigation in depth over there, absolutely none, not without tipping them off. Our overt interest is really the kiss of death as far as any individual is concerned. But he's well trained, and he is loyal. I'd be willing to stake my life on that."

"That's exactly what you are doing," the general said flatly. "That's what we're all doing." He cleared his throat. "I've run into their army boys before. They're tough as horsehide. I can't think their Intelligence boys would be any less. How can you be sure he's not a double agent?"

"He doesn't know what we're doing," Beardon said with a bewildered smile. "He does not have the slightest inkling of our plans. I merely trained him to use a transmitter and gave him a few cautionary procedures to keep him from being discovered. He transmits information, but he thinks this is routine, that we are conducting a scientific census."

"How much is he being paid?"

"Nothing," Beardon said. "I told you, General, he is a man of principle."

The general said nothing more, sinking back into the chair, staring into the fire.

"What are your orders now, Beardon?" the major said quietly.

"I'm due back in Manila the first of March," Beardon said, "or perhaps a little later. But they haven't given me any assignment yet, and it probably won't pop up until late February. Until then I'm on R and R, although I must say that up to now I've had pitifully little of both."

"Get some sleep," the major said. "We'll talk again in the morning."

"Righto," Beardon said. He glanced at the general as if considering some reinforcing remark, then decided against it and smiled at Wilkinson before he crossed the room toward the door, the heels of his highly polished boots clicking against the floor.

General Gibson stood up, a stubborn set to his jaw, massaging his left shoulder with the fingers of his right hand. "He's a queer, isn't he, a homo?"

"Probably," the major said dryly.

"You know that, but you still keep him on?"

"It takes all kinds," the major said. "He's been quite useful on a number of occasions when an ordinary man couldn't have done any good. He has an excellent record."

"I don't trust him," the general said.

"We don't have to trust him," the major said. "Although, if I had to say whether I trust him or not, I'd say that I do."

"I don't think you get what I mean," the general said. "Maybe he wouldn't purposely distort the facts or feed us false information, but damn it, Major, you know as well as I do how emotionally unstable these guys are. I got stuck with a colonel down at Bliss like him. He was with Battalion at the time, a quiet little man, very good at tactics." He stopped short, deciding against the details. "Anyway, his peculiarities damn near loused us all up in an exercise. I hate like hell to think what would have happened if we'd been in the field at the time."

"Beardon doesn't have that kind of responsibility here," the major said. "He's an information source, that's all."

"And that's enough," the general said. "All the data we have comes out of the one man he's trained over there, a fellow homo for all we know. And we're supposed to base our entire operation on the information he sends, which may or may not be reliable. Taking the sex angle out of it, how the hell do we know how well trained that man is? Is he an accurate observer? He's a weak link, Major, and I don't like that."

The February Plan

The major was angry now. He was quite skilled at covering it, but Wilkinson had been with him long enough to know the visible signs, the tightening of the tendons in his neck, the slight flush to his forehead. But there was none of it in his voice. His words were calm, relaxed. "I think you're putting too much emphasis on it, General," he said. "After all, the basic facts are in the public press. Beardon's only confirmed those facts, and his man amplifies them, supplies details. We don't really need the Chinese operative at all. We can operate quite well without him. Now, if you don't want to give credence to his reports, that's up to you."

"I'm not on your neck, Major," the general said calmly. "But we're about to reach the point of no return. And I want to be pretty damn sure before we go ahead."

"It's up to you to make the final decision, of course," the major said. "But if you're open to advice . . ."

"I'm not open to advice," the general said, without rancor. He looked at his watch. "I'd like to see Dr. Smalley in my quarters in an hour."

"All right," the major said. "I'll call him."

"I'll give you the final word in the morning," the general said, dismissing any further discussion. "Have you seen Allenton?"

"He was over at the Hole earlier."

"You might see if you can whistle him up when you get ahold of Smalley."

"All right," the major said. The general nodded and left the room. The major's eyes followed him through the door, his distaste more open now. Wilkinson said nothing, knowing it was not his place to speak first. If the major wanted to make a comment, he would make it without any prompting. He opened a cabinet next to the fireplace and took out a bottle of brandy and two glasses. "Call the Hole and see if you can locate Smalley," he said. "And, as our esteemed general puts it, whistle up Allenton." Wilkinson picked up the telephone and called the Hole. Once he was finished, the major handed him a snifter without comment, sinking down in the overstuffed chair which the general had vacated, extending his feet to the fire, a thoughtful frown on his face. "Well, what do you think?"

"About what?" Wilkinson asked.

"Come off it. You know damn well what I'm talking about. You must have an opinion one way or the other."

"If you're talking about Beardon's Chinese operative, I think the general's right," Wilkinson said. "He is a weak link, but I think the general's making too much out of it."

"The general is a son of a bitch," the major said, glowering into the fire. "But that's what you always run into when you deal with the military on this level. He's used to command, so geared to it that he takes it for granted. And this damn uniform doesn't help a bit."

"Is he likely to scrub at this point?" Wilkinson said. The brandy effused through his throat. He had a slightly giddy sensation, as if he were being etherized. He would have to watch it. The major did not really want any conversation out of him now; he only wanted a sounding board. If that was what he wanted, then that was what Wilkinson would be. That was the name of the game.

The major looked at him sharply. "Of course he's not going to scrub. We've gone too far for that. All this Beardon business is a smoke screen, a bunch of verbiage thrown in to confuse the issue. He's just making it plain that he's in charge and won't tolerate any interference from me. He'll moan about it and dramatize his dilemma, but that goddamn decision was made months ago, and he knows it. He's a zealot. That's the reason I picked him in the first place. It's not easy to work with a man who has a single-track mind. He's not adaptable, there's no give to him; he's as rigid and inflexible as they come. But goddamnit, we have to go along with him because we really don't have any choice in the matter. We're stuck with him. We have to make the best of it."

"Yes, sir," Wilkinson said.

The major sipped at the brandy. His fury expended, his gripes vented, he was ready to change the subject. "Did you talk to Corman and his secretary?"

"Yes, sir."

"Well?"

Wilkinson seized the opportunity, giving his report as if he were emptying his mind of the information. He was convinced that neither Corman nor the secretary really knew anything. If Mitsu had known anything, it had probably died with him. The reports from Tokyo were negative, nothing was developing there that could have stemmed from anything Mitsu had done.

"The goddamned bystanders," the major said, "the accidental intruders. They're always on hand. You can plan an operation right down to the final detail, until it's perfect, and then if you're not careful, people like this can come along and mess you up."

"Any suggestions?"

"Not until after I read your report," the major said. "I'd like it as soon as possible."

"Yes, sir."

"When it's ready, I'll be in communications."

"Yes, sir."

The major stood up. Leaving his brandy glass on the mantel, he went off toward communications. Irritated, Wilkinson stayed behind to finish his drink, staring into the fire. He had somehow expected a project like this to be different, more ennobling perhaps; it was not everyday that a group of men agreed to sacrifice themselves in the name of principle. He had anticipated a metamorphosis in this company, a drawing together, a suspension of differences, but now he knew his hope was unrealistic. Right down to the end, the general would be a man prideful of his position, and the major would insist on paper work as if he could not visualize anything which was not tangible enough for him to hold in his two hands. Nobody would change. There was no sense fighting the problem; the end result was really all that mattered.

He drained the glass and, fighting the inertia which had seeped into him from the fire and the brandy, he went upstairs to get at the report.

2

Corman found himself stumbling over his own imagination. The newspaper was thick and he had no idea what he was looking for, a small item perhaps, or a combination of items which had brought things into perspective in Mitsu's mind. Corman had read no more than fifteen minutes before he realized how difficult this was going to be, not because there were so few news items which might be pertinent, but because there were so many of them.

The lead story on the first page concerned a verbal battle between the Japanese Prime Minister and the Diet over the status of this essentially foreign missile base on Japanese soil. The Self-Defense Department had modified its earlier news release to counter the prevalent rumor of a nuclear-armed Titan II at the base. As soon as conditions permitted, as soon as the base was transferred to the Japanese government, newsmen would be allowed to inspect the base and see for themselves. According to the Prime Minister's chief adversary in the Diet, unless such an inspection were allowed soon, the controversy could lead to a no-confidence vote and an upset of the government.

Corman's pen made a quick question mark beside the article. Could this be the objective of the CIA operation here, the unseating of the Japanese Prime Minister? He doubted it. It would make no sense to remove a pro-American politician and replace him with a radical anti-American. As illogical as it seemed, however, he did not reject it altogether. In the crazy world of international politics anything was possible.

Another story on the front page reported a student demonstration at Tokyo University and printed the speech of a communist agitator denouncing the missile base as another example of American imperialism. He claimed the Americans were using Japan as a double pawn, first as a line of defense against Red China, secondly as a base from which to impose economic sanctions against the People's Republic, interfering with Japan's broadening trade with her sister country.

The February Plan 149

The Americans had corrupted the present government, trading the missile base for these economic sanctions. According to the speaker, the events of the next few weeks could be expected to confirm his predictions.

Again, Corman thought, this was a possibility, but it was hardly an urgent situation which would have called for immediate action on Mitsu's part, precipitating a crisis.

He went through the whole newspaper, listing the subject matter of each article even remotely connectable with the missile crisis, lining them up on a page in his pocket notebook. When he was through, he juggled them around in different combinations, but there was nothing particularly urgent about any of them, either singly or in combination. Finally he worked his way through the paper again, reading every story completely to pick up all the details. And then, in an item buried on the financial page, a familiar name leaped out at him, and he found what he was looking for, sandwiched in a warning to Japanese investors.

The article was an analysis of the Japanese stock market with a particular emphasis on the electronics industry. According to the specialists in the field, Japanese electronics stocks would continue to gain for the next six months, based on the strength of back orders from Europe and mounting sales to the People's Republic of China. But the long-term outlook was not quite as favorable. In a routine announcement Dr. Chien San-Chiang had boasted that within six months the People's Republic would be entirely self-sustaining in the electronics field and that within a year the People's Republic would be a serious competitor in the world market in the manufacture and sale of electronic components.

Examples of the superior electronic items manufactured in Red China would be on display at the celebration of National Science Achievement Day in Lanchow on February 5, at which time all of the senior scientists of the People's Republic would be on hand for the dedication of a new gaseous diffusion plant. Dr. Chien was scheduled to give the major address of the meeting during the morning session, and after a luncheon, the scientists would disperse, each of them flying to a different destination within the People's Republic to conduct local discussion groups and seminars.

Corman blinked. Slowly he put the newspaper down, his mind resistant to the implications. Monstrously logical, morally terrible, the plan was unmistakably clear to him now. The pieces were there, demanding that he put them together. Undoubtedly Mitsu had stumbled across the same article and, in trying to do something about it, had been killed, and Paul had suffered a similar fate. It made sense; they would have to eradicate any outside knowledge.

He checked the masthead of the paper. February 2. Three days to go, seventy-two hours, and he was cooped up here in a ten-by-twelve room, unable to do anything about it. He sat in the chair a long time, mulling the situation over in his mind, examining it from every angle against the possibility that he had made a mistake, that he had caught the major's infection, picking up isolated facts and fabricating them into a distorted actuality. He had made no mistake. The situation was real. He had not invented it; he had merely discovered it. He would have to do something quickly, using the most extreme caution, or what he knew would destroy him and Finley as well.

3

The major could not sleep. The pills he had taken had not worked. As sometimes happened, they had had a reverse effect, making his senses more acute instead of dulling them. He tossed on the bed, keenly aware of the noises in the house around him, the nocturnal creaking of the old and frozen timbers, the moan of the wind, the scurrying feet of mice above the ceiling.

He sat up in bed, berating himself because he could not sleep when he needed sleep so desperately. In his younger years it had not been so, and he had once gone for forty-eight hours straight without closing his eyes, with no loss of power. But he was older now. His nerves were not as resilient; the reservoir was lower. His hand fumbled for one of the cigars he had left on

The February Plan

the night stand, and he lighted it, leaning back against the pillows. He thought about calling Zimmerman to have him prescribe something that might work, but he could not do that, not in the middle of the night, because the word would get around as it always did when there was anything that could be interpreted as a sign of weakness in a superior. No, not tonight. He would catch Zimmerman sometime tomorrow before he made sick call at the detention camp (a half-dozen men down with the flu, faking perhaps, or the forerunner of a wider circle of infection), and he would get a sedative then, casually, making no big thing out of it, nothing that could be used against him.

He flicked the ash off his cigar, contemplating the gray-red glow of the the coal, the one reference point of light in the encompassing darkness. He was fully awake now, and with the wakefulness came a nagging uneasiness, as if something had slipped his mind which he should have remembered, and he crawled out of bed, his feet hitting the cold floor in the search for his slippers. He clicked on the lamp beside his bed and then the electric heater. The coil began to glow cherry-red, putting out a feeble heat against the chill of the room.

He took the time to stack wood in the fireplace, blowing the coals until the half-consumed embers sprang into life again, and then he dressed and took the gray steel file box out of the closet and put it on the desk, unlocking it and lifting out the folder bulging with papers. It went against his conditioning to have these papers in his possession because he had so long operated in a world where a scrap of paper could cost a man's life. He had so thoroughly trained his own memory that he had only to glance at a piece of information to record the words on his brain; when he needed the information, he could recall the printed page and read the words off in perfect clarity.

He did not need these papers now. The whole plan was indelibly fixed in his head, every detail, every nuance, every shading of form and intention, but the file was desperately important. The agency would need it. Because the plan was all here in black and white, from its conception to its present status and a schedule of the final phases. The document would be a testimonial to his skill, an invaluable training aid. It had not been compiled in bitterness or pique; no, he was far beyond that now, although there was perhaps some ego involvement here. After all, he had recognized a clear and present danger and done something about it, on his own, so to speak, knowing that he would never have gotten anywhere with it within the framework of the agency itself, because it had been hamstrung by politics in the past few years, its policy reflecting a political concept of morality. It was now intertwined with too many other agencies that had to be satisfied and mollified and placated. There were too many individuals responsible to, fearful of, and anxious to impress other individuals, until any clear-cut line of action had to be lost in a web of confused personal relationships. He had not allowed himself to be trapped in that web. At the same time, however, he had usurped no power that was not his; he had not created a point of view and persuaded others to implement it. He had merely tapped a reservoir of feeling which was about to burst, anyway, and taken advantage of the force behind it.

He thumbed through the papers, going through Plover's reports from Langley, wondering if there was any way Plover could be spared when this was done, knowing of course that any speculation along these lines was foolish. Plover would fare no better than the rest of them, and perhaps he would do a little worse, if that was possible, because he had operated from inside the agency, and in their ranking of sins, a betrayal of trust was cardinal. Plover was a methodical little man who had been trained as an historian at Yale, a Ph.D. who brought an invaluable sense of history to the agency. He had been assigned to correlate the various international points of view concerning the establishment of a nuclear base in Japan and to estimate what various nations would do about it, how they would react. The principal concern was Russia, of course, because Russia was really the only country with the power to do anything about it.

The February Plan

The night the major approached Plover had really been one of the few sticky moments in the whole operation, the major reflected. He had invited Plover to drop by the Georgetown apartment ostensibly to discuss the status of the Japanese base, the current assignment which would absorb them both. Plover did drop by, but he did little talking. He had a pipe in his mouth and he seemed to spend most of his time trying to keep it lighted, but this was a planned distraction and the major knew it. It enabled Plover to take his time about answering a question, and his mind whirred while his cheeks drew and puffed, and it relieved him of the danger of spontaneity, of responding too quickly.

They discussed the operation. It was routine really, little more than the establishment of a dummy company to facilitate the clandestine construction of the base in Japan. Plover was not worried. Even before he had begun his soundings of opinion in the American embassies abroad, he had a pretty good idea what the end result would be. "I don't think there'll be much reaction from the Soviets," he said. "They know the facts of life. Inevitably Japan will have a nuclear base, undoubtedly in co-operation with us, and the Soviets can't fight over that. They'll kick up the usual protests in the U.N. and the press, and they'll undoubtedly try to stir up something in Japan, whipping up Japanese nationalism and fear of anything nuclear, but that's about as far as it will go."

The major nodded, agreeing, and at that moment decided to take the chance. He knew better than to try indirection, because Plover was a shrewd man and would resent being handled, maneuvered into a political position. It was a moment of great risk for the major because this little man standing by the bookshelves, puffing on his pipe while he browsed over the titles, held the power of life and death in his hands, and it could go either way. Plover could not remain neutral in any practical sense of the word. He would have to move one way or the other, either working with the major or informing against him; his convictions would not allow him to straddle the fence.

So the major had told him what he had in mind,

quite bluntly, and Plover's reaction had been one of mild surprise; he had been in this business too long to be shocked by anything. He merely turned from his perusal of the books, his face quizzical, the pipe still going, and when the major was through talking, Plover sat down, examining the charred bowl of his pipe, taking a small silver tool out of his pocket to ream the smoldering tobacco into an ash tray. "Do you really think it would work?" he said finally.

"I know damn well it would," the major said, relieved, knowing instinctively now that the moment of crisis was past. Plover would go along if he was convinced that the plan was practical. "I have it all worked out. Of course, if they cancel from their end, we would have to abort, but I don't think that's very likely. You're the expert there. When they schedule something, they usually follow through, don't they? It's a matter of face saving, isn't it?"

"Usually," he said, thinking it through, repacking his pipe now. There was still a little doubt in his face. "But why do you need me?"

"That's pretty obvious, isn't it?" the major said. "I have to have somebody here to let me know which way the wind is blowing, internally as well as internationally. Hell, I don't intend to get us into another war, not a big one. If I thought that would happen, I'd forget the whole thing now. But I have the feeling that it won't, that Russia will be overjoyed to see it happen."

"I wouldn't be too sure of that," Plover said.

"That'll be your province," the major said. "You do have the means to find out, don't you?"

"I can make analyses, projections," Plover said. "But they're not one hundred per cent accurate. And what makes you think you can carry off something like this? You only have the first phase of the Japanese project. You'll be working with the military, and they're going to have control after the first sixty days."

"Do you know General Gibson?" the major said quietly.

"Not personally, only by reputation."

"He'll be heading the Japanese project from the military end. I had a report on him this morning. The

Pentagon thinks he sounds off too much, but he's a tough, efficient man, and they don't have anybody else who knows the Japanese situation as well as he does."

The pipe was going again now. "Have you talked with him about this?"

"Not yet, no. I'm scheduled to meet with him after I get to Japan. I'll sound him out first before I put the question to him. But the odds are that he will jump at the chance."

"And if I were to work with you on this, how would I get the information to you?"

"In your routine reports," the major said. "We can discuss methods later, but it needn't be anything elaborate; a simple grouping of words will be enough. If anything goes awry on this end, you can report it. We can cancel at any time. There won't be any divergence from the present timetable until after the missile base is finished, about January fifteenth of next year if we don't run into any delays. We're scheduled to turn it over to the Japanese the middle of February. The only change, of course, will be in programing, and we can do that with no trouble at all, as late as the end of January."

He was simplifying now; he knew it, and Plover knew it as well, because the whole operation would be incredibly complex, involving the screening of men and the selection of a dozen or so at the very least, any one of which, either through a weakening courage or a diminished conviction, could topple the whole house of cards with a single breath. It seemed incredible to him, as he sat there with Plover, that the discussion had such a casual tone to it, as if they were talking about horses or the weather or agency scuttlebutt, when the implementation of their talk would alter the course of world history. This was the only way it could be done, of course, calmly, a routine and dispassionate planning which would account for every detail.

But he knew even as he watched Plover, the thin lips sucking on the pipe, the light of the lamp reflecting on the rimless glasses and obscuring the eyes, that Plover was thinking the thing through to its ultimate end. He was relating himself to it in personal terms, balancing his own life against his convictions, seeing if this was something worth sacrificing himself for. Plover had one advantage; he was a bachelor. He would not have to consider a wife and children in this equation.

"How do you intend to keep this black?" he said. "The Japanese base is going to have the closest scrutiny of the Pentagon as well as the agency."

"That's to our advantage," the major said with a thin smile. "That's the beauty of it, the essence of simplicity. The government's vital concern is in keeping the establishment of the Japanese base from becoming public. All the security efforts are directed toward that. There will be the usual internal checks, of course, the standard internal security, but when it comes right down to it, what could there be to alert them, to arouse the suspicions of either the military or the agency? Your reports? No, your reports will just be routine as far as anybody else is concerned, and your only function will be to warn us if you see anything from this end that might give us trouble. You can do that simply, with a two-word code, something as simple as 'Prognosis unfavorable,' which can be attached to anything, in any context, and I'll pick it up and cancel our project immediately.

"The screening will be a simple matter. We can reject and hold in custody any man we feel is objectionable without giving any reasons. None of them will know what we're up to, and we won't take them in on it unless we're absolutely certain of their political convictions. We must remember that any man who comes in with us can't count on getting out alive, so he would have to be dedicated to the project. Even then, supposing that one of them wanted to back out, he would have no proof of any covert activity on our part. No, I'd say that we have a ninety-per-cent chance of maintaining complete secrecy on this, and as you know, those are very good odds."

Plover sat quiet a long minute and then he stirred, standing up, chewing on his underlip. "I'd like to think about this overnight," he said.

"All right," the major said.

"It's not something that I'd want to commit myself

on immediately," he said, his words measured. "But I can tell you this. I've worried about the Red Chinese for a long time now, and I'm not alone in that concern. We had a projection from Rand yesterday that coincides with my own thinking. Unless something happens it's only a matter of time until they open up on the world. They have peculiar minds, almost as if they'd lost their sense of disaster. In times like these that's a pretty frightening way to think."

Plover had gone along with it as the major knew he would. The recruiting of the others had been almost as easy. From his first meeting with General Gibson, at a geisha party in Shimbashi, there had been no doubt about his co-operation. There had been more give in the general at the beginning, and he solicited the major's opinion on the selection of his personal staff, relying on the major's skill and long experience in evaluating men. There was no room for error in this mission, none, no tolerances to absorb a change of mind, and the project would require an ultimate degree of dedication.

There were times in the middle of the night when every man's defenses were down and doubt crept in, the seductiveness of the ego, the will to survive at all costs. Toward the beginning of this project, when the missile base was still under construction, it would have taken no more than a single changed mind to wreck the insecure structure. The major had taken elaborate plans to insure against that. The detention camp had been a part of the original agency plan, insurance against any possible information leak concerning the missile base until the Japanese government was ready to take over, and the major simply used the facility for his own purposes.

The names of the men he had sent to detention were listed in the file, on the paper the major now held before him. He had appended a critique and detailed reasoning as to why he had rejected each of these men. These explanations would eventually be of great use in training new agents; the current curricula was sadly deficient in the interrogation area. Oh, there was a multiplicity of rules all right, directives, procedures, but nothing which allowed an agent to use his intuition, to measure the answers against the basic man himself, to project the course of a man's actions from his mannerisms and the way he talked.

Captain Ellis was a case in point. The general had picked him as an LCO simply because the general had known him for many years and knew that the captain shared the same political point of view. In his initial interview with the captain, Major Henshaw found that this was indeed true. Captain Ellis was one of those rare individuals in the military who was truly dedicated to the abstract cause of world peace. He had given up a comfortable profession as an electrical engineer to take a commission in the military in the sure belief that there could be no peace without strength. He was willing to do what he could to maintain that national strength.

But he was a bluff and hearty individual, a man with a highly developed sense of humor and a strong attachment to his wife and children in the States (he even insisted on showing the major the pictures he carried in his wallet), and it was on that basis that the major eventually rejected him and had him taken to the detention camp. The general had been furious, not so much for the loss of Ellis (the ostensible reason for his anger) as for the fact that the major had gone against his expressed wishes. From that point the general had been intransigent.

The major read through the Ellis file again, trying to clear his mind and see it for the first time as the director of the CIA would eventually see it. In that light, the major had to admit, going on nothing except the bare facts of the case in front of him, it was possible the director would decide the general had been right in his judgment and Major Henshaw wrong. The major had not expressed himself well. There were too many ambiguities in his statement, too many possible misinterpretations. Well, he would set that right immediately, while it was still fresh in his mind.

The room was still cold; the fireplace was slow to heat the room, and the heater was a poor one. He took a blanket off the bed and put it over his shoulders, re-

The February Plan

turning to the desk to pick up the pen, writing slowly, selecting each word with care, determined neither to make a mistake nor to leave his remarks open to any possible misunderstanding. By the time he finished, he had developed a cramp in his fingers and a tic in a tendon of his right hand, but he disregarded the minor discomfort. He was through with Captain Ellis; they would find nothing to criticize there.

He spread the blanket on the bed again and undressed, carefully folding his trousers on the silent butler, hanging his jacket on the wooden rack. He slipped beneath the sheets again with a pervasive weariness, a mental dullness which he was sure would lead to sleep. But as his mind relaxed, he found himself thinking about his wife. He could see her face, her head canted to one side as she looked at him over her shoulder, with that resigned expression on her face, a weariness of long standing, as if she felt absolutely nothing for him any more, not even disappointment.

Abruptly he forced her out of his mind, shifting his attention to a problem that nagged at him with greater frequency as the days compressed and the time grew short. Ah, the general, that old fanatic, or was he really what he seemed? Or was that dedication of his merely steam, outward fumings that, once vented, would leave him impassive in the end? After all, the same objections which were valid for Captain Ellis also applied to the general himself. For Gibson also had a wife, and he had a son who had graduated from West Point and now served in the Pentagon someplace, and Gibson was an old-line officer, prey to all the weaknesses of the system which had bred these men and sustained them in their rise. Mrs. Gibson was very popular in Washington. Over the years she had been responsible for most of his ascending moves, operating on that informal but highly effective level of command wives.

Now, if this were true, then how much of the public strength generated by the general was truly his and how much had been given to him by his wife? When the chips were down, how much would the general be willing to pay for his beliefs? He would be perfectly willing to sacrifice himself, the major thought—he had the instincts of a martyr—but could he also wreck his son's career and cast his wife into outer darkness, in effect destroying them both? Was the general truly willing to do this?

The general had shown no overt signs to demonstrate that he was not, but the major had been trained in nuances, to pick up the vibration of things before they happened, to detect the predilections in a man, and he was not so sure about the general any more. It could be, of course, that the general was displaying signs of normal caution, attaching as much importance to each step of this project as the major himself did (no, that was impossible; the major demanded absolute perfection, and the general was more pragmatic), and that he was guarding against anything that might go awry. Or—and this was equally possible, considering the circumstances—the general could have had second thoughts about the whole thing and was looking for a way out.

This sparked the major's imagination, set it afire, and he examined the general's alternatives in the new light. If the general decided against the project, if he decided to save himself, could he stop it and emerge unscathed? The major groaned inwardly at his own stupidity, his own lack of foresight. The general was in no way bound to this agreement. There was no way he could be held responsible. If he changed his mind, he could blow the whistle on the major at any time, claiming that he had discovered the major's conspiracy. The general could count on the loyalty of the handful of men who knew his complicity to back him up. He could abort with impunity. In one minute he could wreck something which the major had built with great care over the months.

Well, that was something that could be taken care of, the major decided, and the means were already at hand to bring about the desired effect. He climbed out of bed again, clicking on the lamp, reaching for the telephone. He directed the operator to get Wilkinson for him and then he waited, listening to the spasmodic burr on the other end. When Wilkinson answered, his

The February Plan

voice was slurred. He was not yet fully awake.

"Wilkinson," the major said, "I want you to set up a meeting between Mr. Corman and General Gibson tomorrow. I want it held here in the lodge, in the general's quarters, and I want the whole thing recorded. When they're through, I want you to transcribe the tape personally, and then I want that transcript as soon as you can get it to me. You are to consider the whole conversation black, the whole procedure black. You are to handle it all yourself."

"All right," Wilkinson said, his voice fully alert now. "What are we fishing for, Major?"

"I'm not sure," the major said. "But it should be interesting."

He put the telephone down and went back to bed, but he was fully awake now and he knew there would be no chance of sleep. He lighted a cigar, impatient for the night to be gone and the day to begin. Thirty minutes later his telephone rang and he picked it up to find Strickland, the base security officer, on the line. Strickland was a lean, acerbic man with the face of a hawk and the loyalty of a hound. The major could count on him.

"I'm sorry to disturb you at this hour, Major," Strickland said. "But I just had an alert from my contact in Tokyo. There's going to be a Japanese inspection team from the Diet paying us a surprise visit in the morning, and the general would like you to handle the tour."

"Are they here for any specific reason?" the major said.

"The political climate is growing pretty hot," Strickland said. "I get the impression the Japanese government doesn't know how long they're going to be able to keep this thing under wraps and they want to take over before the information becomes public. I think this delegation is up here to goose us a little."

"We won't sweat it," the major said, thinking quickly. "Are the main generators in and functioning?"

"Of course," Strickland said.

"Well, get some men in there and shut them down. Switch to the auxiliaries for the time being. We are going to be having generator trouble that's going to cause a delay of at least two weeks. When we conduct the inspection team through, I want a lot of men working, and I want it to look legitimate. They're bound to bring in an expert or two on us."

"I'll take care of it, Major."

"And when we get through, I want a steak dinner for the whole delegation in the mess hall, with wine if you have it. Shoot the works on this one. I want it to appear that we are doing everything possible for our allies in this project. It'll help me break the sad news to them."

Strickland laughed. "Will do, Major," he said.

"What time will the inspection team get here?"

"About 0900," Strickland said. "They consider that a polite hour."

"We'll be ready for them," the major said.

By the time he had finished the telephone call, he was feeling fine. Work, positive action, was the strongest tonic in the world, and he was at his best when he was active. Picking up the telephone again, he rang Wilkinson.

"I want you to set up Corman's meeting with the general after the dinner hour," he said. "Let the general know that we think Mitsu may have known everything and that we have to get the information out of Corman to make sure we're protected in this. Let the general know that he's the only man who can do this. That should arouse his vanity and move him along. And I want a car ready at 0730. I think I'd better talk to Corman first and prime the pump a little."

"All right," Wilkinson said. "0730."

2

CORMAN was awakened by the sound of martial music blaring out over the compound, a recording of "The Stars and Stripes Forever," and through the wall of the quonset hut he could hear the barking of commands in the sharp cold air as the prisoners were turned out for morning count. For the space of a brief moment he could imagine that twenty years had evaporated, that he was back in Yokohama again where he had been sent to await assignment on his arrival in Japan, rousing out of bed in the morning to hunt for his shoes and make a mad dash for the morning roll call.

He saw the shuttered window and the closed door, knowing instantly where he was. He went to the door, banging on it with the flat of his hand, and in a few moments he heard the twisting of the key in the lock and a sergeant opened the door. Corman told him he wanted to take a shower. Without a word the sergeant led him down the corridor to the bathroom, providing him with a towel and shaving implements, staying with him in the latrine and the shower room, maintaining a strict silence, while Corman performed his morning ablutions.

At first Corman tried to break him down enough to find out where Finley was being kept, but all his attempts were fruitless, and he finally gave it up. By the time he had returned to his room, his breakfast was waiting for him on a tray, hot oatmeal with cream and powdered eggs and canned ham. He ate little, contenting himself with the coffee, opening the newspaper again to re-examine the story in the light of day. But the facts were still there, the implications still hung together with perfect consistency. He knew he was not wrong.

At eight o'clock there was a polite rapping on the door before it was unlocked and the major came in, smiling as usual, a residue of talcum powder on his freshly shaved cheeks. "Well, Mr. Corman," he said pleasantly, looking around the room as if he had not seen this place before, "I'm sorry to see that you've gotten yourself involved in some difficulty here."

"I suppose I should be surprised to see you here, but I'm not," Corman said.

"As an attaché, I'm in a position to act as a liaison between the government and the military," the major said. "In troubled times like these we need all the liaison we can get." He sat down, lighting a cigar, a rather perplexed smile on his face. "I heard they had picked you up, so I volunteered to come up here and see if I couldn't straighten things out."

"You came all the way up from Tokyo just for that?"

"Hardly," the major said. "I do quite a bit of running back and forth." His tone was light now, as if he considered the whole thing a minor inconvenience which could be righted by discussion. "You're a damned nuisance, you know. If you had listened to me before, you wouldn't be tied up in all this red tape now."

"Red tape?" Corman said. "Is that what you call it?"

"Of course," the major said. "A business like this is so enormously complicated. A great many bureaus and agencies from both governments are involved, so they protect their own special interests by imposing rules and procedures which make it impossible to get anything done. And since the CIA is also mixed up in this, that fouls it up even more. Personally I think they jumped the gun in your case. It was totally unnecessary for them to pick you up. But there's a big controversy raging about whether or not this base is armed with nuclear weapons, and they're afraid you have information to prove it is."

The February Plan

"Then you do have nuclear missiles here. You admit that."

"One," the major said, as if it were a matter of no great importance. "There's been an updating of the mutual security treaty that the United States signed with the Japanese in 1960. We've installed a Titan II here for the Japanese government, but they can't release the news until their people are psychologically ready for it." He checked his watch. "Which reminds me, I have a group of Japanese coming shortly. I mustn't forget that. They're going to give us hell because we're running behind schedule. That's understandable. They know they'll be sitting ducks in the next war unless they have a strong deterrent."

"The next war?" Corman said calmly. "You sound pretty sure there's going to be one."

The major smiled. "That's the military in me, Mr. Corman. We have to operate on that assumption. That's why we're working so hard at this thing. The stronger we are, the less chance there is that we'll have another war. For one thing, it's absolutely vital that we have a string of bases along the Japanese islands as soon as possible. There are certain situations in which our nuclear subs are inadequate. The Soviets are hard at work developing anti-submarine defenses. But there's still no way to demolish one of our hard sites except by a direct hit." He paused, smoking the cigar thoughtfully. "Of course, we have a tremendous stock pile of nuclear weapons in the States and the means of delivering them. But suppose, say, that the Red Chinese decide to open up on Japan? Now, there is a dilemma. According to our treaty, we would defend Japan, of course; we would have to come into it, but none of us wants to see the United States turned into a nuclear battleground. So that particular exchange would be fought from here."

Was the major trying to provoke him into comment, into revelation? Corman was not sure. "Why are you telling me this?" Corman said.

"That's a good question," the major said, smiling again. "Partly, I guess, because the news will come out very soon anyway, about the base, I mean. And secondly, you've had to put up with a hell of a lot of inconveniences, and I think you deserve an explanation."

"And that's the whole reason?" Corman said.

"Do you think there's another?"

Corman was aware of the major's eyes watching him through the screen of smoke from the cigar. "You can save your explanations," he said. "I didn't know anything about your nuclear missiles, and personally I don't give a damn whether you have them or not. I came up here to find out what happened to my son. My intentions haven't changed in the least."

"That's understandable," the major said easily. "Unfortunately I can't tell you anything more than I already have, because I don't have the authority. But I want to help you. Suppose I arrange for you to talk with General Gibson. Do you trust him?"

"More than I trust you," Corman said.

The major smiled. "I don't blame you for that." He stood up now. "It may take a little doing, but I'll see if I can't set it up as soon as possible. I'll be in touch, Mr. Corman."

"I'd like to see my secretary."

"I'm not so sure I can arrange that," the major said pleasantly. "That deals with security here, and that's out of my province. But I'll see. In any event, it won't be too long before the two of you are back in Tokyo." He approached the door, rapping on it with his knuckles. "If there's anything you want—within reason, of course—just let the guard know," he said. "I'll do what I can."

Once he was gone, Corman paced the room, too restless to sit still, knowing that there was nothing he could do at the moment except wait. They had planned this thing with great care, pitting themselves against the force of the United States, and they were not just about to be jeopardized by a single individual whose presence here was more accidental than intentional. He could only hope that he would have an opportunity and the courage to take it if it came.

By afternoon his hope had diminished almost completely. There was no word from the major.

The February Plan

Corman listened to the men exercising on the field, and later he heard the recorded bugle for mess call on the loud-speaker system. Sometime during the afternoon there was a volleyball game outside; he could hear the men yelling back and forth, but he could see nothing. The window was tightly boarded. No light leaked through. The small artificial sun in the wire cage on the ceiling would eventually announce the end of day by winking out at taps, to be lighted again tomorrow morning.

He tried to work in the afternoon, writing in his notebook, but he could not keep his mind on it and finally gave it up, rapping on the door and asking the guard for something to read. He was given a few magazines, most of them months old. The urgency he had felt at the beginning of the day gave way to lethargy.

At seven that evening he heard the sound of footsteps in the hall and his door opened and Wilkinson came in, obviously tired, relatively noncommunicative, to tell him that a meeting with the general had been set up. Immediately Corman's hopes sparked to life again. He put on his overcoat and followed Wilkinson outside to the jeep. The night was pitch-black and the snow was coming down quite heavily, driven by a strong north wind.

The drive was made in silence, with Wilkinson smoking a cigarette and concentrating on the road, apparently sensing no threat in Corman, as if they both knew that there was no reason for him to make an escape and no way to accomplish it, should he try. Wilkinson drove up to the front of the lodge and parked the jeep on the windward side of a clump of cedars. "You mind giving me a hand with the tarp?" he asked Corman. "A snow like this can bury a vehicle in no time."

They pulled the tarp over the jeep, and then Wilkinson gestured toward the front door and allowed Corman to lead the way. Once they were inside, Wilkinson stamped the snow from his boots, nodding to the guard who did not bother to check his badge. "The general's agreed to see you at eight o'clock," Wilkinson said. "You'll have fifteen minutes with him. You'll come this way, please." He led Corman up the stairs to the second floor and down a corridor, passing a small side hall which led to a pair of French doors and a terrace. Finally he stopped, opening a door to admit Corman to a small sitting room. "I know you won't object to my leaving you here to wait for the general. I've got a couple of things to check on." He looked at his watch. "I'll pick you up when you've finished your talk. The general should be along any time."

The door closed and Corman listened to Wilkinson's footsteps receding down the hall. He considered trying the door, but he knew it would be locked. He sat down in a Windsor chair against one wall, intrigued by the sparseness of the furnishings in the general's quarters, two chairs in the sitting room, a cabinet along the wall, and a small game table which served as a desk. Through a half-opened door he could see a single twin bed with blankets folded on it, military style, and a small table bearing a photograph of the general's wife and son. He was not surprised by the monastic severity of the general's quarters; Gibson had never been inclined toward purposeless luxuries.

Why the major had set up this meeting at all puzzled Corman. But then, perhaps the major was not completely satisfied with Corman's story and suspected that he knew more than he was telling. In this case the general would probably ask more questions than he answered.

In a few minutes Corman heard footsteps in the hall and the deep, rumbling bass of the general's voice as he said something to an aide, and then the door opened and the general came in, alone, smiling the odd, pained smile that Corman remembered from Occupation days. "You've got yourself into a hell of a mess," Gibson said, shaking Corman's hand. "I wish we could have met again under pleasanter circumstances."

"You don't wish it any more than I do," Corman said.

The telephone rang. The general picked it up and grunted into it, then jiggled the hook and told the operator to hold all calls until he was directed to do other-

The February Plan

wise. Twenty years had not been easy on the general, Corman decided. He had remembered Gibson as a vital, bearlike man, and the one picture of him Corman had seen in the paper tended to confirm this memory, as if the only real change in the man had been in the graying of his hair. But the picture had not captured his ashen complexion and the tired eyes. The general looked as if the pressures on him had been intense and of long duration. He put the telephone down with an expression of disdain. "I'm going to have a scotch and water," he said. "You want to join me?"

"I could use one," Corman said.

The general went to the cabinet, opening the door to reveal a row of bottles and a small refrigerator. "I hear you're in some trouble with the Intelligence boys," he said, while he mixed the drinks. "I understand you've been giving them fits."

"Inadvertently," Corman said, wanting to ask the old man how this had happened to him, how he had so placated his conscience that he could go along with such a project. "I think I've had grounds to cause a little trouble."

"Maybe so," the general said, handing him his drink, sitting down now behind the game table, leaving his glass before him while he massaged his left shoulder, wincing slightly. "But things aren't that easy any more, you know that. Hell, back during the Occupation, everything was pretty damned simple. You found a problem and you dealt with it, head on. But no more. Everything's all mixed with politics now. That means committees, group decisions." He paused slightly, looking directly at Corman, his mind settling into the subject at hand. "The lieutenant—so he was your son, was he?"

"Yes," Corman said. "Can we speak freely here? Is this place bugged?"

"No," the general said.

"All right then. I want you to be frank with me. My son attacked you with a pistol. That's true, isn't it?"

"Yes," the general said without hesitation. "He got me in the shoulder. Fortunately he wasn't a very good shot."

"Was he trying to kill you?"

"Yes."

"Why?"

"He was brought over here on a project. He didn't know what kind of a project it was. He was to function as a part of the machine, as an interchangeable unit, without ever seeing the larger picture. But he found out. He was working in headquarters and he overheard something. Or maybe he put two and two together. But suddenly he knew what was going on and he didn't like it. So he lost his head and decided to stop the project by killing me."

"And what was this project?"

"The establishment of a nuclear base here."

Corman took a long drink from the glass, trying to calm himself now, to keep his voice even. "Why the hell should he go to such extreme measures over a nuclear missile base?" Corman said.

"That's beyond me," the general said. "I'm no psychiatrist. I don't understand the new crop of radicals, the men who pour gasoline all over themselves and burn to death in protest against one thing or another."

"Do you think he was one of those?"

"I don't know what he was. I only saw him the one time."

Corman felt his stomach tightening now; the drink did nothing to alleviate it. "After he was arrested, what was done with him?"

"You know how these things work," the general said. "We couldn't very well court-martial him because the base was still under construction and we didn't want word to leak out. So we brought him up here to the detention camp. We have a lot of security risks here. And then we sent him back to the States."

"Alive?"

The general looked at him sharply. "Of course he was alive."

And now Corman could restrain himself no longer. "Goddamnit, Gus, don't give me that. It's my son we're talking about. I want to know the truth about him. Don't dissemble with me. I had enough of that from the major."

"All right," the general said quietly, picking up his drink now. "Your son tried to escape from the detention camp. He managed to make it as far as the river before the guards caught him."

"And they killed him."

"He didn't leave them any choice. He was armed. He opened fire on them."

Corman shook his head bitterly. "And that wouldn't do, would it? You couldn't have him found dead in Japan, his body riddled with bullets. That would have taken a lot of explanations all the way around."

"I know how you feel," the general said. "When you start balancing values, weighing things up, nothing seems worth a boy's life. I wasn't in on the arrangements to make his death look like an accident. But I have to tell you this, Corman, I agreed one hundred per cent with what was done. And if it had been my son instead of yours, I still would have agreed with the procedure."

"All to protect security on a missile base?" Corman said, and from the expression on the general's face, the sudden sharpness of his eyes, he could tell that the pretenses were collapsing of their own weight. The general said nothing, drinking the scotch, his hand quite steady, his eyes on Corman, still waiting. And Corman, his suspicions on the verge of confirmation, felt nothing except an unexpected numbness. "How many lives is this project of yours going to cost, Gus?" he said quietly. "A hundred thousand, a quarter of a million? God, can you wipe them out and rationalize it as easily as you rationalize what happened to my son?"

The ice clinked in the general's glass. He studied it for a moment. "You don't know what you're talking about," he said.

"I wish to hell I didn't," Corman said. "Right now I'd gladly accept my son as a thief, an extortionist, anything, if you could use it to prove me wrong. But you can't. I'm a logical man, Gus, and I don't miss much, especially when it's stuck right in front of my nose. My son wrote me a note about the Blue Ants and

February fifth. I thought maybe he knew that the Red Chinese were going to start something then, but that wasn't what he had in mind at all. No, on the fifth of February, two days from now, all of the Red Chinese senior scientists are going to be gathered in one place to dedicate some sort of nuclear paraphernalia. And while they're all there, gathered in that one place, there's going to be a sudden burst of light, so intense it will blind any man who sees it, and then there will be an incomprehensible heat and a sound to burst the eardrums. But none of them will hear it. They will have ceased to exist by then." He stood up now, turning away from the general. "Masterful. In one instant there will be no more threat, no Red Chinese nuclear project, none, because all the men capable of leading it, of building those marvelous devices, will be dead."

"So you have it all figured out," the general said, standing up to refill his glass. "I don't intend to argue the morality of this with you. I just follow orders."

"Do you?"

"Of course."

"No," Corman said, shaking his head. "You can't hide behind the flag this time, Gus. This isn't a government project."

"What makes you think that?"

"If this had been a government project, I would have been bottled up a hell of a long time ago, before I got anyplace close to this base. And if the United States had decided to try something like this, they would have done it from an established site. They sure as hell wouldn't have tried to complete a base under adverse political circumstances just to get off a shot. That wouldn't make any sense at all."

The general sat down again now, pursing his lips thoughtfully. "You always were able to put your finger on a weakness," he said. "All right, the government has nothing to do with this. I'm on my own now. What if I were to tell you that at this National Science Achievement Day the Red Chinese will unveil a new intercontinental ballistic missile, one capable of reaching any point in the United States?"

"Then I would be scared," Corman said. "I would

quake in my boots and say something had to be done about it. But not mass slaughter, not a nuclear shotgun approach. How many civilians are you going to vaporize along with the scientists you're after?"

"How many people died at Hiroshima?"

"It's not the same. We were in a war then."

"And you don't think we're in a war now? Goddamnit, Corman, where have you been? Haven't you read the papers? I can show you reams of material the Red Cross have put out. They have it all figured. They can sacrifice three hundred million of their own people in a nuclear war, and they're willing to do that, because they're convinced they would be the only great power left. There are a hell of a lot of our own people who think that's nonsense, who want to downgrade the Chinese threat, and they're burying their heads in the sand. The Red Chinese believe what they say and they're ready to commit national suicide to prove it."

"And you're going to sacrifice a city now, just as a deterrent? You said it yourself—all you have to go against is a posture of verbal aggression. You can't be sure they're going to use this new missile of theirs."

"Not tomorrow, maybe, not next week, maybe not even next month. But sooner or later they'll come to that point, make no bones about it. That's exactly what they intend to do just as soon as they're strong enough. They're not going to subject themselves to any international disarmament organization." He took another drink from the glass. "From any angle this is the only move that makes any sense. We can't talk them out of aggression, we can't scare them out of it. Now, they're going to lose in the end; with our stockpile we can wipe the whole of China off the face of the earth, kill every living thing, but we're not going to emerge unscathed. Even if they lose, they can take a half-dozen of our cities with them. How many million people would that be? We have to deal with them before they're able to do anything to us."

"And that's been the cry of the war hawks since the beginning of time. You're playing the part of a logical barbarian in this, Gus. You're throwing morality out of the window."

"I don't think so," the general said. "I'm just being realistic. I have an opportunity and I intend to take it. I won't get another. We wipe out their scientific hierarchy and a half-million people along with them. I don't like that part of it any more than you do. But considering everything, the price is a cheap one."

"Not for the people of Lanchow, it isn't," Corman said. "And how do you know that the minute you launch from here, you're not going to draw the United States into an exchange with Russia?"

"We have a number of expert projections," the general said. "The Russians will make a lot of noise about it, but that's all. They've already scrapped their mutual defense treaty with China. They're nervous as hell that they'll have to face a confrontation with China over their mutual border, and that's a strong possibility. They know the facts of life. Unless something is done now, the Red Chinese will start a limited aggression within the year, gobbling up their neighbors directly, testing us. If we're weak enough, they'll keep on gobbling. Within five years or so we won't have any choice. They start it, we may have to, but there will be a full-scale nuclear war."

Corman shook his head in disbelief. "Who spawned this brilliant piece of strategy, Gus? You?"

"It started with some men in the CIA."

"How many of you are in it?"

"Enough," the general said. "That's all a man on the command level ever needs, just enough, no more. And it doesn't make any difference where it started. I believe in it strongly enough that I'm willing to sacrifice myself for it."

"You've been willing to sacrifice yourself for anything as long as I can remember," Corman said. "Give you a cause, any cause, and you'd throw yourself in the breach. So don't give me any of your nobility, General. You're just a martyr looking for a convenient cross."

"I won't debate the point with you."

Corman was tired now, drained. There was no point to further argument. "I want to ask a personal favor, Gus. My secretary knows nothing about any of this. I want you to let her go. There's no way she can jeopardize your project. I don't want anything to happen to her, even accidentally."

"You have the biggest ego of any man I know," the general said, a trace of ironic humor in his eyes. "Did you think I was going to set up a firing squad for the two of you? Hell, I could let you loose right now and deliver you to the Pentagon and let you tell your story to anybody you wanted to see, and do you think they'd believe you? They'd give you a respectful audience, and when you got through, they'd add you to the list of crazy bastards they get in there every day. The world is full of crackpots, and a lot of them have distinguished reputations. I could tell you about one senator I know who used to plague us in Washington because he was absolutely certain the Russians had established a base just across the Mexican border and were getting ready to invade Arizona. No, I've got the advantage here. I haven't done one thing contrary to my orders so far. I was sent here to set up a base and install a missile, and that's all I've done. They could inspect me tomorrow without finding anything wrong. Any deviation from those orders won't come until the last minute, when I have the missile reprogramed. So if you're trying to turn me into a bloodthirsty fanatic anxious to kill everything that moves, you're wasting your time." He picked up the telephone and spoke into it. "We're through here."

"It might have been better if Paul had been successful," Corman said finally.

"I think history will prove me right," the general said.

Corman shook his head. "I don't think there's going to be anybody around left to judge," he said.

2

As Wilkinson removed the earphones from his head and shut down the tape recorder, he had a sour taste in his mouth. He lifted the telephone and rang Sloan, his assistant. "The general's through with Corman," he said. "Pick up Corman and stash him in the interrogation room for the time being. I want to run him around again before he goes back to the camp."

"I'll take care of it," Sloan said.

Wilkinson rewound the reel, taking it off the recorder and carrying it into the room off the teletype center. At the last minute he changed his mind about having it transcribed and jammed it into his pocket, deciding to talk it over with the major before he did anything. He was not particularly alarmed by the extent of Corman's knowledge; he was reasonably sure the knowledge went no further or there would have been repercussions by now. Sooner or later he would have to find out when and where Corman had gained the information, on the off-chance that a security shift would be required, but he would wait for the major's judgment. The major would undoubtedly have ideas of his own.

The major was a peculiar duck, all in all, very jealous of his position and his authority, and he had a top-drawer reputation. There had been a rumor around the Pickle Works after the Guatemalan business, which the major had brought off perfectly, without a hitch, that the director was going to retire and that the major would replace him, and most of the field agents approved of the choice enormously. After all, the major had survived twenty years of hazardous service, and it had cost him a good bit (including his wife, who had divorced him), but he was as tough as they came, a dry, practical man who was closely in touch with the realities of the business. Unfortunately, when the director did retire, the President had decided that the spot demanded an outgoing personality, a diplomat as well as an administrator, somebody to inspire trust in the American people, a well-known name willing and able to do battle with the other Intelligence agencies if necessary, and the major simply did not qualify. So he was bypassed.

Wilkinson often wondered if the major would have conceived this project had he received his promotion. The major had wanted the top spot; he had earned it, and in private conversations he had expressed his bitterness at not getting it. Wilkinson suspected that there was something more in this act than a desire to end a threat to the free world; undoubtedly it contained some elements of spite. In the end it really made no difference, because Wilkinson sincerely believed that this move had to be made, but he was curious about it.

He left word with communications that he would be at the Hole and was about to go out the front door when Knaus stopped him. Knaus was a large, angular man of twenty-seven, a new agent who was very conscientious in his duties and had no real idea what was going on here. He was in charge of the security detail for the lodge and he took his work very seriously. At the moment he was faced with what he considered a grave problem. He had been allotted three men to work in shifts as security guards. One of them, Lindsey, had developed a bellyache and fever during the afternoon and had to be relieved.

Wilkinson cut him short, having no desire to expend any more energy on this minor problem than necessary. "Our main concern in this tinderbox is fire prevention," he said. "What was Lindsey's area?"

"The garages, outbuildings."

"All right. Pull your man off grounds patrol and put him on night watch inside. He won't object to that. It's cold as hell outside. And have your regular night watch make a patrol of the outbuildings every two hours."

Knaus nodded, relieved. "Fine," he said.

Wilkinson went outside, bracing himself against the cold, grimacing up at the snow which seemed to be getting thicker by the minute. He jerked the tarp off the jeep and climbed inside, starting the engine, following the newly bulldozed road that led to the Hole.

As many times as Wilkinson had been in the Hole, he never approached it without a feeling close to awe, considering the enormity of the destructive power in that silo, just waiting to be freed. It was miraculous in a way that this silo existed at all, considering the odds against it, both political and physical, and it was a tribute to the major's skill that it had been finished. For four months the major had followed a killing schedule which led him from the Embassy Annex (where he had established his first control center) to the electronics company (which he had almost single-handedly converted into a CIA headquarters) and finally to the launch complex itself, never letting up for a moment, catching his sleep on the move, driving his subordinates with the same zealous determination that motivated him.

It had been up to the general and the diplomats to work out the details with the Japanese government, and no doubt they had run into some tough going at times, but the real problem was here, in the hard rock of the valley, as the blasting hollowed out the great cavernous cylinder and the network of side rooms and connecting tunnels. By mid-October this hand site had been no more than a leaky excavation with the natural subterranean hot springs keeping the main hole half full of water. But the major had kept pushing, following his own schedule which demanded a launch site by the end of January, ignoring the revised schedule from Washington which now projected the completion of the base for mid-May.

He had supervised the completion of the concrete work and the sealing off of the leaks, the installation of all the electronic equipment, the fuel-storage tanks, the miles of connecting cable and plumbing, and finally the missile itself, at the same time screening the handful of men who would eventually launch it, all of this under the tightest security. Now that the Hole was an accomplished fact, all that showed on the surface was a rather elaborate weather station and a complex of garages which housed the supply trucks and tended to obscure the multiple vents from the labyrinth below.

He showed his badge at the checkpoints and picked up a hard hat before he took the elevator down. At the Launch Control level he got off, exhibiting his badge to another guard, taking the time to climb to the work platform for a look at the missile itself, a hundred and ten feet long, ten feet in diameter, lighted only in the spots where the crews were working on it. Its highly polished skin seemed to gleam, even in the shadows. The air was filled with the muted hissing roar of the ventilating blowers, yet he could hear the voices of the technicians working at the bottom of the cylindrical shaft. One of them was whistling a tune. It seemed out of place here.

Time was passing, the minutes ticking away, and within forty-five hours the great slabs of reinforced concrete would slide away from the top of the Hole and the elevators would lift the missile into the air and the snakelike coils of cable and hose which curled to the bird in such profusion would be cleared away, and on the touch of a button, the hypergolic fuels would be mixed together and spontaneous ignition would occur, the nitrogen tetroxide and the mixture of hydrazine and UDMH exploding with a roar to shake the earth as the missile lifted itself and began to rise, slowly at first, gaining speed as it climbed, rolling to the preset azimuth, making the pitch-over to the programed altitude, leaving a trail behind it in the Japanese sky as it arched slowly to the west and south.

Wilkinson shivered slightly. He turned and went back to the corridor, his heels ringing on the concrete. Showing his badge at the multiple checkpoints, he emerged finally into the larger labyrinth of the Launch Control center. He passed through the console room with its banks of instruments and the large transparent map, crossing it into another hallway, returning the salute of the guard as he ducked slightly to keep from banging his head on the lintel of the communications room.

The major was standing, peering over the shoulder of an operator, watching the tape unreel out of the decoder, reading as the machine translated for him. Obviously the major had arranged a relay from the communications room at the lodge in order to get the evening report from the operator in China firsthand.

Wilkinson waited patiently. The major finished reading and turned toward Wilkinson, only to be handed a telephone by his aide. He listened to it a moment, grunted an order, and then stalked past Wilkinson into a room which had been set up as his private retreat, furnished with a bunk and a worktable. Wilkinson followed after him. The major sat down on the edge of his bunk, kicked off his shoes, and lay down with his arms folded behind his head, chewing on the butt of a dead cigar, studying the ceiling of the concrete bunker. "This has been a day," he said. "That goddamned inspection team didn't leave until 1500, and the general made a drama out of what we knew he was going to do anyway, a long confidential talk about duty and dedication and teamwork." He was silent a moment. "Are you married, Wilkinson?" he said abruptly.

"I used to be."

"What happened?"

"She was killed in a car wreck."

"Any children?"

"No, sir."

"Kids are a pain in the ass. You give them all you have and you try to keep them from killing themselves. You educate them and turn them out into the world and hope that things are going to be all right with them. But in the end they give you more trouble than they're worth."

"You must have children, then," Wilkinson said, a little on edge, not knowing what the major intended, where this was leading. It was the first time the major had talked about his personal life in Wilkinson's presence.

"Two," the major said. "A boy and a girl, both in their teens." He lapsed into silence again, his mouth working the cigar. "Everything's on schedule. The delegations from Shanghai and Canton pulled into Lanchow today. And the Premier has announced his intention of making a speech."

"Then the haul is going to be bigger than we thought."

"Much bigger. Are you familiar with the Young Pioneers?"

"That's their children's organization, isn't it?"

"Yes. In honor of the Premier's visit to Lanchow, they're going to hold a special ceremony, a rally in honor of the dedicated Young Pioneers. Beardon's man estimates that a hundred thousand children from the outlying provinces will be in Lanchow for the day."

"I see," Wilkinson said, suddenly oppressed by the musty smell of the concrete room, the rumbling hiss of the blowers circulating the warm stale air, a confining

The February Plan

awareness that he was surrounded by tons of rock on all sides, closed in. "A hundred thousand children. Is there a way we can change the programing, shift the target center?"

"With a ten-megaton bomb it's all the same. If we get what we want, we get the hundred thousand children as a bonus." His head shifted now on the cushion of his arms. "What do you think about that?"

"I think it stinks," Wilkinson said. "What would any man think about wiping out a hundred thousand children?"

"We're not ordinary men," the major said. "We can't afford to think like ordinary men. If we thought like ordinary men, the dirty work would never get done. Remember that. There's so much dirty work in this world that has to be done, and we're the men who have to do it. And our kind of man is up against a high mortality rate, not because the enemy gets him—no, the odds are good there—but because he gets himself. He has to be born again; he has to get past all the things he's been taught in our society. He has to be reconditioned to see things as they are—not the ideal, not the popular, not the sentimental, but the hard-core essence of things. And that's the real killer in this business, a man's inability to adapt. He plots a course, something that needs doing, and then all of a sudden he runs up against a moral equation he can't solve, a hundred thousand kids, so he blows a fuse. Either he sticks a gun in his mouth and pulls the trigger or he goes out of his head because he can't face the way things are. I could name you a dozen men in the agency who've taken one of those courses in the past two years." He looked at Wilkinson directly now. "So you think this new development stinks," the major said, testing a little, his voice querulous. "That was your word, wasn't it?"

"Get off my back, Major," Wilkinson said. "You don't like it any more than I do."

"Like?" the major said, sitting up, spitting a shred of tobacco onto the floor. "Who the hell said anything about liking? What I like or don't like doesn't have anything to do with this project. A man who 'likes' to kill people, whether those people happen to be enemy or not, is over the brink anyway. That's not the point at all. I don't 'like' killing a hundred thousand children, but realistically, setting aside all sentimentality, I can see that it may be a good thing. Because these aren't a hundred thousand ordinary children; no, they're special cases, the Young Pioneers, the bright ones, the hard ones. Realistically—I repeat that word, realistically—they represent the threat of the next generation. Nits make lice. That's an old quote, but it's true. And I can quote you a dozen historical precedents."

Rationalization, Wilkinson thought, that was what was going on here, not an attack on him, not a testing of his beliefs or his potential, not a lecture, but a demonstration of rationalization in action as the major purged any sentiment from within himself, whipping his mind from acceptance to eagerness.

The major climbed off the bunk as if the depression he had brought into this room had now been converted into nervous energy. "In this business you have to be a pragmatist," he said. "And I look on this development as a practical break. At best, even with a ninety-nine-per-cent success, we could have set them back only twenty years. Now, with any luck, we may be able to remove that threat entirely."

No, Wilkinson thought, a little sick to his stomach, he had been wrong to call this rationalization. The major really believed what he was saying; he did not have to prod himself to acceptance. He had so accustomed himself to this kind of double-think that it took no effort at all for him to accomplish it. Wilkinson felt disgust for the major, but he also envied the major's ability to wrap himself in layer after layer of cottony mental defenses until he felt no shock at all. The mission had to be carried out, Wilkinson could see that, but he was going into this thing with his eyes wide open, accepting the terrible ramifications and the moral responsibility. The major was not. He was deceiving himself that there was a positive advantage to the slaughter of these children. Once it had been done, he would feel no remorse, only an intellectual sense of accomplishment.

Wilkinson thought these things but said nothing. The major was relighting his cigar now. "I don't want this information passed any further," he said. "In the practical view it makes no difference one way or the other." He snapped the lighter shut, extinguishing the flame. He was in good spirits now, obviously refreshed by the brief rest on the bunk. "Where's the transcript of Corman's meeting with the general?"

"There's no transcript yet," Wilkinson said.

"Oh?" the major said, glancing up at him, interested. "But you monitored the conversation, didn't you?"

"I monitored it," Wilkinson said evenly. He told the major everything he had heard.

"So Corman knew everything without the general's telling him?" the major said, intrigued. "I had the feeling that he did. It was just a hunch, but hunches pay off more times than not in this business. Do you think Mitsu knew too?"

"I think so, yes," Wilkinson said. "It occurred to me that we might tighten up our security in Tokyo, just in case."

"The time has passed for that," the major said, inhaling the smoke from the cigar with a half-smile. Wilkinson was puzzled. He had not expected this reaction on the major's part, almost as if he were pleased by the development.

"Then you don't intend to do anything about it?" Wilkinson said.

"I intend to do a good deal about it," the major said, "but we have to approach this logically, we can't run around half cocked. If we start scurrying around Tokyo now, it's a sure tip-off that we're up to something. We can't very well claim we're still maintaining security for the missile base when that secret is already out in the open." He drew himself a glass of water from the small lavatory in the corner of the room, washing down a capsule. "Now, we can be sure that one of two things has happened. Either Corman is the only person who knows what we're doing or somebody on the outside knows as well. But if anybody at Langley had the slightest knowledge, Plover would have tipped me off here. And if there was any stirring in

Tokyo, Watkins there would have picked it up. So if anybody there knows, they're sitting on it. That opens some very interesting possibilities."

"I don't follow you," Wilkinson said.

"That's not important now," the major said. "Who has Corman talked to on this base?"

"No one."

"You know that for certain?"

"He's only had access to the guard. The guard is under orders not to speak to him, and even if he did, the guard couldn't have told him anything. He didn't qualify under 'need to know.' "

"That's very interesting," the major said again. "I want to know where and how Corman got the information. Then I want a transcript of the conversation between him and the general, and you will make that transcription yourself. I want a true copy."

"I don't see any point to that," Wilkinson said. "I have my hands full now."

"Maybe you don't realize the significance of what we're doing here," the major said without rancor. "Not just the shoot—no, that speaks for itself—and not just the political ramifications, whatever they may be. But when we are through here, Wilkinson, every detail of what we have done will assume monumental proportions. They'll go over every scrap of paper, every note, every jotted impression, and I'm going to make sure that it's all there for them, every speck of it. Every turn of the road we've made is on paper, every false start, every mistake—it's all down in black and white." The telephone rang. He picked it up, listened a moment, then returned it to the cradle. He began to put on his shoes. "When you finish questioning Corman, I want it put down on paper too. I'd suggest that you tape it, but I don't think we need go that far." He tied his shoes and stood up, stubbing out the cigar butt, a glowing expression on his face as if, for the moment anyway, things were exactly right. "All right, get with it. Give me a ring when you're through with Corman."

"Yes, sir," Wilkinson said.

By the time Wilkinson reached the surface again and

climbed into his jeep, he found that his stomach was quivering, and he knew he was in for another bout of nerves. He had suffered a spell like this once before, on the night before the Bay of Pigs, and then he had decided to sweat it out, staying to himself as much as possible, but finally it had grown so bad that his voice quavered when he spoke. He had broken it then by drinking a pint of tequila, so doping himself that he was aware of only half of what was going on, but by then it did not really matter. He had finished his part of the mission; he could do nothing more than to wait for the results. This time it was difficult. He still had work to do.

He did not start the jeep immediately. He sat in the cold darkness, smoking a cigarette, thinking for the moment that the whole world had gone mad, sweeping him along with it. He thought of the hundred thousand children and the blast that would obliterate them, and he could not say that he felt any more than an intellectual anger, a cerebral indignation, perhaps because the information itself was so tenuous, a pattern of weak dots and dashes sent by a man he had never seen, cold words printed on paper tape and coming out of a machine. To this extent these children did not exist at all, not as living creatures. They were hypothetical human beings, statistics, a paper complication similar to the hundreds of hypothetical situations thrown at him during his training.

He was angry at himself because he could not care about what happened to these children, felt no real sense of outrage. His primary concern now was with himself and his own fate, a dark future made vividly clear by the major's concern with the records of this operation, a paper monument which would survive him, perfect in every detail. Wilkinson had thought about the personal consequences of this operation many times; he had discussed them with the major in a Tokyo bar, and he had understood fully that he was sacrificing himself for the sake of a larger good, but it had never struck home before with such immediacy. This was not just another assignment with a chance of survival at the end, however small. There was no chance here at all, none, and once that button was pushed, he would be obliterated just as certainly as the half-million people at the other end of that ballistic arc. There would be a trial, undoubtedly, a public hearing to vilify him and the other men who had gone along with the project and to make it quite clear that the United States had not been involved in any way. But in the end, before the year was out, he would die, perhaps by a firing squad, more probably by hanging, and he would cease to exist. He would breathe no more. They would bury him in a box, and that would be the end of him. Now, at this moment, with the snow swirling about the jeep, isolated, shivering in the icy darkness, he did not want to die.

He sparked the engine into life and drove back to the lodge, going up to his room where he kept a bottle of bourbon and pouring himself a stiff drink, trying to dull his nerves. The whiskey gagged him, but he forced himself to finish the first and have another and then lay on the bed until it began to take hold. The quivering eased in his gut; he began to think clearly again. Nothing had changed. The premise of the operation was still valid; everything was the same. For a time his fear had overcome him, but the seizure was passing. He was not a weak man. He stood up, putting on his gun belt, hooking the webbing, his hand steady now. He was all right. The storm was over. He picked up the telephone and asked for Sloan.

"I'm going down to the interrogation room," he said to Sloan. "I may be in there quite a while with Corman, and I don't want to be disturbed."

"You won't be," Sloan said. "When you get through, you might take a look at some of the stuff coming in."

Wilkinson took his time getting to the second floor, giving thought to the approach he should take with Corman, deciding in the end to play it by ear. Corman was an intelligent man, querulous, perhaps, but basically decent. Wilkinson anticipated some resistance but no real trouble. He unlocked the door and went in.

Formerly the room had been used for a library, with shelves from floor to ceiling on three sides and a fireplace breaking up the paneling of the fourth wall.

The February Plan

When Wilkinson first saw the library, he had been enchanted with it, since he was an omnivorous reader, but practically all of the books were written in either Japanese or German, and he was fluent in neither. As he entered, Corman was sitting on a leather sofa near the fireplace, thumbing through one of the volumes. Wilkinson said nothing to him immediately, ignoring him for the moment, going to the telephone and asking that a pot of black coffee be sent up. Only then did he really look at Corman, making no effort to keep the contact light this time.

"Well, Mr. Corman," he said, "you surprised me."

"Oh?" Corman said.

"I thought you understood us a little better than you did. But maybe that's my fault. Maybe I underestimated you."

"You'll be underestimating me again if you think you can get anywhere by beating around the bush," Corman said, closing the book now, putting it down.

"All right," Wilkinson said. "No beating around the bush. I recorded your conversation with the general."

"I see. Was that the general's idea?"

"No. He didn't know anything about it. And you must have some idea of the spot this puts us in." He sat down on the sofa in front of the fire. "We have to know how far this knowledge goes, how many people on the outside share it. So you're going to have to open up. I want to know where you got the information."

Corman smiled slightly. "And you think I'm going to tell you?"

Wilkinson nodded. "Sure. You know the score, Mr. Corman. You can see how the cards are stacked. We're putting our lives on the line here, and we're not going to risk anything just to preserve the civilities."

"I never thought that for an instant," Corman said. "But maybe you'd better understand me too, Mr. Wilkinson. Ordinarily I'm a pretty placid, self-centered man who really doesn't care very much what happens to anyone except himself. But at the moment that doesn't hold true. So anything that I can do to slow you down, then that's what I'm going to do."

"And you really think that your holding out on us can make a difference?"

"You wouldn't be here if it couldn't."

Wilkinson yawned slightly. "Personally I don't think there's any threat at all," he said. "In my book you're a loose end, but the major is a very methodical man, so he bears down on everything. In this case that's going to be you."

There was a knock on the door and Wilkinson welcomed the interruption. He unlocked it to admit Sloan, who had brought the coffeepot and two cups on a tray. He put them down on the table next to the sofa and then beckoned Wilkinson to the door, lowering his voice. "Something's come up I think you'd better know about," he said. "We're getting some different signals from Washington. Plover's not with us any more."

"What?" Wilkinson said, startled. "What happened to him?"

"I don't know. But the contact's changed. We're still getting a lot of routine. They're flooding us with paper."

"Have you notified the major?"

"Not yet. I wanted to check with you first."

"Hold off calling him for the time being. I'll be there in fifteen minutes, half an hour at the outside. And I don't want any interruptions until then."

"What do you think happened to Plover?"

"Beats the hell out of me," Wilkinson said. "But sit tight. If it was anything too negative, we wouldn't be getting a continued signal from them. They're making no queries?"

"None."

"I'll take care of it."

Sloan nodded and left, and Wilkinson turned back to Corman who was standing now, his back to the fireplace, a quizzical expression on his face. "One question," Corman said. "If I tell you what you want to know, what is my status then?"

"Exactly the same as it was before," Wilkinson said.

"And when this project is finished, Miss Finley and I will be released?"

"Yes."

The February Plan

Corman paused as if he was considering it. He eyed the coffeepot. "Do you mind if I have some coffee?"

"No," Wilkinson said. The thought of coffee appealed to him, black, bitter, something to shore up his flagging spirits and equip him to deal with the Plover business. What had happened to Plover? Was this a signal, an indication that the project was coming apart? He turned to the coffeepot and poured a cup full, and at that moment, in his peripheral vision, he saw a stir of movement, the rising arm, and a flash of grim humor passed across his mind as he realized how foolish he had been to be thrown off guard so simply, so obviously. But the impression scarcely had time to record itself in his brain before the poker descended on the back of his head and he thought nothing at all.

3

Corman leaned over Wilkinson on the floor, checking his pulse, relieved to find him alive. His own heart was trip-hammering within him; his mouth was dry. Time now, yes, his chief enemy was time, and he had no idea how soon the telephone would ring for Wilkinson or somebody would come looking for him and discover what had happened. He forced his mind over the incipient panic, taking a deep breath. One thing at a time—yes, that was the only way he could do it. One thing at a time.

Wilkinson had fallen on his face, and Corman turned him over, going through his pockets, taking the ring of keys, sticking Wilkinson's pistol in his belt, going through Wilkinson's wallet and removing the thick sheaf of bills. His fingers touched the reel of tape and he examined it in the light. Luck, blind luck, he thought; it had to be the conversation with the general. Proof. He put it in his pocket, then, convinced he had missed nothing that he might be able to use, he moved to the door, edging it open. The corridor was dark, deserted.

Wait, he told himself as he locked the door behind him. Perhaps he was being too precipitate now, rushed by panic. There was always the chance he could find someone on the base who would believe and help him. Surely all the personnel here would not be members of the conspiracy; that would make the whole thing too unwieldy. But how could he tell? How could he approach anyone here without risking his advantage and his freedom? He could not take the chance.

He moved on, edging his way down the hall until he came to the side corridor he had passed on his way to meet the general. The side corridor was pitch-black, and he groped along the wall until his hand touched the cold glass of a pane, then he took out his lighter and struck a flame. He swore under his breath. There were two ring bolts at the juncture of the French doors. A heavy chain had been slipped through them and fastened with a padlock. He jerked at the chain with his hand, more out of frustration than hope, but the bolts were solidly anchored. He forced himself to stop short, checking the fear that threatened to swallow him. One thing at a time. The obstacle now was that damned chain.

He went back to the library at a dead run, fumbling with the keys and opening the door. The poker was leaning against the fireplace where he had left it. He did not look at the body on the floor. He picked up the poker and took time to lock the door again before he ran back to the French doors. He inserted the end of the poker beneath the chain, gaining leverage against the door facing, beginning a slow, upward pressure. The blunt end of the poker dug into the wood, the wood creaking under the assault, but the chain refused to give. He eased up, breathing heavily, startled to find that his hands were sweating despite the chill in the hallway.

Wiping his hands against his coat, he reversed the angle of attack, slipping the poker beneath the chain from the top, bearing down with all his weight. There was a squeal of outraged metal as the chain began to give, and then, quite suddenly, the bolt tore loose from the door with a loud and splintering crack. He stood rigidly silent, certain that the noise would bring them down on him. Waiting, he heard nothing. He put his hand against the door to push it open. It moved no more than an inch before it jammed tight.

He swore under his breath. First the chain and now the door. The snow had drifted against it on the outside terrace, jamming it shut. He began to work the door, pulling it to him and then pushing it out, but it yielded no more than a fraction of an inch at a time as the snow compacted behind it. The freezing air whistled through the crack, numbing his hands. He took his gloves out of his overcoat pocket and put them on, working the door again, his anger accelerated by desperation. They would find Wilkinson any minute, he was sure of it, and all this effort would have gone for nothing, just because of a few damned cubic feet of snow against a door.

He threw his weight against the door, but still it resisted him, opening no more than a few inches before it froze tight. Muttering to himself, he pushed his hand through the crack, breaking up the obstructing drift, but the snow was almost belly-high outside and he could not reach far enough. The door gave another inch as if to tantalize him. He pulled his arm back in through the crack. His scalp was sweating now; he could feel the moisture on the back of his head.

One more time, he told himself, one more time. He put his shoulder into the crack, and with all his effort, grunting from the strain, he forced himself into it, feeling the door giving little by little, until at last he was almost halfway through, then, pausing momentarily, he gave it everything he had and pushed through. He had ripped his coat; no matter, he had made it, and that was the important thing. He pushed the door shut again, and then, his arms trembling reflexively from the prolonged strain, he pushed his way through the drifted snow, moving very slowly, his hand extended in front of him, anticipating the terrace railing. Finally his gloved fingers bumped against it and he stopped short, his eyes searching the darkness for any glint of reflected light from the house to tell him how much of a drop there was between the railing and the ground. He saw nothing. He would have to assume that the snow was drifted beneath the terrace enough to break the fall.

He climbed over the railing, holding on to the vertical rungs until he was hanging free, and then he let go and fell sprawling in the snow. It knocked the wind out of him. He pulled himself out of the drift and stood erect, pausing to catch his breath, trying to get his bearings. He was on the north side of the lodge. The entrance was on the west. He would have to skirt the house, staying far enough away from it to avoid the possibility of guards, hoping that Wilkinson's jeep was parked on the circular driveway.

The whole thing was impossible, of course, and he knew it. He was a blind man among the seeing, out of his element here, no match at all for the professionals. If he ran into trouble, if he was apprehended, he would not try to fight them. He would surrender immediately. That was only common sense. On foot in these mountains he would have no chance at all. If they did not get him, the country certainly would.

He set out through the darkness at a right angle to the villa, going perhaps a hundred yards before he reached a screen of cedars that broke the wind. From here he could see the reflected glow of the floodlight mounted above the main door, strong enough to penetrate through the falling snow as far as the circular driveway. The jeep was there, the snow piling up on the tarp, giving it the appearance of a white island against a dark hedge of low-growing firs. He started walking again, staying in the shadow of the trees until he reached the hedge, following it as far as it went before he raised his head to check the front of the house. The frosted windows glowed with light, staring at him like luminous eyes. Perhaps there was a watcher behind one of those windows; it made no difference. He had to take the chance. Moving into the open, he made a run for the jeep, ducking behind the side away from the light, lifting the edge of the tarp and opening the door on the driver's side.

Taking off his right glove, he fumbled through the keys until he found one to fit the ignition, intending to start the engine before he removed the tarp, in the hope that it would muffle the sound. He turned the key and ground the starter. From somewhere beneath the hood came a low, straining moan. Cursing to himself, he tried it again. This time the reluctant starter turned over the engine, sluggishly, with great effort. He worked the choke feverishly, trying to coax the engine into life. It caught once, spluttered, died. He tried it again.

This time the engine caught and held. He raced it once before he scrambled out of the jeep to grab at the tarp, pulling frantically against the heavy bank of snow that held it down, finally breaking it free. He rolled it back and dumped it on the ground, glancing toward the house. There was still no sign of movement. He climbed back into the jeep, closing the door. He shifted into gear. The jeep moved around the driveway and into the narrow road. Once he was a hundred yards from the house, he turned on the lights.

When the needle rose on the temperature gauge, he turned on the heater, feeling the rush of hot air against his feet. It was ironic, he thought, that the very weather which had permitted his escape would also be responsible for his capture. The swirling snow reflected in his headlights, so obscuring his vision that he was forced to keep the jeep at a crawl, taking for his reference points the trees which flanked the twisting road on either side. Time had already run out. Undoubtedly they had found Wilkinson by now; the alarm would be going out. By the time he reached the main gate, the guards would be expecting him.

He thought about Finley and wondered what he would have done about her if things had not happened as they had, if she had gone back to the States and he had followed later. Most likely he would have arranged with Henderson to have the publishing house offer her a job for so much money she couldn't turn it down. Then he would have insisted that she take it, for her own good, and it would have ended there. But now things had changed and he was no longer sure he wanted it ended. It was a damn strange time to be thinking about Finley, he thought, when there was nothing he could do about it. At the moment there was no certainty that he would ever see her again. There was no chance of his getting her out of the detention camp, and even if there had been an opportunity, he did not have the time. The tape took precedence over everything else, even his own safety. If they caught him now, it was very likely they would kill him out of pure expediency. He thought of Paul, running for his life along the river, and he felt now what Paul must have felt then.

He forced his attention back to the road. Leaving the hills, it had begun to flatten out, and he slowed the jeep even more, looking for the intersection with the main road. Then he saw the vague pattern of the red warning poles sticking up through the snow and a warning sign reflected in the headlights dead ahead, and now he could see the cleated tracks of the truck traffic that marked the main road. He turned to the right, getting the jeep wheels in the tracks, increasing his speed.

In a few minutes he slowed down again, peering through the windshield, looking for the luminous patch in the snow that would mark the searchlights at the gate. The snow had begun to lighten, but the visibility was still extremely poor, and he was no more than twenty yards from the lowered crossbar when the guard shack took shape in the storm, the powerful lights haloed by the snow.

There was no roadblock, no sign of frenzied activity. Instantly the hope sprang alive within him. Two guards emerged from the shack, one of them flailing his arms across his chest against the cold, the other lighting a cigarette, his hands cupped about the flame, his rifle slung over his shoulder. They sauntered from the shack, and Corman could tell that they were expecting nothing more than a routine check. They would give this jeep a cursory inspection and get back to the warmth of their coal stove.

Corman jammed the shift into second. The first guard raised his hand, cautioning Corman to stop. Corman gunned the motor, flattening the accelerator, and the jeep leaped forward, almost hitting the man who leaped away, falling backward in the snow. The second guard grabbed at his rifle and brought it up to fire, but Corman saw no more than the sweep of his arm before the jeep smashed into the barrier, splintering the heavy arm which broke and gave way, deflecting the jeep at an angle across the icy road. Corman fought the wheel. At the very edge of the ditch the jeep came around and lurched back into the center of the road again. The snow closed in behind him, obscuring the guards.

They would call ahead and block the road at Chuzenji, he knew that, and then they would begin to close in on him from both directions. But he was still alive, and that was more than he had expected. He still had a chance, a small one to be sure, but he would make the most of it.

3

THE major stood at the upper level of the Hole, watching the technicians below him work on the guidance system, moving on the platform around the dissembled nose, hovering over the exposed mass of wiring like white-suited surgeons over the exposed belly of a patient. There was something about one of the technicians that reminded him of Massad, the cant of the head perhaps, the hawklike nose, and although he could not see them from here, the alert eyes, so dark brown they were almost black, holding a glint of perpetual good humor. The man looked enough like Massad to be his brother.

It could not be Massad's brother, of course, because the Massad business was over and done with and only a handful of people had known what had happened to the Lebanese agent, and even the major's closest associates had never suspected him, because Massad was his closest friend. But they could not know that Massad was also a defector, that he was selling out in Beirut, peddling information like tinware, and in the end the major had had to dispose of Massad himself, when the two of them were alone, at dinner, and the major had said nothing at the time, making no charges, no recriminations, because argument was senseless and the evidence spoke for itself, so he had simply raised his Service Special over the low table and shot Massad through the head. The body had been disposed of completely, secretly, so that Massad would never be found, not a trace of him, because all of Lebanon was one big complex family, everybody was related to everybody, and they read each other's thoughts and knew what was going on. When Massad had come into Beirut, under cover of darkness, his visit surrounded by the tightest security, he had awakened in his hotel room to find a hundred relatives camped on the lawn, patiently waiting for him to get up, and some of them had traveled a hundred miles or more. There had been no leak in security. They just knew.

The major fretted, glancing at the general who stood beside him. "That technician down there, the Lebanese," the major said. "Who is he?"

"Kouri," the general said. "He's Syrian, not Lebanese."

"It's all the same," the major said. "What do you know about him?"

"Just that he's one of the best men I have. If you like, you can go through his personnel files."

The major said nothing, restraining his irritation. He checked his watch. They were two hours and twenty-three minutes behind schedule now and falling farther behind all the time. Even now Dr. Smalley and his men were waiting to move in the moment this crew was finished. Most of the thirty-six hours remaining would be gobbled up by the critical tests of the circuits and equipment.

"We're going to have to speed this up," the major said in a low, intense voice. "This crew is going to have to be out of here within the hour."

"They're coming along," the general said laconically.

The February Plan

"We've cut the standard procedure time in half as it is. They're working as fast as they can."

"Nobody ever works as fast as he can," the major said flatly. He turned and stalked off to the elevator, taking it down, fuming inwardly. With a clear field, without having to work with the military and a general who seemed to be developing a dragging reluctance, he could have kept the project well ahead of schedule. They would not be fighting for time now.

When he reached his communications room, he was greeted with a stack of dispatches which Simmons handed him from the coding machine. He carried them into his office and sat down at his desk, putting them to one side while he called Strickland.

"Strickland," he said, "there's a man named Kouri on the roster. I want him kept under surveillance."

"Yes, sir."

Once that was done, the major glanced through the pile of papers. There was a long dispatch from the China operative, a detailed listing of some of the men who had already arrived in Lanchow. He put this to one side and picked up the latest weather forecasts. The three-day forecast was excellent. The sky would be perfectly clear over Lanchow with a temperature in the twenties and a variable north wind five to fifteen knots. The weather at the launch site would be equally good, scattered high clouds and no wind at all.

He looked up as Smalley came into the office. Smalley was a mild-mannered little man, middle-aged and balding, and he had the habit of pinching the bridge of his nose when he was tired. The major had never related very well to members of the scientific community; he always had the feeling that even as they talked with him their minds were somewhere else, lost in a world of mathematical abstractions which the major could not understand. Smalley, however, was a different matter. The major found him fairly easy to handle. Ordinarily he was calm, extremely matter-of-fact about his business, but at the moment his forehead was beaded with perspiration and he exuded an air of nervous tension. His eyes kept darting down to his watch. The major turned on an easy, relaxed smile.

"Don't worry about it," the major said disarmingly. "They're almost through out there. You'll be able to get your crew to work in about an hour."

"That's trimming it pretty close," Smalley said. "I just hope that we're not rushing this too much. If I had my way, I'd have a minimum forty-eight hours of tests before ignition."

"And if I had my way," the major said easily, "I'd give you forty-eight hours."

Smalley nodded, rubbing the back of his neck with his hand. "Do you suppose we could get some sandwiches and coffee for my crew?"

"Just call the mess hall," the major said. He handed him the weather forecasts. "These should cheer you up."

Smalley looked at them briefly and then put them back on the desk. "It could be worse, I guess," he said. "But I would have preferred a perfectly still day." He paused, calculating. "Five knots will carry the fallout far enough south to wipe out Lintan, Lunghsi, Wutu, and Pingwu. Fifteen knots, and it's almost certain we'll get Chengtu and Chungking as well. There are almost two million people in Chungking."

Now the message was coming through; now the major could read the doctor like a book, the frown of doubt, the persistent twinge of conscience at the prospective casualties. "It's enough to give a man second thoughts, isn't it?" the major said. "I can't blame you for that. I've had second thoughts myself."

Smalley looked at him with an expression of startled relief, as if he was grateful that he no longer had to hide his feelings. "It never occurred to me that you would question," he said to the major. "But then, I never thought I'd fall victim to the epidemic of scientific guilt that's going around, and I have. It's a monstrous thing we're doing, Major. We can call it by any name we like, but reduced to essence, it's just that, a monstrous thing."

"Yes, it is," the major said, leaning back in his chair, giving Smalley his head, letting him wallow in his feeling of self-abnegation.

The February Plan

"I keep wondering, even at this late date, if there isn't another way."

"If there is, nobody in our government has been able to find it," the major said. He waited to see if Smalley was going to comment, but Smalley said nothing, retreating into a thoughtful silence, and the major decided this kind of speculation had gone far enough. It was time now to bring him back into line again, to focus him on the job at hand. "It's a hell of a world," the major said. "An imperfect world, and that's the problem. Hell, everything would be simple if all the international problems could be solved by discussion, by sitting down around a table. But that's never worked, because we have moral standards and people like the Red Chinese don't. I don't blame you for wanting to shy away from a stinking mess like this. I do too. But I know this represents our only hope and we're the ones who have to do it. We've been given the opportunity. It may be the only one."

Smalley nodded. It did not take much to bring him around. "Well, we've chewed on that long enough," he said. "That won't get us anywhere." He picked up the weather forecast again. "Is there any chance we can adjust our launch time to a more favorable wind?"

"We can't ask for perfection in a thing like this, can we, Doctor?"

"Not perfection—I don't ask for that. And it's not likely we could get a perfectly still day this time of year. But long-range projects a new front and a wind shift sometime in the next seventy-two hours. It would be a lot cleaner if we could have a south wind that would blow the fallout into the Gobi Desert."

"Cleaner, perhaps, for them, but far deadlier for us," the major said. "That would be the most costly breeze in history as far as the United States is concerned. The Soviets have a mutual treaty with Mongolia. That would involve them long before anybody would have a chance to explain to them what had happened. Have you got a kill prognosis for me yet?"

"In the ten-megaton range I think we're sure of a kill," Smalley said. "A complete denial. The standard deviation is negligible at this range."

"That's what I wanted to hear."

Smalley nodded, turning as if to go, stopping at the last minute. "One more thing," he said. "I've heard the rumor that the Chinese are turning this science celebration into a children's day. How many children are going to be involved, Major?"

"None," the major said instantly.

"Oh?"

"It was just a rumor, nothing more."

"I see," Smalley said, satisfied.

Once Smalley had left the room, the major picked up the telephone and called Simmons in, making no effort to contain his anger. "From now on," he said, "any information coming in here from any source, and I mean any source—no exceptions—is to be considered black. Do I make myself clear? It will be brought directly to me. It will not be discussed with anyone by the man who takes it."

"Yes, sir."

He dismissed Simmons and then sank back in his chair, left with a residue of anger and no place to vent it, feeling besieged from every direction, inundated by trivia. More than one project had gone down the drain because a man had changed his mind, defected at the last moment and not done his job. The major felt that he was having to bind the whole mission together single-handedly. He felt a sudden surge of fatigue. He would have to pace himself now, taking care of one problem at a time and dismissing it before he went on to the next. No holdovers of anger, no accretion of emotion that could weigh him down. Everything neatly compartmentalized. He could do it.

He called for a pot of black coffee, and when it came he took two benzedrines, settling back to wait for them to relieve the dullness he felt within him. Everything was still all right. They were behind schedule, but they would catch up. His luck had been phenomenal so far. No one had cracked; security was tight; there was no indication that the Overseas Intelligence Department of the Red Chinese government had gotten wind of the project. No, that was not luck, that was a tribute to his skill, to the soundness of the plan. The Chinese

The February Plan

were still in the dark, plunging ahead with their plans; all of the reports confirmed this. Two trainloads of children had already arrived. Those damn children, he thought.

The telephone rang. He picked it up to find Sloan on the line. "I'm sorry to disturb you, Major," Sloan said, "but we're getting a lot of communications that call for confirmation."

"Oh?" the major said. "I'd better have a look at them."

"There's one more thing," Sloan said. "About an hour and a half ago Plover closed out on us. Now, I don't know who's dispatching there now, but from the style I'd say it's Anderson."

"Is Wilkinson on it?"

"No, he's still tied up with Corman."

"Get him down there. I'll be there shortly. And don't send anything to Washington until you hear from me."

"Yes, sir."

The major put down the telephone, refilling his coffee cup, lighting a cigar, perplexed. Something was going on back there, but he could not second-guess it. He would have to sit tight, evaluate the new dispatches before he could make any rational judgment. He sorted through the papers on the desk quickly, pocketing those he wanted to add to his file, and as he was standing up to leave, the telephone rang again. The major picked it up. Sloan was on the line again, his voice so controlled that Henshaw knew something was wrong even before he got to the specifics. "Wilkinson's badly hurt," Sloan said. "Corman's missing."

"Missing?" the major said. "What do you mean, missing?"

"Apparently Corman jumped Wilkinson during interrogation. He hit him with a poker and then took his keys. He drove off in his jeep. I just got a call from the main gate. He broke through there about three minutes ago."

"I'll be there immediately," the major said. He severed the connection, refusing to allow himself to feel, only to think and act. He rang Strickland, who had just received an alarm from the gate. "I want the Japanese Rural Police alerted," Henshaw said. "I want the road blocked at the Kunoko and Chuzenji ends. I want telephone service in the whole area cut off; make it lines down by ice. I don't want Corman to be able to contact anybody outside our control area."

"Yes, sir," Strickland said.

"Can you get a helicopter into the air?"

"We can fly it, Major, but in this weather it's not going to be worth a damn to us. He's going to have to stay high to avoid the trees and the power lines. And we have zero visibility."

"Get one up anyway and send him out to the plain. I want the highway covered at the intersection with the base road. Maybe we'll have a break in the weather."

"Yes, sir."

"And get a weasel out. In this weather you should be able to catch him before he reaches the main highway."

"Yes, sir."

He put down the phone, yelling for Simmons, telling him to have a car ready in two minutes and to have the general meet him at the surface. By the time he reached the surface, he found the general waiting for him. He told the general what had happened. "Now, the question is," the major said finally, "what pattern is he likely to follow? What is he likely to do?"

"He'll probably head straight for Chuzenji," the general said calmly. "Unless I miss my guess, he'll try to get word through to the American ambassador. He doesn't have much use for the military."

"Yes," Henshaw said, peering through the snow toward the building where the doors had been rolled back to reveal the headlights of the car. He only half heard the general and paid little attention to his remarks. The major's mind was busy sorting facts, planning, taking in the evidence of his senses concerning the weather and the chances that the snow would let up by the time the helicopter reached the highway. "We're launching in thirty-three hours and eighteen minutes," he said, almost as a murmur.

The February Plan

"That's the one thing to keep in mind. And nothing's going to stop that, nothing."

The car approached through the snow. Henshaw opened the rear door and climbed in without a backward look. In another moment the car moved on. The general stood looking after it, watching the red sparks of the taillights diminish and die in the distance. He shook his head and turned to go below.

2

By the time the major reached the lodge, he was calm again. There was nothing like an attitude of calm when things were going wrong. It was oil on the waters, an ameliorative, an infectuous restorative. When he entered the communications room, he settled down behind a desk and lighted a fresh cigar, radiating an expansive confidence as he asked Sloan for the new dispatches from Washington, aware that Sloan was awaiting his reaction.

Sloan had been right—Plover was no longer doing the sending, but the major was more concerned over the content of the dispatches. It seemed that a crisis had developed in the Japanese government. One of the members of the Diet had just released the information that there was a nuclear missile at this new base. The CIA doubted that he was basing his announcement on hard fact, and the best guess at the agency was that this particular member of the Diet was bluffing, trying to force the Prime Minister's hand. The bluff had worked; the Prime Minister could stall no longer.

The Prime Minister would have to release the full facts about the missile base immediately. In order to give him a firm psychological base from which to maneuver, both governments had decided that the base should be turned over to the Japanese immediately. A token force of Japanese technicians would arrive at 1500 tomorrow afternoon, 4 February. The full complement would arrive on the morning of the fifth. The announcement would be made in Tokyo on the afternoon of 5 February, and an inspection team, to include both members of the opposition and the press, would arrive at the base at 0930 on 6 February.

The major and all of his agency staff were to leave the base by tomorrow noon, leaving the members of the military and civilian work force to complete work on the base as soon as possible. General Gibson would assume joint command of the base at that time with a Japanese military man who was yet to be named. This was the basic information. There followed pages and pages of specifics, technical details, and the major scanned them cursorily before he pushed the papers away from him and leaned back in his chair, looking up at Sloan who was waiting for him to finish.

"They want an immediate confirmation," Sloan said, harried.

"I'm sure they do," the major said. "We live in an immediate world. Everything's split-second now. How long will it take you to get me through to the director on a direct line?"

"Fifteen, twenty minutes, maybe."

"I want you to do that pretty soon," the major said. "But we have another problem on our hands that takes precedence, don't we? Now, I want you to start from the beginning on this Wilkinson business and tell me everything you know. And sit down, son. We're not going to gain anything by sweating this."

Sloan nodded, feeling easier now, since the major did not seem to be particularly upset by something he considered a calamity. Sloan laced his big hands and began to talk while the major jotted notes on a piece of paper. When Sloan was through, the major stood up, putting out his cigar. "Is the base surgeon here yet?"

"Yes, sir, he's upstairs with Wilkinson."

"Then maybe I'd better see what's going on. Start on that direct call. And let me know when it comes through."

"I'll do that."

The major went upstairs to Wilkinson's room. Wilkinson was lying on his bed with Colonel Zimmerman leaning over him, wrapping a bandage around his head. The major did not go in immediately. He stood in the shadows by the door, mentally sorting through all the

The February Plan

disparate elements of the current situation, looking for possible combinations. His mind was sharp now, his thinking clear, burning with a clean, hot flame. No precipitate conclusions, no jumping in feet first; he must eliminate the possibilities one by one until the truth was left isolated, standing alone in perfect clarity.

He walked to the side of the bed opposite Zimmerman, his teeth working against the dead cigar, looking down at Wilkinson, who lay with his eyes closed, his face deathly pale, a small dribble of saliva hanging in the corner of his mouth, catching the light of the lamp. Zimmerman glanced up at the major for an instant, and then his sharp eyes went back to the job at hand.

Was there something significant in the furtive swiftness of that glance, the major wondered? Did it imply reluctance, a desire to conceal? Eyes were traitors. A man might have mastery over his facial muscles, perfect control, but if you watched him closely under stress, his eyes always betrayed him. The major had always distrusted Zimmerman, a scarecrow of a man, tall, lean, uncommunicative as he went about his duties, a perpetual squint to his eyes. One telltale flick of light in the pupils, that was all it took. The staging of a scene, the appearance of truth. How simple it was to feign unconsciousness.

"How is he?" Henshaw said, watching carefully for Zimmerman's response.

"He'll be all right," Zimmerman said. "He's got a nasty cut on his scalp and a mild concussion, but no skull fracture."

"A cut," Major Henshaw said musingly. "I want to see that wound, Colonel."

"You want to what?"

"I want to see the wound," the major said firmly. "Take the bandages off."

For a moment Zimmerman's eyes were incredulous. His long fingers froze with the roll of gauze in the air. Back-lighted by the lamp, it had the appearance of gossamer, as if he were spinning a web. "What the hell for?" he said.

"There's no reason why I shouldn't see it, is there, Colonel?" the major said, with a strained smile.

"No reason except that it doubles my work."

"Then do it," the major said. "I want to see the wound."

Reluctantly Zimmerman unwrapped the gauze from around Wilkinson's head. He lifted the bandage, very gently. Henshaw leaned over to examine the wound in the light. It was not very long. It had been stitched. "How many stitches, Colonel?" he said, blocking Zimmerman's view.

"What the hell are you talking about?"

"I just asked you how many stitches."

"Seventeen," Zimmerman said. "Now, get away from him and let me get this bandage on."

Seventeen stitches, yes. Henshaw backed away. One possibility had been eliminated. Good. He did not relish the thought of having Zimmerman involved in this. There were half a dozen men down with the flu in the detention compound. A doctor was indispensable on a project like this, where there was so much chance of injury. The major went to the window and looked out into the night, holding his hand against the pane to get rid of his own reflection. The snow was as heavy as ever. He willed it to lighten, thinking of the helicopter already in the air.

He turned back to Zimmerman. The last piece of adhesive was going into place. "I want to talk to him," he said. "Give him something to bring him around."

"He needs all the rest he can get."

"There are other needs that supersede his," Henshaw said. "I have to talk to him. I'm ordering you to bring him around."

Zimmerman took a hypodermic kit out of a bag, stripped away the plastic, and prepared the injection. Once he had finished, he looked to Henshaw again. "It'll take a few minutes."

"Fine," the major said. "I'll wait. Good night, Colonel."

Zimmerman snapped his bag shut. For a moment Henshaw thought he was going to say something and he watched him carefully, the tightening of the muscle in the jaw, the slight constriction of the throat as he swallowed. But he did not speak. He turned and went out,

The February Plan

closing the door behind him, leaving the major alone with Wilkinson.

The major sat down by the bed, watching Wilkinson's face, waiting while the color returned, bit by bit. The facial muscles began to twitch with the stirrings of consciousness. "Can you hear me, Wilkinson?" he said softly. He waited a minute and then repeated the question. "Can you hear me, Wilkinson?"

The eyes opened slightly. The pupils were dull. The lips parted almost imperceptibly, and Wilkinson stirred. He raised himself up slightly before the pain caught him and forced his head back down to the pillow.

"Major?" he said weakly.

"Where did Corman go?" Henshaw said, hoping to catch him unaware. There was always a moment when a man's mind was just on the edge of consciousness when he was unable to marshal his defenses.

"Major?" Wilkinson said again. "What happened to me?"

"You don't remember?"

"No."

"You were interrogating Corman. He caught you by surprise, hit you on the head," the major said. He paused to light the cigar again, giving Wilkinson time to get his bearings. The smoke was harsh against the major's throat, but he felt eased by it. "Would you like a glass of water?" he said.

"No," Wilkinson said. His voice was more responsive now. "I was stupid," he said. "Goddamn stupid all the way around."

"You're beginning to remember now."

"Yes."

"An unfortunate business," the major said, taking his time, relaxing in the chair. "But we'll catch him without too much trouble."

Wilkinson was startled. "He got off the base?"

"Yes."

"How?"

The major shrugged slightly. "It seems that one of Knaus's men is sick. So he rearranged his security schedule, took off his outside man."

"I suggested that."

"Oh?" the major said calmly.

"How did Corman get past the main gate?"

"He rammed through the barrier. The guards saw the jeep, assumed it was you. By the time they knew differently, Corman had already broken through." He was silent for a moment, thinking. "A nasty business," he said quietly. "The whole goddamned thing. Before I came with the government I was a lawyer, did you know that?"

"No."

"My father was a very poor man, an immigrant from Liverpool, and he was always running afoul of the law. He looked on laws as something the authorities created to harass him. And from the very first day I went to school he had it in the back of his mind that I was going to be a lawyer, so I could take care of all the poor bastards like himself who never knew what it was all about." The major smiled. "But by the time I graduated from law school, the old man was dead, so I decided to go with the government. And I never really regretted it, not until today. Not until this business of the Chinese children."

Wilkinson was confused now—his eyes said as much—not only by the abrupt change of subject, but by the major's new attitude. "I thought you were all for it," he said. "Nits make lice, remember?"

"I have to be all for it if I'm to go through with it," the major said reflectively. "But I don't like it, any of it." It was working now, just as the major knew it would. Weakness could not grow unless it had the proper climate. "Do you want out Wilkinson?"

"Who doesn't want out?" Wilkinson said. "I don't want to die any more than the next man."

The major accepted this, assimilated it, abandoned the subject of the children in favor of the new course. "That's true. None of us want to die," he said. "I don't want to die myself, but maybe it's a little easier for me. I'm older and I've been in this business a hell of a long time. I got used to the thought of dying quite early. But now that it appears to be inevitable, I'm not so sure. And I imagine most of the men who came along on this project feel the same way."

"I've never heard any of them discuss it."

"They don't have to spell it out. Men aren't that much different basically. There's an instinct in all of us for self-preservation, a natural antipathy toward death. So, to that extent, what we do to save ourselves can't be held against us." He poked at a wreath of smoke with the glowing tip of his cigar. "I checked with Sloan before I came up here. The tape of Corman's conversation with the general isn't in the files."

"The tape?" Wilkinson's brows furrowed. "You told me to take care of that myself."

"Did you transcribe it?"

"No, I decided to talk to Corman first."

"Where is the tape now?"

Wilkinson's hand moved down to his side and then he realized the coat had been taken off him. "It's in my jacket."

The major's eyes flicked over the room. He stood up slowly and walked over to the chair where the jacket was hanging. "Which pocket?"

"The left side."

The major's fingers explored the empty pocket. He turned it inside out and held it up for Wilkinson to see. "It's not here now. But maybe Corman took it. He took everything else you had. So it's possible he took the tape as well, isn't it?"

"It's possible," Wilkinson said, his eyes suddenly wary. "What are you getting at?"

The major ignored the direct question. He walked over to the window again, aware that Wilkinson's eyes were following every movement he made. The snow was still falling, still drifting down in the cold black sky. "Did Corman know what was on the tape?"

"I used it as a lever to pry information out of him," Wilkinson said defensively. "It's a standard interrogation technique. You would have used the same method yourself."

"Did you get your information? Did you find out?"

"No, Sloan brought the coffee. Corman jumped me right after that."

"And caught you off guard."

"Hell, I didn't anticipate anything like that. He knew he couldn't get off the base."

The major turned slightly, preserving his façade of calm reason. "But he did," he said. "He did get off the base."

"And that was a pure fluke. He couldn't have known he would."

"Not ordinarily, no," the major said. "But look at this from my point of view. He arrives here on this base, and at that time we can presume he was clean, that he didn't know anything, because if he had known on the outside, he would have taken an entirely different course of action. He would never have come here. He's not a stupid man. Now, he arrives, and sometime between his time of arrival and his interview with the general he learns everything. And from your own statements, you say that he talked to nobody except you."

"As far as I know. Look, Major . . ."

"Let me finish," the major said firmly. "Now, looking at this from your point of view, I suppose the whole thing makes a kind of sense. You decide that you want out because you get an attack of nerves. But how are you going to accomplish it? There's no chance of a physical exit on your part, none at all, because you know the rules in a thing like this, and all of us are to some extent expendable. If you had even tried to leave here and break security, you know damn well you would have been shot. And I suppose that there was still a kind of honor involved, too, in that you couldn't defect out of simple cowardice. Very few of us could manage that." He was feeling very good now, enjoying himself as all the pieces dropped into place, one by one, interlocking, unshakable. He did not even look at Wilkinson now. His attention was turned inward, marshaling his facts, regimenting the circumstances into straight lines.

"Why in the hell would I have gone to all that trouble?" Wilkinson said angrily. "If I had intended to use Corman to get myself off the hook, I could have told him everything back in Chuzenji and sent him to the authorities."

"They wouldn't have believed him, you know that.

The general said as much in his talk with Corman. You're a perceptive man, Wilkinson. You know it wouldn't have worked. And even if there was a chance it might have, you couldn't have taken it. Because you were under orders to bring Corman and the woman back here."

"You're wrong, Major. You have a lot of circumstantial evidence, but that's all you have."

"I have the truth," the major said, beginning to feel some irritation at the interruption. "You had no chance of bringing it off until Corman had something tangible to show to the authorities, and that tape was it. Suppose he gets that tape into the hands of the American ambassador within the next twenty-four hours, a recorded conversation with General Gibson in which the whole thing is spelled out, step by step? What do you suppose our government is going to do about that? Do you suppose they're going to develop a wait-and-see attitude and allow things to follow a steady course? Hell, no, they're not. They'll overrun us in a minute, swamp us before we can move. Believe me, Wilkinson, I've been in the business a long time and I know all the angles." He tried to read Wilkinson's face now. It was not difficult. A feigned stupefaction, a pretended incredulity. "You gave permission to Knaus to call in his outside guard. Your jeep was conveniently available for Corman to use. All it costs you is a blow on the head, a mild concussion and a little pain, and the whole thing is over. The project is canceled and you have a life insurance policy." He sat down again. "One more thing, the woman—what have you done about her?"

"I haven't done a damn thing about her. She doesn't know anything."

"You're sure of that, are you?"

"Dead sure."

"And it didn't occur to you she might be far more than she seems to be, did it? Well, I'll take care of it." He relaxed his tone. "I want you to know, I understand your motivations."

"Goddamn your understanding," Wilkinson said.

"It wouldn't work, of course," the major said, "even if Corman managed to get through to the authorities.

Your life would be forfeit, just as much as anybody else's. But he won't make it. We will catch him. And you can make it easier for us to do that. I want you to tell me where Corman has gone, what his plans are, what your deal was with him. Hell, I want to be lenient with you. I want to believe that you had a momentary loss of nerve. That could happen to anybody. And I want to know who was in this with you. Did you discuss it with the general? Did he arrange that display of ineptitude at the gate? Was it his idea to have this mission aborted? What part does the woman play in all this?"

Wilkinson was calm now. He shook his head. "There's no conspiracy, Major."

"Then it's all my imagination," the major said, with a faint smile. "You expect me to rack it up to coincidence, the whole thing."

"You're really around the bend," Wilkinson said finally. "Far gone."

The major fixed him with his eyes. Training, he thought, conditioning. He could not really expect Wilkinson to confess. He was lying too well now, his face under perfect control, following a predictable course from outrage to denial to accusation. The telephone was ringing. With a sigh the major picked it up.

"I have Langley on the line."

"I'll be right down."

He put the telephone down, standing up, facing Wilkinson. "I'll talk to you again later," he said. "But I want you to remember one thing. Nothing is going to stop this mission, absolutely nothing."

He went downstairs to communications, going into one of the smaller rooms, sitting down at the desk, trying to empty everything out of his mind except the facts pertinent to the call in front of him. He picked up the telephone. "This is Henshaw," he said to the operator. "Connect me."

"Yes, sir."

There was a slight buzz on the line, and he could picture the circuits being connected, the whisper of electronic joinings. In his vaultlike office at Langley, the director would be sitting at his desk, chewing

The February Plan   213

thoughtfully on the edge of his folded glasses, the telephone pressed closely to his ear, the perpetual corporation frown creasing his forehead, the mass of papers in front of him to keep his memory refreshed. Ah, that would be a sight, the major thought, and he would give all he had to see the director's face when the news finally came through of the launch and he realized he had been outfoxed by the man who should have occupied that expansive seat of power. The major would see that the director had first look at the collection of papers concerning the project along with the final report, but then again, the director would never be able to appreciate the finer intricacies. No, only a man who had been with the agency over the long haul could fully understand the beauty of the operation.

"Henshaw?" the voice came over the line, vague, distant, slightly distorted.

"Yes, sir, this is Henshaw," the major said.

"What's the trouble?"

"No real trouble at all," the major said, extemporizing now, letting his imagination take wing, improvising, functioning in milliseconds to come up with something logical, indisputable. "Since there's a matter of policy involved here, I thought I'd better pass it along for what it's worth. We've run into a little trouble with the nuclear installation. There was a small accident, nothing serious, but we've had a leakage of some radioactive materials in the Hole, and it's going to take us a while to flush it out and cool it down."

"My God, was anybody hurt?"

"One of the technicians suffered a minor burn, nothing serious. However, it's going to take about twenty-four hours to get things back to normal here. Considering the current timetable, I thought I'd better get the information on to you."

"The advance Japanese team is due in there tomorrow, at 1500."

"I know."

The director was thinking now. "That's all we need," he said, "an atomic incident with Japanese personnel. Twenty-four hours, you say?"

"Yes."

"Has the general sent this information to the Pentagon yet?"

"No, sir. He's had his hands full."

"Very well, I'll take it up with State. I'll see if the Japanese government can't hold off until the afternoon of the fifth."

"That's all the time we need," the major said.

"Send me a full report," the director said. "And in the meantime, you can get ready to clear out of there. I don't want any direct contact between our men and the Japanese team. As far as anybody is concerned, this is a straight military deal."

"I understand. One more thing, sir," the major said, as an afterthought. "Has something happened to Plover?"

"Plover?"

"He was handling the dispatches from that end. One of my boys thought he detected a change in style early today."

"Hold on." The line was empty for a moment, and then the director was back, obviously after checking with somebody in his office. "You can tell your man he was right. Plover had a heart attack this afternoon."

"Serious?"

"I'm afraid it was. He died before we could get him to emergency."

"I'm sorry to hear that."

"I'll be in touch," the director said, and then the line went dead. The major put down the phone. A hell of a note, he thought, that Plover had died now, before fruition of the plan, but then again, perhaps it was best. The last link with Washington had been removed. Plover was always a cautious man. He would have left nothing tangible behind him to connect him with the project. The major picked up a pencil and wrote out what he had told the director, jotting down the time of the call, so that it would all be a part of the final record.

Quite suddenly he felt sick to his stomach, a little woozy in the head. He went to the water cooler and pulled one of the paper cups from the dispenser, exam-

The February Plan

ining it carefully before he filled it with water and took another of his pills. Sloan had appeared through the hall door now, and the major welcomed his presence. Sloan was an uncomplicated, quiet individual whose mind was centered in his machines. He was a stocky man with a sandy thatch of hair and pale gray eyes. There was no hostile independence in Sloan, no quirks; he followed orders well, and the major perceived in him a great strength of character. He gestured to Sloan with a nod of his head and went back to the desk, waiting for Sloan to join him.

"I've taken care of the Washington business," he said in a low voice. "Now, I want you to do something for me."

"Yes, sir," Sloan said, his ruddy face gleaming with curiosity.

"I want you to stay close to communications from now on. Sit on it. If Wilkinson makes any attempt to communicate with the general, or vice versa, I want the conversation recorded and you're to notify me immediately. But no guard on Wilkinson's room. He's in no shape to go anywhere, and there's no sense wasting a man."

Sloan's face was puzzled, but he did not push the question. "Yes, sir. Do you mind my asking what happened to Plover?"

"He had a heart attack," the major said simply. "He's dead."

The telephone on the desk rang. Sloan picked it up, listened a moment, and then handed it to the major. "It's for you," he said.

Strickland was on the line from the Hole. "We've just had a report from the helicopter, Major. He's spotted a burning vehicle in a gorge off a side road about seven miles southwest of the base road intersection."

"Is it a jeep?" the major said.

"The pilot couldn't tell," Strickland said. "The snow's too thick, and he couldn't get close enough. But I have a hunch it is. I think Corman decided to get off the main highway, took a side road, and missed a turn in the storm. I think that's where we'll find him."

"Send the weasel down there right away," the major said. "Get a crew down to the wreck. I want a confirmation."

"It's a pretty deep gorge. It may take a little time."

"Two hours, three?"

"About that. Maybe a little longer."

"All right," the major said. "Have you carried out my orders concerning the telephones and the Japanese police?"

"Yes, sir. The trunk line is down this side of Chuzenji. Since all of the calls from this area feed through there, we have a complete blackout between Chuzenji and Yunoko. We should be able to hold that for a six-hour minimum. And the Japanese police already have a roadblock this side of Chuzenji."

"Very good," the major said. "I don't think we're going to need it, but there's no sense taking chances. Now, if you need me in the next hour, I'll be over at detention. I'm going to have a little chat with the woman."

3

The major had never done well with women and he knew it. In his occasional critical self-examinations he realized that in his adolescence he had been a sexual predator and that basically he had an antipathy toward all women, primarily perhaps because he had never fully understood them. They were moody creatures, subject to shifting currents of the psyche which he could never chart, and he was never comfortable around them because he could not trust their reactions.

Both of the women he had loved or trusted (the two words were equatable in his mind) had betrayed him as he had suspected that they would, eventually, holding that opinion in one corner of his mind even as he entered into a relationship with them. Mildred had been the first, and he had married her because it was important that he should be married at the time, but there was no real strength within her, no real understanding of the nature of a man, and in the end she had drifted away from him into a liaison with a naval

The February Plan

officer, more from his performance in the bedroom, the major suspected, than from any quality of intelligence. And then there had been Bianca—oh, the fires of sensuality that burned in that woman; how exquisite it was with her, with a fervor that aroused his dormant ardency and brought it to an equal flame. Yet, in the end, she had betrayed him as well, and quite through necessity he had turned off his emotions, battened down the sentient hatches and ordered her killed, thinking at the moment that her body was being placed in the black waters of the lake, gently, a victim of a boating accident in the public eye, that a painful phase of his life had ended and would never trouble him again.

There had been others, of course, because this business placed a great reliance on women, and the sexual urge had brought more than one otherwise inaccessible and unapproachable man into line, but the major had never had many personal dealings with these women, not in a way which would truly involve him, instead contenting himself with using them in the same way he would use any object which offered a possibility of accomplishing his ends.

It was not clear to him why his mind had drifted into these channels, except that Miss Finley disturbed him as no other woman had in some time, in that there was a quality in her which reminded him of Mildred when they had first met, a kind of hostile indifference. It struck him the moment the guard opened the door to Miss Finley's room; there was in her eyes the same expression that might have greeted the entrance of a servant. There was nothing positive here for him to work with. If she had turned to him with hope, he could have capitalized on that, or if there had been hate or anger, he could have worked either of them just as well. They would have dictated an angle of approach which was now lacking, and he would be forced to plan his own.

She was combing her hair, and the false bun of hair lay coiled on the dressing table which had been provided for her. Her own hair fell down about her shoulders, ash blond, the fine strands glittering in the lamplight, and despite the tailored form of her suit he could see the full convexity of breast, the well-turned leg. A controlled vanity, yes; the basic woman subdued, in check, a logical mind, or so she would regard it. Fine.

He smiled. "I hope I'm not interrupting you, Miss Finley?" he said.

"No," she said, her thin fingers placing the comb on the surface of the dresser with a firm click. She sighed slightly. "If you're here to ask questions, I can't tell you any more than I did the other man."

"No questions," the major said pleasantly, taking out a cigar. "Do you mind if I smoke?"

"No."

"I'm Major Henshaw from the American Embassy," he said, lighting the cigar. "I'm sure Mr. Corman has spoken of me."

"Many times." Was there opinion registered there? Had Corman infected her with his distrust? The face was passive, tired. He would have to make his own path.

"This is an embarrassing situation for all of us," the major said, "and the government is anxious to expedite a solution. That's why I'm here. But I'm going to require your co-operation."

"My God," Finley said. "How much more co-operation can I give you? Look, I've told you the truth about everything. Mr. Corman came up here to find out about his son. That's all he's ever wanted. And I can't understand why you try to make more out of it than that."

There it was, the major thought, a pattern was emerging, a foundation he could build on. "His son, yes," the major said, "an unfortunate business. If it hadn't been for the son, of course, none of this would have ever come about. I can understand why Mr. Corman would want to find out about his son; that's a natural parental instinct, and I suppose there was a little guilt involved too. I understand that Mr. Corman travels a lot."

The abruptness of the last statement forced her a little off balance. "Travel?" she said.

The February Plan

"Abroad. His last book, for instance—he never could have written that without spending some time in Europe."

"He was in Paris last year for a few months."

"Paris only?" the major said pleasantly.

"No, he was in Spain for a while and then in Germany."

"East or West?"

"Why ask me these questions?" she said. "I'm sure he'll tell you himself. He has nothing to hide."

"That seems to be a debatable point," the major said musingly. "I can tell you now, Miss Finley, that you are under no suspicion at all. I'm sure you have no part in this affair, and the government shares that belief."

"What affair?" she said, baffled. "I don't know what you're talking about."

"Of course not," the major said. "I didn't expect you to. And I'm not free to give you all the details. But I can say that the government has had its eye on Mr. Corman for some time."

"Why?"

"We suspect that either wittingly or unwittingly he is being used by the enemies of the United States."

"That's ridiculous."

"Is it? Were you along on his European trip last year?"

"No."

"Then how do you know what he did over there?"

"He dictated tapes, sent them to me, and I transcribed them."

"And you say he wasn't in East Germany?"

"I didn't say that."

"Then he was?"

"I didn't say that either."

It was working now, the major reflected, an old and very classic method of interrogation, but still very reliable. She was confused, almost to the point of wringing her hands, anxious to defend Corman. The alarm was sounding, but in her confusion she was running to the wrong wall. "You don't need to hide it from me," the major said. "We know he visited East Germany."

"As a tourist, maybe. I don't remember."

"And who did he meet there?"

"If I'm not sure he went to East Germany, how could I possibly know who he met there?"

"And after his trip to Europe, he began to discuss plans to visit Japan, isn't that right?"

"No," she said flatly, her expression of relief saying that she was on solid ground now. "He did not plan to come to Japan at all until he got the note written by his son."

"Mitsu sent him that note, didn't he?"

"He didn't meet Mitsu until we got here. He didn't even know Mitsu existed. As a matter of fact, I picked Mitsu's name out of an English service directory for tourists."

Now the major paused, concentrating on his cigar, shaking his head with great certainty as if he believed none of it. "You certainly can't expect me to believe that. The meeting between Corman and Mitsu was prearranged."

"No."

"They were assigned to work together against an American project here."

"No, he hired Mitsu to find out what had happened to Paul."

"A simple investigation," the major said with a smile. "Hardly the kind of case to lead to all that activity in Tokyo. Mitsu knew what we were doing all along. So did Corman."

"You're wrong," she said, highly distraught now. "Believe me, Major, whatever you're thinking about Mr. Corman is not true. He knew nothing. He still probably doesn't. Mr. Mitsu was upset because he had read something in the paper, but he wouldn't tell me what it was. No, I bought a copy of that paper for Mr. Corman and brought it up here to him. He still didn't know what was going on. You have to believe that, Major. If the government thinks Mr. Corman is disloyal to his country, they're mistaken."

There, the major thought, that had the ring of truth to it. Simple. The truth laid bare with one stroke of the scalpel. "Which paper?" he asked.

The February Plan 221

"The English edition of *Asahi*."

"For which day?"

"The day Mitsu was killed."

"And you say you brought a copy of that paper to Corman?"

"I did bring it to him."

"And he read it."

"I don't know whether he read it or not."

Possible, the major thought, trying to remember if that was the day the story had appeared concerning Japanese electronic stocks and the meeting of the scientists in Lanchow. Yes, it could be. And the man following Corman had reported that Corman had asked the librarian about the phrase, the Blue Ants, and uncovered Chien's name. Yes, it could fit quite well; this was the way things happened, tags and scraps of information. The Suzuki girl—any loopholes there? The major wondered. He thought not. No, she was in the south of Japan with her father, and her father was truly ill, and she had long since passed the point where she might be troublesome. "Well," the major said finally, "it could be that the government is wrong. They have been before. They will be again."

"They are wrong," she said, her hand smoothing her hair again now. "I know Mr. Corman as well as any person living. I know what he is, and he certainly isn't disloyal to his country."

She reveals herself, the major thought, complimenting himself on his ability to pick up the seemingly meaningless and translate it into the significant. She shifted slightly on her chair, crossed her legs, and there was a touch of color in her cheeks. Defense in the name of love, he thought, much more than secretary, and they were undoubtedly bedding down together, and there would certainly be a responsive depth of feeling in Corman which might prove extremely useful. The major stood up now, looking around the small quonset hut which still bore some traces of its former use as a supply room. A cot had been supplied her and a makeshift dressing table, and in the rear there was a toilet. "These are terrible quarters," he said. "I'll see if I can't have something more suitable arranged for you."

"I don't care about the quarters," she said. "I just want to get out of here, Major. I want to see Mr. Corman."

"If what you say is true, and I don't have any real reason to doubt you, that shouldn't be too long. These things happen, Miss Finley. I hope when it's over you will understand and not be too harsh in judging us. We all want what's best for the country, after all."

"Mr. Corman is all right, isn't he?"

"Quite all right," the major said. "Upset, belligerent, but that's understandable, considering the circumstances." He put out his cigar in an ash tray. "Is there anything you need?"

"No."

"I've appreciated your being so frank with me," the major said, going to the door and knocking on it. "It may clear up a number of problems."

On his way to the car his mind was perfectly clear and he smiled to himself. One could never tell what one was going to pick up in an interview, and the men who went in to gather support for a particular point of view were handicapped, blinded by their own preconceptions. She had been most helpful, he decided, most helpful indeed.

4

CORMAN heard the sound and he stopped walking, listening, craning his neck to peer up into the black sky, his eyes squinched almost shut against the blowing snow. It was the spluttering of a small helicopter and it was off somewhere to the east, but in the storm he could judge neither height nor distance. They had

The February Plan

probably found the jeep by now—that would account for the presence of the helicopter, and the pilot was undoubtedly circling, radioing in his report of the fire burning at the bottom of the gorge.

It was going to take a while for them to get a ground crew in, and he had been given a momentary reprieve, but he did not know how long it would last and he could count on nothing. He pulled the coat up around his neck and began to walk up the side road again, telling himself that he had made the right choice, letting the jeep go off the sharp edge of the gorge, taking to foot in the darkness and a temperature that must be hovering close to zero. But on the other hand, there had really been no choice at all, because that same helicopter that now hovered above the gorge would have picked up his lights on the road and called for ground forces to block him.

There had been recent traffic on this side road. His jeep lights had picked up tire impressions, clean and sharp in the snow, before he abandoned it, and he hoped that they would lead him to a house perhaps, or a shrine, or a habitation of any sort. If he had any luck at all, he would find a telephone there.

By the time he had walked an hour, he was half frozen, his feet were numb, and he was fighting despair. He forced himself to keep moving for another fifteen minutes, and then he gripped the fingers of his right glove in his teeth to pull it off, groping with numbed fingers for the lighter in the pocket. He clicked it into flame and stooped down to examine the tire tracks again to make certain the vehicle had not turned off. It had not. As he straightened up, extinguishing the flame, he saw the light, a hundred yards ahead and somewhat to the right, a bright wink in the snowfall as if a door had been opened and closed. Summoning his last reserves of strength, he pushed up the road toward it.

As the distance lessened, the vague shape of a building took form in the darkness, and he could see that it was a Japanese inn, a low building sitting in a grove of pine trees up the slope from the road. There was a glow of light from the shuttered windows, and a pale lantern marked the entrance. He followed the driveway, his feet dragging now, totally unfeeling, stopping short when he reached the car, a red Triumph parked near a low wooden fence. He tried the doors, but they were locked. He could see no keys in the ignition. The car had not been here long. Only now was the snow beginning to stick on the rapidly cooling hood.

He approached the doorway, ringing the bell, and in a moment the door slid open and a little woman in a gray kimono appeared, bowing to him, chattering in a pleasant, sibilant Japanese, admitting him to a hallway, kneeling to help him remove his shoes, assuming that he was here for a room. He made no attempt to explain his presence here, and she demanded none. She put his shoes on a polished wooden rack. Apparently business was poor tonight, Corman noticed. There were only two pairs of shoes on the rack, army oxfords and a pair of expensive red pumps with stiletto heels.

"*Koshundenwa motimasuka?*" Corman said, asking for a telephone. The woman sighed, displaying an apologetic smile. There was obviously no telephone, and his Japanese was insufficient for him to ask where the nearest phone was. But it made no difference. He was near the end of his reserve and he could go no farther.

"*Itto no heya misete kudasai,*" he said. The woman bowed again and led him into a central hallway, stopping at the first door, sliding open the door to admit him. The room was small, clean, relatively warm. Corman nodded at the maid to signify his approval and then stood to one side as the maid took the bed quilts out of the closet and unrolled them on the reed floor. She tried to help him with his coat, displaying the traditional kimono of the inn for him to wear, but he shook his head and with a smile declined, and she left the room to bring him the registration card and a tray of food.

Corman sat down on the floor, exhausted, his face still aching with the cold. He began to massage his feet, keeping them near the charcoal hibachi, and bit by bit the circulation was restored, and with a return of feeling came the pain. He knew rationally that it was over, that he had made his grand effort and that it had not been enough. He had been defeated, not by anything they had done to stop him, but by the limitations of his own body. He would stay awake only until after the maid had brought the registration card, and then he would sleep, knowing that they would catch up before long, even more keenly aware of the pressure of time than he was. The day after tomorrow—no, it was after midnight now; technically today was the fourth and tomorrow would be the fifth—and the general would have his way and the shot would take place, probably toward midday, early afternoon perhaps. Thirty hours. He would never have been able to make it in any event.

He dozed off, coming to with a start when the maid came in with a tray of food and a pot of tea, handing him the registration card with a deep bow. He filled it out, using a fictitious name, and then insisted on paying her for the room in advance, trying to make her understand that he would be leaving early in the morning. He was not sure that she did, but finally she accepted the money and left. He poured himself a cup of tea, cradling the thin porcelain in his hands for warmth a long time before he drank it. He was surprised to find that he was ravenously hungry, and he ate everything on the tray, the bowls of tempura, the sour pickled turnips, the bowl of rice. Once he had eaten he felt somewhat better, and he knew he would have to go ahead and make the try, even if it failed.

Everything was against his success, of course, and foremost on the list was his own inadequacy and lack of experience. He had led a fairly sedentary life, and the battles he had survived had been intellectual and emotional ones. Aside from the business part of his career, which occupied relatively little of his time, he had spent his life dealing in fictional terms, the synthesizing of experience, and there was little similarity between the way he would have imagined his current predicament and the way it actually was. His feet hurt; his throat was raw; he was still chilled to the bone, and he had difficulty thinking. He wanted to do nothing. His chief enemy was inertia.

He pulled the lamp closer to the table and began to

go over the things he had taken from Wilkinson. There was an identification card with Wilkinson's picture on it. Corman could not use that. He examined the pistol, breaking open the cylinder. It was fully loaded. He snapped it back into place, laid the pistol to one side, and picked up the reel of tape. Now there was his weapon—not indisputable proof, because in these days of such expert technological fakery there was no absolutes, but enough to make them check it out. He would have to get the tape into the hands of the American ambassador himself, not to one of his subordinates. The general had mentioned a Tokyo contact, and he could very well be attached to the Embassy. Yes, the ambassador, and Corman would have to get to Tokyo with the tape.

But how to do it—that was the problem. And then he thought of the sports car sitting in front of the inn and the shoes in the entryway. Two people had come here in that car, and it was his guess that one of them was an American officer. Perhaps the officer would listen to him, help him, but even as he considered the possibility, his mind turned back to the thought of his own welfare and the nagging temptation to save himself.

He thought of Finley and, using her as a solid reference point, he projected a new life for himself once he got back to the States, a more meaningful life now that he had someone to share it. He could have it for the asking. He could walk back down that road and turn himself in to any one of the men investigating the wrecked jeep. They would take him back to the base and things would be as they were before. Once the launch was made, he and Finley would be released. Very well, he bargained with himself, he would view this unknown man in the room down the hall as his last chance. If he could get no help in that direction, he would give up.

Loading his pockets, he put the gun in his belt and slid back the door. The hallway was deserted, dark except for a small lamp burning at the far end near the entrance to the bath. He heard the sound of muted voices and he stood listening until he could determine a direction. The sound was coming from the left. Closing the door behind him, he went down the corridor in his stocking feet, stopping at the first door to listen before he went on to the next. The third room was occupied. He heard the subdued lilt of a woman's laughter, the indistinct, rumbling voice of a man.

Corman knocked lightly on the door and instantly all sound died within the room for a moment, and then he heard a whispering consultation and the man's voice answered. "What do you want?"

"Are you American?" Corman said. "I need to talk to you. It's very important."

"Come back in the morning," the man's voice said. "Go away." There was a slight slur to his words and Corman could tell that he had been drinking, and from his tone of voice Corman knew instantly that the woman in the room was not his wife. Corman groaned inwardly.

"I know it's late," Corman said. "But this is very important. Just give me five minutes of your time, that's all I ask."

"Get the hell out of here," the man said.

Corman took the pistol out of his belt and then, reaching out, he grabbed the door and slid it open. The woman was young, sitting in her slip by the low table, her red hair glinting in the lamplight, a sake cup in front of her. The man was standing near the table. The inn kimono draped over his shoulders looked incongruous with his crew cut and unmistakably American look. In that moment, as the door slid open, they froze as if they were part of a tableau.

"Don't move," Corman said. "And no noise, please."

He came into the room, sliding the door closed behind him. The man's face was befuddled, his expression more confused than angry. "What is this?" he said. "What's going on here?"

"I meant what I said," Corman said. "I'm sorry to break in, but I have to talk to you."

The girl's eyes flicked to Corman, completely unintimidated.

"Get out of this room," the man said, and Corman

could detect the army in his voice now, the ring of command, as if he was used to immediate response when he spoke.

"You don't understand," Corman said. "I have to talk to someone, and you're the only Americans in this inn." He saw the uniform hanging on the rack near the closet door, the eagles glittering in the light. "Neither of you is going to get hurt, Colonel."

"I don't talk to any man at gun point," the colonel said, but Corman saw the resolute glint in his eyes and realized he was not going to listen at all, that while he stood there, rubbing his hands together, he was shifting to put himself between Corman and the girl while his mind raced ahead, projecting himself heroically. Corman shook his head desperately, knowing what the man was going to do even before he did it. The colonel lurched forward awkwardly, reaching out to grapple for the pistol in Corman's hand, and, quite reflexively, Corman brought the gun up and hit the man on the side of the head. The colonel fell heavily to the floor, half out, moaning slightly. The girl screamed once before Corman caught her, pinioning her from behind, putting a hand over her mouth to muffle the next scream while he stood listening, his heart beating wildly, expecting to hear the shuffling feet of the maid in the hallway at any moment. He heard nothing.

"Now listen to me," Corman said to the woman. "I didn't want to do that, but I didn't have any choice. Now I don't want to hurt you, but I can't take the chance of getting caught. Do you understand me?"

The girl nodded and he released her. She stood looking at him, breathing heavily. The colonel was stirring slightly now. "He'll be all right," Corman said. "But I'm going to have to ask you to tie him up."

"You expect me to help you?" the girl said.

"You don't have any choice," Corman said. "Get one of the inn robes out of the closet and tear it into strips."

The girl glared at him a moment and then shrugged and went to the closet. She was well shaped, in her early twenties, not at all self-conscious in her black slip, a type of woman he had seen many times before.

The February Plan

She had a slightly petulant lower lip and bored eyes, as if nothing in life really interested her greatly. Corman could not help but think that he was doing the colonel a favor now. The affair would not survive this indignity, and the colonel would be better off for it. She took out a robe and began to tear it into strips.

"Is that the colonel's car out there?" Corman said.

"Mine."

"Where are the keys?"

"His pocket, I guess." She had torn three long strips off the robe. "Is this enough?"

"Yes. Tie his hands behind him."

She shrugged and moved to the colonel who was just beginning to come around now, his eyes half aware of what was going on, but still too stunned to do anything about it. Corman found the keys in the colonel's jacket which was hanging next to the girl's dress and a full-length mink coat. The colonel's overcoat was lying on the floor.

Once the colonel was bound, Corman inspected the strips, found them tight, efficient. The girl stood watching him. "Now I suppose you're going to tie me up too." she said. It was not a question.

"No," he said, on impulse. "Put your clothes on. I'm taking you with me."

"You're making a mistake," she said evenly. She eyed him coolly for a moment and then began to get dressed. Keeping an eye on her, Corman gagged the colonel and then collected the colonel's uniform, carrying it to the far side of the room, emptying his pockets in a pile, undressing hurriedly, putting on the uniform. It was a trifle large, but he could count on the overcoat to conceal the misfit. He went through the pockets, discarding everything except a wallet, money, some mimeographed orders, and a pack of cigarettes. Gathering up his own things, he stowed them away, transferring the pistol to the right pocket of the overcoat.

The girl was dressed now, wearing a tight black sheath which looked completely out of place here, the mink coat draped over one shoulder. Whatever nervousness she might have felt was under full control now, but her eyes were still defiant.

"Let's get a few things clear," Corman said, putting on the colonel's hat. "I have nothing to lose, you remember that. We're going out of here without any noise. None. If we run into the maid, you're not to say one word. We're going to pick up our shoes at the entry and we're going out to the car. Do you understand?"

"Yes."

He led the way, opening the door to check the hallway before he waved her through. When they reached the entryway, he put on his shoes in a hurry, afraid that the maid might appear at any moment. She did not. The woman put on her red shoes, and he had the feeling that she was not going to give him any trouble. He opened the outside door, bracing himself against the cold. "All right," he said. "Let's go."

At the car, he opened the door from the driver's side. Without a word she got in and slid across. Once he was in, he clicked on the dash light to acquaint himself with the gears and then turned on the ignition. The motor caught immediately, and he turned around and drove out onto the road.

"Now," he said, once they were headed east. "What's your name?"

"Ginger will do."

"I want your full name."

"Ginger Stevenson," she said. "Mrs. William Stevenson. May I have a cigarette?"

He gave her the pack he had taken from the colonel. She struck a match and lighted it for herself. In the brief flare of the match he could see that she was more curious than afraid.

"I want to know where you came from tonight, what time you got to the inn, how you got connected with the colonel."

"Are you just curious or do you have a reason?"

"I may have to do some talking at the roadblock. I don't want to be tripped up."

"My husband is a captain in the IG," she said. "We came up to Nikko on a party. We're due back in

The February Plan

Tokyo the day after tomorrow."

"And where does the colonel fit in?"

"I met him at the bar earlier this afternoon. We had a few drinks."

"Where did you go from there?"

"We drove on to Chuzenji and had a few drinks there."

"And how did you decide to come out here to the inn?"

"Come on now," she said chidingly. "I don't have to draw you any pictures, do I?"

"Yes," he said.

She shrugged. "We decided to go to bed, but we couldn't very well take a room at one of the big hotels. You know how the army is. So we drove out here."

"What time did you arrive at the inn?"

"About an hour before you broke in on us."

"What do you know about the colonel?"

"He's stationed in Yokohama; he's on leave; he has a wife in the States, and he's prowling. That's all I know about him."

"What's his name?"

"Armbruster, Henry J. His friends call him Hank."

"When you drove out from Chuzenji, did you see a roadblock?"

"No." She smoked her cigarette in silence for a moment. "What are you going to do with me?"

"I don't know. Does that frighten you?"

"Nothing frightens me. What are you running from? What did you do? Did you kill somebody?"

"No," he said. "Do you know about the missile base near here?"

"I don't keep up with things like that."

"Well, there is one," he said. "And it's been taken over by a group of conspirators who intend to launch a nuclear warhead against a Chinese city tomorrow. I won't go into details, but I have to get to Tokyo if I'm going to have a chance of stopping them." She said nothing, continuing to smoke her cigarette. "You don't believe that?" he said.

She shrugged slightly. "I don't know."

"It happens to be true."

She said nothing more, and he was amazed by the lack of reaction in her, as if it really made no difference to her one way or the other. He concentrated on the road. After twenty minutes he saw the blinking lights through the screen of snow and he slowed down, his stomach tightening as the Air Force truck took shape ahead and to the side of the road. There was a crew of men around it, and a winch on the rear of the truck was slowly grinding a cable down into the gorge. They had not blocked the road, and for a moment he thought about gunning the accelerator and shooting past the men who stood at the side of the truck, but he knew that would be a fatal mistake. A colonel would be interested in what was going on. Corman slowed the car. "I don't want a word out of you," he said to the woman. "Not one word."

As the car stopped, an Air Force sergeant detached himself from the group of men and approached the car, saluting when he saw the uniform. Corman began to breathe easier. The sergeant's face was not familiar. Corman returned the salute.

"What's going on here, Sergeant?" Corman said.

"An accident, sir."

"Anything I can do to help?"

"Nothing, sir. Everything's under control."

Corman nodded. The sergeant saluted again. Corman shifted into gear again and the car moved down the road.

"You're nervous, aren't you?" the woman said, her voice slightly amused in the darkness. "That shook you up, didn't it?"

"Yes," he said.

"They'll kill you if they catch you, won't they?"

"Very likely. I don't want to talk any more."

He could feel the shrug of her shoulders in the darkness, and it occurred to him what a terrible mistake he had made in bringing her along. She reminded him of a self-centered girl he had known in Darien, Connecticut, who had lived in a perpetual search for excitement, driving too fast, drinking too much, interested in nothing except as it affected her, experimenting with sensations as if bored by anything

The February Plan

commonplace, feeling happy only when she could test everything and everybody around her to the limit. He had never understood her, and despite the fact that she was good in bed and a lively companion, he could not stand the nervous tension she generated and had soon left her for a quieter way of life. A few months later he read in the papers where this glowing girl from Darien had been found dead from an overdose of narcotics. Ginger reminded him of the girl from Darien—not physically, no; that girl had been blond, very small, but emotionally they were sisters. They had the same hunger for the different. Once he reached Chuzenji, he would have to find a way to leave her behind.

He reached the main highway, turned south, bracing himself for the test that lay ahead, anticipating the roadblock long before he actually saw it. The Japanese police had erected a partial barrier across the road, letting the traffic through one car at a time, and Corman found himself behind an ancient bus which would have blocked him in, even if he had wanted to make a run for it. He could count at least six Japanese officers around the two parked patrol trucks, all of them armed.

A Japanese policeman descended from the bus, waving it on, beckoning to Corman to pull up. He was a short man with a round face, and he came up to the car with a flashlight, shining it first on Corman and then on the girl.

"What is your destination, please?"

"Nikko," Corman said.

"May I see your identification, please?"

Corman took out the colonel's wallet and removed the mimeographed orders, handing them to the policeman who flashed his light on the paper. "Very good, Colonel Wilcox," he said, handing them back. "But there will be a delay, I am afraid. The road to Nikko is closed by the snow at the moment."

"How soon will it be opened?"

The Japanese smiled and shrugged. "Sometime tomorrow, I regret. When the snowplows can clear it. You may proceed."

Corman eased the car forward. The lights of the

roadblock faded behind him, and he pulled off on the shoulder of the road, clicking on the dash light to look at the orders. They were made out in the name of Colonel Lawrence A. Wilcox. He looked at the girl. She smiled. "You're pretty quick on your feet," she said.

"I should tie you up and dump you in the snow right here," he said angrily.

"You could do that," she said, snubbing out her cigarette. "But I don't think you will. I helped you through the roadblock, you know. I could have spoken up and they would have had you there, just like that. You wouldn't have had a chance against all those policemen, and you don't look like the type to fight it out."

"Why didn't you?" he said.

"I left Nikko with the colonel this afternoon because I was bored, looking for something different," she said simply. "And this is it. Maybe I can help you."

"Why?"

"For kicks," she said. "What else?"

He turned off the dash light and edged the car into the road again.

2

The major sat in the communications room, watching the men, listening to the whirring clatter of the machines. How much better it would be if he did not have to deal with men at all, if they could be replaced by machines that would accomplish the same function. If a machine broke down, the point of error could be tracked and repaired, the circuits restored, and you could predict its reliability. Not so with a man; no, you had no way of knowing what went on in that tissue labyrinth of brain cells, that complicated psycho-chemistry, no way of predicting what erratic behavior would pop up, no way of charting the secret currents of thought.

Twenty-nine hours. He put an X on the paper, circling it, projecting that X onto a mental image of the

The February Plan

city. Target, ground zero, the Worker's Science Hall, a scant eighth of a mile from the stadium in case they decided to use it, a quarter of a mile from the gaseous diffusion plant, no matter at all these small distances. They were all within the circle. Probable error, ± 4 miles (on the Pacific Range, fired from Vandenburg, the error had been 9, infinitesimal considering the power of that fireball), but still, if he had been given the choice, he would have preferred two missiles, double the chance, with one targeted for the river itself, the natural valley, cutting out the city like a curved scalpel scooping out diseased tissue. But one would do it. He was grateful for the one.

As Sloan approached, a troubled expression on his face, the major turned the paper upside down. Sloan's clothes were rumpled and untidy, as if he had been sleeping in them. His upper lip was beaded with sweat; his armpits were ringed. "We have a report back from the search crew," he said. "They didn't find a body in the wreckage of the jeep. Apparently Corman jammed it in low gear, pointed it toward the gorge, and jumped."

"So the wreckage is clean," the major said with a tight smile. "And where did you get this information?"

"From security. From Strickland."

"And that's his story, is it?"

"Not his story," Sloan said, a trifle bewildered. "I monitored the dispatch from the truck myself. Strickland just repeated it to me."

"I see," the major said. The pencil began a tattoo against the desk. "A radio message—now how much credence can we give an authority like that? Are you sure, for instance, that the message came from the radio on the truck?"

"Yes," Sloan said. "It was coded."

"Do you know any of the men who searched the wreckage? I mean, do you know them well?"

"Peters and Johnson. I know them pretty well."

"Do you trust them?"

"Yes. I've worked with both of them, Johnson in West Germany, Peters in Italy. Maybe you'd better fill me in, Major. What point would they have in falsifying a report about Corman?" The major studied him carefully, admiring Sloan's technique, the precisely timed blunt question which was supposed to trigger an equally candid answer. How old was Sloan—thirty-five, perhaps? Not nearly old enough to work something like this on a man with the major's experience. "What do you think, Sloan?" he said.

"I can't see that they'd have any reason at all."

"Are you afraid of death?" the major asked bluntly.

"Of course," Sloan said.

"Then there's your answer," the major said. "Dedication is one thing, Sloan, but we're all human beings, and anyone can have a change of heart. It could happen in anybody. Now, suppose for the sake of argument that one of those men on the truck decided that he wanted out. And suppose he found Corman's body there and realized that that particular threat to security was finished, done with. But, if he could persuade us that Corman's body was *not* found, that he had somehow escaped, then there would be a small chance that somebody here would change his mind and call off the mission. Because we can do that at any time, you know. We can cancel the whole project and turn the base over to the Japanese as scheduled, and that's that."

Sloan looked at him quizzically. "That's pretty farfetched, Major."

"Maybe so," the major said. "But you have to guard against the little things, the subtle things. That's the only way you can cut down the odds against error. Now, the project is most secure as long as it is contained in this base. If we mount a full-scale search for Corman, disperse our men, so to speak, then there's a greater chance of something leaking out. That's elementary logic. It would be very easy for someone to try to use that against us." He looked off toward the machines. "I want you to talk to Johnson and Peters separately. Make a comparison. I want a report as soon as you can get it."

"All right," Sloan said, but he was obviously not pleased by the order. The major watched him walking away. He carried himself too rigidly, not enough give

The February Plan

to the knees, not enough spontaneous swing to the arms, as if he were holding himself in. That could come from fatigue. It could also come from a sense of relief that he had carried off a deception and gotten away with it.

The major leaned back in the chair and lighted a cigar, smoking it casually. He owed it to himself to have the cigar; it was his reward. He also owed it to his men to let them see that he was relaxed, unconcerned—proof that everything was going well.

The blue smoke wreathed about his hands lying on the desk blotter, palms up, and he regarded them with admiration as if they were not his, seeing them objectively; yes, it was necessary to preserve a perspective, and these hands were steady as a rock, not a tremor in the tendons of the fingers, the tips sensitive, reliable. The question was, could these hands of his do the job when so many lives depended on them? He was certain that they could; he had no doubt.

The fuse was highly sensitive, yes, and behind that ring of polished mirror metal was a spring, tightly wound, like the spring in a fine clock, and when the cylinder was pulled out, even so much as an inch, the spring would expand and the bomb would explode, so it was vital for his left hand to ease out on the cylinder until the index finger of his right hand—oh, that well-trained, perceptive digital member—could ease over the unburred lip of metal and keep the spring tight, safe, until his left hand, operating independently, could lower the cylinder to the ground and then go back to remove the firing pin and render harmless the ingenious treachery of the spring. The report would read, with characteristic simplicity, "Bomb disarmed. Hansberry."

His mind jerked to with a start. He withdrew his hands from the table, disconcerted. That bomb had been disarmed in Algiers ten years ago; he had not used the name "Hansberry" in nine. Fatigue, he thought. Insidious. He raised himself from the chair, standing motionless for a moment, testing himself, daring any part of his body to betray him. He removed one of the pills from the silver case he always carried.

He turned the pill over in the light of the lamp until he could see the faintly stamped S of the pharmaceutical house, and then he checked it again, pressing it against his tongue, reassured by the metallic, bitter taste.

He waited, watching the water cooler until Phillips, who was approaching it, had removed a paper cup from the dispenser on the wall, held it beneath the spigot, pressed the button with his thumb, gulped the water down. Safe. Phillips returned to his desk. The major drew a cup of water from the bottle and washed the pill down, standing in the doorway of the teletype room, watching the rows of machines chattering away as if they generated the information they transmitted, hundreds of words a minute, keys clicking, carriages turning, whacking back to begin again. Millions of words, a ceaseless tide, an inundation of ink. Phillips tended them, moving from one to the next and then to the next, occasionally ripping off a rectangle of paper and handing it to a man at the computer. Reynerson was his name. He was bald-headed. His scalp shone unhealthily in the fluorescent light.

The major's mind was clear now; the fatigue had fled away from him.

He wrote out a dispatch in longhand concerning the accident in the Hole, leaving it purposely vague and ambiguous, and then he appraoched Phillips with it. "I want this typed up," he said. "Get one copy over to the general right away and then send the dispatch to Langley."

"Yes, sir," Phillips said. "What priority?"

"Immediate," the major said. "And tell Palnau I want to see him right away."

"Palnau?" Phillips said, mystified.

The major blinked. "Forget it," he said. "When Sloan gets back, I'll be in my room."

"Yes, sir."

He went up the stairs to the second floor, angry with himself. Palnau was dead, buried at sea off Hong Kong, nonexistent, how many years? His heels clicked along the wooden corridor, the wrong material. He had ordered quarry tile for his house, a burnt red, indestructible, assured that the tile would outlast both

The February Plan

him and the house. A thousand years from now, what would they make of it, those archaeologists who dug down and found the bare pattern of that tile along a wall-less hallway, a corridor leading from nowhere to nowhere.

He opened the door and made a tour of his room, clicking on the lamps and the electric heater against the musty chill, rubbing his hands together briskly, setting a fire in the fireplace, watching the flames lick up around the small logs from the wood box. He laid out his writing things on the desk—blank paper, a bottle of ink from which he would fill his pen—then he took out his bulging file of material and thumbed through it on the off-chance that his memory might be sparked by it to remember something he had forgotten. But everything was all there, concise up until this moment, all contained, everything taken care of. He examined his pockets, finding the rumpled dispatch from the Chinese operative, and he smoothed it out for insertion in the folder, first deciding to add his comments at the bottom. "Unnecessary complication," he wrote in a cramped hand. "Kept black. No further action."

Once that was out of the way, he was now up against a greater difficulty, one which he had been avoiding because he had not yet found the words to put it in, and he knew that when they were studying this report back in Washington, they would seize on this critical action, examining it from every angle, and he would not have them shaking their heads and saying, "The major made his mistake here," or Goddamnit, why would he do something like that?" He would not give them that satisfaction, no, not one ounce of it. This report had to be perfect, just as the operation itself had to be without flaw, so that when the thing was done, long after he himself was dead, there would be that undercurrent of legend within the agency, or if talk of it were suppressed, a legacy of legend surrounding this one magnificent exploit.

"I have too much ego," he wrote on the paper, communicating with the men of the future whose faces he could not see. "This should be watched most carefully in men selected for later programs, for in our business a man must be able to submerge himself, lose all sense of identity and personal will, and I have never been able to do that. Or perhaps there should be a balance struck, so that a man still strives for perfection and in perfection gratifies that unquenchable instinct for self-glorification which might jeopardize a project."

He read over the words he had just written and decided to let them stay. Yes, they were important; they deserved a place here. He plunged on, recording in black ink the basic weakness of an operation like this, the desire for survival that watered down a man's determination. He recorded his suspicion of the general, of Sloan (he would save Wilkinson for a more exhaustive treatment), and of most of the men connected with the project. If he had this to do again, he would never make the prospects seem so final, and he would leave at least one small mental loophole which a man's hope for survival might wiggle through, one little out, a way that a man could participate in something like this and remain alive when it was done.

For all of them knew that at the end they would be killed, that there was no possible escape from the consequences of their actions, and this made them balance the virtue of the act against the price they would be forced to pay, and this could only lead to self-doubt. He scribbled rapidly, furiously against the paper, led by this recommendation into his ideas about the trial which should follow the launch. It should not be held by the United States, nor should the United States insist on supervising, overseeing, controlling, for it must not appear in any way that the United States was trying to cover her complicity or foreknowledge. No, it would be best if the defendants in this trial were turned over to the United Nations or some international court, perhaps The Hague, where the enemies of the United States could prosecute with undiminished vigor, and the subsequent executions should be suitable to the crime. He paused, scribbling suggestions. "Garroting? Hanging? Guillotine?" Something heinous, yes, an extreme ignomy.

But he was getting off the subject. He was here to

The February Plan

defend his point of view concerning his current actions—facts, not subjective feelings, not recommendations concerning his own demise. Security, yes. He recorded Corman's escape in detail, Wilkinson's complicity. Then why had he not arrested Wilkinson, put him in detention? "I feel that Wilkinson is part of a larger plot," he wrote, "one point in a circle, and it would be of greater jeopardy in this project to confine him—that is a part of their plan—for by confining him, isolating him, the rest of them could function in complete safety. But this way I feel certain Wilkinson will implicate the others."

He blotted the ink on the paper and leaned back in the chair, capping his pen, putting it back in his pocket, incredibly tired now, comforted by the thought that there would be an end to all this, and very soon. A little over twenty-four hours and he would be through here, leaving the mop-up to Ladish, and he would apply for a month's leave and take Mildred and the children to Florida for a while. The hot sun, the warm beach, the incredible luxury of being himself. But first there was the chore of the President's palace, that ancient and beautiful building which had been stripped of its ornamentation by the revolutionaries, reduced to a marble barracks by the bearded barbarians, with garbage piled in the corners and dog shit on the floors. The executions would be held at sea—no better place, the weighted sacks cleaving the water, leaving no mark except a ripple.

He took off the webbed belt and the holster, laying them beside him on the bed as he stretched out. His head was beginning to ache now. In the flickering firelight he saw a tiger on the wall opposite the foot of his bed, a great striped Bengal moving through a screen of bamboo with delicate leaves and gently swollen joints. He sat up, shaking the cottony thoughts out of his head. There was work to be done. Corman, of course, Corman. He must find out whether Corman was among the quick or the dead.

There was a discreet rapping on the door. The major swung his legs off the bed, standing erect, pulling the jacket of his uniform down. "Come in, Ladish," he said.

The door opened and Sloan came in. The major blinked at him. "What do you want?" the major said.

"You asked for an immediate report."

"Yes, of course, Sloan. What did you find out?"

"I checked out Peters and Johnson. There's no discrepancy there. The wreckage was clean."

The telephone rang. The major's eyes moved to it and then to Sloan and finally to the belt and pistol lying on the bed. Sloan's eyes were wary, a little bewildered as the telephone continued to ring and the major made no move to answer it. "Would you like me to get it?" Sloan said.

"Yes, you answer it," the major said.

As Sloan crossed the room to pick up the telephone, the major stepped to the bed, slinging the belt around his waist, fastening it, checking the pistol in the holster. He would have to be very careful now.

"It's the general, Major," Sloan said, extending the telephone toward him.

The major nodded, taking the telephone from Sloan, continuing to watch him. "Yes?"

"Major, I want to know what in the hell is going on," the general said angrily. "I just got a call from the Pentagon asking about the radioactive leakage. They wanted to send a team of specialists in here from the States to take care of it."

"I sent you a duplicate report on that," the major said.

"I don't have any goddamn duplicate anything."

"Sloan was supposed to get it to you." He told the general what had happened, the emergency of the revised schedule which had demanded an immediate stall, the story he had used. "I'm sorry about the mixup."

"You should be," the general said. "It damn near cost us the shoot. But I covered and said I'd fill them in."

"I'm sure they have it by now," the major said. "I sent a dispatch to Langley."

There was a pause on the line. The general was

thinking. "Major," he said, "I want you to close down your communications there, have them relayed over here. I want our communications consolidated. That should take care of any more mix-ups."

"I don't think that's practical, General."

"Don't put me off. I've checked with our boys here. It's a simple matter. I want it done. We're not in any rivalry, Major. We're both after the same thing. And I don't want any more mistakes."

"All right," the major said. "I'll take care of it."

He put down the phone and it rang again almost immediately. This time it was Strickland. "We've had a report on Corman," Strickland said. "He went through the Chuzenji roadblock about twenty minutes ago."

"How did he get through?"

"He took the uniform off a colonel who was shacked up with a woman in an inn west of the highway. He took the woman's car and forced the woman to go along with him, and when he showed the colonel's papers, the Japanese officers at the roadblock didn't suspect a thing. We wouldn't have found out about it except that the maid found the colonel tied up and reported it to the police."

"I want an immediate block on the Nikko toll road," the major said.

"I've already set it up. But the road's snowed in anyway and won't be cleared for a while."

"Put our men on it, for God's sake. I don't want Corman slipping through again."

"Yes, sir."

"I want an immediate blackout of all telephone and telegraph between Nikko and Tokyo."

"There's no way we can do that, Major, not without a hell of a row with the Japanese government. They have a lot of official lines running on that trunk."

"Then set up a monitor. I don't give a damn how you do it, but I want it done."

"Yes, sir."

"Do you have men tracing the car?"

"I've got a team on it, but I don't expect anything soon. I put a block on the Ashio road, in case he plays a long shot and tries to make it out that way. But there are a hundred places where he could hole up. It may take some time to flush him out."

"I'll take charge of the search myself," the major said. "I want a dozen of your men to meet me at the toll roadblock within the hour."

"Yes, sir."

Putting the telephone down, the major lighted a cigar, demonstrating his calm. "I want all our communications moved to the Hole," he said to Sloan. "I want all our lines maintained and I want it accomplished without a moment's breakdown in communications. Can you do that for me?"

"Yes, sir. I think so."

"Now, I want a car from the motor pool with a two-way radio and a driver-operator."

"Yes, sir."

"If there are any more calls from Langley for me, you will relay the code number to me. If I think it's important enough to interrupt my work for, I'll come here to complete it. And one more thing—under no circumstances will the military be permitted to dominate our communications. They would like to take credit for this whole operation if we give them half a chance. But we're going to see that they don't get it. That's all, Sloan."

"Yes, sir."

As Sloan left the room, the major sat down again at his desk and opened the folder, recording the general's command and the time. He put the folder away and then he put on his overcoat and went downstairs to await the arrival of his car.

3

Once he had reached Chuzenji, Corman stopped the car on the lake road, looking through the glove compartment until he found a map of the area, very much aware of the girl sitting beside him, watching every move he made. He spread the map out on his knees under the dash light to study it. The odds were against him now that the Nikko road was temporarily closed. He could wait for it to be cleared, knowing it was the fastest route out of here, but that would take far too long and he could not wait. Once the deception was discovered, they would block off the Nikko road at both ends, trapping him in the middle. The guard at the toll booth would undoubtedly remember the car and the red-haired woman. He abandoned the idea. There was another road twisting to the south beyond Chuzenji toward the town of Ashio, feeding into a network of backroads. He put his finger on it. "Have you ever been down here?" he asked Ginger.

"Once," she said.

"What are the roads like?"

She shrugged. "Pretty bad," she said. "I was looking for a fortuneteller who's supposed to have one clear eye into the future. We never did find her. But then, none of the roads were marked and my driver was drunk. And speaking of refreshment, is there anyplace around here where we can get a drink?"

"No," he said. He shifted the car into gear and moved off into the darkness, driving through the darkened village. He got lost twice before he found the Ashio cutoff. The sky lightened in the east and the sun pulled itself over the mountains, and his luck ran out. He shifted the tiny car into low, following a poor road which twisted up a precipitate grade, the ice thickening on the roadbed with each foot of added elevation, until finally he rounded a hairpin curve to find that he could go no farther. The road ahead was under ten feet of snow, the result of an avalanche which had sheared off the steep slope above it. He groaned inwardly, glancing at the girl. She was wrapped up in the mink coat, dozing, her face barely visible above the collar.

Well, he thought, it made no sense to fight the problem. He lighted a cigarette, trying to think it through. The immediate problem was the girl and what he was going to do about her. It was likely that the alarm would be out very shortly anyway, and if he let her out here, it would take her at least an hour and a half to walk back to the village to report what had happened to her to the police, and she would be a distinct liability to him if he decided to take her along. She was completely unpredictable, and the acquiescence she had displayed so far was likely to change momentarily when she decided she had had enough of this particular game and wanted out.

On the other hand, she represented the only tangible chance he had. He would have to dump the car now and find a way to get back to the hotel, hoping that the sailor would still be there and that he could be persuaded, by either money or patriotism, to co-operate. But if the sailor was not there, if his plans had worked out and he had gone away with his Japanese girl, then Corman would be completely on his own again. In that case the girl would be indispensable, if he could bring her around to his point of view. He would have to take her along.

He shifted the car into reverse, backing it around to the shoulder of the road, inching forward until he had room to back again, and then he straightened it out and went down the mountain toward Chuzenji. He had lost valuable time and the protection of darkness, but still it was not too late. He would find a deserted side road, dump the car in the lake, and then figure out an inconspicuous approach to the hotel.

By the time he reached the village, he found that he had reckoned without the change which the warm sunshine had brought to Chuzenji. The patrons of the inns and hotels, after being shut in by bad weather for so long, had spilled out into the countryside with a vengeance. The hiking paths were swarming with them. The traffic was quite heavy in the village itself, the cars stacked up behind a crawling snowplow which was clearing the main road, and he found himself boxed in behind a truck full of skiers on their way up to the Yunoko slopes, a group of young Japanese in brightly colored sweaters. They grinned and waved at him as he crept along behind them. Ginger had come awake by now, blinking the sleep out of her eyes a little glumly, lighting a cigarette. "Where are we?" she said.

"Back in Chuzenji. The Ashio road was closed."

"You're doing fine then," she said, peering out the window at the sun, taking a pair of sunglasses out of her purse and slipping them into place. "They're bound to have discovered the colonel by now." She smiled

The February Plan

slightly. "I feel sorry for him, you know that? He had quite an ego, not to mention his id—oh, that galloping id."

He grew tenser by the minute. The time margin was stretching thin, and the alarm was certainly out for him by now. At any moment he could expect to run up against another roadblock or a patrol, and in this tangle of traffic he would have no room to maneuver. At his first opportunity he spun the steering wheel sharply to the left, skidding into a snow-covered road which he was certain would take him to the lake.

"It would make this more interesting," she said, "if I knew who was after us."

"You name it," he said, breathing a little easier, now that he was away from the crowds. "The military, the Central Intelligence Agency, the Japanese police."

"All because of this bomb business," she said in a matter-of-fact voice.

"Yes."

"What's your name? You never did tell me."

"Phillip Corman."

She did not recognize it. "Is that your real name?"

"Yes."

In a few minutes he rounded a clump of snow-covered trees to see the lake glistening in front of him and he stopped the car. "I think you'd better come with me," he said.

"What are you going to do?"

"I'm looking for a place to dump the car."

"And you don't trust me enough to leave me here, is that it?"

"That's it," he said. He opened the car door for her and helped her out, leading the way up the road to a slight promontory which offered him an unobstructed view of the lake. Below him, a hundred yards away, was a wooden pier which ran perhaps fifty feet out into the water. In better weather it was a base for the red and blue rowboats which were now upended in the snow along the banks, but now it was deserted. He took Ginger back to the car and then drove to the pier before he stopped. "All right," he said, "climb out."

"How can you be sure I won't make a run for it?"

He glanced at her shoes. "I don't think you can move very quickly in those heels."

"You'd be surprised," she said with a smile. She got out of the car and stood to one side of the pier, using the time to examine her face in her compact mirror and put on fresh lipstick. He shifted into gear and very slowly inched the front wheels onto the wooden planking. At that moment he heard a shout and turned to see a troop of what appeared to be Japanese Boy Scouts streaming out of the woods and running down the slope toward him. They were shepherded by a tall, middle-aged Japanese who carried a walking stick and wore a helpful smile.

"Get back in the car," Corman said to Ginger, pushing open the door on her side. For a moment she appeared to hesitate, looking toward the boys as if she had no intention of doing what he said. He took the pistol out of his pocket, holding it low where she could see it but the boys could not. "I mean it. Get in."

She sauntered toward the car, easing herself into the seat. He put the pistol back in his pocket and jammed the shift into reverse, stepping on the accelerator. The tires whined and then caught. The car shot backward into a snowbank. Cursing, Corman shifted into low. The wheels spun helplessly. He looked up to see the scoutmaster approaching, scolding the boys gently, telling them to stand back, not to touch the car. Corman looked to Ginger. "I mean it, keep your mouth shut. Let me do the talking."

The scoutmaster came up to the side of the car, smiling as he bowed to Corman. "May I inquire if you are having difficulty, sir?"

"I seem to be stuck," Corman said.

"You would permit assistance, sir?"

"I'd appreciate it very much."

The man examined the car, stepping over to peer at the back wheels, straightening up before he gave orders to his boys. He stood back, leaning on his walking stick while the boys clambered into the snowbank, putting all their weight against the back of the car, rocking it free. Corman gunned the engine. The car pulled away

The February Plan

and he kept it moving, honking his horn in response to the boys who stood waving and cheering behind him.

"What time is it?" he said, as they approached the highway.

"Ten o'clock."

He would have to assume that they knew he was past the roadblock now. He could not risk another chance at the lake.

"Tell me something," she said. "Would you have shot me back there at the lake?"

"I don't know," Corman said.

He drove across the highway and cut off into a narrow lane toward the Chuzenji Temple and then followed an even narrower road off that, attracted by the roof of a country house he could see through the trees. There was no smoke coming out of the chimneys, and the snow on the approach road had not been disturbed. Pulling up to the front of the house, he stopped the car and got out to have a look around, taking the keys with him.

It was a European-style house, fairly small, with steep gables and a fieldstone chimney, a summer place. Apparently it had not been occupied for many months. Behind it he found a garage with the snow piled deep against the doors. Moving the car around where he could keep an eye on the girl, he spent a half hour getting the garage doors open, only to find the narrow space completely taken up by the hull of a sailboat, mounted on a small trailer. It took him another half hour to wheel the sailboat out of the garage and replace it with the car.

He had just closed the garage doors when he heard the spluttering whir of a helicopter, and he pulled Ginger back beneath the eaves of the garage. The sky was becoming overcast again, with a bank of gray clouds rolling in from the north, turning the sun into a steel-gray disc. He spotted the helicopter flying rather low over the trees, some distance to the west. It had the markings of the American Air Force.

He glanced toward the house. There was a screened porch on the rear. "We'll stay here awhile."

He pushed a hole in the screen, inserted his hand,

and unfastened the latch, but once he was on the porch, he found the house locked tight. He broke a window with a stick, clearing the glass away from the molding before he stepped over the sill, pushing through the hanging draperies. The room was dark, and all of the furniture was covered with sheets. He opened the door for Ginger. She noticed the fireplace immediately. "Do you think we could have a little heat?"

"No," he said flatly. "Somebody might see the smoke." He flipped a switch, trying the electricity, but it had been disconnected. He looked around for a telephone, but there was none. "We won't be staying here very long. We'll see if we can find anything to eat and then we'll move on."

He led the way through the dining room into the kitchen. He told her to sit down, and then he began to go through the cupboards methodically, finding nothing more than a few assorted cans and a container full of what appeared to be coffee. He found a pot and an alcohol burner beneath the cupboard, and he stepped outside to fill the pot with snow before he set the burner on the table and struck a match. Once the coffee was making, he sat down at the table to open the cans. One of the cans contained beans, the other two asparagus. He sluiced the beans onto two plates and put one of them in front of her.

"I'm not hungry," she said.

"Eat them anyway," he said. "We have a long way to go."

"Where are we going?"

"You'll find that out when we get there." He wolfed the beans down hungrily. She began to eat halfheartedly. "Were you going to ask those Boy Scouts for help?" he said.

She thought about it a moment and then shook her head. "I don't think so. If I had gotten away, I'd never have known what had happened to you, would I? I mean, it isn't the kind of thing to ever hit the papers, is it?"

"No. Out of curiosity, what will you tell your husband when this is all over?"

"Nothing," she said. "I don't explain myself to any-

The February Plan

body." She stood up, going over to the cupboard to search out a pair of cups, bringing them back to the table. Despite the predicament he was in, he found his interest piqued, his curiosity aroused, and he knew the writer was at work again. She was a beautiful woman, but she was much like so many of the Hollywood starlets he had seen in whom every movement was a practice in sensuality, as if they were imitating something they could never really achieve.

"What's his name?" he said.

"Who?"

"Your husband."

"Ralph."

"And Ralph doesn't give a damn what you do."

She poured the coffee into the cups. "He's West Point. Have you ever met the boys from West Point?"

"Yes."

"Then you know the type. The crew-cut boys in gray, who live for their service record and what goes on it. So he can't afford to care what I do as long as I don't get mixed up in anything. I mean, *really* mixed up in anything. He wanted to leave me in the States when he came over here, but I've always been interested in Zen, the contemplation of contemplation. But it's nothing, really nothing." She tasted the coffee, grimaced. "That's terrible," she said. "What's in it?"

"Chicory," he said. He heard the whirring of the helicopter again, this time quite close, and he went to the window, pulling back the curtain to peer into the sky, but he could not see it. Apparently it had flown directly over the house. He was not sure how much the helicopter pilot could see from the air, whether he could make out the fresh car tracks leading to this garage or the disrupted snow around the doors, but Corman had no illusions about the safety of this house. The longer he stayed here, the greater were the odds that he would be discovered. It was logical to assume that the major would seal off all roads out of this area that had not already been blocked by snow. He would set up checkpoints on all public transportation, and once he was sure Corman was bottled up in the area, he would bring in enough Japanese police to supplement his own force and begin a house-to-house search, concentrating on the heavily populated northwest quadrant of the lake.

Corman stood at the window a long moment, and when he turned around, the girl was gone. Her high-heeled red shoes still sat under the table. He went through the kitchen at a dead run, stopping short when he reached the living room. In the dimness of the room the girl was a dark form against the sheet covering the divan.

"What in the hell are you doing?" he said, catching his breath.

"Oh, come on," she said chidingly. "I want you to make love to me. Does that surprise you?"

"No, it doesn't surprise me," he said. "But this isn't the time or the place for it."

"Anyplace is the time for it," she said, a little impatiently. "Any time."

For the space of a second he was tempted, her presence there on the divan, her willingness, filling him with a pang of mental desire, for sexual arousal and a sense of danger were kindred emotions, and he was curious to know what she would be like. But he had passed that now; he was beyond the need for anything she had to offer him.

"Get up," he said flatly. "We're moving on now."

4

The major rubbed his gloved hands together, frowning at the dark and heavy sky, his breath steaming in the cold air. He turned back toward Ito with an expression of weary distaste. Ito was competent enough, the major supposed, with twenty years' service in the National Rural Police, and the roadblock was up to book standard, the police trucks angled to let the cars through, one at a time, but if the major had been doing it himself, he would have put the block farther down, near the toll booths. He did not mention it. His dissatisfaction was not really with the Japanese. He simply did not like to wait.

"How long has this road been open?" he said to Ito.

"Two hours now."

"You're absolutely sure they didn't get past you before I got here? Corman might have come through alone. He could have ditched the woman somewhere."

"He has not come through," Captain Ito said. "Traffic has been very light. No Caucasians."

The major turned back toward the pewter-colored lake which glinted dully through a stand of trees. Beyond it he could see the mountains, half obscured by the omnipresent mists. His vision was obfuscated by this goddamned weather; his eyes refused to register images sharply; his mind felt as dull and leaden as the lake.

Where was Corman? In the banks of trees perhaps, in one of the many country houses scattered around the coves, in one of the temples or shrines or inns, holed up, and he remembered a puzzle from his childhood, a page of simply drawn outlines of trees and a river, convoluted waves and complicated leaves, and below it was a list of objects hidden in that picture, the face of Abraham Lincoln, a log cabin, a shovel, a stovepipe hat. Try as he might, turning the picture to every conceivable angle, he could locate none of the objects, and his father had tried as well, studying it for what seemed like hours with equally fruitless results and the final conclusion that the puzzle-makers had made a mistake. There was nothing more to the drawing than what it appeared to be.

In this real landscape which confronted him now there was no such chance of mistake. Corman was trapped, and sooner or later he would be flushed out by the men looking for the car, that stab of red against the drab white, that bleeding wound of color in the snow. He had issued orders to shoot on sight—a shame, really, since that would preclude any chance of interrogating Corman in depth, but he could not take the chance that Corman would be picked up by one of the men who had not been included in the project. Odds were that Corman would not be able to subvert a trained agent, but there was a feeling of crisis in the air now, preoperation jitters, and he did not want any risk involved here, no matter how small. So Corman would be shot and this stray woman interrogated to see if he had passed anything on to her. Complications, the ever-widening ripples, but he would accept them. He would deal with them.

He turned on his heel, walking back to his car, refusing to get into the back seat because the motor was running and the interior of the car would be warm, and that was a seductive danger to a tired man. He opened the door only long enough to get his map case out of the back seat and then he closed it quickly, spreading a map against the cold side of the car, leaning against it, drawing lines to indicate the movements of his men.

Too slow, he thought, too goddamned slow as they flushed out the roads on the plain west of the lake, working back toward the highway and the village, another team making a sweep to the south. He could hear the crackling of the radio as the helicopters checked in, as the ground teams chatted back and forth.

He felt no excitement at the tightening of the net, knowing how laboriously ineffective these things could be, because this was one area in which a man could not have full control and there was always the element of chance and the possibility of human error. Wolkenstein came to mind, a large, hairy man with the mentality of a jack rabbit who had slipped through the lines of searchers again and again, simply because a man could not be efficiently observant every minute, because no mind could ever retain full alertness over long periods, and eyes sometimes saw without registering and ears took in sounds without hearing. At the end of that search in the Bavarian Alps, Wolkenstein had been found, of course, because one man was nothing against large numbers, but he was dead by then, frozen to death against a tree as if he had tried to embrace it for warmth, slumped to his knees at the snowy root, the face dead-white, hoary with frost that interlaced his beard with glittering strands of ice. How many dead men had the major seen in his career? How many of them had he been personally responsible for killing? Into what grotesque attitudes had they fallen in that parody of sleep? How many expressions were there for the fact of death, which in the end could not change or soften it but only impute to it an aura of impermanence, to pass away (slipping into shadows, as if not to be found again), to expire (the last breath released, containing the soul), to be wiped out (as if man were a mark, a stain, a smear). In the end it was all the same.

The net was tightening, but the major did not have time to wait now. He had not expected Corman to be so resourceful; no, there was often a wide gap between a man and his writings, and the imagination which ran free in the latter was rarely discernible in the former. When a man ran, when he felt pursued, it was a rare individual who did not panic, who could remain separate from the thought of his own imminent extinction, and he usually trapped himself. But Corman had not done this. The major would have to mentally upgrade the strength of Corman's resources, re-evaluate his potential. In this new view it was not likely Corman would be driving around in the outlying country, aimlessly hoping for an opening. No, he would ditch the car somewhere close to the center of population. That was his only hope. Since the car had not been spotted, it was logical to assume he had already gotten rid of it.

The major closed his map case and walked around the car to the field radio. "I want a shift in operations," he said to the operator. "I think Corman ditched the car in the lake somewhere this side of the river, where the highway parallels the lake shore. He couldn't have done it without leaving tracks. I want every foot of the shore gone over. Have Rover One move up from the south and commence the search north from the Chuzenji Temple. Rover Two is to start at the river on the north and come around south. After you relay the orders, pack up. We're going to move into the village. He's someplace close, we can count on that. And we're going to get him."

"Yes, sir," the radio operator said.

5

Sloan made one last tour of the communications room, testing the relays, making certain that everything was operative. It was his third check of the circuits and he knew it was ridiculous to be such a perfectionist, but that was the way he was. He had a strong affinity for his machines; he felt a proprietary interest in them, a love for them, and he took great pride in his ability to keep them functioning perfectly. When he was finished, he locked the door to the communications room and went upstairs to his quarters, feeling a little guilty about taking the time, but knowing that he was not likely to have another opportunity to write to Sister Angela, and it was important that she should understand why he was a part of this.

There was a chill in his room, but he did not mind. He would not be here long enough to light a fire. He had never been much of a letter writer or a man to put what he felt into words. He took out a sheet of paper and wrote laboriously, "Dear Sister Angela: By the time you read this, you will have heard many things about me, about what I have done. Some of them will undoubtedly be true, but I will not have the chance to explain why I did them." The pen faltered, scratched against the paper, and stopped. He read over what he had written and then crumpled the paper and dropped it on the floor. It was no damn good, he knew that, and he could hardly explain to her what he did not fully understand himself. He had never been vitally concerned over international politics or relating things to himself in abstract terms. He was a practical man, good with his hands, and that was about the size of it. And he had listened to the major and become convinced that this had to be done, not because of any stabilization of the balance of power in the world, but because he was convinced there would be another war unless it was done.

There was a bronze plaque set in the base of the flagpole in the square in front of the Home, and every morning when Sister Angela ran up the flag, she would ask the children to pray for the boys overseas, that their names would not be etched on the blank surface, that God would spare them. It was an excruciating time for him, for at this same ceremony she occasionally announced the name of one of the boys who had been killed, and once she had cried openly when there were five names to be announced at one time, and the tears ran down her cheeks until she could no longer continue. And once a month the plaque was taken out of the flagpole base, and Mr. Kukler, who was an excellent engraver as well as a teacher in shop, would add the latest names. Sloan had been ten at the time, and he had never been a communicative boy so he had never been able to tell Sister Angela how his heart ached for her when she stood at the morning ceremony or how he wept in the darkness of his room over something which he did not fully understand.

In essence, he supposed, it was as good a reason as any that he should have been willing to go along with the major, doing his part to slow down the creeping procession of metal plaques around that cement base, the casualties of Korea, Vietnam. Perhaps, at least partly due to his efforts, there would never be a plaque for the casualties of the Great China War.

In the end he simply wrote her a note to tell her that he loved her and was grateful, and then, on a separate sheet, he wrote a document that could be considered a holographic will, leaving all his assets to the orphanage after his death and telling her where to find his insurance policies and the key to his safety deposit box where he had a considerable sum in cash. He was sure there would be a considerable legal wrangle about this, and perhaps his insurance would not pay off under the circumstances, but the Home would at least get his savings and the lawyers could take appropriate steps to get the rest.

He signed both the letter and the will and put them in an envelope, putting Sister Angela's name on the front of it and the address of the orphanage. He left the envelope on his desk and was about to leave his room when the telephone rang. He picked it up to find Wilkinson on the line. "Thank God, I caught you," Wilkinson said. "I've got to talk to you. Come up to my room for a few minutes."

"I'll be right there," Sloan said.

He mounted the stairs with faltering steps. He had

never felt very much at ease around Wilkinson and thought him a little overbearing.

He found Wilkinson in bed, looking rather glassy-eyed and more than a little distraught, holding his head perfectly rigid on the pillow as if he was afraid it would come off if he moved it. "Thank God," Wilkinson said again. "I've been trying to reach you over at the Hole."

"I had to make a final circuit test," Sloan said, sitting down in a chair near the bed. "How are you feeling?"

"Terrible," Wilkinson said. "I can't move my head without seeing double. Zimmerman gave me something for it, but it just made me sick to my stomach. Now I have to know what's going on. Where is the major?"

"He's out after Corman," Sloan said.

"I knew it." Wilkinson groaned slightly. "Goddamn-it, I knew he was going to blow this thing. I knew it, but there wasn't anything I could do about it. How long's he been gone?"

"He left here after he talked to you."

"How many men has he got out there in the field?"

"I don't know for sure," Sloan said. "He's got most of security out there, fifteen or twenty of Strickland's men. And I know he alerted the Japanese police."

"He'll blow security higher than a kite with an operation like that. He's taking a hell of a chance. Get on the radio and see if you can't talk some sense into him."

"That's not likely," Sloan said.

Wilkinson was perceptive—he had to give him that—picking up this one expression of doubt and amplifying it immediately. "Then you've noticed it too," he said.

"It's been pretty obvious," Sloan said. "He's been calling everybody by the wrong names and he suspects everybody of trying to undermine him."

"I'm no expert on things like this," Wilkinson said thoughtfully, "but I think he's paranoiac."

"I don't know," Sloan said. "It may be that he's just worn-out. The way he drives himself."

"No, it's more than that. A man gets exhausted and

The February Plan

his mind slips a cog, maybe, but not like this. I've seen cases like this before, never as pronounced as this, but similar. It has to do with killing, I think. The major spelled it out for me. A man only goes so far in this business and then something snaps. I think it was the business of the children."

"The children?" Sloan said.

"The Chinese are holding a children's rally along with the science day. They're bringing a hundred thousand of them into Lanchow."

Sloan blinked. "A hundred thousand?"

"So he had his own personal dilemma right there," Wilkinson went on, thinking it through, paying no attention to Sloan now. "He originates a project, believes in it so completely he's willing to give his life for it, and then something like this comes along and his mind balks at it. He can't give it up, and at the same time he can't go through with it. So his mind snaps and so distorts things that it appears he is being forced to give it up, that he has no rational control over what's happening."

"You're sure about this children business?" Sloan said. "That's been verified?"

"He's had more than one dispatch from the Chinese operative," Wilkinson said. "He's got to be stopped, Sloan, you know that." He started to rise up from the bed, but the dizziness caught him and he sank down again. "I'm afraid you're going to have to do it," he said, irritated. "Goddamnit, the one time that I'm really needed, I can't even move."

"I'm going to have to do it?"

"At this point there's nobody else."

"I see," Sloan said, but he did not really see at all. He was seeing in his mind's eye a hundred thousand children all packed together in one place. He had been at a ceremony in the Imperial Plaza one summer in Tokyo where the children from the provinces had gathered to pay their respects to the Emperor, and from a vantage point in the Dai Ichi building he had looked down on the crowds, the swarms of them, the girls in bright flowered kimonos, the boys in their school uniforms, but he could not remember just offhand how many of them there had been. There could have been a hundred thousand of them there that day, very easily. "Maybe we could work a crisis in communications; that might bring him back."

"He's a shrewd man," Wilkinson said. "He's been at it long enough to know every trick in the book."

"Then I don't think he'll be taken in by that."

"There's only one answer," Wilkinson said, turning his head very slowly on the pillow to look at Sloan. His voice was quite steady. "You'll have to kill him."

"I don't know," Sloan said. "What about Corman? Do we just let him go?"

"Damn Corman," Wilkinson said. "He never was a real threat except in the major's mind. The Japanese police will keep him contained until it's too late for Corman to be of any harm to us. We're not talking about any long hauls. We shoot tomorrow. He has no time left. And the Japanese police aren't going to listen to any of his charges. They have a strong respect for anything official, and at the moment I'd be willing to bet you that the major has ordered them to shoot on sight. So we don't have to worry about Corman." He closed his eyes as if the dizziness was giving him trouble again. "That pitiful bastard," he said.

"I think we should notify the general," Sloan said.

"He's got his hands full," Wilkinson said. "We'll notify him after we take care of the major."

"And afterward, what comes next?"

"You come back here and sit tight; that's all we can do. From here on in it's the general's ball game, and all we can do is to see that he gets his turn at bat."

Sloan nodded. "Is there anything I can do for you before I go?"

"No. Zimmerman's due back here within the hour. You'd better get with it."

Once Sloan was outside, he took the time to light a cigarette. He was sick to his stomach. A hundred thousand children, and he was on his way to kill the man whose conscience could not take the thought of such multiple slaughter. It was inconceivable. His mind searched frantically for any way to bring this thing to a halt, to stop it now, but he had not been trained for such a capacity as this and he had been on enough projects by now to know that, once begun, they seemed to carry along of their own momentum, crushing obstacles. There was no possibility of calling anybody even if he had known whom to call, because he himself had helped plan the disablement of the local telephone lines and the monitoring of the Tokyo trunk. Even on his own communications system he would have difficulty getting through to Washington, and should he manage it, it was doubtful that anyone would believe him. No, there was nothing he could do about it, absolutely nothing, and he had never been independent enough to operate on his own. There had always been someone to give him orders before, to specify his actions, and he had orders now. He might not like them, he might rebel against the awful consequences, but he would carry them out. The major would be removed. The launch would go as scheduled.

He went down to his room again and, picking up the telephone, asked for a car to be sent around. The dispatcher told him there would be a brief delay since most of the vehicles had been commandeered by the major. Sloan did not push it. In his most patient voice he said he would wait.

6

Once he left the country house, Corman fell into a kind of stupefied nightmare that persisted throughout the afternoon. In the back of his mind he had now formulated a plan. He was not more than seven or eight miles from the hotel, and there was still perhaps twenty-four hours left before the launch, all the time he needed. He would get to the hotel and contact the sailor and offer him a great deal of money to take the tape to Mitsu's office in Tokyo. Mitsu's brother would know how to handle it and what to do with it, and the proof would be presented to responsible American officials who would take the initiative and put an end to the business at the base.

He left the house about noon, keeping the girl in front of him, following the path that wound from the rear of the house through the trees toward the crest of a ridge that angled in a general northerly direction and offered the hope of leading him toward the hotel. The girl was openly hostile now, sullen; she was discovering that what had seemed exciting to her in the car, the danger of the chase, had now turned into hard work and discomfort on foot. Her shoes offered little protection against the snow; her feet were wet and cold, and she was obviously miserable. They had not gone more than a hundred yards before she sank down against a rock wall, glaring up at him.

"Oh, come on," she said. "You don't expect me to go on with this. My feet are freezing. Let me go back down to the house. I'll give you as much time as you want before I go back to Nikko. I won't say a word to anybody."

At first he was sorely tempted. He was dead on his feet and he did not see how he was going to summon up enough energy to make it to the hotel on his own, much less with the girl in tow, but he simply could not take the chance on leaving her behind. He glanced up at the sky, the heavy overcast. The temperature was dropping. Very shortly it was going to be bitterly cold again, now that the sun was hidden.

"No," he said. "I'm sorry about this. I never should have taken you in the first place. But now that I have, you go all the way."

She wrapped her fur coat about her and with a flounce stood up and began to move up the path again. He followed close behind. They rested again in a dense grove at the top of the ridge, and he watched the helicopter moving far to the south, an insect against the clouds, making a lazy sweep from the mountain to the lake before it banked and came back again, following a pattern. He pushed on up the ridge, relieved to find the hiking trail deserted. The tourists had come out with the sunshine, and now the deepening cold had driven them back indoors again. Occasionally, through the early part of the afternoon, he heard laughter from the valley below, or the echo of childish voices yelling at one another, and at one point he saw a group of beginning skiers on a slope near the foot of the ridge, a

The February Plan

family, it seemed, a man and a woman and two children, and beyond them was a small house with smoke curling up from the chimney. Presently, when they had had enough of the snow, they would go inside where it was warm and the woman would put dinner on the table. He glanced around. Ginger was watching the family, too, and he could read her face; her thoughts were transparent. "You won't try it," he said quietly. "You'd never make it down the slope. And if you think that the man down there would risk his own wife and children to help you, forget it."

"You're a real bastard, aren't you?" she said, without much force. "I don't give a damn one way or the other, don't you know that? I'm not going to turn you in."

"I need you as a reserve, remember?"

"If you think I'm going to help you, you're crazy. I won't turn you in, but I won't lift a finger to help you."

He said nothing more. He waited for her to precede him up the ridge and then he walked close behind her. The going was cold, monotonous, and occasionally a flurry of snow fell, driven by a gust of wind, only to stop abruptly. He thought of Finley and wondered what she was doing at this moment, whether she had been informed of his escape. Probably not. She would be calm in any event, he knew that; there was a basic wisdom and strength to her. When this was over, he decided that he would ask her to marry him. It would not be the best thing for her, because he was set in his ways, egocentric, subject to moods of depression and occasional anxiety, but with her help perhaps he could get beyond the vagaries of his own nature.

At four o'clock he stopped short in the shelter of a giant fir, sinking down on the sheltered side of the massive trunk. The snow had started blowing again, and he was exhausted. "We'll take a break here," he said to her. She sat down beside him, taking a cigarette out of her purse, lighting it. "How much longer are we going to keep this up?" she said. "Where are we going?"

"To a hotel," he said, all talk an effort now. "There's a sailor there who's going to take something to Tokyo for me. At least I hope he's going to be there. And if he's not, then you're going to have to do it."

She exhaled the smoke. "Not me."

"I think you will," Corman said.

The snow was beginning to settle in the fine hair of the mink coat she wore, and her eyes were sharp as they studied him, and he realized that despite the condition of her feet and the fact that she was equally as exhausted as he was, there was a reserve of strength in her which he seemed to lack. She was gauging him, still looking for her chance.

"Do you think I'm going to stick my neck out for you?" she said.

"Not for me, no," he said. He stood up. The wind had stopped again, but the snow was falling, and as he was about to move on, he heard the crackle of a filtered voice from somewhere in the distance, a voice on a loud-speaker, and he moved on up the path, looking for a break in the trees where he could see down into the valley to his left. When he found it, he stopped short. He was looking down on what seemed to be a religious institution, a church of some sort with a multitude of smaller buildings dotted over the fairly level plain. The area was swarming with Japanese police who moved from one building to the next, directed by a man with a bull horn from a police truck. They were searching for him, he knew it instantly. Suddenly he heard the woman shouting, and he turned to see her starting down the hill, waving at the men in the valley. He was after her instantly, running back up the path and then down the uneven slope, slipping, falling down the side of the mountain, tackling her in the snow, pinioning her threshing arms and legs, clapping a hand over her mouth to keep her quiet. She struggled for a moment and then lay still. He raised his head up, peering through the bushes toward the valley.

The bull horn was drawing the men back to the truck now. Apparently the girl's attempt had gone unnoticed. He waited until he heard the sound of the truck sputtering into the distance and then he took his

The February Plan

hand off Ginger's mouth. "You're hurting me," she said.

He climbed off her, helping her to her feet, picking up one of her shoes and handing it back to her. He was breathing heavily now from the sudden exertion. "I don't want any more of that," he said.

She brushed the snow off her coat. "Did you expect me not to try?" she said, but for the first time he could see past the veneer, past the querulous petulance, the offhanded manner with which she had treated everything thus far, and she was scared, quite frightened by all this. She would never admit it, but she was, just the same.

"From now on you'll do exactly as I tell you," he said. "Now come along."

At the end of an hour he realized he had followed the ridge much too far to the north and found himself looking down on the far side of the village, and they were forced to retrace their steps. Night was coming on and the storm was growing worse by the minute. Twenty minutes more and he would be quite lost, unable to see anything at all. He came across a side path that wandered off on an abutting ridge to the west and he followed it, towing the girl by the hand, trusting that he would come out somewhere near the hotel before the last trace of light was gone from the sky. Finally he rounded a screen of snow-covered bushes, and there below him he saw the back of the hotel, its lights gleaming in the darkness, its parking lot almost deserted. He sat down on his haunches, keeping his hand on the girl's arm, trying to think. His reserve of strength was gone and his mind was dull.

Logically the major would have checked the hotel sometime during the day on the off chance that Corman might have returned here, but it was unlikely, considering the limited number of men the major had to work with, that he would have left more than one man here. That man would probably use the lobby as his base. Corman had no way of knowing this for sure, of course, and the man could very well be somewhere near the rear of the building, but the time for options was past. If they stayed here on the ridge much longer, the descent would be dangerous.

"We're going down to the hotel now," he said to Ginger, "and in through the service entrance. We'll take the service stairs to the third floor. If we run into any of the hotel staff on the stairs, you're going to remember that we're guests. I'm very tired now and I'm not going to try to run you down any more. I'll simply kill you and have done with it. I mean what I say. Now do you believe that?"

"Yes."

He stood up with effort, leading the way down the path and across the parking lot, opening the door with caution, peering into a deserted hallway. There was a staircase to the left. He heard the chattering of Japanese voices and the sloshing grind of what he took to be washing machines. Through a half-opened door down the corridor, their bodies wreathed by the steam from the machines, he saw a group of Japanese women folding sheets.

Taking Ginger by the arm, he hurried her into the stairwell and then looked her over. She looked terrible. Her hair was caked with snow and the fur coat was dripping. One look at her and anybody would know that she was not an ordinary guest who had been out for a stroll.

"What are you looking at?" she said.

"Never mind. There's nothing we can do about it now." He led the way up to the third floor, edging the door open into the corridor, closing it again quickly as a Japanese couple came out of a room and walked toward the elevator, a businessman and a woman in a kimono. They were arguing, the staccato growl of the man's voice occasionally punctuated by a sharp response from the woman. In a moment Corman heard the vibrating whir of the elevator through the walls as it climbed to the third floor. He waited until he heard the elevator descending, and then he led the way into the corridor.

He stopped at room 312 and rapped lightly on the door. There was no response from inside the room. Finally he tried the knob and was relieved to find that it

The February Plan

was unlocked. He pushed it open, allowing the girl to precede him before he closed it, clicking on the lights. Herbert Fields was not here, but he was very much in evidence. There was a half-empty bottle of bourbon on the dresser, and in the bathroom his shaving things were laid out above the lavatory. The bed was perfectly made, so Corman could assume that the sailor had not been back here since noon. The girl dropped her coat in the middle of the floor and then kicked off her shoes and sat down on the edge of the bed, massaging her feet. Corman took off his coat.

"You mind if I have a drink?" she said, eying the bottle on the dresser.

"We could both use one," he said. He found two fresh glasses in the bathroom and he poured a slosh of whiskey into each. "Water?"

"No," she said. "Straight."

He handed the glass to her and she sipped at it, lying back against the headboard now, looking at him. "So what comes now?" she said.

"We wait until the sailor who rented this room comes back."

"Do you know where he is?"

"No."

"Is he a friend of yours?"

"No."

"Then how do you know he's coming back at all?"

"I don't know for sure," Corman said. He downed the drink, gagging slightly at the raw whiskey against his throat. "I shared a cab with him on the way over here from Nikko a few days ago. He was coming up to spend some time with a Japanese girl."

She finished her drink. "Is there a tub in the bathroom?"

"I think so."

"Do you mind if I have a hot bath? I'm half frozen."

He went into the bathroom to check it. There was an exhaust fan in the ceiling but no windows. He came out into the room again. "All right," he said.

She extended her hand with the empty glass. "Another drink?"

"How many does it take to get you drunk?"

"More than there is in that bottle. Why?"

"I can't afford to have you drunk," he said. He poured her another drink and she carried it into the bathroom, closing the door behind her, but he heard no click of a lock. He poured himself another drink and sat down in the chair, stretching his legs out in front of him. Despite the warmth of the room, he was still chilled to the bone, and the whiskey was doing little to ease him. He picked up the telephone.

"This is Herbert Fields in three-twelve," he said to the operator. "Have there been any calls from Tokyo for me?"

"No, sir," the operator said. "I'm sorry, but the connections with Tokyo have not yet been restored."

"I see. Thank you." He put the telephone down, listening to the water running in the bathroom. He had been hungry earlier, but it had passed now, and he only considered the thought of food because it was likely to be a long night, and for a moment he thought about calling room service and having something sent up, but he decided against it. The one call to the switchboard had been risky enough. He could not compound it.

She turned the water off in the bathroom and he heard her splashing in the tub, and in a few minutes he heard the water draining. He lighted a cigarette. Shortly she emerged from the bathroom, her hair piled up on her head. She was wearing one of the bathrobes provided by the hotel with a large red calligraphic symbol on the back, and she had a fresh scrubbed look about her, as if by the ritual of the bath she had undergone a personality change. She poured another drink in her glass and sat down on the edge of the bed. "How about food?" she said.

"Sorry. We can't risk it."

She seemed to accept this. "Cheers," she said, and she emptied the glass, smiling slightly now. "Who in the hell would believe this?" she said, and he realized now from the tone of her voice that she was slightly drunk. "I start out to cheat on my husband with a colonel who has a roving eye, and I end up in a hotel twenty-four

The February Plan

hours later with a crazy civilian. You know, I think you really are crazy."

"Where is your husband?" Corman said quietly.

"A hotel in Nikko. Why?"

He did not stir from his chair. "The telephone lines into Tokyo are down," he said. "Now, I don't know whether you can get through to Nikko or not, but you can give it a try. Go ahead, call your husband."

She looked at him, startled, as if she hadn't heard him correctly.

"I can call him?"

"Or the police, anybody you like."

She did not move. "Oh," she said. "You've really flipped, haven't you? You drag me around all day and threaten to kill me and then all of a sudden you hand me the telephone. Why?"

"Does it make any difference?"

"Hell, yes, it makes a difference. What's the point?"

"You were right. The sailor may not get here at all, and I can't afford to wait for him. So when it comes right down to it, you're going to have to trust me. Because when you walk out of here, you can go straight to the police and I'm dead."

"You're going to let me walk out of here?"

"Yes. I could spend the rest of the night trying to talk you into it, but I don't think it would change anything. I'm taking a short cut. If you want to turn me in, you can do it now. I won't stop you."

She pressed the rim of the empty glass against the pink flesh of her lower lip, studying him. He had given her the advantage and she had taken it. Her eyes were shrewdly confident. "Then you're serious about this bomb business."

"Hell, yes, I'm serious."

"And there really is a missile base?"

"The American government built it for the Japanese," he said. "They've armed it with a nuclear weapon and their big concern is to get the Japanese people to accept it. But that's not the real problem. No, the general who supervised construction of that base is going to use that missile for another purpose. Tomorrow he's going to fire that missile on Red China in the hopes of wiping out the Chinese scientific community and their nuclear capability." She had pursed her lips now, drawing up one knee to hug it, and he could not tell what she was thinking. "Doesn't that make any difference to you?"

"Doesn't what make any difference?"

"That they're going to wipe out a quarter of a million people at the very least tomorrow, that they could start a war."

"And how did you find out about it?"

"That's a long story. It's not important. The only important thing is that I get the proof to the American government. I have a tape that will prove what I say, everything."

"And you want me to take it somewhere."

"Yes. Take it to your husband. Tell him to listen to it and get it to the American ambassador in Tokyo. Tonight. It has to be tonight."

She sat up on the bed again, thinking, and then she picked up her glass again and went back to the bottle. "How do I know that what you're telling me is the truth?"

"Why else would I go to all this trouble?"

"Because you're crazy," she said, smiling, pouring her glass half full. "I really think you are. Way out. But it's the crazy people of the world who are the most interesting. I'm a little that way myself."

"You saw those Japanese police out in the field, the helicopters, the roadblock. Why in the hell would they all be after me if this wasn't true, if I didn't have the power to stop them?"

She sat down on the bed again, making no effort to pull the edges of her robe together, not from forgetfulness, no, but out of design, quite aware of how she looked and how she was dressed and what she thought and felt, as if the whole world was centered in her and there was really nothing else to be considered. Everything would be balanced against how it made her feel or what she wanted. She really had no concept of what was going on in the world and did not particularly care.

"Suppose I take this tape," she said. "O.K., suppose

I get out there with this tape and the men who are out to catch you catch me instead. Now what are they going to do to me?"

"You can bluff your way through it," he said. "They won't do anything to you." He stood up, walked over to the bed, and sat down on the edge of it while she moved over slightly to give him room. He was aware of the smell of her now, scrubbed clean, warm, and he had but to reach out his hand and place it on the swell of her breast beneath the robe, and he could have her, not only physically, but mentally as well, because this was the way she could be handled, capitalizing on the remnant of fear within her, the doubt, and the attraction of danger. She lay there, looking at him, and he saw that her fingernails were painted silver, long, shining in the lamplight like miniature daggers.

"You're crazy, you know that," she said, reaching up to run the back of her hand against his face.

"You're going to do it, aren't you?" he said, quite certain of himself now.

"I don't know. Come down here to me."

"A quarter of a million people are going to die unless I can do something about it," he said. "Now, I want you to get up and get dressed." He stood up, finishing the rest of the bourbon in his glass, aware that she was studying him from the bed.

"How would I get to Nikko?" she said. "If they're combing the bushes for you, they're sure as hell going to have the roads blocked."

"You'll go downstairs and out the back way. Then you'll catch the bus for Nikko, everything casual, nonchalant. I may be wrong, but I don't think they'll expect anything like this. As far as they know, you're the unwilling victim of a kidnaping. If you had a chance to get away, you'd go straight to the authorities. You wouldn't calmly get on a bus and go back to Nikko."

"And what will you be doing all this time?" she said.

"I'll give you enough time to get going," Corman said. "I feel pretty sure they'll have an agent in the lobby someplace, and I'll have to distract him. Once he thinks he has me pinned down, he'll notify the major and they'll call off their dogs. They're not going to pay any attention to you. I'll tell them I left you tied up someplace in the woods."

She got up off the bed again now, bringing her clothes out of the bathroom, laying them out on the bed, stripping off the bathrobe and beginning to dress as if she did not care whether he was in the room or not. She began to chat now about nothing in particular, about what she was going to say to her husband when she got back to Nikko, about the fact that his leave was up tomorrow and they were going back to Tokyo, where she could expect to be bored to death.

"You still don't believe me, do you?" he said, a little startled.

"That doesn't make any difference, does it?" she said. "I mean, you want this tape taken out of here; that's all you care about, isn't it?"

"I've got to know whether you'll do it. If you believe what I told you, then I think you'll carry through with it."

"Then you really can't know, can you?" she said. "Let me tell you something, friend. I don't really give a damn whether a hundred million Chinese get fried tomorrow. I'll either do it because it's something I want to do or I won't do it at all."

She slipped the dress over her head now and slipped a scarf over her hair, taking time to put on her lipstick before she put the mink around her shoulders. "You'd better give me the tape."

He gave her the tape and she put it in her purse, still eying him speculatively, as if she still could not figure him out. He checked his watch. "There's a Nikko bus leaving in about eight minutes," he said. "Do you have any money?"

She nodded, and he checked the hall, then picked up his coat and led the way to the stairs. Once they reached the service entrance, she stopped him, putting her hand on his arm, as if for a moment she had something serious she wanted to say to him, but then she thought better of it. "I think you're crazy," she said. "But the whole world's gone crazy, right? Take care."

And she was gone. He stood in the hallway a long moment and then he followed it toward the lobby, trying to quiet the nervousness within him. He passed the hotel offices and reached the door which opened into the lobby, and then he paused, lighting a cigarette while he had a look. There was a bar off to the left someplace, and he could hear the odd cacophony of a Japanese trio playing American jazz.

There was an American couple in the bridge game at the right side of the lobby, both of them overweight and middle-aged, grimly playing cards against the Japanese couple as if the honor of the United States were at stake. He discounted them as possibilities. The man rarely looked up from his cards except to glare belligerently at his wife.

Corman watched a group of young Japanese drifting across the lobby toward the bar, and then he saw the man he was looking for. The man was obviously American, tall, slightly bald, dressed in a conservative blue suit. He was sitting in a chair across from the main entrance, leafing through a magazine without really seeing it, occasionally glancing at his watch or lighting another cigarette as if he had maintained this vigil a long time and was bored with it, anxious to be relieved. Corman made another visual tour of the lobby in case this man might not be alone, but he saw no possibilities. It was doubtful the major had gambled two of his urgently needed men on a long shot like this.

Corman put the overcoat over his arm, bringing out the pistol beneath it, and then he walked across the lobby, moving very slowly until he was immediately behind the man in the chair. "Don't turn around," he said quietly. "Keep your hands on the arms of the chair."

The man froze instantly and Corman moved around him, sitting down in the chair across from him. The man made no attempt to bluster his way out of the situation. He eyed Corman coolly, deliberately, as if it made no difference. "Good evening, Mr. Corman."

"Stay exactly as you are," Corman said. "You make one move and I will shoot you. What's your name?"

"Fairfax." He glanced at the overcoat and the protruding muzzle. "You're being very foolish, you know."

"Maybe I am," Corman said. "Do you know what they're doing at the base, Fairfax?"

"Nice try," Fairfax said. "But I'm with the operation all the way."

"Then I won't waste my time," Corman said. "Where's the major?"

"Here in Chuzenji. He has a field headquarters in one of the Nikko-Kanko cottages. If you want to talk to him, I'll be glad to take you to him."

"No," Corman said, "I want you to call him. I want him here alone."

"He won't agree to that."

"Let's leave that up to him. Tell him I'm in a reasonable mood and open to bargaining. He won't get hurt. There's a telephone room at the far side of the lobby. Get up and walk toward it very slowly."

The man did as he was told, with Corman close behind him. Over the hotel loud-speaker he could hear the sibilant voice of a woman calling out a last call for the Nikko bus, first in Japanese and then in English. Corman opened the door of the telephone room. "Inside," he said casually. "No sudden movements, please."

Once they were inside, Corman closed the door. "Now," Corman said, "sit down. Put your pistol on the table in front of you."

The man shrugged, complied. "What did you do with the woman, Mr. Corman?"

"I left her behind," Corman said. "Now make the call."

Fairfax eyed him dryly and picked up the telephone, speaking in Japanese.

"Keep it in English," Corman said. "And don't underestimate me, Mr. Fairfax."

Fairfax nodded. "Give me the Nikko-Kanko, extension six-one-two." He waited patiently. "Major Henshaw, please."

"Exactly what I told you to tell him, nothing more, nothing less."

"Major, this is Fairfax. I'm with Corman over at the Chuzenji-Kanko. He would like to see you here. He says to inform you that he's in a reasonable mood and open to bargaining." He paused, listening. "Yes, sir," he said. "He wants to see you alone." He hung up. "He'll be right here," he said to Corman.

"That's fine," Corman said. "Now we're going to the coffee shop, Mr. Fairfax, and we're going to wait. Don't make the mistake of thinking that I won't kill you if I have to. I don't feel I have a great deal to lose."

"All right," Fairfax said. "I won't make that mistake."

5

AFTER the call from Fairfax the major remained in his chair, savoring the taste of triumph, looking across the room at Strickland. Strickland was drawing a red X through another grid on the map, another block searched, another area flushed out. He was wearing headphones plugged into a radio slung from a strap across his shoulder, and his face had the remote expression of a man listening to secret voices. Once in a while his eyes flicked from the map to the major. The major did not miss this significant shift, no; Strickland was looking for the first hairline crack, the first sign of weakness, but he would not see it. The major had never felt better, more alert, more fully in control.

He stood up now, nodding to Strickland, beckoning him over. Strickland removed the headphones, letting them rest around his neck, the muted crackle of voices and static leaking out of the earpieces. The major would not give him the news immediately, no; there was a delicious felicity to suspense, to the prolonging of a pleasurable event. He withdrew a comb from his pocket and ran it through his hair. He needed a shave as well (he liked to maintain a presentable appearance at all times), but this need was not pressing. His ability to grow a beard was considerably less than normal. He supposed it was hereditary. After all, his father had never been particularly hirsute, and even at fifty, the age at which he had died, he had never had to shave more than once every two or three days. The whiskers lay on his cheeks like down, silky, almost transparent.

"You want to talk to me, Major?" Strickland said, openly impatient.

"Yes," the major said. "Call in your units."

"Call them in?"

"I want the Chuzenji-Kanko Hotel surrounded."

"You've located Corman?"

The major nodded, returning the comb to his pocket. "Fairfax just called me. Corman's at the hotel and he wants to surrender, but only to me, alone. He's a bright man, yes, and I have to give him credit for being more perceptive than I thought he would be. Of course, this doesn't bode well for Fairfax, overlooking him that way, perhaps even co-operating with him. His tone of voice implied that. But even the best of men can be corrupted. It's an infection, Strickland. Sometimes it takes a man against his will. What do you know about Fairfax?"

"He's one of the best," Strickland said. "I've worked with him off and on over the past ten years."

"A man's track record means nothing in the long run," the major said. "I've seen dedicated men change on the spur of the moment, in an instant, the flick of an eyelid."

"I'd stake my life on Fairfax," Strickland said, and the major recognized that gauging look in his eyes, the light constriction of the blue-gray pupils. "This has gone on long enough, Major. I think we had better get everything out in the open, for the good of everybody concerned."

"In the open?" the major said, smiling now. "Of course."

"I had a call from Wilkinson. He said Sloan was coming down here to consolidate things."

The major blinked. "Consolidate?"

"That's the term he used. He wouldn't specify."

The February Plan

"No, of course he wouldn't specify, not in a radio message."

"Then you know what's going on."

"I make things happen. I am the instigator here, remember?"

"Are you? Look, Major, I get the feeling that Sloan is coming down here to take over. That's the long and short of it."

"That's what you think, is it?"

Strickland said nothing for a moment. He was weighing his thoughts, a poor quality in a security man, the major reflected, a great weakness. He should be functioning automatically now, not groping around. "It might not be such a bad idea," Strickland said quietly, finally. "I think you're a very tired man. You don't know what you're doing. You've made a dozen slips in the past three hours. You've called me by a half-dozen different names. I'm sorry, Major, but I think you're out of it."

"Out of it?" the major said calmly. "You're forgetting, Strickland, I originated this project. I planned it, every damn step of it, and I recruited the men to carry it out, and I can't very well be out of it. It can't function without me, you know that." He stopped short. There was no sense arguing with Strickland, not on an obvious point like that. "So you have judged my mental capabilities and found them wanting. And you think I'm irrational."

"At times, yes."

"Am I irrational now?" he said steadily.

"I don't know," Strickland said. "You may be lucid now, but you may not be lucid a minute from now. If we were under the agency now, I think the DFC would have grounds to have you relieved."

"But there's no DFC here," the major said, "no provisions for anybody to be relieved. We're all in this together, you know. I will bear the brunt of the responsibility in the final report, of course. I may need to mention the point you raise, not that it has much bearing on this project, because from here on in the agency will keep a much tighter control, but it does raise interesting points as far as being clandestine is concerned.

At what point in a clandestine operation, where there is no contact with Washington, can a subordinate take over? Very interesting." He blinked, reaching for a cigar, but his pocket was empty. The rest of his cigars were back at the base. He had brought ten boxes with him from the States, meaning to ration them over the length of the operation, but he could not remember how many of these boxes were left now.

He was fairly certain he was down to his last box and he tried to picture it in his mind. He had put the box on the table next to his bed, scooping out a handful of cigars which had gone into his pocket. His hand had scraped along the bottom of the box, he was sure of that, and since he invariably took six cigars at a time, he could assume that the box still contained three or four. This was a logical assumption.

When he emptied a box, he always discarded it, and he remembered quite clearly that he had closed this box and replaced it in the bureau drawer. Indisputable proof. A few cigars would last him until he got back to Tokyo. The tobacco shops were quite complete there. He would not be able to find his favorite cigars, of course, but he would pick up a substitute until he could get back to the States. "Do you have a cigarette?" he asked Strickland.

Strickland handed him a pack, saying nothing, as if he was still waiting for an answer. There was always somebody waiting for an answer, an explanation, as if everybody lived in a perpetual state of confusion, unable to see for themselves, needing him to interpret lift for them. The major lighted the cigarette, sucking the smoke into his lungs. It was most unsatisfactory, no substance to it. He felt as if he had ordered ale and been served water.

"I'll admit it, Strickland," he said quietly. "I'm very tired and I'm getting along on pills and coffee. And there are occasional mental lapses, yes, a confusion of names once in a while, nothing severe. But I've been on so many operations, Strickland—thousands of them; none of them the same, but all of them similar—and the cover names change. I may have to remember ten names for the same man over a period of years." He sucked at the cigarette again. "But my mind is quite clear now. I'm fully aware of what is going on. Sloan is coming down here, but only because I asked him to. There are so many details, so very many, that require attention, and frankly I can't keep up with them all. So in one respect he will be functioning as my DFC, and in another he will be working as a co-ordinator. Because the real problem is no longer at the base; no, from here on the launch is purely mechanical, one, two, three. The real problem is here."

He pinched the unsubstantial cigarette between thumb and forefinger. "The communists are very shrewd, Strickland. That's the one thing you must never forget. They're deceptive, masters of illusion and cover because they have no strong sense of national identity, no religion, no strong personal attachments. I can testify to that. Oh, I've known thousands of them, some of them quite well, in all parts of the world. It pays to know your enemy. They shift around, dissemble, as naturally as you breathe, and their lies are quite convincing. Perfection, sometimes."

His hand brought the cigarette to his mouth and allowed the smoke to be extracted. "They've known about our plan, even from the beginning. The lieutenant who broke into the company, Corman's son, he was the tip-off, the giveaway, because the act was so irrational, it was perfect, you see? Suppose he had killed the general; things would have ended right there, perfection itself. They would then leak the whole story to the press, distorted, of course, to suit their ends, to make it appear that an idealistic young officer, unable to bear the thought of such wholesale destruction, had murdered his commanding general." He jabbed the cigarette toward Strickland to underscore his point. "You see the beauty of that? They would make it appear that the whole plan was conceived by the United States Government. It would have been quite a propaganda coup for them."

"You're saying the lieutenant was a communist?"

"Of course," the major said with a sharp laugh. "But he wasn't a good enough shot, no, and we took him instead of his taking us. So they had to try something else. Yes, these people are very shrewd, never obvious, so they sent one of their best-trained agents, Corman himself. Perfect logic, because Corman was not only an agent but also the lieutenant's father, and he had a double motivation and a perfect cover. I must admit, I was taken in by him myself, because it seemed so natural. I'm a father myself and I could picture myself in his place, torn up over the death of his son. I'll be frank with you, Strickland, I never for a moment suspected him. Not at all. That was where I made my mistake. It's those situations which appear most normal that you should suspect the most."

He stubbed out the cigarette, almost savagely, shaking another from the pack, lighting it with the lighter Mildred had given him. So much of what he had came from her, and he had given her so goddamned little, all in all, a weakness within himself that he could not ascribe to devotion because there was no connection, none, and to be truthful with himself, totally candid, he had always loved her enormously but had never been able to relate properly, so she had been quite right to leave him, quite right. He looked up at Strickland who stood over the desk, his face partially obscured by the smoke—how old was he? In his early forties perhaps, a long way to go, and it was desperately important for him to understand, to develop his defenses, to stay alive. Yes, life was important; he must never lose his taste for it. For all men were too soon dead and gone, and after forty the pace increased and the years flashed by like a freight train, and a man rationalized his readiness, his acceptance, but only because there was nothing else he could do about it.

"If these men were communists," Strickland said, "why didn't they inform the Red Chinese what was going on? Why didn't the Red Chinese cancel? Or why go to all that trouble, when they could have tipped us off to the American government and washed us down the drain?"

The major laughed again. "They have canceled, don't you see? Oh, that's the most beautiful part of the whole plan. There is no scientific meeting at all, no Chinese missile, no hundred thousand children. Perfect,

perfect. They took us and we didn't even know what was going on. They hoodwinked us. They let Corman be captured and then arranged his escape. But they never wanted us to cancel our plans. Not at all. We fire a missile and there won't be anything at the other end, nothing, because they have evacuated everything, and they are poised for counterattack, to wipe us out with complete impunity, and they'll attack the United States with complete justification in the eyes of the world, because it will seem that the United States fired first. Foolish, we've been sucked into it, playing their game. And that's the reason why we must find Corman. He knows the details, everything that's going to happen."

"I think you need a good long rest," Strickland said sympathetically. "I want you to wait here for a few minutes, Major. I'll be back." The major waved his hand vaguely to acknowledge, knowing the moment when Strickland left the cottage, but having heard nothing of what he had said. The major paid no attention to anything beyond the smoke of his cigarette. His mind had turned inward and he was listening to the sounds of his own thoughts, carefully, not missing a word, knowing he was close to an absolute truth he had never known before. "I must find Corman," he murmured. "Corman will know it all."

There was a shadow in his mind, something vaguely remembered, something he was supposed to do. Yes, the telephone call, Fairfax; yes, Corman was over there at the Chuzenji-Kanko, waiting to tell him what he wanted to know. He stood up, checking his service revolver, clicking the cylinder open with an expert flick of his finger and snapping it shut again. His mind was leaden; his body was almost insensate. He put on his topcoat and muffler, and his legs carried him toward the door as if he did not control them at all. Once he was outside, he felt better, his mind scourged by the icy wind. He considered taking the car, but he decided against it. He needed the walk, the bracing stroll to get the blood pumping again, and the other hotel was not far away. He walked briskly, picking up a gnarled piece of wood along the side of a fence to serve as a walking stick, throwing it away once he reached the Chuzenji-Kanko.

He went into the lobby, looking around, but there was no trace of Corman or Fairfax, and near the fireplace sat a Japanese couple with their two small children, all lined up on a couch, and they were chatting back and forth, pretending that they had not noticed him, that they had not been waiting for him, alert to signal Corman that he had arrived. But no matter, it made no difference. An old Japanese man was reading a newspaper near the desk, pausing occasionally to pinch a tiny whiff of tobacco into the chrome bowl of his pipe. Did his eyes flick up from the page to signal the major as he passed? The major could not be absolutely sure, but it was entirely likely. The agency would not have sent him here without a backup; no, that would have been highly irregular.

He paused at the entrance to the dining room. On the far side, at a table against the wall, were Corman and Fairfax. One of Corman's hands rested beneath the table, and the major could be sure there was a gun in that hand. Back to the wall, the oldest illusion of safety, but even in that crowded room Corman would be an easy target through the windows, and the bullet that killed him would make no sound at all, just the tinkle of glass where it came through the window and the impact against flesh, an almost imperceptible whispering thud that could go unheard unless you were listening for it. And that was what Corman wanted, of course, somebody to take him out here and now before there was a chance for anything to go wrong, for an inadvertent word that would cause his plan to go awry, but he would not be allowed that luxury, no.

The major crossed the dining room, weaving his way through the tables. There was a large Japanese family occupying a table immediately in front of Corman's, three generations at least, perhaps four, chopsticks clicking at the rice bowls, a pattern of conversation. Extremely clever, the major thought, that Corman had put this family here, as if he thought in some way that it would appear he was trying to protect himself. And Corman himself looked terrible, close to exhaustion, his face lined, but there was still a terrible defiance in his eyes. The major held his hands away from his body, speaking in a conversational voice so as not to alarm the Japanese family. "Well, Mr. Corman, it's been quite a day, hasn't it? I got your call. I'm sorry I'm late, but there were a number of details to handle." He smiled pleasantly. "I'm not armed, Mr. Corman."

"Well, I am armed," Corman said. "I have a gun under the table. Sit down, Major."

The major pulled out a chair and sat down, glancing at Fairfax. He had never seen Fairfax ruffled, but Fairfax was certainly ruffled now, unsettled, his eyes ill at ease. "Are you all right, Major?" he said.

"Perfectly well, thank you," the major said. He looked to Corman again. "We won't be needing Fairfax here, will we? I am here now, after all." He looked back to Fairfax. "You'd better report to Strickland. Have him begin removing the roadblocks."

Fairfax glanced at Corman. "Go ahead," Corman said.

Fairfax stood up without a word, clearly undecided, then he walked across the dining room and went into the lobby. The major relaxed, picking up a menu, rubbing his eyes to bring them into focus. He would be needing glasses one of these days—a damn nuisance to a man in the field, but he would learn to get along with them. A waiter materialized at his elbow, and the major gave him a glance and then returned to a quiet study of the menu. "Just *sushi*," he said to the waiter. "*Sushi* and tea, lots of tea, very hot, very strong." The waiter departed. The major smiled. "I've grown very fond of *sushi* since I've been here. When I smoke too much, it's about the only thing I can taste. Do you have any cigarettes, Mr. Corman? I ran out of cigars." Corman slid a pack across the table. The major removed one, lighted it, inhaled the smoke. "I don't like cigarettes, but they have to do." He removed a shred of tobacco from the end with his thumbnail. "Now, Mr. Corman, I have a great deal of admiration for your boys."

"My boys?"

"Let's don't pretend, Mr. Corman. I know your team is here."

"What are you talking about?"

The major nodded toward the waiter who was standing near the kitchen door, a boy in his early twenties. "Let's take him, for instance. He's watching this table. Now I know he's not one of ours, so that makes him one of yours."

"He watches all the tables," Corman said. "He's a waiter."

The major shrugged. "A waiter then, nothing more. Have it your own way. But maybe I'd better explain, Mr. Corman. I know what you're doing. I've been onto it for some time."

"Oh?" Corman said, startled.

"That's better," the major said, smiling. "But I wouldn't feel too bad about it if I were you. We can't control our reactions all the time. I would really enjoy watching you work, Corman. But time's running out and I have to know what you're up to. So I'm going to have to have some straight answers out of you. For those straight answers I can guarantee you immunity, even a reverse cover if you want to go back. I know you're an agent, Corman. I know you intend for us to carry out our assignment here, so you'll be admitting nothing that I don't already know, not in the larger sense. You will just be supplying me with the details. For instance, your secretary."

"What about my secretary?"

"I talked with her earlier this evening. Now, one thing disturbs me about her. If she has been with you ten years, then she must know what you are—there is no way she could keep from knowing—and yet when I talked with her, I had the impression that she did not. Now, either she is extremely clever at this or you are extremely clever in preserving your cover."

Corman shook his head, tired. "What in the hell are you up to, Major?"

"Information, that's all. You can't change things, Corman. I am going to cancel the shoot."

"Cancel?"

"You don't expect us to carry through, do you?" He

glanced up as the waiter served the *sushi* on a small plate, putting a pot of tea on the table before he retreated. The major's nostrils were seduced by the fragrance of the tea and he lifted the porcelain lid and glanced into the pot, knowing that he could not drink it, no more than he could eat the *sushi* on the plate, because the waiter was in this with Corman, and how many ways there were to poison foods now, tasteless, odorless, with the terminal effects of stroke or heart failure, leaving no trace, carrying a man into a deep sleep from which there was no waking, and for an instant he was tempted to go ahead and drink the tea and be out of it. An old temptation, to be resisted now as it had been before, but he felt the fatigue rushing in after it again, and he wondered briefly if there had been something in the cigarette. He crushed it out.

Corman was staring across the room. The major's eyes followed his gaze and he saw Strickland and Sloan approaching, and if one part of his mind was irritated at their interruption, the rest was grateful. They could carry on now. They could take over. Everything had been done for them. They approached with caution, and the major knew the pistol was shifting beneath the table to cover them. But they scarcely paid any attention at all to Corman. They were looking at him.

"Hello, Major," Sloan said. "How are you feeling?"

"I'm glad to see you, Sloan." He wanted to extend his hand to Sloan, but the hand refused to obey the command and stayed on the table.

"We're taking over here, Major," Sloan said. "You need a rest."

"Yes," the major said. "Yes."

Strickland was looking at Corman now. "We're going to take you out of here, Mr. Corman. Now, the hotel is surrounded and we can take you out by force if we have to. But it's possible a number of innocent people will get hurt."

"You can't take me anyplace," Corman said. "Not without the tape and the woman. And if you try to get me out of here, there's going to be a hell of a fight and you'll end up with neither."

Sloan shrugged slightly. "Send the major back to the

base, Mr. Strickland, and start moving your roadblocks. I want to talk with Mr. Corman."

Strickland nodded, touching the major on the shoulder. "No, not yet," the major said, and the tiredness seeped down inside of him, like hot wax. He felt that he would topple from the chair unless he made the effort to stiffen himself, to hold himself erect. "We are going to scrub the mission, Sloan. That's the only way. There is no loss of honor involved in this, none, because we couldn't have known what they were up to. I will explain all that in my notes. I must have time to bring them up to date, to explain why we're canceling. None of us are afraid to die; we've proved that, quite conclusively, I think. But sometimes discretion is the better part of valor."

"I'll take care of it," Sloan said. "You can be sure of that."

"Of course, yes." All done now, finished, and he stood up, his vision blurring, no longer able to see Strickland at all, knowing he was there only because he felt the hand on his arm, propping him up. "It's all there somewhere, but I can't make any sense out of it, none of it. You can write that down for my report. The major has gone blind. He can't see any more. And when you turn in my report, put down my real name. Hensley. W. P. Hensley. They must make no mistake. They must know who I am."

"Yes," Sloan said. "They will know who you are."

Half leaning on Strickland, the major crossed the dining room and disappeared into the lobby. Sloan sat down. Corman was staring after the major. "What's wrong with him?" he said.

"Occupational fatigue," Sloan said. "That's a hell of an understatement. He's just had too much. You mind if I smoke?"

"Go ahead." But Corman had tightened now, and his eyes would be watching Sloan's hands very carefully and the finger would rest a little tighter against the trigger. Sloan made certain that his movements were slow, carefully defined. He took the cigarettes out of his shirt pocket and lighted one with a match from the table, and he knew he should begin the questioning, trying to locate the woman and the tape, wrapping everything up, talking Corman out of using the pistol, but he knew quite suddenly that this was not what he was going to do at all. The major had been raving, but the major had also been right; this mission could not be allowed to happen, and Sloan's last chance of stopping it was sitting across the table. "I want to help you, Mr. Corman," Sloan said quietly. "Things have gone too far as it is, but if we work together, there may be a chance."

"A chance of what?"

"Do you have the tape?"

"I'm not naïve enough to carry it around with me, if that's what you mean."

"But you can put your hands on it."

"We can assume that."

"That would be proof enough," Sloan said speculatively. "We wouldn't need anything else. Where had you intended going with it?"

"To Tokyo."

"Who were you going to see?"

"You expect me to tell you?"

"Who were you going to see? There isn't much time."

"The American ambassador."

"Yes," Sloan said, "that'd be best. He could take immediate action on it." It would be worth a chance. He would take Corman out and dismiss the driver, taking the wheel himself. The roadblock would have been shut down by now, and there would be no slight confusion as Strickland rounded up his security forces and got them back to the base. Sloan was not sure how long it would take to get to Tokyo in this weather. Four hours, perhaps. Yes, it was worth the chance. "All right," he said, "we'll go to Tokyo. Now, where is the tape?"

Corman smiled thinly. "You're all the same, aren't you?"

"What do you mean?"

"I've been conned at the hands of an expert," Corman said, reaching out for the tea left by the major. "And I can say, the major put on a first-class performance."

Sloan blinked. "Performance? You think he was faking?"

"Wasn't he? Isn't this all designed to soften me up?"

"No," Sloan said, feeling the pressure of time now. "Look, Mr. Corman, everything has changed. The Chinese are bringing a hundred thousand children into Lanchow tomorrow for a special children's celebration. What started as a pre-emptive strike is going to turn into a slaughter. That's what unglued the major."

"But the general is unconvinced," Corman said firmly. "He's still going ahead."

"Yes."

"So that leaves it up to us," Corman said, pouring the tea. "You and I. We're the only ones who can stop it."

"What the hell do I have to do to convince you?"

"Nothing," Corman said. "You can't. Your group killed my son. I've been lied to, kidnaped, chased, hounded, financially ruined by your group. So why the hell should I take your word for anything?"

"You think that's the reason I'm offering to help you?"

"Yes," Corman said. "You want the tape and you want the woman."

"To hell with them both," Sloan said, completely frustrated now.

"If you want to stop the shoot, why don't you go to Tokyo yourself, talk to the ambassador?"

"Would he believe me?" Sloan said, stubbing out the cigarette. "He'd listen all right, and maybe he'd provide a stenographer to take down my story, and then he'd go into the other room and call the general at the base and ask him what the hell was going on? That's exactly what would happen."

"There are men on the base who don't know what's going on. Tell them."

"It's too late for that," Sloan said. "They're all in detention by now. The hard-core boys are in control. Everything extraneous has been stripped away."

Corman was thoughtful now, his eyes assessing.

"You might as well take me back to the base," he said, "because you're not going to get either the tape or the woman. I told her everything and she believed me. She took the tape out of here."

"When?"

"I won't tell you that."

"Where did she go?"

"I won't tell you that either. But you have her name, don't you? That gives you a chance of stopping her."

"Yes," Sloan said. "The colonel gave us her name." He lighted another cigarette now, refusing to allow himself to feel relief, not yet, not until he was sure. "Can she get anybody to listen to her?"

"Her husband's West Point. They'll go to the ambassador," Corman said. "I think he'll listen."

Sloan nodded. "Then that takes care of that."

"And you're not going to do anything about it?" Corman said testily. "If you push, you just might have a chance." His eyes drifted up to the clock above the cashier's head. "No, you don't really have any chance at all. She's there by now."

"Yes," Sloan said. He had the sudden desire, not felt for many years, to find a priest and confess himself, to rid himself of the onerous burden which he felt was resting on his soul, not so much the guilt of complicity as the crime of weakness. Even as he had been too weak to fight this thing in the beginning, he was too weak to follow through now. He should take Corman and go to Tokyo, to see the ambassador and prepare the way for the tape. But his resolution had drained from him now.

"How's my secretary?" Corman said.

"She's all right."

"It would have been a better pitch if you had worked her into it somehow," Corman said. "If you had appealed to my sense of gallantry. I'm surprised you didn't think of that."

Now Sloan saw Strickland coming across the room again. As he approached, Sloan looked up at him. "There's nothing to worry about," Sloan heard himself saying. "He left both the tape and the woman up on the ridge."

"Is that what he told you?" Strickland said.

"That's what I told him," Corman said instantly, the faintest touch of incredulity in his eyes.

"It won't work, Corman," Strickland said. "I just came from the local Japanese police station. The woman dropped by there about twenty minutes ago."

"I don't believe you," Corman said.

"It took a little time for her to get the Japanese police to believe her," Strickland said. "She had a couple of drinks after she left you, and that didn't make her any more convincing. But they finally had sense enough to get in touch with us."

"No," Corman said. "That's not true."

Strickland reached into his pocket and his fingers withdrew the reel of tape until Corman could see it. "We have the tape," he said. "Now, make up your mind which way you want it, Corman, easy or difficult. Because we're taking you back."

Sloan studied the glowing tip of his cigarette, half wishing now that Corman would make a fight of it and the pistol would go off in his hand and Strickland would go down, and then Sloan would grab the tape and they would make a run for the car. It was better than doing nothing, a loss by default. The smoke curled up from the lengthening ash. He heard the thud of metal against wood, and his hope died. Corman's fingers had loosened. The pistol had dropped to the floor. It was over.

6

IT was over, Corman thought, leaning back against the car seat, watching the lights of Chuzenji fade through the rear window, giving way to the blackness of the snowy plain. He had done what he could, and considering everything, it was a minor miracle that he was still alive. He could have died during his escape from the villa, dropped by a bullet from a sentry he could not see, or he could have been killed at the gate in the wild flurry of fire from the guards. He could have frozen to death on the road or been killed by the colonel if perhaps the colonel had been a little less drunk. There had been many chances for death to snatch him, and he had somehow eluded them all.

He sorted back through the things that had happened, trying to see if he had taken a wrong turn, but he could find nothing he could have handled differently except the girl perhaps. Maybe he could have been more persuasive had he not been so tired. No, he could not have changed her. She was set, already conditioned to a specific course of action.

Full circle and back to the starting point and nothing had been accomplished, and the launch was still on. Paul had tried to stop it and was now dead; Mitsu had died in his attempt; there was nothing more Corman could do. He had earned the right to withdraw into a consideration of his own welfare. There was no reason for them to kill him now; he was harmless, and by tomorrow at this time it would be over and he would face nothing more strenuous than the post-morten interrogations, the government probings, the depositions and the questionings. But he would be back with Finley and he could pick up his life again. He would go ahead and sell the Connecticut house and perhaps the New York apartment as well, not with any specific goals in mind, but only a desire to change the pattern of his life which had become so suddenly unsatisfactory to him.

And yet, even as he allowed himself the luxury of acceptance, he knew it was not possible. He could not give up, let things slide. Somewhere in the darkness of his lethargy was a glowing spark of stubbornness, of indignation, that all his rationalizations could not extinguish. It was not only the project and the enormous monstrousness of it, or his son's death, but something more egotistic, more personal. He had been abused, degraded. From the beginning they had expected him to do nothing, to go along, to be swept up by the strength of their patriotic zeal, to surrender his individualism to their group action, expecting that one man would be easily contained, no threat to them. It was foolish that ego should enter into this, and he knew it, but there was still a slight glimmer of hope within him that something could be done, and he had to follow it through.

He had one ally, Sloan, the indecisive man who now sat in the front seat of the car next to the driver, his head a silhouette against the reflected lights from the road ahead. It had taken courage for Sloan to lie to Strickland; this was proof enough of his sincerity. Corman leaned forward and tapped Sloan on the shoulder. "Do you have a cigarette?" he said.

Sloan handed him a pack. Corman shook one out and lighted it, studying the driver in the flare of the match. He was fairly young, an Air Force lieutenant with a jutting jaw and alert eyes, concentrating now on the road and the hazard of the snow. "I've been thinking about what you suggested," Corman said to Sloan. "I think it might be a good idea. I mean, I have nothing to lose by co-operating with you now, do I?"

Sloan gave him a look, but in the darkness of the car Corman could not interpret it. "It's too late for that, Mr. Corman," he said.

"I don't know," Corman said. "It's never too late to make up for pigheadedness, is it?"

"I don't know what you could say that would be of any use to us," Sloan said, obviously for the benefit of the driver.

"There's something I haven't told you," Corman said. "The major and I had a deal, Mr. Sloan."

"I don't believe it," Sloan said.

"I don't think you can afford not to believe it."

Sloan shrugged, looking to the driver. "We'll go to the Hole instead of detention," he said.

"Yes, sir," the driver said.

Corman's hope came alive again. He could make no plans; he would have to wait and see what happened. He finished the cigarette and stubbed it out, leaning back against the seat, dozing past the main gate, coming fully awake only when the car had reached the Hole. There was some dispute between Sloan and the guard at the first checkpoint, and Corman could see them arguing in the light of the headlights, apparently over Corman's admission to the Hole, but Sloan prevailed. When he came back to the car he was carrying an identification badge which he handed to Corman without comment.

There was no more trouble. The lieutenant parked the car near the entrance to the air lock, and in a few minutes Corman found himself in the elevator, plummeting down in a sickening drop. The elevator stopped; the door slid open. They passed another sentry in the corridor and followed a long tunnel, stopping at a door marked Intelligence. "Thanks, Lieutenant," Sloan said. "You'd better stand by. I'm going to need you to take the prisoner up to the detention camp in an hour or so."

"Yes, sir," the lieutenant said.

Sloan opened the door, leading Corman across a room filled with banks of communications machines and coils of multicolored wire which snaked along the side of the concrete floor as if all the instruments here had been assembled in a hurry. One of the men looked up from his console to speak to Sloan as he went by, but Sloan waved him off, opening another door at the far side of the room, ushering Corman in and closing the door behind them. The room was small and there were boxes of electrical equipment and rolls of wire along the walls, leaving little space for a single desk and two chairs. "We won't have much time," Sloan said, breathing with slight difficulty as if acclimating himself to the new atmosphere. "Security is going to chew my ass for bringing you down here as soon as the guard at the gate makes his report."

"All right," Corman said, trying to think logically over his fatigue. "What can we do?"

"What can we do?" Sloan said. "Not a goddamn thing, that's what we can do. Our only chance was back there in Chuzenji."

"I don't believe that," Corman said. "There's bound to be some way to put this base out of commission."

Sloan was pale now, disturbed. He mopped the sweat off the back of his neck with a handkerchief. "There's no way to do it, believe me."

"How about electricity? Where does it come from?"

"We have our own generator."

"Is there a way we can knock it out?"

"No," Sloan said instantly. "Even if we destroyed it, there's an auxiliary that would cut in immediately. Everything's double system here. In the time it'd take us to get at any single element they'd be swarming all over us."

"The air conditioners."

"No good. Their only real function is to filter following an enemy attack. A fresh-air system would work just as well, and there are separate blowers for that."

"If you don't intend to do anything, say so," Corman said angrily. "Send me to detention and get it over with."

"There's nothing we can do here," Sloan said.

"What have you got to to lose?" Corman said. "If they launch, you're a dead man. But you find a way to stop the shoot and you have a chance to live." Sloan had been brought up short by the impact of the new thought. "I don't think the government will prosecute a man who tries to undo what he knows was wrong," Corman said, amplifying.

Sloan nodded, but the despair had not lightened on his face. "There just isn't any way." He sat down in a chair, his fingers picking up a piece of wire from the floor, bending it, as if the physical activity gave him comfort. There was the sound of a distant horn bleating through the labyrinth now, more of a vibration than an actual noise.

"What's that?" Corman said.

"They've finished fueling," Sloan said.

And then it was there, quite clear in Corman's mind, as if he had known all along what needed to be done. "The missile," he said.

"What about it?" Sloan said.

"Do you know anything about the guidance system?"

"Nothing."

The February Plan

"But you could throw it off enough to keep it from getting to the target."

"That's no good," Sloan said. "There's still the bomb."

"All right," Corman said, backtracking. "Now we're getting somewhere. We'll take it one step at a time. How is the bomb exploded?"

"By an altitude sensitive fuse," Sloan said. "It's set for three thousand feet, I believe."

"Can you deactivate it?"

"I don't know."

"Can you disable the bomb so it can't be fixed within twenty-four hours?"

"I don't know that either."

"But it's possible you could?"

"Possible."

"Then that would stop it, the whole thing?"

"Yes. There would be no point to the launch without the bomb."

"Then that's what we will do," Corman said, realizing with a start that he had been leaning over Sloan, browbeating him with questions like a hostile witness on the stand being harassed by an attorney. He straightened up, feeling better now, more alert than he had been in days, brought alive by the danger which now confronted him. "All right," he said. "How do we get to the bomb?"

Sloan spoke in a monotone, easier now that someone had taken hold and he was merely following orders again, discussing the layout of the Hole almost as if he were explaining a diagram to an apprentice electrician. He ran his finger along the surface of the desk, the oil of his finger tip leaving a mark as he explained. The corridor they had just passed through, if followed in the other direction, led to a service well, a pod-shaped excavation around the cylinder which held the missile. He was not sure how this was guarded according to the book, but the security system had had to be revamped for a minimum force, so the usual procedure had no relevance here. There would be two checkpoints to be passed. The first was the armed guard who was stationed just beyond the elevator on the approach to the service well. Beyond him, around a bend in the corridor, immediately outside the heavy door to the service well, there was a second guard.

"None in the service well itself?"

Sloan shook his head. "Not after fueling."

"Then when will they arm the bomb?"

"I believe the critical mass has already been dropped in," Sloan said.

"Is there an alarm system?"

"Each guard has a telephone box at his station. There is also a light on one of the consoles in control that goes on if the door is opened to the service well after fueling."

"Can the door be locked from the inside?"

"No."

"How long would it take them to reach the service well if the light went on?"

"A few minutes, no more than that. They'd check with the guards first, to make sure there wasn't an electric malfunction."

"How long will it take you with the bomb?"

Sloan shrugged. "I have no idea."

"Is there any possibility you might set it off by messing with it?"

"I don't think so," Sloan said.

"Can you disable it before they reach us?"

"I don't know. I've never seen the device. I just don't know."

"I've gone as far as I can," Corman said. "Do you have any idea how we get past the guards?"

Sloan studied the wire in his hands, twisting it into a knot before he dropped it on the floor. "We may have to kill them," he said quietly. "Have you ever killed a man, Mr. Corman?"

"No."

Sloan took the pistol out of his holster and slipped a silencer onto the muzzle. "The whole trick," he said, not looking at Corman, "is not to think about it. You shoot the man in the middle of the chest, not the head. You shoot him and you don't think about it." He put the pistol back in the holster. "It may not be necessary to kill them. We'll see. But you leave the guards to me. I'll take care of them."

"Are they your men? Will they recognize you?"

"They're military." Sloan stood up, and Corman could tell that much of his indecisiveness was gone now. He went through one of the boxes, taking out the tools he would need, a few small wrenches, pliers, cutters, nothing as exotic as Corman supposed he would need for a job like this. He wrapped them all in a leather pouch which he tied, sticking it under his belt. He found a flashlight on a shelf and tested it. "This is all I'll need, if I'm going to be able to do it at all." He took a deep breath. "We'll go out the same way we came in," he said. "You follow my lead. If we're stopped in the corridor, you're my prisoner and I'm taking you back to the detention camp."

Corman nodded. Sloan opened the door and led the way across the room and out into the corridor, with Corman preceding him. Their footsteps were hollow as they walked down the tunnel. Corman's resolution began to weaken, and the thought occurred to him that this was not really happening at all, that he had so long existed in his imaginary fictional world that this tunnel and what awaited him at the end of it were merely projections of his own thoughts. He blinked, half expecting that he would open his eyes and find himself at the termination of a nightmare, but the tunnel still stretched ahead of him, with the bulk of Sloan casting elongated shadows on the floor.

They passed a guard, a big, burly man with the stripes of a master sergeant on his shoulder. He scarcely looked at them as they passed. They rounded a corner, the elevator dead ahead, and beyond that, half shadowed by the light mounted in the wall to his back, there stood another guard, on the telephone now, and Corman noticed that while he was talking, he scratched his shoulder, absently, his fingers tracking down an itch. He put the telephone back into its container and turned toward them as they approached. Young, early twenties, prideful in his uniform, ignorant in his youth. "Control just called, Mr. Sloan," the guard said. "They're having trouble with one of their circuits and they want you there right away."

"I have a prisoner to take back to the compound," Sloan said.

"You can drop him off at security."

"You'll have to call them back," Sloan said, an odd edge to his voice. "Tell them to get in touch with Cutter."

The young man turned, and in that instant Sloan drew the pistol and hit him across the back of the neck with it, just below the terminal arc of the protective helmet. The man sagged and slid down against the wall. Sloan did not give him a second glance. He began to move down the corridor at a fast pace, still not running, while Corman followed, his stomach churning, feeling that he was going to be sick. He rounded the corner, following Sloan, and in that instant they met the second guard who was proceeding toward them, and in that moment their luck went sour.

The moment the guard saw the pistol in Sloan's hand, he grabbed at it, catching the arm just as the gun fired with a strange whacking noise that sent a bullet ricocheting against the concrete walls. They grappled and the pistol fell to the floor near the door. Corman scooped it up and turned to help Sloan, but at that moment a shot rang out from the guard's pistol and Sloan died on his feet. Corman plunged ahead to the door with the alarm horn bleating through the tunnel. Grabbing at the wheel, he turned it and pulled the door open as the guard fired after him.

Corman went through the door and closed it behind him, blinking in confusion, thinking he had come into another corridor only to realize that he was in a ring-shaped room and that behind the cylindrical wall which confronted him was the missile. He could hear voices now, yelling, but he had no idea where they came from. He spotted an iron staircase and climbed it, emerging into a room with a ceiling like a quonset hut, and there, through an open doorway, he saw the missile itself, the nose dun-colored in the dim light.

He moved to it as if in a dream, stepping out on the work platform, and quite suddenly he knew what he

The February Plan

must do. He heard the door opening on the floor below, the chatter of voices. Deliberately now he moved around the missile until it was between him and the entrance. Then he raised his pistol and pressed it against the metal skin.

"Corman," a voice came from below, probing, feeling him out. "Come out of there, Corman. You haven't got a chance."

"No," Corman said quite calmly. "I want to see the general. Here."

"That won't work. Come on down, Corman."

"I'm not going anywhere," Corman said. "I have the pistol pressed against the missile. Now I don't know what kind of effect that pulling the trigger is going to have, but if the general isn't here in five minutes we're all going to see."

"Corman, for God's sake."

"Five minutes," Corman said. "Five minutes and I pull the trigger."

2

The general sat alone in his room, writing a letter to his wife concerning his impending death. He had written many of these letters before on the night before a particularly hazardous mission, or when it was highly likely that his position was going to be overrun, or when he had a premonition that the pattern of bombs which seemed to hit England at random was going to catch him, and he had always destroyed them the morning after with a feeling of relief. It was foolish, of course, because there was no need to explain himself to Elna. They had been married thirty-five years and she knew him as well as any woman could ever know any man, and there was nothing he could tell her in these letters that she did not already know, that he loved her, that he was grateful for her, that he wished life could have given him more opportunity to be with her.

The letter he was writing now was different. He knew for one thing that it would become a public document and that every word he put down would be carefully analyzed and eventually released to the public media, and he would have to exonerate her here, to disassociate her as a wife from any preknowledge of what he was doing. She would understand, of course, because she shared many of the same views and had the same sense of alarm about the highly hazardous world in which they found themselves. It was likely that she would rise to his defense once the trial began, and he did not want this to happen because he wanted no defense, no rationalization. The deed itself would be sufficient, an end to itself.

"I take full responsibility for what has happened," he wrote on the paper. "I initiated the idea, I recruited sufficient men who shared my point of view to man the launch, I personally deceived the inspection teams who came to make progress reports on the construction of the base, and in the end I alone touched off the launch. Ordinarily it takes two men working in tandem to fire a missile of this sort, duplicating a complicated sequence in order to fire. This procedure was set up to prevent any man from going berserk and instigating an action like this in the heat of his irrationality. But I have simplified this. Only I know the way the console is programed. There is but one key and that one is mine. I repeat. It was my act and mine alone. Whether this will lighten the eventual sentence of the men who cooperated with me in this, I don't know. I sincerely hope that it will. I say for them that they acted from the highest degree of patriotism, recognizing the danger and the political limitations which prevented our country from seizing a highly volatile initiative. I would have preferred that my country had done this and that I was acting directly as an instrument of my country, but this was not possible."

He looked up at the sound of the emergency horn, and then, quite calmly, he capped his fountain pen and reached for the telephone just as it rang.

"What's going on, Allenton?" he said.

"I'm not sure," Allenton said. "All I know is that Corman's in the Hole. He's on the service platform and he has a pistol. He's threatening to shoot into the missile unless he can talk to you."

The February Plan

"I see," the general said. "How the hell did he get there?"

"Sloan brought him down for interrogation."

"Where's Sloan now?"

"Dead."

"I'll be right there," the general said. "And turn off that damn alarm."

"Yes, sir."

The horn died almost instantly. The general moved down the corridor at a half run to the Intelligence room where Allenton and Strickland were leaning over a diagram. Allenton glanced up as the general came in. Allenton was sweating. "All right," the general said. "What's the picture?"

"He's here," Allenton said, pointing to the cutaway diagram, "on the service platform. The damage he can do depends on his knowledge of the missile structure. How much does he know about one of these birds, General?"

"I don't know," the general said. "Give me the alternatives."

"We are presuming that he has Sloan's forty-five," Allenton said. "Now, if he fires into the warhead, it's possible there will be a small explosion from the charge. The odds are about even that this explosion would touch off the fuel tanks in the missile itself and consequently the storage facilities."

"The bomb," the general said quietly.

"Smalley says there's no danger of nuclear explosion."

"Can he guarantee that?"

"The odds are minimal. He doesn't see any way it could be touched off by a pistol shot."

"Which means he's not quite sure."

"Yes."

"All right. How about leakage?"

"That's possible. He could cause a rupture and we'd get radioactive leakage."

"Go on."

"If he shoots into the guidance system, we're fairly safe, at least from any immediate explosion."

"From explosion, yes," the general said. "But if he

goes that far, if he actually fires into the missile and gets no result, what's to keep him from firing again in a different spot?"

"Nothing," Strickland said adamantly. "I think we're wasting time. We have to keep him from firing at all."

"Maybe," the general said, shifting his eyes back to Allenton again. "You have more?"

"Yes, sir. If he fires into the fuel tanks, we have an almost certain probability of explosion."

"All right," the general said evenly. "Then we keep him from firing." He looked to Strickland now. "Do you have any ideas?"

"He's immediately below the concrete doors," Strickland said. "There's a chance we might flush him out with gas."

"Do you have any gas that works instantly?"

"Rapidly, but not instantly," Strickland said. "We might work out something with the blowers."

"But he would still have time to get off a shot?"

"Yes,"

"Two shots?"

"Probably."

"Then that's out."

"It seems to me security would have covered an eventuality like this," Allenton said, glaring at Strickland. "What the hell have your boys been doing with their time?"

"That's enough," the general said firmly, and Allenton's anger died instantly. Recriminations had their place, but only after the fact, never during it. "He wants to talk to me."

"You can't go in there, General," Allenton said insistently.

"I don't see that you have any alternative to offer me," the general said. "Give me your pistol, Major."

"Sir . . ."

"Your pistol."

Allenton handed it to him. The general stuck it in his pocket. "I qualified for the all-Army team when I was stationed in Manila," he said. "That was a good many years ago, but I don't think I've lost my touch."

"Let me talk to him first," Allenton said.

"I appreciate the gesture, but no."

"If anything happens to you," Allenton said, "this launch goes down the drain."

"I know Corman quite well," the general said. "He's a very stubborn man. If he asks for a general, he's not going to be satisfied with a major." He walked to the door. "To be on the safe side, I want you to follow the evacuation procedure."

"Except for a backup team," Allenton insisted.

"No exceptions," the general said. "And that's an order."

He went out the door and down the hall.

3

Corman had now moved around the missile to the point where he could see the door and yet keep himself shielded from any sudden attack. His logic told him that they would not try to rush him—no, not when such an attack might set off the volatile monster beside him. The stakes were too high for that. But his imagination was running rampant, and he had difficulty controlling it and stilling the incipient panic that distorted his senses, seeming to make them more keen, until his ears picked up the slightest whisper, the shuffling of feet, and his eyes burned from staring at the circular wall around him and the heavy cement slab above his head. He could expect attack from any quarter, and he must be aware of everything at once; he could not let them take him. He wiped his face with his free hand, feeling chilled here, damp, and he checked his watch again. Only a minute had passed and on first glance the sweep second hand appeared not to be moving at all, and he shook the watch and held it to his ear. It was a long moment before he heard the tick, and it seemed as if in that second his heart had stopped, missed a beat, and he was waiting for it to resume.

They had not called out to him now for the past thirty seconds, but he could hear the muffled murmur of their voices, just the tone of them, not the words. The horn had stopped, and then, before long, the blowers stopped, too, and he had to get past his fear before he could think of a logical reason for their turning off the blowers. They were not trying to suffocate him; no, that was impossible, for there was no way they could seal off the air from this particular portion of the Hole and squeeze him in a vacuum. They had shut off the circulating air because they took him seriously. If there was an explosion here, they wanted to contain it, limit it, and even now they would be closing doors along the corridors to keep the fire from racing down it. He doubted that it would be effective. He had read someplace about an explosion in a silo in Kansas, and if he remembered correctly, there had been heavy casualties and the whole facility had been gutted, charred. The same thing would happen here.

He looked at his watch again. Three minutes had passed. He was sweating heavily now, the water oozing out of his scalp and pouring down his face. Was it hotter in here now? Were they trying to trick him? Had the light dimmed slightly? Was there now a pronounced whispering from somewhere deep in the Hole beneath the platform? His hand tightened around the butt of the pistol.

"I meant what I said," he said in a conversational tone of voice. "Three minutes."

"The general's on his way," a voice came from somewhere below him.

Were they trying to stall him now? Had someone, in a flurry of mental scurrying, decided to send for Finley, to bring her here in the hope that he would do nothing to endanger her life? No, they would not have time for that. They would have to take it as it came, no elaborate stratagems, nothing that required time for execution. Time was the one thing they did not have.

Now he heard the sound of footsteps and the scrape of feet on the iron steps. His finger edged the trigger, waiting, and then the voice called out, "Corman, this is Gibson. I'm coming up."

"By yourself," Corman said. He shifted further around the missile, still keeping the door in view, and in a moment Gibson's head came out of the shadows and then the rest of him emerged into view. He stayed

The February Plan

very near to the door, and there was an attitude of impatience about him, as if he regarded this more as an inconvenience than jeopardy.

"You're alone?" Corman asked, his words sounding hollow in the vault.

"Yes," the general said. "You seem to be one up on me, Corman."

"You're not going to launch this missile, General."

"Maybe not," the general said, his voice a little tired. "But sooner or later it'll have to be done. I was in Germany at the time of Munich, Corman, and there were a lot of sound bright men who said Hitler should have been stopped when we had the power to do it easily. But there were too many idealists who said, 'Let's wait and see what's going to happen,' and their way seemed to be easier. So we paid a hell of a price for stalling around, a hell of a price."

"I'm not going to discuss politics with you," Corman said.

"Not politics, life and death," the general said. "That's what it boils down to."

"Your boys have worn me down, General. I'm too tired to listen."

"We're all tired," the general said. "It's been a long, hard, dirty grind. A hell of a lot more work than intrigue."

"And now it's over," Corman said. "I've stopped you, General."

"That remains to be seen," the general said.

"You doubt that I can pull this trigger?"

"I don't know for sure," the general said. "That depends on how tired you are. Unless you're completely exhausted, you won't. Because that would put you in the same league with me. You don't like something and you're willing to kill a lot of people to stop it, including yourself."

"No," Corman said. "It's not like that."

"The only difference is a matter of degree. You can kill me, a hell of a lot of good men, and yourself, and you can accomplish your end. I would be killing a lot more people, but the stakes are a hell of a lot bigger too."

The general's arguments were specious, and Corman knew it, but he could not quite find the flaws in his reasoning. He had never been fast on his feet, and his mind was more deliberate, perhaps because he was oriented to the written word rather than the spoken. But on the surface what the general said *seemed* to be true, and he had to fight against believing it. This was his weakness, an attraction toward any way out that would not involve his own extinction.

"And what do you get out of this?" the general said, as if reading his mind. "You blow us all to hell and no one will ever know what really happened here. But I'll compromise with you. You put down that pistol and come down to my quarters and we'll talk about it seriously. God knows I don't look on myself as omnipotent. You know me. I never have. If there's any mistake in my reasoning, if you can show me any other way this thing can be done, then I'll call off the project here and now."

Canny, Corman thought, the general was shrewd, offering him more familiar ground, the trade of the gun for words, of violence for logic, but he knew nothing would be accomplished by it, nothing at all, and he would only be giving in to the desire for self-preservation. "No," Corman said. "No discussion. But I'll give you fifteen minutes to get your men out of here."

"And then what?" the general said, more firmly now. "Do you pull the trigger? What in the hell would be gained by that? You would just be destroying the weapon, not the man who was going to use it. That would just be delaying things, wouldn't it? You blow up the Hole, we can cover that. We can make you out a madman, cover our tracks, and make another try somewhere else. So all you'll accomplish is to kill yourself. You're not thinking straight, Corman. You need to get us all."

"Then you won't evacuate?"

"No."

"Then I'll stay," Corman said. "I'll stay right here."

"That's twelve hours."

"I'll stay."

The February Plan

"And what then?"

"You have to elevate this missile out of the Hole before you fire. At the first sign of any movement it's all over."

The general wavered slightly now, as if he had leaned forward to say something and then decided against it. "Do you mind if I talk to my men?"

"No," Corman said.

The general turned and went through the door into the shadows so quietly he resembled smoke flitting out of a grate. Corman's right hand was trembling now with the strain of holding up the pistol. He shifted it to his left, knowing he had made a mistake by backing down, by delaying, by postponing the inevitable action, for he had revealed his weakness, the strength of his own ego which would not allow him to destroy himself unless there was no other way.

In a few minutes the general was back again, calling out to let Corman know he was coming. He materialized in the door again. "All right," he said without equivocation. "I've talked it over with an adjutant. He tells me we could get you out of here, but not without a hell of a risk of explosion, and that's no good. So I've decided to play it your way."

"You'll call it off?"

"I don't think I have any other alternative," the general said.

"And I don't believe you," Corman said flatly. "I've known you too long for that."

"I've never risked my men in a battle where I didn't think I had a chance," the general said. "And don't kid yourself that the war will be over. No, you will be held for twenty-four hours, or long enough for us to cover our tracks here, and then you and your secretary will be sent back to Tokyo. Now, if you can get anybody to believe your account of what happened here, that's fine. I don't think you will. And that leaves us free to try somewhere else."

Oh, the gentle seductiveness of words, the temptation to take words for acts, the symbols for reality, and he wanted to believe, to get out of this oppressive hole, to have it done with. "And what's to keep you from taking me if I give up this position?" Corman said.

"My honor," the general said quietly. "Have you ever known me to lie?"

"No."

"A man of principle doesn't change. If we make a bargain, I'll stick to it."

"It's not enough," Corman said. "Not in circumstances like these."

"I have evacuated the Hole," the general said. "If you like, you can keep me as a hostage. We can go to the control room and wait."

"What's wrong with this place?" Corman said. "I've got the missile here, and that's a hell of a deterrent in itself."

"But what if you slip?" the general said. "What happens if you sneeze or fall asleep or relax for a moment and there's an accident? A couple of million dollars go down the drain for no reason at all." He paused, waiting. Corman said nothing. "If you want more insurance, I'll give you the key to the console. The missile can't be fired without it. Now, if you can think of any better insurance, you tell me and I'll arrange it."

"You really mean this, don't you?"

"Yes," the general said.

The pistol began to lower in Corman's hand, almost of its own volition, and he stepped from behind the shelter of the missile, feeling a great and guilty relief. "You walk in front of me," he said. "Very slowly."

"Yes," the general said.

He went into the dimness of the outer circular room just as the general was beginning to descend the stairs, and he suddenly knew that something was terribly wrong because the room below had been darkened and the general was descending into blackness, leaving him in the light, a perfect target. He brought the pistol up and fired, just as the general was turning toward him, and the bullet caught the general in the chest and knocked him backward against the railing, and it was only then that Corman saw the pistol in his hand, a heavy black pistol that slid from his fingers and rang against the iron stairs as it fell. The general did not fall. He slid down to a sitting position, heavily, and stayed there, and all that Corman could think was not that the general was dead but that he had been forced to lie, and that compromising his honor must have been the hardest thing he had ever done.

In a moment the door opened below and Corman saw Allenton in the wash of light from the corridor as he came in. Corman raised the pistol, but Allenton ignored him, rushing to the general, leaning over him with a look of bafflement, as if he could not believe that something he had considered so indestructible was now gone.

"Has the Hole been evacuated?" Corman asked, his voice strained.

"Yes," Allenton said, deflated now, no trace of resistance in his voice.

"Then I want you to go with me to your communications room," Corman said. "We are going to send some messages."

7

THE debriefing was about over and Corman was impatient to have it done with. He lay on the couch, smoking a cigarette and looking across the room at Hill who reminded him more than anything else of an IBM man, clean-cut, vigorous, soft-spoken. For three days they had been cooped up here in a suite at the Imperial, and Hill had never relaxed a moment. Never once had he loosened his tie or taken off his jacket except when he retired for the night. Hill and his damn machine, the tape recorder that rolled incessantly, catching every scrap of conversation, every question and response, while Hill sat next to it, smoking one cigarette after another, grinding one out in the ash tray only after he had lighted the next. The tape recorder continued to whir even when he was interrupted by a telephone call or when one of his men came into the room to pick up one of his scribbled notes or bring him a transcription of previous material which he wanted to go over again.

Corman had been forced to relive every moment, examine in detail every second he had spent on the base, exhume every scrap of remembered conversation, over and over again, as they dredged his memory for any pieces that might be useful to them. And Corman knew it would not end here. These tapes would be transcribed and fed into another team of men who would analyze every word he had said, fitting his view of the facts in with their other sources, trying to accomplish what Hill called "a deep analysis."

Corman had only been allowed to see Finley very briefly, on the morning the American team had arrived at the base to take over. It had been done efficiently, Corman thought, and with remarkably little malice or rancor, considering the circumstances. Hill had been the first man into the Hole and he seemed to know what he was about, bustling with efficiency, directing his men to shut down the suspended countdown, deactivating machines, assigning agents to take care of Allenton and the men aboveground, latching onto Corman himself and shepherding him up the elevator, introducing his credentials belatedly, only after the important things had been taken care of. He was from the Defense Intelligence Agency. On the way to the waiting car he filled Corman in on the procedure which would be followed here.

Corman's call to the ambassador and Allenton's confirmation had set the machinery in motion, and the DIA detachment in Tokyo had been notified immediately. Even before the team arrived in Chuzenji, the individual assignments had been made. There would be interrogations of everybody even remotely connected with the project, a very time-consuming business which unfortunately would have to include those innocent of any complicity here. Corman listened until his patience was exhausted and then interrupted. "My secretary is being held at the detention camp," he said. "I want to see her."

"I'm sorry," Hill said, immediately apologetic. "But that's going to have to wait awhile."

"I don't think you understand," Corman said, tired and irritated. "I haven't gone through all this just to be swept up in the routine of another government agency. Now, either I see her first, or you don't get one goddamned word out of me."

Hill thought this over. Leaning forward, he tapped the driver on the shoulder and told him to go to the detention camp. He turned to Corman again. "I can give you a few minutes," he said.

"Let's get one thing straight at the outset," Corman said. "You're not giving me anything. You're not granting me any favors because it's not in your power to either grant or withhold anything. I'm a free American citizen and I'm willing to cooperate with you, but only because that's the way I want it to be. Understood?"

"Yes," Hill said.

It seemed strange, Corman thought as the car crept through the snow-covered hills, that the gates were all opened, the checkpoints deserted, the fences looking almost insubstantial now that they no longer held anything in or out. At the compound the trucks had already arrived. The prisoners were lining up to get aboard, falling back into the old familiar disciplines. Freedom was a relative term.

He was allowed to meet Finley in the privacy of the room he had occupied in the headquarters hut, and the minute she came into the room and saw him her bewilderment turned to relief and she came into his arms. "What's going on?" she said. "What's happened to you? You look terrible."

"I don't have time to explain it all now," he said. "But I wanted to see you immediately, before the questioning starts."

"Questioning?"

"We'll be going to Tokyo separately," he said. "And we won't be together for a few days. But I wanted you to be thinking about something."

"What?"

"I don't quite know how to put it," he said. "But the long and short of it is, I want to marry you." She pulled away slightly, looking at him, startled. "Don't interrupt, not yet," he said. "I had it all thought out. When we got back to New York, I was going to arrange an offer for you from Henderson for so much money that you couldn't turn it down, and then I was going to insist that you take it, for your sake. That was going to get me out of a sticky situation. That would have been better for you, and it still would be, I believe that. I'm an egocentric man, set in my ways, and it's not likely I'm going to change. You'll be letting yourself in for a lot of grief."

"I've known your weaknesses for a long time," she said quietly. "But if you'd made all those plans for me, why did you change your mind?"

"I won't say I can't live without you," he said, "because I don't believe that. But I don't want to live without you, let's put it that way. I love you."

"That's all I needed to hear," she said, putting her arms around him again.

"But I want you to think it over. Look at it realistically."

"I see things a lot more realistically than you do. Your idea of realism is a dirty teacup."

"All right, then," he said before he kissed her. "I'll see you in Tokyo, as soon as possible."

He had expected the questioning to last a day at the outside, and now it had lasted three and they were approaching the end of it and he was impatient to be gone. As they neared the end of a reel, Hill fell into an unaccustomed silence, as if all the questions had been asked too many times and any fresh methods of approach had long since been exhausted.

"Tell me something," Corman said. "How do you know you've got all of the conspirators?"

"That's the reason for this intensive questioning," Hill said. "When we put all this together, if there are any of them we haven't got, he'll leave a trace. He's bound to. No man's invisible. He can't play a part in anything without leaving a mark."

"Then that makes your job pretty impossible, doesn't it?"

"How?"

"You can't cover this whole episode, make it seem like it never happened."

"It won't be so difficult," Hill said. "There will be an official government version to explain what happened here, and it should hold up very nicely. Nobody's going to care enough to poke any holes in it." He picked a sheet of paper off the desk and handed it to Corman. "We're going to release this today."

Corman glanced at it. It was an announcement by the United States Government that General G. V. Gibson had been killed in an accident at the Chuzenji Missile Site in the performance of his official duties. "So you turn it into routine," Corman said.

"Exactly. His body has already been taken back to the United States. There will be a funeral Friday with full military honors. He will be buried in Arlington."

"And the major, what will you do about him?"

"The CIA has a hospital in upstate New York. I imagine the major will spend the rest of his life there. And he's no problem for us. As far as the world is concerned, the major never really existed at all."

"And none of this bothers you?"

"Why should it?"

"That the general comes out with full military honors, for one thing."

"He's dead," Hill said simply. "That's all that counts. There are a lot of traitors and more than one fanatic buried in Arlington. That's a convenient symbolic disposition. Because if anybody in government hears about this five years from now, they'll think to themselves, no, that couldn't be true or the general wouldn't have been buried in Arlington."

"But they're all not dead. What do you do with Wilkinson and Allenton and the rest?"

"That's not my province. The CIA will take care of their own, and the military personnel will be handled by the Pentagon."

"And they'll be killed," Corman said flatly.

"I don't know."

"What else can you do with them? You can't try them in the normal way, because you can't afford to have their testimony made public. What would it do to our international relations to have it known that a group of Americans were almost able to launch a nuclear attack on their own? And you can't really punish them without a trial, not officially, because you'd have too many relatives and friends on your neck, demanding to know the facts. So you'll have to dispose of them one by one."

"I wouldn't know about that," Hill said evenly. "But after all, they surely must expect that to happen. They're all traitors in the strict legal definition of the word. All of them took an oath to uphold the Constitution of the United States, to obey orders. They betrayed a trust."

Corman shook his head. "The general was right," he said in a low voice.

"I beg your pardon?"

"The general was right," Corman said firmly. "Not in his projected attack on China—that was monstrous—but something he said. He accused me of acting on the same principle that motivated him. He said I was willing to suspend ethics, morality, to kill a hell of a lot of men, just to stop something I believed should be stopped. And that was true. Hell, I'm against killing, but I was willing to kill. And you're operating the same way, Hill, and maybe the whole damn government is too. Technically these men are traitors and they have to be killed—that's mandatory—but the law says that there is a procedure to be followed, a form. But if the law is observed, then international relations are upset. So you choose not to observe them. And to that extent you are just as guilty as the rest of us. All in the name of expediency."

"I won't argue that," Hill said. "It's a mean, rough world, Mr. Corman."

The tape had run out now, the loose end flapping against the machine. Hill reached out and turned it off.

"And in the end it's very man for himself," Corman said.

"Not quite that extreme, I think," Hill said, standing

up now. "The old codes of ethics, of morality, don't work any more, and we've had to come up with some new ones. They're tougher, not so idealistic, highly imperfect, but maybe we can learn to live with them." He paused now, thoughtfully. "I've gotten to know you pretty well in the past three days, Mr. Corman, so I'm not going to try to order you not to say anything about what has happened here, because I know that would lead to a hell of a fight, and neither one of us is in any mood for that. You know what's at stake here. And you know that if you try to make an issue of it, the government will deny everything and come up with convincing proof to counteract it. In the end you would only be hurting yourself."

Corman stood up, stretching. Finley would be waiting for him and they would be married tonight, and a whole new life was waiting for him, but he was not sure now that it would be as calm as he had projected it to be. He was disturbed now and he had things to think about, and he was no longer the same man he had been when he first set out to find out what had happened to his son. He could no longer sit by and let things happen, no longer accept without questioning, no longer wait for time to correct the obvious wrongs of the world. "All you're saying to me, in effect, is that I can't fight city hall," Corman said.

"That's about it," Hill said with a smile.

"Well, I don't know. I'll have to think about that." He shook Hill's proffered hand, but there was little politeness in it. It was more like the touching of gloves at the beginning of the opening round. "We'll keep in touch with you from time to time," Hill said.

"You won't have any trouble knowing I'm around," Corman said. "No trouble at all."

And he opened the door and walked out into the hall.

A NOTE ABOUT THE AUTHOR

James Hall Roberts is the pseudonym for a successful free-lance television scriptwriter who lives with his wife in the suburbs of Los Angeles. Under this pseudonym he is also the author of *The Burning Sky* and *The Q Document*.